"Captain Widderich, listen to me," Diocletia said. "An inspection will find those coasters' papers in orders. That means any damage you do to cargo or craft will come out of your performance bond, and could result in revocation of your letter of marque. And any harm to the crew will be treated as an act of piracy."

"And who's gonna know? Lot of room for ships to get lost out here."

"The court of inquest will know. Based on my testimony and that of my crew."

Tycho risked a glance at Yana, who was watching their mother intently.

"You'd turn on yer own like that?" Baltazar asked. "You ain't no Jupiter pirate."

"No, I'm not. None of us are anymore. And that includes you, Captain."

· BOOK THREE ·

THE JUPITER PIRATES

THE RISE OF EARTH

BY JASON FRY

HARPER

An Imprint of HarperCollinsPublishers

The Jupiter Pirates: The Rise of Earth
Text copyright © 2016 by Jason Fry
Illustrations copyright © 2016 by Jeff Nentrup

Library of Congress Control Number: 2015958592
ISBN 978-0-06-223027-0

Typography by Anna Christian
❖
17 18 19 20 21   OPM   10 9 8 7 6 5 4 3 2 1
First paperback edition, 2017

FOR MOM, KRIS GILGER,

& SUSAN VALENTI,

THREE CAPTAINS WHO TAUGHT

THIS MIDDIE

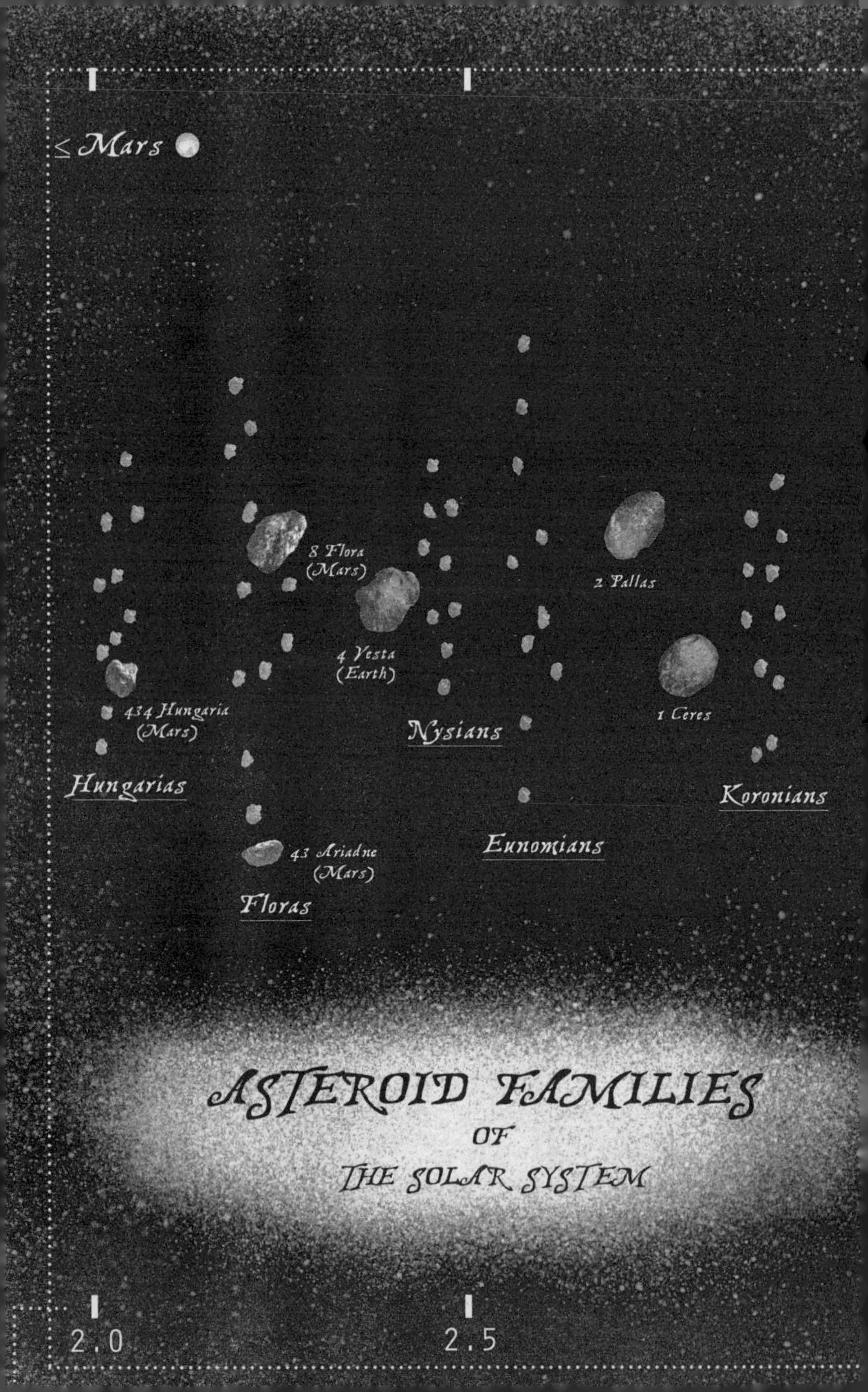
≤ Mars
8 Flora (Mars)
4 Vesta (Earth)
2 Pallas
1 Ceres
434 Hungaria (Mars)
Nysians
Hungarias
Koronians
Eunomians
43 Ariadne (Mars)
Floras
ASTEROID FAMILIES
OF
THE SOLAR SYSTEM
2.0
2.5

Jupiter ♃

153 Hilda
(Jovian)

121 Hermione

65 Cybele

Hildas

2:1 Kirkwood Gap

10 Hygiea
(Earth)

Themistians

Cybeles

3.0   3.5   4.0

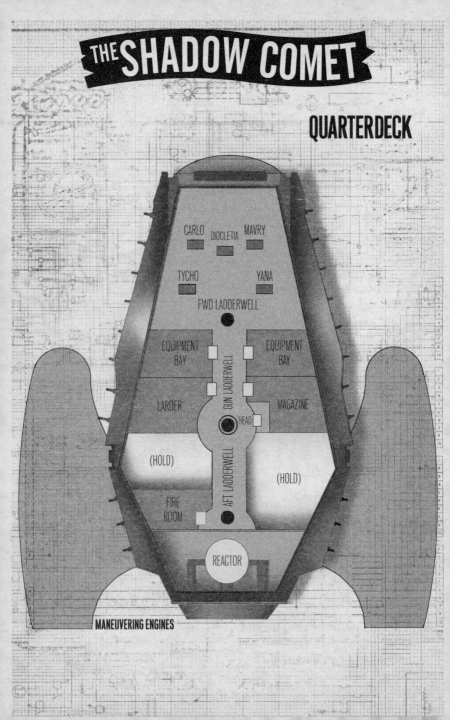

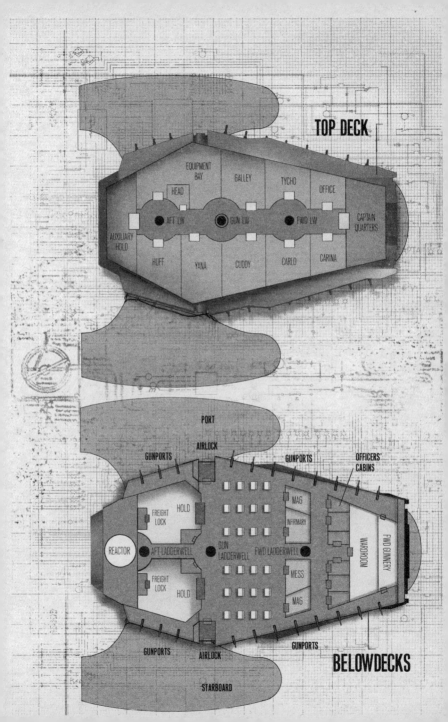

TOP DECK

EQUIPMENT BAY

HEAD

GALLEY

TYCHO

OFFICE

AUXILIARY HOLD

AFT LW

GUN LW

FWD LW

CAPTAIN QUARTERS

HUFF

YANA

CUDDY

CARLO

CARINA

BELOWDECKS

PORT

AIRLOCK

GUNPORTS

GUNPORTS

OFFICERS' CABINS

FREIGHT LOCK

HOLD

MAG

INFIRMARY

REACTOR

AFT LADDERWELL

GUN LADDERWELL

FWD LADDERWELL

WARDROOM

FWD GUNNERY

FREIGHT LOCK

HOLD

MESS

MAG

GUNPORTS

AIRLOCK

GUNPORTS

STARBOARD

CONTENTS

1

THE RELUCTANT CAPTAIN

Your fuel-efficiency calculations for the simulated journey from Callisto to Neptune are incorrect . . . again," Vesuvia said in her cool, dispassionate electronic voice.

It was the "again"—combined with the brief pause preceding it—that made Yana Hashoone angry.

The computer program that the *Shadow Comet* used to communicate with her crew was a stern taskmaster. Vesuvia had insisted it was an ideal time to test sixteen-year-old Yana, despite the fact that it was only an hour into the morning watch, with the rest of the bridge crew asleep in their cabins on the top deck and most of the crewers snoring in their hammocks one deck below.

Yana was the only member of her family who actually enjoyed the solitude of the middle and morning watches. Her twin brother, Tycho, and their older brother, Carlo, spent that time doing homework, but Yana preferred to tackle her studies in her cabin after dinner. While everyone else was sleeping, she'd read old tales of Earth on her mediapad or run battle simulations in which she tried to turn famous commanders' historical defeats into successes. A silent quarterdeck was perfect for such pursuits, with no lights except those of her crew station and the main screen displaying a readout of anything the ship's sensors might scan.

"Let me point out—*again*—that doing these calculations by hand is pointless," Yana said, tapping at her keyboard. "See my screen? That sensor indicator displays the fuel efficiency. It's currently ninety-four point one percent, resulting in a lovely shade of emerald green. Exercise successfully concluded. Now leave me alone."

"Since you prefer a real-world exercise, the *Comet* is currently cruising in the Hildas, four days, nine hours, and eleven minutes out of Ceres on its way to Jupiter," Vesuvia said. "Based on this—"

"Is it possible you think I've sustained a head injury? First you think I can't read a sensor indicator, and now you think I don't know where we are."

"Please do not interrupt," Vesuvia sniffed. "Since you indicate you are aware of the *Shadow Comet*'s position, and are presumably also aware that the *Shadow Comet* has followed this course before, please tell me what level of fuel efficiency is the historical norm for this heading."

Yana sighed and tapped at her keys, but Vesuvia wasn't finished. "You appear to be determining fuel efficiency for the current heading. The request was for the historical norm."

"Which is why I was *querying the Log*," Yana said, hastily switching over to that input screen. Some parts of the Log were captain's eyes only, but most of its records were available to any member of the bridge crew. They summarized thousands of voyages made over hundreds of years.

As Yana typed, the access prompt for the Log flickered and vanished, replaced by an error message.

"It seems the Log is unavailable," Vesuvia said. "Perhaps battle damage has severed linkages somewhere."

"That's a dirty trick, even for you."

"Severed information linkages are a known hazard of combat situations," Vesuvia said, sounding pleased with herself. "As are interrupted fuel lines, damage to engine baffles, and other perils. An officer faced with such a situation must be able to do more than read a sensor indicator—she must also be able to verify that a sensor indicator is providing accurate information."

Yana sighed and folded her arms, glaring at the main screen.

"All right, have it your way," she grumbled, then reached for her keyboard. "But first let me run a quick sensor scan."

"Sensor scans run automatically every ninety seconds," Vesuvia objected. "Anomalies are reported to the watch officer immediately."

"And what if *you're* the one who isn't providing accurate information?" Yana asked. "Shouldn't an officer verify that you're performing those automatic scans correctly and communicating them properly?"

"Your stalling tactics are—" Vesuvia said, then stopped. "Sensor contact."

"That isn't funny."

"The sensor contact is not simulated. It has just entered the long-range sensor cone. Initial readings positive for metallic signature and ion emissions."

Yana leaned forward to stare at her scopes. This wasn't an exercise—it was real.

"The heading is for Saturn," Yana said. "Distance to sensor contact?"

"Eighteen thousand kilometers and closing."

Not so long ago, a heading for Saturn wouldn't have meant anything special. The ringed planet's moons were officially members of the Jovian Union, whose government the Hashoones served as privateers. But two years ago, a group known as the Ice Wolves had proclaimed Saturn's independence, then backed up their claim by defeating a hastily assembled task force of Jovian warships—a task force that had included the *Comet*.

Some called the Ice Wolves revolutionaries, because they were seeking freedom from the Jovian Union just as the Jovian Union had once sought freedom from the government of Earth. Others called them pirates, and charged that they were part of a plot hatched by Earth to regain control of her former colonies.

Yana liked arguing about such things—it made family dinners more entertaining. But this wasn't the time for it. The ship out there could be loyal to Earth, registered with the Jovian Union, or pledging allegiance to the Ice Wolves.

If she was Earth's, the *Shadow Comet* could seize her as a prize, with the possibility of a big payday. If she was Jovian, Yana would have to let her pass—under the terms of the Hashoones' letter of marque, only enemy ships could be attacked.

And if the ship out there was loyal to the Ice Wolves? Well, that was the kind of question that led to arguments at dinner.

"Seventeen thousand kilometers," Vesuvia said.

"Tactical readout on the main screen," Yana said. "Sensor and communications data on my monitor. And shut off the autopilot—I'll take the sticks."

"Acknowledged," Vesuvia said as lights began flashing on Yana's station.

A U-shaped control yoke whined and rose from beneath her console. Yana closed her hands around it and pressed her feet against the pedals below the console. The *Comet* could be steered from any of the five stations on her quarterdeck. Normally, that job belonged to Carlo—just as communications was generally Tycho's job. But both of them were still asleep on the top deck.

Yana twitched the control yoke to port and the *Comet* rolled obediently in that direction.

"Controls green," Yana said. "Charge up the communications mast. Don't display colors—black transponders."

"Acknowledged."

Every starship had transponders that identified her allegiance to other ships. But unless on a heavily patrolled spacelane or near port, starships rarely broadcast that allegiance openly, for fear of attracting enemy privateers—or, worse, pirates who'd attack any vessel, without regard for the law. So civilian starships typically hid their true loyalties, showing no allegiance or claiming a false one.

"Query the bogey's transponders," Yana said. "And do you have a sensor profile yet?"

"No response to transponder query. Still building sensor profile. Shall I beat to quarters?"

"I'm thinking."

If that was a hostile ship out there, the *Comet* would need all hands, including crewers manning the gun emplacements below and a full complement on the quarterdeck. Beating to quarters now would ensure everyone was decently awake if the *Comet* had to fight. On the other hand, it would be humiliating to rouse the entire ship just to make small talk with a Jovian freighter. Tycho would yawn theatrically all day, while Carlo would mock her mercilessly until they reached Jupiter.

"Fifteen thousand kilometers," Vesuvia asked. "Have you reached a decision?"

"I have. Detach from the long-range tanks, plot an intercept course, and open communications channels. But that will do for now. I want to take a look first."

"Acknowledged. Disconnecting fuel lines. Stabilizers disengaged."

Yana felt a bump, and then the *Comet* shook slightly as Vesuvia broke the connection between the sixty-meter frigate and the massive, bulbous fuel tanks she used for long-distance travel. With the *Comet* now free to maneuver, Yana pushed down on the control yoke and the privateer dipped her nose and accelerated away from her tanks.

"This is the *Shadow Comet*, operating under letter of marque of the Jovian Union," Yana announced, the sensor masts broadcasting her message into space. "Unidentified craft, activate transponders and respond at once."

There was no response but the hiss of static.

"Fourteen thousand kilometers," Vesuvia said. "Sensor calculations complete. Profile fits modified Galicia-class caravel, confidence eighty-four point three three percent."

A caravel was a small freighter, perhaps thirty or forty meters larger than the *Comet* and relatively speedy. But the Hashoones' ship was faster, Yana thought with a grin.

"Unidentified caravel, we are on an intercept course," she said. "Activate transponders immediately."

The *Comet*'s bells rang out—a *clang-clang*, followed by a brief pause and a single *clang*. Three bells meant it was 0530. The bells struck every half hour, whether the privateer was sitting peaceably in port or trading broadsides with an enemy in deep space.

As the bells died away, Yana heard footsteps behind her. She turned and saw Diocletia Hashoone—her mother and the *Comet*'s captain—descending the forward ladderwell. Her eyes were puffy with sleep. Right behind her came Yana's father, Mavry Malone.

Yana started to ask what her parents were doing on the quarterdeck, then stopped herself—no self-respecting officer could sleep through the familiar rattle and bump of a starship detaching from her long-range tanks.

"Modified Galicia-class—she's ignoring my hails," Yana said as Diocletia studied the tactical screen with a practiced eye.

"Well that's rude," Mavry said, flopping into his chair at the first mate's station, then putting one foot on the console and yawning.

"She's heading for Saturn?" Diocletia asked.

Yana nodded, automatically rechecking her sensor scans.

"That could mean anything these days," Mavry said as they heard new footsteps behind them.

"Hang on—transmission's coming through," Yana said. "She's flying Jovian colors."

"Of course she is," said twenty-year-old Carlo, peering over his sister's shoulder. "Ask for the current Jovian recognition code."

"*Thank you*, Carlo," Yana said. "I've handled an intercept before, you know. Would you also like to remind me about the difference between port and starboard?"

"Well, Yana, take your left hand—"

"Behave yourselves," Diocletia said as Carlo settled into his chair and began buckling his harness. "Where's Tycho?"

"Right here," Tycho said sleepily, his footsteps a bit tentative on the ladder.

"Nice of you to join us, little brother," Carlo said, his grin causing the pale scar on his right cheek to flex.

Tycho grunted, refusing to be baited, but Yana saw spots flare in his cheeks, beneath his haystack of dark hair. Tycho was frequently the last to the quarterdeck except for their grandfather, Huff. And Huff had an excuse—he needed to attach his cybernetic limbs and power up his systems.

"Vesuvia, I'll take the controls," Carlo said.

"Belay that," Yana snapped. "My starship."

"Don't be ridiculous—"

"Members of the bridge crew will obey the officer of the watch or return to quarters," Diocletia said without taking her eyes off the tactical screen.

"Twelve thousand kilometers," Vesuvia said.

"Tyke, monitor communications—let me know if she tries to call for help," Yana said. "Unidentified caravel, acknowledge transmissions before I start knocking pieces off of you."

"Hold yer fire, *Comet*," a voice grumbled over the speakers. "Our commo board's slow to warm up. This be the *Lampos* out of Ganymede, runnin' freight from Ceres. We're bound fer Titan—an' we're on a tight schedule."

"We won't keep you, *Lampos*," Yana said. "Transmit the current Jovian recognition code and we'll be on our way."

Silence.

"Eleven thousand kilometers," Vesuvia said.

Yana looked at Tycho, who shook his head.

"*Lampos*, transmit the recognition code," Yana said.

"We just did, missy," the caravel's captain growled.

Yana covered her microphone as Huff Hashoone descended the ladderwell, his metal feet clanging as they struck the rungs. Nearly half of Huff's body was metal—the rest of him had been blasted away in a terrible battle when Yana and Tycho were babies. One side of his face was a mass of scarred flesh, while the other side was a bare skull of gleaming chrome. The old pirate's artificial eye blazed white as he stared at the screen, and the wicked-looking blaster cannon screwed into his metal forearm twitched in response to its master's thoughts.

"*Lampos*, we are not receiving your code," Yana said. "Retransmit immediately."

"We *are* transmittin'. P'raps yer sensor mast is faulty, missy."

"Call me missy one more time and I'll turn your ship into a debris field," Yana said, then shut off her microphone. "Vesuvia, diagnostics on all sensor masts."

"I already checked," Tycho said. "Our gear is functioning normally."

"Ten thousand kilometers," Vesuvia said.

Yana reactivated her microphone. "*Lampos*, we claim your vessel under the articles of war governing interplanetary commerce. Heave to and prepare for boarding. Vesuvia? *Now* you can beat to quarters."

2

WHAT THE *LAMPOS* CARRIED

A few years earlier, Yana would have been nervous. But experience had made every operation aboard the *Shadow Comet* routine and comforting—even the preparations for battle. First came the squeal of the bosun's pipes from belowdecks, ordering the crewers to lash up and stow their hammocks. Then sensor light after sensor light turned green, indicating the crews were at their assigned guns and ready to fire. Even the complaints of the *Lampos*'s captain as the caravel shut down her engines were familiar.

And in the middle of the tumult, four bells rang out—a *clang-clang*, followed by another *clang-clang*. It was 0600.

Yana descended the ladderwell from the brightly lit quarterdeck into a maze of girders, the only illumination the dim red light of battle stations. She smelled fuel and cheroot smoke. All was quiet—the crews were at their guns, while shot boys waited for the order to fetch new munitions from the ship's magazine, sealed off by thick fearnought doors. Through the gloom Yana could see the bright lights of the wardroom, its mess table turned into an operating theater for Mr. Leffingwell, the *Comet*'s surgeon. He and his loblolly boys were busy setting out surgical instruments that they hoped not to use.

The boarding party awaited Yana at the port airlock, led by Grigsby, the *Comet*'s warrant officer and the below-decks boss. He was tying his white dreadlocks behind his head, brilliantly lit tattoos oscillating up and down his dark-brown arms.

"Mistress Hashoone on deck," Grigsby barked, and the dozen crewers saluted.

Yana nodded at them as Grigsby handed her two chrome musketoons. The weapons' weight felt reassuring. They'd been in her family for generations, used by the ranking officer in countless boarding actions.

"We're boarding a caravel," Yana told the crewers as they checked their own carbines. "She was flying a Jovian flag but never transmitted the recognition code—tried to say our sensor mast wasn't receiving."

"Heard that tale before, Mistress Yana," muttered Higgs.

"Silence there," Grigsby growled, his mouthful of chrome teeth gleaming.

"Their heading was Saturn," Yana said.

The tough, scarred men and women surrounding her went quiet. Most were veterans of the defeat at Saturn. They'd seen their fellow crewers die during the *Comet*'s desperate flight through the planet's rings, pursued by Thoadbone Mox and his fellow Ice Wolves. And they'd wanted revenge ever since.

"We're playing this by the book, though," Yana said. "I'm not dying because some accountant panics at his ship being boarded. We all want payback, but today that means taking a Saturnian cargo and ship and turning them into livres to spend in Port Town. You hear me?"

"Three cheers for Mistress Yana!" yelled Dobbs, the *Comet*'s pale master-at-arms, his ever-present cheroot dangling from his lips. The other crewers took up the cheer as Yana checked the power levels on her musketoons.

"We're ready, Captain," Yana said into her headset.

"So are we," Diocletia replied. "You are green for boarding."

Yana nodded at Grigsby, who stepped forward with Dobbs and a crewer named Cartier, weapons raised. Klaxons wailed as the *Comet*'s inner airlock door opened. Through a window in the outer door Yana could see the

Lampos's own outer door was shut. A docking ring of tough but flexible rubber connected the two ships, sealing them against the vacuum of space.

Carbine raised, Grigsby thumbed the control that opened the *Comet*'s outer hatch. The temperature plummeted and gooseflesh rose on Yana's forearms. The moisture in the docking ring froze into crazy zigzags of rime on the surface of the *Lampos*'s hatch.

"Open her up, Mr. Grigsby," Yana said, thumbing her musketoons' safeties off.

The *Lampos*'s outer hatch screeched open, revealing the inner airlock door still shut. The Comets muttered angrily.

"This here captain's a right hard horse," Grigsby said.

"Tycho, patch me through to the caravel," Yana said, shivering in the chilly lock while her brother opened the communications channel. "Captain? Are you going to open the starboard airlock, or are we going to burn through it?"

The inner hatch grumbled upward, wind rippling the clothes of the Comets as the air in the two ships mingled. No one was waiting on the other side of the lock—ahead of them, a passageway led deeper into the caravel.

They were halfway down the passageway when the first Lamposes appeared. They were big men in dark-blue coveralls, their belts crowded with tools. The Comets met them at the caravel's belowdecks junction, where a ladderwell led upward. Yana peered down each passageway, then up the ladderwell. It should lead to the bridge, she thought, trying to remember the ship's schematic. She wished she'd taken more time to study it.

"Hands up, you lot," Grigsby growled at the caravel's crewers, waving his carbine emphatically.

The freighter's crewers obeyed—slowly, smiling in an effort to be reassuring. Yana looked around, wondering why she felt nervous.

It felt like there were too many Lamposes all of a sudden. Where had they all come from?

It's an early-morning intercept and *a green freighter crew, that's all. Still, you'd think they'd have enough sense to hold still and keep their hands up.*

There were Lamposes behind them now too, Yana realized. She felt a trickle of sweat run down between her shoulder blades.

"Take me to the captain," she said to the crewer who looked least confused. "Right now."

"He's on his way down, miss," the man said, the accent Saturnian. He smiled broadly. There was something strange about his face. The cheeks and forehead were tan, but the upper lip, jaw, and chin were pale.

Yana shot him.

Then she fired at the man behind him as the two ships' crewers came together, cursing and screaming. The boom of the guns was startlingly loud in the narrow passageway.

"Back to the *Comet*!" Yana yelled, squeezing off another barrage of shots. Grigsby kicked free of a *Lampos* crewer's arms, his carbines roaring. The air was thick with smoke, pierced with deadly lines of laser fire.

"There's another ship coming in!" Tycho said in her earpiece. "Looks like a cruiser at intercept speed. But what's that noise?"

Yana didn't reply. Cartier stumbled and then was propelled backward, knocking her onto her behind as a laser blast zipped through the space where her head had been a split second before. The crewer behind her screeched in agony. Yana scrambled free of Cartier and grabbed his arm, dragging him backward. He felt strangely light.

"Leave him!" Grigsby barked. "He's gone!"

Yana looked down at Cartier and winced. She let go of the dead man's arm and stumbled backward as Dobbs and Grigsby filled the corridor with blaster fire. She tripped over a fallen Lampos, dropping one of her musketoons, and had to crawl over a gasping spacer to retrieve it.

They were still ten meters from the *Comet*'s airlock.

"Yana, what's happening?" Tycho demanded.

"Ambush!" Yana yelled, scrambling to her feet again. "They're Ice Wolves! We're almost back to the lock—get ready to cast off!"

She felt the impact before she saw the laser beam—it spun her halfway around and knocked her down again, the brilliance of the light leaving gray spots in her vision. She picked up the musketoon, annoyed that she kept dropping it. Closing her fingers around the gun sent pain shooting through her shoulder. Then Grigsby had grabbed a fistful of her jumpsuit and was propelling her down the passageway toward the *Comet*.

"Let go," she protested, but Grigsby kept hauling her along. She stumbled over the uneven decking in the docking ring, then cried out in pain as Grigsby grabbed her injured shoulder. Dobbs was kneeling in the *Comet*'s outer lock, firing past them. His cheroot glowed red in his teeth. There were Lampos bodies on the deck around him.

"That's everybody," Grigsby said, ducking as a beam of light zipped past them, deeper into the dim red confines of the *Comet*. Yana saw a bright white spark in the gloom and realized it was her grandfather's artificial eye. Huff was stomping toward the airlock, the flesh-and-blood half of his face dark with rage.

The *Comet* shuddered, and a deep groan echoed through the ship. Yana tried to shove a body over the threshold of the inner lock so it could close. She could barely move her arm.

"Yana?" Tycho asked. "We're taking fire from that cruiser. She's flying Saturnian colors."

"We're back in the lock!" Yana yelled. "Disengage, Tyke! Do it now!"

Klaxons blared inside the airlock.

"Get out of the way!" Grigsby yelled at Dobbs, bending to yank at the legs of a dead Lampos lying in the path of the *Comet*'s inner hatch. The frigate shook again under the impact of cannon fire.

Huff reached for Yana, but she waved him away, pushing the body blocking the outer hatch, then had to duck as a laser blast from inside the *Lampos* struck near her head.

Then the *Comet* disengaged from the Saturnian ship.

Both airlock doors descended instantly but caught on the bodies of the Lampos crewers. Motors groaned and a hurricane of air roared out through the gaps, whisking a pair of dropped carbines into the void. The suction slammed Yana against the outer door face-first and pinned her there.

"Airlock malfunction," Vesuvia warned.

"Tyke!" Yana screamed, spitting out blood as she struggled to reach one of the handholds used during extravehicular maneuvers. "Manual override! Open the inner hatch!"

Grigsby was trying to brace himself against the wind as he pulled on the legs of the body blocking the inner hatch. Through the outer hatch Yana could see the hull of the *Lampos*, perhaps twenty meters away. Several of the caravel's crewers were floating in space outside the airlock, kicking feebly.

"The inner door!" she yelled, praying that Tycho could hear her. If he opened the outer door by mistake, she and Grigsby would die.

The inner door rose and the tide of escaping air yanked the dead crewer free of its path and slammed Grigsby against the outer hatch next to Yana. She tried to tell Tycho that the lock was clear, but her brother must have been watching on the security camera, because the inner door immediately slammed shut.

The remaining air in the lock vanished into space and the suction disappeared. A puff of breath froze onto Yana's nose and mouth and her eyes stung as their moisture boiled into vapor.

Grigsby grabbed her by her upper arm, near where the blaster bolt had struck. She yelled but it made no sound. The belowdecks boss pulled her body against his, his other hand closing around one of the handholds. Then he nodded up at the camera.

The outer hatch rose, leaving Yana staring over Grigsby's shoulder into space. Beyond the *Lampos* she could see a bright dot moving against the darkness of the void. It flashed—once, twice, three times. It was the cruiser, she realized—and it was firing at them.

Grigsby was kicking at something, chrome teeth bared in a grimace. She dragged her eyes away from the cruiser and saw the body blocking the outer door's path. It was almost impossible to concentrate—her chest felt like it was trying to cave in on itself, and her vision was going gray.

She forced herself to move slowly and ignore the agony in her shoulder. She got her foot under the dead crewer's side and pushed. The crewer's heavy body moved a bit. Then the *Comet* rolled to port and the body slipped out into space.

The outer hatch slammed shut. Grigsby let go of the handhold, and he and Yana slumped to the deck inside the airless lock. Yana's eyes turned to the inner hatch.

Her vision was hazy and the door seemed kilometers away.

It opened. Yana gasped, drawing in greedy lungfuls of air, then began to cough. She fumbled with her headset as Huff rushed to her side.

"I'm fine, Grandfather," she managed. "Trap—it was a trap! All port guns fire on the caravel!"

"Belay that," her mother said calmly. "Carlo, take evasive action. Mr. Grigsby, if you can hear me, please get my daughter to the surgeon."

Yana hissed in pain as she climbed slowly up the ladderwell from belowdecks. She found Huff in his usual spot by the ladderwell, his magnetic feet locked to the deck between her station and Tycho's. Her twin brother's eyes jumped to the thick bandage on her shoulder.

"You all right?"

Yana nodded, picking irritably at the crust of dried blood ringing her nostrils. Diocletia turned in the captain's chair.

"What did Mr. Leffingwell say?"

Yana waved dismissively, wincing when the motion sent a bolt of pain down her arm.

"I'm fine. It's a bad burn is all. A session of tissue regeneration on Callisto should restore full mobility."

Carlo turned from his station to listen. The *Comet* had evaded the Ice Wolves' cruiser, reached her long-range tanks, and was speeding away from her near-disastrous encounter with the *Lampos*. Mavry was in the fire room, running diagnostics on the damage inflicted by the Saturnian cruiser's cannons during her getaway.

"And are you fit to resume duty?" Diocletia asked.

"Of course I am," Yana said, then dissolved into a coughing fit. She held her breath, trying to force her body to obey her.

"Good," Diocletia said. "Now, I countermanded your order to fire on the *Lampos* because—"

"Perhaps we should discuss this in the cuddy," Yana said.

"We'll discuss it here."

"And if I don't want to discuss it here?"

"You'll discuss it where the captain of the ship tells you to. Yana, *think*. When I agree a conversation should be held in private, *that's* when you should worry. We're discussing this on the quarterdeck because your brothers need to hear it, too. Now sit down."

Yana settled into her chair, working her arm into the sling Leffingwell had given her.

"You started a firefight on the *Lampos* before Tycho told you about the inbound cruiser," Diocletia said. "That means you saw something. What was it?"

"Beards. The crewers aboard the *Lampos* had shaved off their beards—the lower halves of their faces were still pale. They were Ice Wolves. They stalled for time while the cruiser came to intercept us, and tried to trap our boarding party so we couldn't disengage."

"Arrr, the caravel was bait, an' the cruiser were the hook," Huff growled.

"And they almost landed us," Tycho said.

"Almost," Diocletia said. "You had your eyes open and kept your head fighting your way clear. We lost three Comets, but we could have lost everything."

"And then you let the *Lampos* go," Yana said, coughing again.

Mavry emerged from the aft passageway leading to the fire room, wiping his hands on his jumpsuit.

"Gosh, kid," he said. "You look terrible."

"Nice to see you too, Dad."

"Our first priority was to get to safety," Diocletia said. "We don't have the firepower to slug it out with a cruiser. And remember, we're missing the dozen hands we sent off as Mr. Richards's prize crew. If that cruiser had been carrying pinnaces, we'd be space dust now."

"Which is what that caravel should be," Yana said. "Then the next Saturnian captain would think twice about helping the Ice Wolves."

"And you're sure the captain of the *Lampos* was helping them willingly? Did you inspect the bridge? What if the Ice Wolves captured the *Lampos* and forced her crew to cooperate?"

Yana looked away unhappily.

"We're not pirates, Yana," her mother said. "And we're not in the vengeance business. You were right that there were Ice Wolves on that ship. But if you'd been wrong about the rest, you could have been hanged."

The thought hung over the quarterdeck for a moment.

"Arrr, every pirate's life ends with the carbine or the gibbet," Huff said.

"Like Mom just said, we're not pirates, Grandfather—we're privateers," Tycho said.

Diocletia nodded. "And remember, there are powerful people who would like to put us out of business, not just on Earth but also on Ganymede. Any mistake we make helps them make their case."

"Can we not talk about gibbets and carbines?" Carlo asked. "Personally, I'm planning to die in bed, at a very old age."

"Me too," Mavry said. "Preferably after overindulging on plum duff and some good Ganymedan brandy."

"There's summat to what yeh say, Mavry my lad," Huff said. "'Tis a tad less heroic, but p'raps an excess of grog ain't a bad alternative to the hangman."

Tycho found his sister drinking a jump-pop in the cuddy.

"What do you want?" she demanded.

Tycho rolled his eyes. "Sorry to offend you. I just wanted to see if you're okay."

"I'm fine. Just been a busy day."

"How's the shoulder?" he asked, sitting across from her.

"It hurts," Yana said, coughing again. "Mr. Leffing-well explained it to me—the laser superheated the water in the tissue around the point of impact. Cooked it, basically."

"Yuck, boiled sister. And what about the rest of you?"

Yana's fingers explored her puffy face.

"I'll live. Broken nose and a mild concussion. Mr. Leffingwell says the swelling is from decompression, and it'll go down in a couple of days. The annoying thing is this stupid cough—bits of ice irritated the respiratory passages. Anyway, it could have been a lot worse."

"Thank God it wasn't," Tycho said, reaching over to squeeze her hand. Yana squeezed back.

"Still, it was bad enough. Grigsby had to carry me out of the *Lampos* like a little kid. And you heard Mom—she didn't agree with anything I did back there. Now I'll get written up in the Log."

The captaincy of the *Comet* had been handed down from one Hashoone to the next for as long as the ship had existed. Diocletia had taken over from Huff fifteen years earlier, and one day she would name either Tycho, Yana, or Carlo to succeed her. She watched every decision her children made, recording their successes and failures in a protected part of the Log.

"Mom didn't seem mad," Tycho said. "It was more like she was afraid."

"Mom's never been afraid in her life."

"You know better than that."

Yana waved that away, then grimaced. "What would you have done back there, Tyke?"

Tycho's teeth worried at his lip.

"It's weird these days," he said. "There are all these

rumors about Earth warships conducting operations in the asteroid belt. And nobody can figure out what's happening with the Ice Wolves—"

"I can help you with that part—they just tried to kill us."

"I know, but before that we hadn't run across them in months. After the Battle of Saturn they had a perfect chance to put pressure on us, and squeeze us between them and Earth, but they mostly haven't."

"All very interesting, but I didn't have time to convene a meeting of the Diplomatic Corps. I had to do something. So I did. And it was the right thing."

"I didn't say it wasn't."

"No, but you were thinking it. I could tell." Yana sighed and shook her head. "I guess if Mom thinks I was wrong and you think I was wrong, it doesn't matter what I think."

Tycho cocked his head at his sister, curious.

"Oh, don't play dumb," Yana said. "You're the one who found the *Iris* cache, and Carlo's the self-proclaimed best pilot in the Jovian Union. Which leaves me, the bad pirate daughter. The one who's always wrong and never listens."

"You're being way too hard on yourself," Tycho said. "Well, except for the never listens part."

Yana winced at the pain in her shoulder. "Whatever. As soon as Mom picks one of you to be the new captain, I'm getting my own ship."

Tycho shook his head.

"You know that's impossible. The Jovian Union won't allow it, and family tradition—"

"I don't care about either of those things anymore. There's no way I'm spending the rest of my life forgotten on Callisto, Tyke. I'd rather die than live as a nobody."

3

THE PRIZE CREW'S TALE

The Jovian cruiser *Sparrowhawk* lurked above Callisto, bristling with weapons and surrounded by pinnaces. A hard-eyed lieutenant ordered the *Comet* to hold her position for half an hour while he pored over the frigate's recent navigational records. The sound of fifes and horns bounced up the ladderwells to the quarterdeck, accompanying spacer songs that sounded more enthusiastic than melodic. Free of their duties, the

Comets were turning the last hours of the cruise into a shindy.

"What's the holdup?" Carlo demanded, peering down at the *Comet*'s unoccupied docking cradle. "They already checked our flight logs at Ganymede."

Tycho gazed out at space beyond the viewports. Ferries were gathered around the docking cradle, their running lights blinking red and green, waiting for the privateer to muster out her crewers. Below, on the cracked beige surface of Callisto, a cluster of tunnels and domes marked Port Town, the moon's largest settlement.

"Lot of ships out there," Huff growled. "Bet some of 'em are Jovian Defense Force, lookin' for spacers to press."

"You're probably right," Diocletia said. "Yana, Tycho, write up exemptions for our crewers. The Defense Force will need to approve them, but they'll still make a press gang think twice about taking one of our people."

"And what if some of our crewers want to serve?" Tycho asked.

Huff snorted. "No self-respectin' Comet would run from a privateer to a military ship. Spit-an'-polish uniforms and gettin' told what to do all day? Arrrrr. That's why press gangs carry truncheons—can't win the argument without 'em."

"I can't believe some of the old hulks they're recommissioning," Mavry said, peering at his terminal. "That pocket cruiser we saw back at High Port was a modified Ocelot-class. Where'd the Defense Force get her, a museum? And remember those two corvettes at 617 Patroclus? Converted coasters, by the look of them."

Diocletia nodded. "Remember the last time there was all this saber rattling, right before Yana and Tycho were born? If a hull would hold air, the Defense Force claimed it and painted a name and number on the side."

"Which means they'll pay good livres for any ship we can bring in as a prize," Yana said.

"Hope that includes the cargo hauler we captured a couple of weeks back—the one Mr. Richards brought in," Mavry said. "Though the prize paperwork for her hasn't been filed with the admiralty court yet. That should have been taken care of when the prize crew reached Ganymede."

"Mr. Richards wouldn't overlook something like that," Diocletia said.

"Maybe the Defense Force seized the hauler—like they've tried to do with the *Hydra*," Yana said, her voice muffled and strange because of her still-swollen nose.

Tycho followed his sister's eyes to the deadly-looking pirate ship moored in her docking cradle. The *Hydra* had once belonged to Thoadbone Mox, the unrepentant pirate who'd betrayed the Hashoones and his fellow Jupiter pirates at the Battle of 624 Hektor. The Hashoones had captured the *Hydra* from Mox four years earlier, though Huff had let the pirate go for reasons he'd never made clear to anyone's satisfaction.

It had been a grave mistake—Mox had signed on

with the Ice Wolves, and nearly destroyed the *Comet* at the Battle of Saturn. The Ice Wolves had expelled Mox from their ranks for disobeying orders, and no one had heard from him since, but Tycho was grimly certain he was still out there somewhere.

"At this point I almost wish the Defense Force *would* seize the *Hydra*," Diocletia said with a sigh. "Better that than paying docking fees for a ship we can't touch."

"Incoming transmission," Vesuvia said.

"Finally," Mavry said.

"You may proceed, *Shadow Comet*," said the lieutenant. "*Sparrowhawk* out."

The Comets belowdecks let up a ragged cheer as Carlo grabbed the yoke and brought the privateer down to her docking cradle for the first time in five months. It took an hour for Yana and Tycho to muster out the hands, issuing their exemptions and warning them to beware of press gangs. But then the last crewer hoisted his chest and passed through the port airlock to a waiting ferry, and the *Comet* was empty of all but her bridge crew.

The Hashoones gathered their own gear and climbed down the aft ladderwell to the gig. Carlo unlatched the little craft from its socket in the *Comet*'s belly and let it plummet down Callisto's weak gravity well, fast enough to make Tycho's stomach turn flips.

"Easy on the sticks," Diocletia complained. "We're not shooting the Kirkwood Gap here."

"Sorry, Mom," Carlo said with a grin, easing up on the controls and tapping the gig's retro rockets as it settled on the landing pad, so gently that Tycho barely felt the bump.

"Show-off," Yana muttered, and Carlo offered her a mocking bow.

The Hashoones tramped down the corridor to Port Town's transportation hub, where their grav-sled was waiting in its stall for the brief trip to Darklands. Tycho was so busy debating the legality of press gangs with Yana that he didn't notice Mavry had come to a halt and collided with him.

Grigsby was standing in the corridor, his duffel bag at his feet and a grimmer-than-usual expression on his face. Behind him stood a knot of morose-looking spacers, hats in their hands. Tycho recognized them as the Comets who had been sent aboard the captured cargo hauler weeks earlier.

"I don't suppose you're here to welcome us home," Diocletia said.

Richards stepped forward, eyes downcast. "'Fraid not, Captain. It's my duty to tell yeh we lost the prize, ma'am."

Tycho and Yana traded looks. The cargo hauler had been flying Earth's flag, and while she wasn't the stuff fortunes were made of, she'd been worth enough to make the *Comet*'s last cruise a moderately successful one. Without her . . .

"Lost the prize?" Diocletia asked. "How did this happen, Mr. Richards?"

"She was recaptured, ma'am. A rescue ship from

Earth intercepted us a day out of 153 Hilda. Frigate by the name of the *Gros-yoo*."

"Gesundheit," Yana said, earning a stern look from her mother.

"We couldn't outrun her, Captain," Richards said. "Not much in the solar system could. She took back the prize and her captain made us give our parole. Then he hailed a liner heading for Jupiter and put us on it."

"An Earth captain paroled you?" Diocletia asked.

Tycho understood his mother's surprise. Earth regarded privateering as thinly disguised piracy. Many captains in His Majesty's navy would have taken the *Comet*'s prize crew prisoner. But this one had allowed the Comets to return to Jupiter.

"I was surprised meself," Richards said. "We thought we was bound for the brig, but this captain was a right decent cove, Earthman though he was. He turned us loose, and the *Gros-yoo* took the prize back to the asteroid belt."

"I've never heard of an HMS *Gros-yoo*," Mavry said. "Are you sure you're pronouncing that correctly, Mr. Richards?"

"Maybe not, but it's summat like that. 'Cept the *Gros-yoo* ain't no navy ship, sir. She's a privateer, she is. Carryin' a letter of marque from Earth."

"That's impossible," Huff said. "Earth ain't issued letters of marque since the Third Trans-Jovian War."

"Seen the papers meself, Captain Huff. Weren't forgeries, neither—I know a Port Town special when I see one. These had a holo-seal and everything."

"We believe you, Mr. Richards," Diocletia said. "And you have my thanks for making your report in person. That was no enviable duty."

Richards ducked his chin gratefully as Diocletia turned to the other Hashoones.

"Let's get back to Darklands," she said. "Sounds like there's a lot to discuss."

4

HIS MAJESTY'S PRIVATEERS

Yes, the privateer is real," said Carina Hashoone, Diocletia's sister. "She's called the *Gracieux*, and her captain is Jean-Christophe Allamand. He's retired from Earth's navy. Spent most of his career chasing Martian blockade runners in the Floras."

"So the commission is legitimate," Mavry said.

Carina nodded. "Yes, and there are five others, all issued within the last six weeks. These new privateers have taken at least three Jovian vessels, all in the Cybele asteroids, and have rescued two Earth and Martian vessels taken by our privateers before they could be condemned at admiralty court. These letters of marque have been issued by Earth's new war minister, Threece Suud."

Tycho gaped at his aunt. Four years earlier, Tycho and Yana had discovered evidence linking Suud—then a secretary in Earth's diplomatic corps—to payments made to pirates preying on Jovian ships. That had led to the Hashoones capturing the *Hydra* and discovering labor camps in which Jovian citizens were working as near-slaves. Earth's government had been badly embarrassed, and Tycho had assumed Suud's career was over.

"Well, this changes things," Mavry said. "Commissioning privateers is a lot more serious than saber rattling."

"Let them stuffed-shirt Earthmen come across the Kirkwood Gap—we'll give 'em what-for," Huff said, accepting a cup of tea from Parsons, Darklands's gray, dignified majordomo. Huff's forearm cannon sensed the old pirate's agitation and began to spin, seeking a target. Parsons glanced mildly at the weapon and glided away with one eyebrow raised.

"If they're in the Cybeles, they're already across the Gap, Grandfather," Carlo pointed out.

"Don't think that isn't being discussed, Carlo," Diocletia said. "On Ganymede they think—"

Carlo's reaction brought his mother up short—he crossed his arms over his chest, scowling, then turned away to look at Carina, who was blowing on her cup of tea.

"Do *you* think it will come to war, Aunt Carina?" he asked.

Tycho glanced inquiringly at Yana, who raised her eyebrows, clearly surprised. Diocletia drummed her fingers on the tabletop.

Carina ran her thumb around the rim of her teacup, frowning, and Tycho could guess what she was thinking. Carina knew a captain's authority—to say nothing of a mother's—extended well beyond her ship. After all, Carina had been Huff's choice to succeed him as captain, but vowed never to go into space again after learning her fiancé, Sims Gibraltar, had died from radiation poisoning suffered at 624 Hektor.

"I believe your captain was answering that," Carina said finally.

"Apparently my opinion isn't valued on this particular subject," Diocletia said in a low, dangerous voice, not looking at Carlo. "Go on, Carina."

Carina sipped her tea. The only sounds were the chuff of Darklands's air exchangers and the plinks and clinks of silverware and plates from the kitchen.

"War would be a disaster for the Jovian Union," she said finally. "Earth can build more ships in a month than we can in a year, and a trade blockade would starve us. And though things have been quieter than expected—recent unpleasant events notwithstanding—we still have to contend with the Ice Wolves. Losing Titan to them would be nearly as bad as a war with Earth."

"I hadn't heard about anything happening at Titan," Mavry said.

"As far as we know nothing is," Carina said. "But on Ganymede there's a lot of worry that it's the Ice Wolves' real target. Titan is the economic engine of the entire outer solar system. If we should lose it . . ."

Her voice trailed off and she shook her head.

"Here's what I don't understand," Yana said. "Earth knows we're caught between two enemies. So why not take advantage of that?"

"Because a war would be a disaster for Earth, too," Carina said. "Any disruption in the delivery of raw materials from the outer solar system—particularly from Titan—would cost their corporations trillions of livres."

"It all comes down to money, doesn't it?" Yana muttered disgustedly.

"Of course it does," Carlo said. "For us and everybody else in the solar system. Don't be naïve, sis."

"I'm not naïve—I just think there are more important things than money."

"Such as?"

"How about freedom? And self-determination? And not wanting to be bullied?"

"People don't worry about that stuff unless they have enough livres to feed their families," Carlo said with a sniff.

"That's enough, you two," Diocletia growled before Yana could reply.

"His Majesty's forces would have trouble defeating us," Mavry mused. "Their supply lines would be too long to defend, and Earth's task forces can't operate indefinitely without fuel and food. We'd prove a tougher opponent than our old friend Mr. Suud might think."

"Yes, we would," Carina said. "But that brings us back to Titan. Earth's fleets could get all the fuel they needed if they occupied it—which a lot of His Majesty's ministers would consider worth a war. If you ask me, that's what's kept the Ice Wolves quiet. Seizing Titan could ensure their independence—but it would also lead to Earth's intervention."

For a moment there was no sound but the squealing of Huff's agitated blaster cannon.

"Fortunately, you can bet Earth's war ministers have considered this same dilemma," Carina said. "If His Majesty wanted to retake the Jovian Union, he'd be signing a declaration of war, not letters of marque. And we have to remember, Earth has problems of its own—the Martian separatists blew up a military communications array on Deimos last month. Issuing letters of marque is a provocation, and a dangerous one. But it's still only a provocation."

"So it won't be war," Tycho said.

"I didn't say that. Nobody wants a war, but sometimes everybody gets one anyway. Dangerous events have a momentum of their own."

Carina smiled and nodded at Parsons, who'd re-appeared to place a platter of sandwiches on the revolving server in the center of the table. The sandwiches were real bread, with ribbons of in vitro beef peeking out.

Tycho spotted Yana eyeing a particularly robust-looking sandwich and hastily spun the server before she could take it. He grinned triumphantly at his sister, then looked over to see his father had nimbly intercepted the sandwich as it passed in front of him.

"Fortunately, there's some good to come out of all this trouble," Carina said. "The Jovian Union is offering rich commissions on prizes seized in the Cybeles, and paying a premium for ships willing to serve as escorts."

Huff's face twisted in disgust.

"Escort duty? Playin' shepherd for a bunch of tea wagons ain't pirate work—more like deep-space babysit-tin'. Talk to me when there's a bounty on this Jean-Chris What's-His-Name."

"The way Captain Allamand is taking ships, that will be soon," Carina said. "And whatever bounties there are, in the Cybeles you'd be well positioned to collect them."

Huff grunted, scratching his bearded chin with the muzzle of his blaster cannon.

"There's something else, too," Carina said. "The Jovian Defense Force hasn't been able to recruit enough privateers, so they've issued new letters of marque. I don't have the whole list of recipients, but I know the Widderich brothers each got one, as did Canaan Bicker-staff and Kanoji Ali."

Mavry and Diocletia exchanged a surprised look.

"I've heard of the Widderiches, but not the others," Tycho said. "Who are they?"

"Straight-up pirates, the whole lot of 'em," Huff murmured, his face a half-living, half-metal grin.

"Pretty much," Mavry said. "All of those captains were either denied letters of marque when piracy was outlawed or lost them because they couldn't stay on the right side of the law."

"So this is what we've been reduced to," Carlo said, his lip curling in disgust. "Letting known pirates fly our colors. It makes us look bad by association."

Yana rolled her eyes at Tycho.

"Arrr, I'm in," Huff said, bringing his metal fist down on the table. "Always liked 65 Cybele—'tis a lively little rock, an' this company will make it livelier."

"And where do the loyalties of this lively little rock lie at the moment, Carina?" Diocletia asked.

"Publicly, the Cybeles are trying very hard to not be on anyone's side right now," Carina said. "A declaration of allegiance would dam up the free flow of livres. And right now they're flowing very freely indeed in that part of the solar system."

"Uh-oh, money. Does this mean Yana's going to make a speech?" Carlo asked.

"Yeah, a short one," Yana said. "You're an—"

"That's enough," Diocletia snapped. "It's decided, then. We go where the opportunities are. And right now that means the Cybeles."

"But no escort duty, Dio," Huff said. "Nothin' worse than a tea-wagon captain what thinks he's spotted a pirate—"

"I'm not fond of escort duty either, Dad. But if something's profitable, I'm not ruling it out. After all, I have no personal objection to livres."

"Except when there are too many of them in other people's pockets and not enough in ours," Mavry said.

"True," Diocletia said. "I never have liked that."

The lowermost level of Darklands was reserved for the family crypt.

No one was actually buried there—like most spacers, the Hashoones were horrified by the idea of spending eternity entombed in rock and dirt. The family memorials were digital—holograms of Hashoones who'd died decades or centuries earlier, their smiles preserved for descendants they'd never met.

Tycho heard the low buzz of his grandfather's voice as he descended the short flight of steps into the crypt—Huff always spent a few hours in the crypt after the *Comet* returned to Callisto, communing with his ancestors.

Tycho coughed politely to make sure he wouldn't surprise his grandfather. Huff's eye was a brilliant spark in the gloom, beneath the bluish glow of a towering hologram.

"Lemme guess, lad," Huff said. "Carlo hoggin' the flight simulator again?"

"Like always. I hope I'm not interrupting."

"No, lad," Huff said softly, tapping keys on the holographic display. "Jes' renewin' old acquaintances. Ol' Johannes fought a number of dustups in the Cybeles, did yeh know that?"

Tycho looked with distaste at the image of Johannes Hashoone, his great-grandfather. Eighty-five years earlier, Johannes had been the ringleader of a crew of pirates who had stolen a fortune from the mail boat *Iris*—a fortune that had been lost until Tycho figured out that Johannes had hidden it from his fellow Jupiter pirates beneath the Hashoones' own homestead, in the lightless ocean beneath Callisto's crust. In solving that mystery, Tycho had also discovered that Johannes had ambushed and killed his friend Josef Unger, leaving his ship broken on the surface of a comet.

"Yeh don't think kindly 'bout ol' Johannes, do yeh, lad?" Huff asked.

Tycho hesitated, but then his ancestor's cocky grin made him angry.

"No. He was a cheat and murderer."

Huff stared silently up at the image of his father. Tycho realized he was almost eye to eye with his grandfather. When had that happened?

"I'm sorry to say it, Grandfather, but it's true," he said more quietly.

"He was both those things, 'tis true. I tried to convince meself yeh was wrong about what yeh found. But yeh weren't, lad."

Suddenly Tycho felt ashamed. Huff had been a

midshipman on Johannes's quarterdeck. He'd learned the pirate's trade from him, and spoke of his father with barely concealed awe. Now Tycho had ruined the memories Huff held dear.

"I suppose it was a different time . . . ," Tycho mumbled.

"No it weren't. I don't know why Father did what he did, and there ain't no way to ask. All I can think is he must 'ave had his reasons."

Tycho turned to look at his grandfather and found Huff still staring up out of the shadows at the bright image of his father.

"I ain't sayin' they was good reasons—but killin' just for the pleasure of it? Arrrr, that weren't like Father. Somethin' made him do a thing he didn't want to. Been in that situation meself."

Tycho paused. He imagined himself calmly asking his grandfather about the Battle of 624 Hektor. Had he and Thoadbone Mox really been the ones who distributed software to the other Jupiter pirates—software that had hidden a jamming program that left the Jovian craft helpless when Earth's warships attacked? If so, had Huff known what the program concealed? Did he really think Oshima Yakata was a traitor because her ship hadn't been affected? And if not, why had he spent more than a decade telling people that she was?

But Tycho knew he wouldn't ask any of those questions. That he couldn't.

After all, Tycho had secrets of his own now. Like the fact that he'd conspired with a Securitat agent named

DeWise, who'd met him on Ceres and all but handed him the bulk freighter *Portia* as a prize. Or that Tycho had pocketed the data disk he'd discovered in the *Iris* cache and given it to DeWise in return for a clear title to the *Hydra*—an agreement the Securitat agent had broken.

Tycho hadn't spoken with DeWise since then, and had sworn he'd never cheat again in pursuing the captain's chair, no matter how the Securitat or anyone else tried to entice him. But he still worried that his family would discover what he'd done. If that happened, he knew, his pursuit of the captaincy would be over—you didn't lie to your crewmates or steal from them, because no starship could operate effectively if her crewers didn't trust each other.

And if those crewmates were also your family?

The family is the captain, and the captain is the ship, and the ship is the family.

He and Yana had first heard that in the cradle. The Hashoone retainers who'd taught him the spacer's trade belowdecks had recited it regularly. And his mother had quoted it whenever his disagreements with Carlo or Yana had become a problem on the quarterdeck. And yet he'd ignored it when it really mattered.

But then Tycho shook his head, glaring up at Johannes.

No, he thought. *I've made mistakes and done things I'm not proud of. But I'm not a murderer. I would never do anything like what you did.*

Tycho turned to his grandfather, but whatever he'd

been going to say died away. Huff looked shrunken and tired, like the weight of the metal half of his body was dragging the rest of him down.

"I've never been to 65 Cybele, Grandfather," Tycho said, trying to think of something to dispel the gloom. "What's it like?"

Tycho saw his grandfather's shoulders lift.

"Arrr, it's as close as yeh can get these days to how things used to be. Plenty of prizes for a crew what keeps their ears open and their hands on their carbines."

"Well, that's good," Tycho said. "Still, I wonder if these new privateers are a bad idea—for the Jovian Union and for us."

"Bah, 'tis long overdue, lad. Solar system's gotten too civilized—give me pirates o'er bureaucrats an' lawyers any day."

Huff grinned at his grandson.

"Captured my first prize near 65 Cybele, y'know," he said. "Just a little coaster out of Mars, name of the *Emerald*, but she had a full hold. I was on the quarterdeck for a middle watch. *Emerald* tried to run, so I beat to quarters, blasted off her sensor masts 'fore she could call for help, then led the boardin' party. 'Twas Grigsby's first boardin' party, come to think of it—we'd been belowdecks together. Crew of the *Emerald* raised a little ruckus when we came aboard. Lemme see if I can find the scar. . . ."

Huff looked down at his metal forearm and frowned. His blaster cannon twitched.

"Arrr, it was on me left hand—I forget what pieces

'ave gone missin'. I can still feel that hand, did yeh know that? Itches at night summat fierce."

"You never told me that," Tycho said. "I'm sorry, Grandfather. That must be awful."

"It ain't no shindy," Huff grumbled. "Strange, to 'ave a thing what's gone pain yeh. Ain't had that hand for fifteen years, but I'll wake up during the middle watch an' need to scratch it, an' I can't."

5

THE CAPTAIN'S CHAIR

There's another one of those poor dirtsiders," Yana said.

The droopy-eyed man was walking back and forth beneath a display urging viewers to join the Jovian Defense Force, the weight of a hologram emitter and power pack causing him to slump. A virtual Jovian flag waved proudly above his head, rippling in an imaginary breeze.

"What's that make, three of them?" Tycho asked.

"Plus the guys with mediapads at the transportation hub," Carlo said.

"We could enlist," Tycho said with a grin. "Imagine Grandfather's face if we came back with crew cuts and JDF uniforms."

Carlo didn't smile back.

"On the lower levels we might get pressed," he said. "And if they're recruiting this heavily, you can bet there will be crimps about, too—filling their clients' crew rosters by force."

"Any crimp so much as looks at me sideways, he'll regret it," Yana said.

"Can we not have another incident like the one on Pallas?" Tycho asked.

"Why not?" Yana asked. "That turned out okay."

"I think you're safe, sis," Carlo said. "I doubt the JDF's desperate enough to press one-armed spacers quite yet."

Neither Tycho nor Carlo had grumbled when Diocletia ordered them to accompany Yana to the treatment center. The wait for Carina to finish negotiating the terms of their commissions in the Cybeles had left everyone at Darklands stir-crazy and snappish.

The treatment center was on one of Port Town's upper levels, which were clean, brightly lit and well patrolled. It wasn't like that farther down—the deeper precincts were a dim, frigid labyrinth prowled by gangs that preyed on the poor and broken residents. Tycho wondered how many able spacers a press gang would find down there—the upper levels seemed like a much richer hunting ground, their tunnels thronged with men and women whose plentiful tattoos and rolling gait indicated they made a living aboard starships.

The Hashoones reached the treatment center without incident, and the doctor inspected Yana's shoulder, which remained blistered and an angry red. She peered at the burn through a full-spectrum monocle, then nodded with satisfaction.

"My compliments to your ship's surgeon, Mistress Hashoone," she said. "A couple hours of platelet regeneration should restore full mobility. I'm afraid it will scar, though."

"Occupational hazard," Yana said with a shrug, and the doctor's eyes jumped to Carlo's right cheek, creased by a laser beam aboard the *Hydra* four years earlier. Tycho felt a twinge of regret that he had no scars of his own.

The doctor wrapped Yana's shoulder in a cuff connected by tubes to a humming machine. Yana grimaced as the cuff tightened and the machine began to whine.

"The discomfort will fade in a few minutes," the doctor said, then excused herself, leaving the siblings alone.

All three of their mediapads chimed. Tycho managed to dig his out before Carlo. He eyed the screen, then pumped his fist.

"Mom wants engines lit at 0930 tomorrow. I can't wait to get out of here."

Carlo made a face.

"What?" Yana asked. "I know you're as ready to get

out of here as we are—you didn't even run piloting sims this morning."

"Oh, I want to get out of here. It's what we're getting into that worries me."

"Yeah, I sure hate privateering," Yana drawled as the machine continued its work. "Too much excitement for me. If only I could sit on my butt in an old mine, flying a pretend ship and ringing Parsons for more tea."

"Very funny," Carlo said. "Obviously the situation in the Cybeles is unstable. Here's my question: Will our sending a bunch of unreformed pirates there make it better or worse?"

"We're not the ones who created the instability," Tycho said. "Earth did that, with its provocations."

"Provocations responding to provocations, as it's been for centuries."

"You've always been great at explaining why we're wrong, Carlo," Yana said. "You ever think about why that is?"

"Because you two give me so many opportunities to practice?"

"Ha. Cute, but no. It's because criticizing is all you can do—you never bother coming up with answers of your own."

"Of course I do," Carlo said. "I just don't feel like sharing them with you."

"I don't think that's it," Yana said. She leaned forward, eyes narrowed. "Quit playing games, Carlo. We all know the solar system's a mess. If you're so smart, how would you fix it?"

To Tycho's surprise, their brother smiled.

"By making peace with Earth. A real peace. One that takes everything into account—our interests, Earth's, and those of the outer planets."

"Does that include the Ice Wolves' interests?" Tycho asked.

"The Ice Wolves are part of everything, yes."

"At the moment I'm against making peace with them," Yana snapped.

"I thought you were all about freedom and self-determination," Tycho said.

"I was until they tried to kill me."

Tycho shrugged. "Well, if you're going to take it personally . . ."

Yana glared at her twin brother, then turned back to Carlo. "So your answer is we surrender."

"Of course not," Carlo said. "But Earth *is* the dominant power of the solar system. It's crazy not to acknowledge that."

"Then why doesn't His Majesty actually act like the solar system's leader, instead of its biggest bully?" Tycho asked.

"Good question. Perhaps if we abandoned our provocations, we could have that conversation with him."

"Provocations like what?" Yana asked. "Like privateering?"

"Yes, like privateering."

The three of them were silent for a moment while the machine whined and worked.

"This isn't about what's happening in the Cybeles," Yana said quietly. "You want to abandon the family business."

Carlo crossed his arms over his chest.

"Let's be honest about what the family business is. We're *pirates*. Nobody will say it, but it's true—and giving these new letters of marque to a bunch of rogues just proves it. After 624 Hektor they came up with a new name for what we do, but it's the same profession."

"That isn't true and you know it," Tycho said. "We follow the rules of our letter of marque and abide by the laws of interplanetary commerce. Pirates don't do that."

"That's a little speech we've all memorized," Carlo said. "But we're the only ones who interpret the laws that way. Unless you want to count the Ice Wolves, which isn't the company I want to keep."

"What about Earth, since they have privateers of their own now?" Yana asked. "Here's what I don't get, Carlo—you want to be captain, but you think we shouldn't be privateers anymore. So what's the point?"

"How much longer do you think there will be privateers?" Carlo asked.

Yana and Tycho glanced at each other, puzzled.

"As long as there are Hashoones," Yana said, and after a moment Tycho nodded in agreement.

"I don't think so," Carlo said. "The current situation can't continue."

"And why not?" Tycho asked. "Have you noticed there are a lot more privateers now than there were a month ago?"

"That's just another sign of how unstable everything is. We need to think about what happens the day privateering ends, because it'll be here soon. And we need to be ready."

"So what do *you* think comes after privateering?" Tycho asked his brother.

"Nothing," Yana said. "If privateering ends, we have nothing."

"Why should that be true?" Carlo asked, his voice rising. "We've got a fast ship that's tough in a fight, a highly skilled crew, and a long service record."

"And that gets us what?"

Carlo hesitated, and Tycho knew he was debating how much to share with them.

"A place in the Jovian Defense Force. *If* we play our cards right. After privateering ends, the JDF will bring the best privateer bridge crews into the military as officers. The question is, will we be able to take advantage of it?"

Yana leaned forward, causing the machine strapped to her shoulder to squall a warning as the tubes began to stretch too far. She scooched back on the examining table and glared at Carlo.

"You know, you could have just joined the JDF in the first place," she said. "That would have saved us all a lot of trouble. I just don't get how you can still be so in love with them. Don't you remember what happened at Saturn?"

"Of course I remember what happened at Saturn."

"Then you remember that to the JDF, we're *auxiliary* units. Expendable."

"That was the opinion of one commander who was unfit for duty."

"Please," Yana said. "Admiral Badawi never had an original thought in his life. They all think that way. If privateering is coming to an end, there's *nothing* waiting for us. We're useful tools of the Defense Force, that's all. If a day comes when they no longer need us, we'll be thrown away."

"Now you're being paranoid," Carlo said.

"Am I? Speaking of paranoid, why haven't you shared this opinion with Mom and Dad? Or with Aunt Carina, since you think she knows better than them?"

"There's no point talking about it with Mom and Dad. They're from another time—one they can't admit is going away."

"I don't think that's it. I think it's because you're scared."

Carlo snorted. "Scared? Of what?"

"Of not becoming captain, of course."

"Really? And who am I going to lose to? You?"

"No, not me," Yana said, then inclined her head at Tycho. "Him."

Carlo flipped his hand dismissively, but he wouldn't look at his brother and sister. His eyes jumped everywhere in the medical chamber—from the hissing equipment to the doctor's computer console to the humming lights— but they avoided his siblings' faces.

"The crewers like Tycho," Yana said. "He listens to them, while you can't be bothered. And he sees things. He makes connections. You don't. All you do is fly."

"I fly a lot better than either of you do," Carlo snarled. To Tycho's surprise, he sounded more hurt than angry.

Yana heard it too.

"You *are* scared," she said. "Because you know Tycho's catching up with you."

"Tyke's had some lucky breaks. But it won't be enough. I'm twenty, and the two of you are just sixteen."

"That doesn't matter and you know it."

Now Carlo turned to look at them.

"That's where you're wrong, Yana. Mom's getting old."

"Mom's what, forty-five?" Tycho asked. "That's not exactly ancient."

"It is in our profession. You know what they say, there's regular years and then there's captain's years. She's not going to be captain forever—I don't think she *wants* to be captain forever. If there's no more priva-teering, and she steps down, who would she pick as her replacement? It wouldn't be you, Yana, and it wouldn't be Tyke either. It'd be me. For the good of the family, you both need to accept that."

6

THE DEFENSE FORCE REQUESTS

Tycho could never sleep the night before his family returned to space. He woke a little after 0400, blinking at the simulated starfield on the ceiling above his bed, and scrubbed at his eyes. He'd just given up and decided to get out of bed when his media-pad chimed softly on his desk.

Curious, Tycho padded over, halfheartedly trying to restore order to his pile of dark hair. The sender's recognition code was a nonsensical string of characters. He went to delete it, then stopped.

The subject of the message read *Cybeles*.

Almost unwillingly, Tycho opened it. He already knew who'd sent it.

> I'M SORRY WE'VE LOST TOUCH. THE SITUATION IN THE CYBELES IS DANGEROUS. PERHAPS I COULD BUY YOU A JUMP-POP AT THE PLACE WE USED TO MEET?

Tycho stared at the message as if it was radioactive. He went to delete it, then changed his mind and began typing angrily.

> THE LAST THING MY FAMILY NEEDS IS ANY MORE OF YOUR HELP. YOU'VE PROVEN TO ME THAT YOU'RE A LIAR AND A CHEAT. DON'T CONTACT ME AGAIN.

DeWise must have been at his console—Tycho wondered idly where that was—because the mediapad beeped just a few seconds later.

> TYCHO, THIS ISN'T ABOUT YOU AND ME. WHAT'S HAPPENING IN THE CYBELES THREATENS ALL OF US. WE NEED YOUR HELP—AND YOU AND YOUR FAMILY COULD USE OURS.

Tycho shook his head.

Forget it, he typed back, then waited for the next beep.

YOU KNOW HOW TO REACH ME IF YOU RECONSIDER.
PLEASE DO. UNTIL THEN, STAY AWAY FROM THE ICE
WOLVES. LEAVE THEM TO US.

Tycho archived the conversation with DeWise in an encrypted section of his mediapad only he could access, then sorted through his clothing and gear again, though he knew everything was in order. He pawed halfheartedly through his T-shirts and jumpsuits, then sighed and left his quarters, hoping to beat Yana and Carlo to the downstairs bathroom. Darklands's water-recycling system was old and creaky—if you waited too long for the shower, the water would be tepid and faintly greasy from traces of soap.

Tycho's quarters opened onto a long spiral ramp that led down from Darklands's airlock on the surface of Callisto to the living room and kitchen far below, passing bedrooms, storage areas, and simulator rooms. The homestead had begun as the central shaft of a mine excavated four centuries ago, when the Hashoones' ancestor Gregorius had arrived from Earth. Here and there along the ramp, slabs of iron sealed off tunnels leading deeper into Callisto's crust, dug before the mine was exhausted. When that happened, Gregorius's great-grandson Lodovico Hashoone had bolted weapons onto his motley collection of ore boats and convinced his miners to sign on as pirates. Some of their descendants still served the Hashoones as retainers.

Tycho found Yana one level down, outside the

simulation room. Tycho thought about racing past her to get to the shower first, then noticed she had her head cocked to one side, her expression intent.

"How's the eavesdropping, sis?" he asked with a smile. Sound bounced up and down the old mineshaft of Darklands in odd ways, and by chance the simulation room was perfectly positioned for a person to hear what was happening a level above—or a level below, where the bedroom shared by Diocletia and Mavry opened onto the ramp.

"Quiet," Yana chided him, not the least bit embarrassed at being caught. "Mom and Grandfather are exchanging broadsides."

Tycho joined her, resting his elbows on the railing and peering down into the living room, which was dominated by the giant steel water tank that tapped into the lightless ocean many kilometers below.

"—wish I hadn't lived to see the day a Hashoone would take some Securitat spy aboard the *Comet*," Huff growled from the next level down.

Some Securitat spy? Tycho stared down into the living room, trying to stop his hands from shaking. *No. It can't be. They* wouldn't.

"Like I told you the first time, Mr. Vass isn't with the Securitat," said Diocletia, sounding angry and tired. "He's an intelligence minister with the Jovian Defense Force."

Tycho blew his breath out in relief.

"Shh," Yana said.

"Intelligence means he's a spy," Huff growled. "And spies are all the same."

"You know that isn't true," Mavry said. "The Securitat and the JDF barely work together since what happened at Saturn."

"That's what they want yeh to believe," Huff said, his voice rising. "This Vass will break into the Log an' copy the lot, give all our secrets to the Securitat."

"Vesuvia's systems are secure—unless we're talking about rogue programs you put in there without telling anybody," Diocletia said sharply.

"Arrr, that's a low blow, Dio. Thought we agreed to let that be."

"When did we do that? I haven't forgotten about it— just like I haven't forgotten how you let Thoadbone Mox go, for some reason you've never seen fit to explain."

"The daughter I raised wouldn't 'ave needed it explained. I let Mox go cause he's a Jupiter pirate—the last of us, maybe. He deserves better than dyin' in a court-room because some politician's declared us extinct."

"How romantic. And do you recall how Mox paid you back for this act of pirate brotherhood? I remember he tried to kill us at P/2093—and nearly succeeded at Saturn."

"Piratin' is a dangerous business. But it's better than playin' ferryboat for the JDF. No matter how many livres some bureaucrat dangles in front of yeh."

"Agree with Grandfather there," Yana muttered to Tycho.

"How many times have we had this conversation?" asked Mavry. "Huff, there's nothing wrong with livres that don't involve someone shooting at you."

"Agree with Dad there," Tycho said, and his sister rolled her eyes.

"Except these livres are for lettin' a spy aboard our ship," Huff growled. "At least keep him away from the kids."

"And how would I do that, exactly?" Diocletia asked. "It's three days to the Cybeles—shall I tie our guest into a hammock for the duration?"

"Second best to marchin' him out the airlock, but that would do."

Then the old pirate's voice changed, and Tycho had to strain to hear him.

"Seen these Securitat types operate too many times, Dio—seen 'em be the ruin of many a good pirate. Keep him away from the kids. Is that too much to ask?"

Tycho stared down into the living room. He realized he was looking at the very spot where he'd stolen the data disk for DeWise.

"All three of our kids have their faults, but I've never worried about their loyalty," Mavry said, sounding offended.

"Arrr, I know they're good kids, Mavry. But ain't nobody born bad. Them Securitat types spin their webs, an' little by little they wrap yeh up. Until yeh can't find yer way out, an' yeh realize they own yeh."

"You two are up early," a voice said very close by.

Startled, Tycho turned to see Carina standing on the ramp. One hand was around a mug of steaming tea. The other was on her hip.

"You're not the first middies to discover that spot, you know," she said. "But you might be the first to be so embarrassingly obvious about it. Yana, I hope you run sensors a little more carefully than you monitor your own surroundings."

Tycho wondered how this would look in the Log— two midshipmen spying on their parents.

Yana sighed. "What happens now?"

Carina raised an eyebrow.

"Officially, nothing. Unofficially, you're volunteering to prepare the articles for the Cybele cruise, while your brother will make sure all hands sign those articles."

Yana crossed her arms over her chest and hung her head. She disliked all pixel work, but preparing the written agreement for each cruise was her least favorite assignment. Tycho stifled a groan—he'd have to spend an hour and a half standing by the airlock belowdecks waiting for the ferries returning the Comets from shore leave in Port Town, explaining the articles to crewers who had no interest in reading them, and clarifying minute points of order with the hands who fancied themselves space lawyers.

"But Mom assigned the articles to Carlo," Yana objected. "What will I tell him?"

"That you're the kindest, most generous of sisters. Why would that surprise him? Now I believe your captain wants engines lit by 0930, so get moving."

At the *Shadow Comet*'s port airlock, Tycho finished entering the last retainer's name into his mediapad and deactivated the screen.

"Full complement aboard and all hands have signed the articles," he said wearily into his headset. "I'm coming up."

Up by the bow, the bosun's pipes shrilled out an order, followed by the sound of a lone bell—it was 0830, an hour to engines lit.

Tycho stepped around a new crewer dangling a malodorous hunk of dried fish in front of the ship's cat, who sniffed at it suspiciously before walking off in disdain. He ascended the ladderwell and emerged on the brightly lit quarterdeck, where his parents were running diagnostics and Carlo was testing the flight controls. Next to Tycho's station, Yana was quarreling with Vesuvia about how to deal with a stuck sensor mast, while Huff was in his usual spot between Tycho's and Yana's stations, forearm cannon jerking irritably.

Carlo turned around as Tycho stepped off the ladder. He grinned, then stretched languorously.

"Thanks for the extra sleep, Tyke," he said, resting his sneakers on his console. "Really nice of you and Yana."

"Belay that," Diocletia said, and then her gaze fell on her younger children. "I decided not to ask Carina what trouble you two managed to get into so early in the morning. You're too old to be stealing cookies out of the pantry."

"That's my department," Mavry said.

"Were you up early running a piloting sim, Tyke?" Carlo asked. "Figured out how not to fly into Jupiter yet?"

"What part of 'belay that' was unclear?" Diocletia asked. "Our passenger, Mr. Vass, just left Port Town on a ferry. When he arrives, you two will give him a tour of the ship and get him settled in his cabin. I want you both back here at 0915."

"Aye-aye," Tycho said, then hesitated. "What cabin is he using? I suppose he could bunk with Mr. de Pere— he's most junior in the wardroom."

"A JDF minister sharing a cabin belowdecks?" Diocletia asked with a raised eyebrow. "I don't think they'd care for that on Ganymede. Mr. Vass will take Carina's old cabin."

Shocked faces turned to Diocletia. Carina's cabin had been empty since 624 Hektor.

"Have you all gone deaf? Mr. Vass will use my sister's cabin. I just made it ready myself."

It was Huff who spoke first. "Yer givin' my daughter's cabin to . . . to a *spy*?"

"Let's please not refer to our passenger as a spy. But yes, that's exactly what I'm doing. It's been fifteen years since Carina swore she'd never set foot on the *Comet* again. I don't think she's changing her mind."

Huff sputtered, his forearm cannon pinwheeling crazily.

"The solar system's changing," Diocletia said. "Time we accept that. If we can't start with something as obvious as this, what chance do we have of accepting things that are really important? Now, I trust my order is clear?"

She looked at each of her family members in turn. Mavry put up his hands in acquiescence. Carlo offered his mother a nod. Tycho looked down at his sensor board, then nodded hurriedly when he felt his mother's eyes lingering on him. Yana shrugged. But Huff just stared at his daughter, his artificial eye blazing white.

An alert sounded on Tycho's sensor board.

"Inbound ferry requesting docking permission," Vesuvia said.

"Granted," Diocletia said, gaze still fixed on Huff. "Direct the pilot to the port airlock and ask him to hold—in case my father decides he would rather return to Port Town."

For a moment the quarterdeck was silent except for the chug of the *Comet*'s air scrubbers.

"I'm goin' to me cabin before yeh rent it out to the next spy," Huff said.

Then he turned and clomped up the ladderwell to the top deck, his metal feet ringing out like hammers. Tycho watched his grandfather vanish, trailing a stream of invective.

"Tycho?" Diocletia asked. "Are you joining your sister belowdecks?"

"What? Oh—of course, Captain."

Tycho started to rise from his seat, but he had forgotten to unstrap his restraints and fell back into it. He fumbled with the straps, trying to ignore Carlo's laughter, then followed Yana down the ladder. Crewers and retainers touched their knuckles to their brows, and Tycho and Yana nodded in return.

The *Comet* shook faintly as the ferry's docking ring aligned with the privateer's, sealing the two craft together. The lights around the airlock blinked green.

"You do the talking," Tycho said to Yana.

"No way! That's your job!"

"Why is it *my* job?"

"Yana, your microphone's hot," Diocletia said over their headsets.

Yana stabbed guiltily at her headset's controls while Tycho closed his eyes in dismay. They both heard their mother sigh.

"I don't know why everybody's getting along like cats in a sack today, but it needs to stop. You two can help by not embarrassing us for the next fifteen minutes. Tycho will greet the minister. Is that clear?"

"It's clear, Captain," Tycho said with a final glower at his sister. "Quarterdeck, we are green to receive our passenger."

"That's better," Diocletia said. "Vesuvia, open her up."

The inner airlock door rose smoothly into the ceiling. Standing in the ferry's airlock was a little man with close-cropped white hair and a neatly trimmed beard, his eyes a bright blue. He carried a large canvas valise and wore a neat formal tunic and trousers—not a military uniform, but the garb of a government official.

"Masters Hashoone, my name's Vass. Nehemiah Vass," he said in a crisp voice. "Permission to come aboard?"

"Granted, Mr. Vass," Tycho said. "I'm Tycho Hashoone, and this is my sister, Yana. Welcome aboard the *Shadow Comet*."

Vass extended his hand to Tycho, then bowed to Yana.

"You can leave your bag, Minister," Tycho said. "One of our crewers will take it to your cabin."

Vass set the large valise down gratefully. As Yana closed the airlock, he peered beyond Tycho into the dim depths of the privateer's lower deck, where crewers were rushing among the maze of struts and girders. Somewhere aft they heard Grigsby directing a string of impressively awful oaths at a crewer who'd done something to trigger his wrath.

Vass looked surprised by the paint-peeling torrent.

"You'll discover things can be a little . . . *informal* belowdecks, Mr. Vass," Tycho said. "Um, our captain's ordered engines lit at 0930, but we can show you around first if you like."

Vass brightened. "I would like that very much, Masters. I've never been aboard one of our privateers."

"Then follow us," Tycho said. "We'll show you to

your cabin and then give you a tour of the quarterdeck. The ladderwell is this way."

"But what about this level?" Vass asked. "I'd like very much to see it as well. If there's time, of course."

Tycho and Yana looked at each other, surprised. The bells clang-clanged for 0900 and Vass jumped at the sound.

"It's been a while since I was aboard a starship," he said. "I forgot about all the racket."

"We hardly notice it by now," Yana said.

"You'll get used to it too," Tycho said. "So this is the port side of the ship. There are eleven gunports on each side, eight fore of the airlock and three aft. Behind the gunnery ladderwell you'll find the main hold. And if you'll come this way, Mr. Vass, we'll show you the magazines, infirmary, and the mess."

Crewers rushed around them in a blur of glowing tattoos and clouds of cheroot smoke, muttering greetings and touching their knuckles to their foreheads. Vass had to dodge a giant crewer with a mohawk who emerged from the head and gaped in horror at the sight of two members of the bridge crew.

"That ladderwell leads to the quarterdeck," Tycho said as the big crewer smacked his knuckles to his scalp and fled. "And these are the cabins used by the below-decks officers."

"They're much smaller than the ones aboard a military vessel," Vass said. "Are your quarters down here too?"

"No," Yana said. "We're bridge crew, so we berth with the rest of our family on the top deck."

"That's where you'll be staying as well, Mr. Vass," Tycho added. "And this is the wardroom. The below-decks officers eat here, but during combat this room is cleared and becomes the surgeon's operating theater."

Vass nodded distractedly, peering at the crewers surrounding them.

"But these people can't all be officers. Where do they sleep?"

"In hammocks," Yana said. "Back on the main portion of this deck."

"I didn't see any," Vass said, retreating to look up into the maze of struts and girders they'd passed through earlier. "Where are they?"

"We need to hurry, Tyke," Yana said in a low voice. Tycho shrugged helplessly.

"Right now they're stowed for departure," Tycho told Vass. "The crewers lash them to their footlockers, which are magnetized so they can be attached to the girders. 'Lash up and stow,' we call it."

"Ah. Can I see?"

Yana reached out to grab a young crewer's shoulder. "You there. Would you unfurl your hammock for a visitor?"

"Which I jes' stowed it," grumbled the crewer, who wasn't more than a year or two older than the twins.

Yana took a step back, astonished.

"Yana, he's new," Tycho said hastily—the crewer's

name escaped him, but Tycho had read the articles to him less than an hour before.

"Pardon, Master Hashoone," the young man muttered, raising his knuckle to his forehead. "Didn't see yeh there."

Yana stepped forward until her nose was a millimeter from the crewer's.

"I see you've met my brother. I'm Yana Hashoone—bridge crew. Now, do I need to repeat my order?"

Before the crewer could say anything, Grigsby emerged from the passageway that led to the wardroom.

"What's this then?" he asked.

"Mr. Vass, this is Mr. Grigsby, our warrant officer," Tycho said.

"Pleasure," Grigsby muttered, but his eyes were fixed on Yana and the crewer.

"I didn't mean to cause any difficulty, Masters," Vass said. "Perhaps we could continue the tour later?"

"What's your name?" Yana asked the young crewer.

"Immanuel Sier. Signed on this morning out of Port Town."

"You don't sound Jovian, Mr. Sier," Yana said.

"Mum came to Port Town from Enceladus," Immanuel said, raising his chin to stare back at Yana.

"A Saturnian?" Yana asked. "Who doesn't salute and talks back to officers? Like we don't have enough problems these days?"

"Yana, Mr. Sier signed the articles and has been read in," Tycho objected.

"I'm Saturnian—and what of that?" Immanuel demanded. "Bein' Jovian don't make yeh better'n me, miss."

One of Grigsby's big hands closed around the front of Immanuel's jumpsuit and dragged him away from Yana.

"That's *Mistress Hashoone*, crewer," Grigsby growled, his eyes bulging. "You make your apology right now, Mr. Sier—or I'll throw you to the crimps."

"Meant no disrespect, Masters," said Immanuel, his knuckle rising slowly to barely graze his brow.

"'Meant' ain't what matters on my deck," Grigsby rumbled. "And now you'll come with me."

Vass stared after Immanuel as Grigsby propelled the unfortunate crewer toward the wardroom.

"Um, as we were saying, Mr. Vass, once we're under way the crewers will tie up their hammocks between the girders here and sleep in watches," Tycho said. "We have seven aboard the *Comet*—the first watch starts at 2000 and lasts four hours, followed by the middle watch, morning watch, forenoon watch, afternoon watch, first dog watch, and second dog watch."

Vass frowned. "Is that right? Wouldn't that be twenty-eight hours?"

"Nicely done, Minister," Tycho said. "Most dirtsi . . . um, *visitors* don't notice that. The dog watches are two hours each."

Vass craned his neck to peer around their cramped surroundings. "Even with the watches, there can't be enough room here."

"Each crewer gets half a meter," Tycho said. "You get used to it. I thought it was cozy when I was an apprentice."

That had been true . . . eventually. But first there had been nights spent hoping the crewers around him couldn't hear him sniffling—or, worse, the glassy-eyed middle watches in which he'd made mistake after mistake and been corrected by glowering, gigantic men and women who'd been rated able spacers decades earlier. How many times had he sworn that this was the last day, that tomorrow he'd ask to see his mother and plead for her to send him back to Darklands?

"But you said your quarters were elsewhere," Vass said. Tycho noted with amusement that they'd struck a tacit agreement to ignore his still-fuming sister.

"Now they are. But as apprentices we slung hammocks belowdecks with the rest of the crewers. You stay here, learning your trade, until you're rated able spacer and made midshipman."

"I see. And how long does this apprenticeship last?"

"As long as it needs to. I was read in on my eighth birthday—that's the usual practice—and needed a little over two years to make able spacer. And now are you ready to see your cabin, Mr. Vass?"

"A moment more, if you please. How many crewers from this level will be promoted to the bridge crew you talked about?"

"None of them," Tycho said. "Bridge crews are drawn from the family."

"That's not always true," Yana objected.

"Well, sometimes a bridge crew needs to be filled out while the younger members of a family are still apprentices," Tycho said. "In a situation like that, a captain might go down the ladder to fill a position, but everyone knows it's temporary."

"Dad came up from belowdecks," Yana pointed out.

"By marrying Mom. He only spent as long as he did belowdecks because Grandfather insisted on it."

The bells clanged again.

"My sister and I are due on the quarterdeck," Tycho said apologetically. "Yana, I have to run communications with Perimeter Patrol. Perhaps you could show Mr. Vass to the top deck?"

Yana nodded and led Vass aft, heading for the rear ladderwell. Tycho climbed up to the quarterdeck, blinking at the bright light.

"You're late," Diocletia said, without turning. "I trust you managed to give Minister Vass a simple tour without causing some kind of incident I'll have to deal with?"

Tycho just sighed.

7

SERVANTS OF THE UNION

Spirits lifted aboard the *Shadow Comet* once the privateer reached her long-range fuel tanks and accelerated away from Jupiter. Tycho filed the signed articles for the cruise and waited for Vesuvia to confirm that she'd archived them alongside centuries of similar documents amassed under generations of Hashoone captains.

It was spooky to think of all the records in Vesuvia's memory banks, reflecting all the people who'd spent anywhere from days to decades aboard the *Comet*. Mr. Sier and three other crewers, for example, had just made their first appearance in those files. Tycho and Yana's first cruise was in there too, of course, along with Carlo's, and their parents', and Huff's. And those of countless other crewers and retainers, middies and captains. The records contained the names of dirtsiders who'd washed out after a single cruise and spacers who'd arrived centuries ago and now had descendants belowdecks. They preserved the names of boys and girls fated to win the captain's chair and less fortunate apprentices who'd been killed by a moment's inattention or bad luck.

Tycho looked around the quarterdeck. Mavry had the watch and was coolly scanning his instruments, his well-worn boots up on his console. Carlo was in his usual place, hands on the control yoke. He shoved the yoke to starboard but the *Comet* didn't respond, a giveaway that he was deep within a simulation. Yana was belowdecks having her shoulder looked at by Mr. Leffingwell, while Diocletia had retired to the captain's stateroom. And Huff was still sulking in his cabin.

Tycho yawned and excused himself, climbing the ladder to the top deck. The passageway connecting the family cabins was quiet and dim. He thumbed open the door to his cabin and crawled into his bunk, fumbling to set an alarm on his mediapad, and was asleep almost at once.

He awoke not to the alarm but to four bells—it had to be 1400. Blinking, he struggled out of his bunk and saw that the passageway was illuminated by a square of light from the cuddy. He'd missed lunch, but some soup would do nicely.

Tycho poked his head in and found Vass sitting at the table where the Hashoones gathered for meals. Scraps of bright white paper surrounded his mediapad, and a steaming mug of something sat at his elbow.

"Master Hashoone," the minister said. "I never thanked you for the tour of the lower level. It was illuminating."

"My pleasure, Mr. Vass," Tycho said, still a bit sleepy. "Are you hungry? Mr. Speirdyke won't arrive in the galley for a few hours yet, but I could make you some soup."

"No thank you, Master Hashoone. I had a little something in my cabin. I hope my inquiries didn't cause a problem for that young crew member."

"Mr. Sier? He caused his own problems."

Vass hesitated. "If I may ask, what will happen to him?"

Tycho yawned and stretched. "Belowdecks discipline is Mr. Grigsby's department. But I can guarantee you Mr. Sier won't make that mistake again."

"I see. The mistake, I take it, was being insubordinate to a member of the bridge crew?"

Tycho nodded as he sorted through the packets of soup mix.

"It may not seem like a big deal. But aboard a ship, discipline is everything. Every member of the crew has to follow orders from his or her superior officers, without question. If anyone fails to do that, or even hesitates in doing so, it could mean all our lives. So obedience must be absolute."

"Understood. Though—and forgive me if I'm overstepping my bounds, Master Hashoone—your sister did escalate the argument."

Tycho allowed himself a smile. "Escalating arguments is one of Yana's specialties."

He hesitated but supposed there was no harm in letting Vass know the rest of what had happened. "Mom—Captain Hashoone—always says that obedience flows more easily in response to respect and trust. Which is why she ordered Yana to go down and apologize to Mr. Sier. She said Mr. Sier had been insubordinate, but had the excuse of not knowing whom he was addressing. My sister, on the other hand, was rude—and there's no excuse for that."

Vass nodded.

"It's very interesting seeing the workings of a privateer up close," he said, waving vaguely at the scattered papers in front of him. "Quite different from scouring reports to try and figure out what's happening in the Cybeles, Master Hashoone."

"So what *is* happening in the Cybeles?" Tycho asked as he tore off the corner of a foil packet and poured the soup mix into a mug. "Oh, and you can call me Tycho."

"Well, Tycho, what's happening is only obvious once it's over," Vass said with a smile. "Until then, you ask different people and you get different answers. Right now when President Goddard asks what to do about the Cybeles, the Jovian Defense Force tells her one thing but the Securitat tells her something else."

"What is it that you and the Securitat disagree about?"

"How we keep the Ice Wolves from getting control of Titan and the outer planets, but without going to war with Earth. All of which might be at stake in the Cybeles."

Tycho looked up from pouring hot water into his mug and gave a low whistle.

"The entire future of the Jovian Union, in other words," Vass said with a smile. "Before the Battle of Saturn we advocated a cautious approach, while the Securitat thought a show of strength would put down the Ice Wolves' rebellion and discourage Earth from meddling. President Goddard sided with them—and she's regretted it ever since. But I don't need to tell you that—you were there."

Tycho nodded grimly, remembering the screams of the dying crewers belowdecks at Saturn.

"But wait a minute," Tycho said around a spoonful of soup. "It wasn't the Securitat commanding the task force at Saturn. It was you—the Defense Force. You treated us like hired guns—*irregulars* was the word Admiral Badawi used—and abandoned us when things went bad."

Vass nodded and shut his eyes, pinching the bridge of his nose.

"Yes," he said simply. "To Badawi's shame and ours.

We have our own disagreements, Tycho. Some people in the JDF think we need to build a Jovian navy that could hold off an Earth invasion. One that's organized the way Earth would organize it—and to them, that means JDF-commissioned warships with navy crews. Not privateers that they can't control."

"But Earth just started commissioning its own privateers," Tycho objected. "And the Jovian Union issued a bunch of new letters of marque."

"We live in interesting times, don't we?" Vass said with a chuckle. "That's because some of us in the JDF think an arms race with Earth would be madness. I happen to be one of them. A few big warships and support craft is about all we can afford, so we have to be creative. We have to rely on . . . well, 'irregulars' might not be the worst word."

"So you can't make up your minds even within the Jovian Defense Force?"

Vass smiled. "Does your family always agree about what to do?"

"Fair point."

"The Securitat knows it made a mistake at Saturn and is now determined to crush the Ice Wolves. We in the JDF think it's far more important to prevent Earth from getting control of Cybele."

"How would Earth get control? With an invasion fleet?"

"No, with livres. Earth's ministers are pouring money

into the Cybeles in an effort to buy off the people who run things there."

Tycho knew what Yana would say: *As usual, it all comes down to money.*

"So why haven't they taken control already?" he asked. "We can't possibly match what's in their treasuries."

"Because it isn't that simple. Independence has worked out well for Cybele—its financiers and merchants make a pretty good living playing Earth and the Jovian Union against each other. The same goes for their shipwrights—who may, in fact, be the key to everything."

Vass took a sip from his mug, then continued.

"Cybele's shipwrights might be the best in the solar system. They'll build anything you're willing to pay for—and have done so for centuries. Cybeleans built some of the first long-haul ships for prospectors in the outer solar system, and since then they've moved on to ore haulers and tankers . . . but they'll also make cogs and caravels. And small craft with oversized engines and heavy weapons."

"Pirate ships, you mean."

"In the Cybeles, they'd say that's the customer's business."

"So they build ships. Why does that make them the key to everything?"

"Because Earth is offering Cybele a contract to build warships for its fleets. That could lead to a supply depot. And then a naval base."

"A naval base that would be on our side of the Kirk-wood Gap."

Vass looked grave. "That's correct."

"And we can't match what they're offering."

"No, but we don't have to. Cybele wants to keep its independence. Its leaders know they risk losing it by making a shipbuilding deal with Earth. So we can win by offering them a deal that's good enough to outweigh the risks."

"And what deal is that?"

"Raw materials. We're trying to negotiate a deal, but it's off the table if Cybele takes the shipbuilding contract. So Earth is trying to make its offer impossible to refuse by throwing livres at the Cybeleans and demonstrating its power—but without sending warships across the Kirkwood Gap and risking a war. That's how we wound up with privateers flying Earth flags, and commissions for our own privateers."

When Tycho shook his head, Vass flashed a surprisingly boyish grin. "Now throw in the Securitat and Earth's intelligence agencies and a whole pack of diplomats. An interesting situation, wouldn't you say?"

"That's one word for it," Tycho said. "What's the Securitat doing on Cybele, then? You said they wanted to fight the Ice Wolves."

"For now, we're working together—President Goddard has ordered them to support our mission on Cybele."

"And are they?"

"You don't approve of the Securitat, do you?"

Tycho realized his expression must have betrayed him. "I don't like the way they use people. It's dishonorable. I prefer to see my enemies coming. They'll shoot at me, but at least I'll get a chance to shoot back."

"Your enemies?" Vass asked, his bright-blue eyes narrowed. "Do you put the Securitat in that category?"

Tycho felt his cheeks flush. "You don't approve of them either. You just said you disagreed with them."

"That's frequently true. But we have the same goal—to defend the Jovian Union and its citizens. And the Securitat believes in that as passionately as my colleagues in the Jovian Defense Force do. The Securitat's efforts have saved many lives, Tycho. Without them, we might now be caught between two enemies, each emboldened by the other's strength."

"That doesn't make their methods okay, though," Tycho said. "At least not to me."

Vass looked down at the table. Outside, something clanked in the passageway.

"The Jovian Union needs the Securitat. It can do things the Defense Force can't—things we like to imagine we wouldn't do," he said quietly.

The clanking noises stopped. Tycho held up his hand, but Vass wasn't finished.

"The thing about the Securitat is they're an organization trained to learn secrets, ferret out threats, and eliminate those threats without anyone knowing," the minister said. "The danger for a group like that is it can start seeing threats everywhere, and turn secrecy to its own—"

Huff Hashoone strode into the cuddy. Vass looked up at the half-metal pirate, eyes jumping from Huff's blazing artificial eye to his forearm cannon, which had stopped spinning and was now pointed in Vass's direction.

"What're yeh doin' in here, Tyke?" Huff growled.

"Speaking with our guest," Tycho said, putting his mug down. "Mr. Vass, this is Huff Hashoone, my grandfather."

Vass stood and extended his hand. "Captain Hashoone," he said. "It's a pleasure. Your reputation precedes you."

Huff eyed his outstretched hand like it was something that had been fished out of the bilge.

"Arrrrr, yeh ain't worth goin' to the gibbet for. But I catch yeh talkin' to any of my grandchildren agin an' yeh'll go back to the Securitat on crutches. Yeh got that, Mr. Vass?"

"Grandfather, he doesn't work for the Securitat," Tycho protested.

"Don't care who he works for—a spy's a spy."

Huff took one step forward, the motors in his mechanical legs whining. Vass retreated until his shoulders were against the wall of the cuddy. Huff advanced and tapped the minister in the chest with the muzzle of his forearm cannon.

"Yeh leave my grandchildren alone, Vass," he said. "Don't make me say it agin."

Vass slowly reached up and moved the deadly fore-arm cannon aside so it was no longer aimed at his face.

"That's better," he said. "Don't make me say *this* again, Captain Hashoone: Besides being a guest aboard this ship, I am a member of the Jovian Defense Force on a vital mission to Cybele. Like you, I am fighting for the freedom and security of the Jovian Union. I will speak to anyone aboard this vessel whose insights will help me do that—whatever your opinion on the subject."

Huff stared at the little man in disbelief, his blaster cannon whirling madly. Before he could speak, there was a bump above their heads and the *Comet* shook slightly. Huff and Tycho automatically looked up, then at each other: the privateer had separated from her long-range fuel tanks.

"Sensor contact," Vesuvia said. "All crewers to stations. Bridge crew to quarterdeck."

"You'd better get to your cabin, Mr. Vass," Tycho called over his shoulder as he hurried out of the cuddy. "And strap yourself in."

Alarms began to blare as he reached the forward ladderwell.

8
ABOARD THE *ACTAEON*

V ass stopped Tycho just as Tycho put his hands on
the outside of the forward ladderwell's rungs. Huff
was clomping out of the cuddy behind them, his
artificial eye a spark in the gloom.

"Can I observe from the quarterdeck?" Vass asked.

"During an intercept?" Tycho asked. "I doubt Mom
will allow it."

Vass looked at him hopefully, and Tycho shrugged.
"Come on, then. Just don't fall down the ladderwell."

Tycho propelled himself down the ladderwell, descending to the quarterdeck in a controlled fall—and nearly kicking his sister in the head as she arrived from belowdecks. Vass descended more cautiously, then looked around the quarterdeck.

Diocletia wasn't on deck yet. On the main screen, a cross represented the *Comet*'s position; a flashing triangle indicated the unknown ship, with a dotted line representing its current heading.

"Um, Dad, Mr. Vass would like to observe the intercept," Tycho said.

Mavry cocked an eyebrow.

"I'm not sure you meet the height requirements for this ride, Minister."

"I assure you, First Mate Malone—"

"Just kidding," Mavry said. Then his face turned serious. "But if anyone on this quarterdeck gives you an order, Mr. Vass, you need to follow it instantly. Understood? All right, then. Tycho, get our guest a harness and show him how to use it."

As five bells rang out, Tycho helped Vass into a harness, having to tighten the straps considerably to fit the minister's elfin frame, then secured him to the ladder, yanking on the harness until he was confident Vass was unlikely to hurtle across the quarterdeck or plummet belowdecks.

"Ready to take sensors," Yana said. "What have we got?"

"Freighter of some sort, heading for the inner solar

system," Mavry said without turning around. "She's running hot—every dial on her bridge must be hard right."

"Not hot enough," Carlo said. "Plotting an intercept now. I'll hand over navigation once it's locked in, Tyke. If you're ready, of course."

"Play nice, kids," Mavry said mildly. "Tycho, holler when your board's green. We'll hail on all frequencies."

Slow, deliberate steps sounded on the ladder. Diocletia stepped onto the quarterdeck, looking quizzically at Vass where he stood trussed to several rungs.

"Mr. Vass wanted to observe the intercept," Mavry said. "I said yes."

"Of course you did," Diocletia replied, unconsciously capturing her hair with a hair band as she walked to the captain's chair, eyes fixed on the screen.

"Intercept course plotted," Vesuvia said. "Ten thousand kilometers to intercept."

"Sensor profile complete—she's a Chital-class freighter," Mavry said. "Confidence level ninety-eight point two. Yana, scan her engine signature for a match in the registry."

"Already doing it. Querying database now. Sing out if you've got a match, Vesuvia."

"Acknowledged."

"Ready to hail," Tycho said. "Standard intercept procedure?"

Mavry glanced over at Diocletia. "Captain?"

"Not awake yet. Check back in a minute."

"Standard procedure, Tycho," Mavry said. "Vesuvia, display colors."

Tycho checked his microphone. Behind him came the sharp reports of Huff's metal feet on the ladder rungs. The half-cyborg pirate grunted disgustedly at the sight of Vass and took his normal spot on the other side of the ladderwell, magnetic feet locking to the deck. The lights on his chest were flashing yellow.

Tycho allowed himself a smile as he activated the control that would transmit his voice across the void to the freighter. He'd figured his grandfather wouldn't be able to resist being on the quarterdeck for an intercept.

"Unidentified freighter, this is the *Shadow Comet*, operating under letter of marque of the Jovian Union," Tycho said, the words smooth and familiar. "We have you on our scopes and have locked in an intercept course. Activate transponders and respond immediately."

"Heading indicates Ceres," Yana said. "But confidence level is only eighty-four percent."

"With sloppy piloting like that, I'd hate to see their fuel bill," Carlo said.

"Target craft has activated transponders," Vesuvia said. "Jovian colors. Still scanning engine signature."

Tycho's fingers flew over his keyboard. These were his favorite moments aboard the *Comet*—his entire family working smoothly together thanks to years of practice, anticipating each phase of the intercept and adapting to anything unexpected.

"A Chital?" Huff asked. "Arrr, probably one of ours then."

"She's transmitting," Tycho said. "Patching it through."

"Transmission acknowledged, *Shadow Comet*," said a grumpy male voice, the accent Jovian. "This is the *Actaeon*, out of Io. Bound for Ceres."

"Nice to see you, *Actaeon*," Tycho said. "Please transmit the current Jovian recognition code."

"Give us a second to decrypt and initiate code sequence," the *Actaeon*'s captain said.

"Recognition code received," Vesuvia said. "Matches current Jovian code."

"And the engine signature matches the *Actaeon*'s," Yana said. "Confidence level ninety-nine point nine nine nine all the way to infinity. She's ours all right."

Diocletia's fingers drummed on her armrest. Then she leaned forward, eyes fixed on the screen.

"My starship," she said. "Tycho, make conversation. Yana, pull the *Actaeon*'s registry records. I want her home port and the name of her captain. Vesuvia, scan her long-range tanks and cross-reference the results with the standard capacity for that model. I want a fuel-level estimate at ninety-percent confidence."

"Acknowledged," Vesuvia said.

"What's all this about?" Vass whispered to Tycho. "The ship is clearly Jovian."

"Not now, Mr. Vass," Tycho said. "One moment, *Actaeon*. We're, uh, having a problem calibrating our code recognition. Should take us a minute at most."

"She's registered on Io," Yana said. "Captain is Pius Wildasin."

Mavry whistled. "Get that man a nickname."

"Belay that," Diocletia said. "Tycho, patch me through."

"You're transmitting."

"Captain Wildasin? This is Captain Diocletia Hashoone."

"Was something wrong with our code, Captain Hashoone?"

"We're still calibrating. But I recognize your voice, Hans. I never forget a fellow Callistan."

"Hans?" asked Vass. Tycho shushed him.

"Um, I don't believe we've met, Captain Hashoone," the *Actaeon's* captain replied. "My name is Pius . . . and I'm from Io."

"My mistake, Captain Wildasin," Diocletia said. She shut off her microphone and frowned.

"Are you ordering us to heave to, *Comet*?" Wildasin asked.

"Arrr," Huff said, the familiar word a low, satisfied purr.

Diocletia turned in her chair, smiling. "I am now. Tycho, give the order. Vesuvia? Beat to quarters."

"Fuel-level estimate is not complete at desired confidence level," Vesuvia objected.

"That's all right—you can beat to quarters anyway."

"*Actaeon*, we invoke our right to inspect your

vessel under the articles of war governing interplanetary commerce," Tycho said. "Heave to and prepare for boarding."

"I don't understand—" Vass began, but Tycho shushed him again.

Belowdecks, the bosun's pipes shrilled out and the sound of running feet and rolling machinery echoed up the ladderwell.

"This is outrageous, *Comet*," Captain Wildasin said. "There's no cause for detaining us! Continue and I will file a protest with the commercial oversight board!"

"You have that right, of course," Tycho said. "Our order stands. Heave to immediately or you will be fired upon."

"Light fingers on the triggers, Mr. Grigsby," Diocletia said. "Let's try to take her back intact."

"The lads won't break anything, Captain."

"Ion emissions dropping to zero," Yana announced. "She's stopping."

"Now can you explain, Master Hashoone?" Vass asked. "The vessel's Jovian."

"The *vessel's* Jovian," Huff said. "But there's a prize crew on board what ain't."

"Fuel level estimated at forty-four percent," Vesuvia said.

"Forty-four percent?" Vass exclaimed. "That means the freighter wasn't heading for Ceres at all!"

"She was probably headed for Jupiter when she was

seized," Diocletia said from the captain's chair. "When the *Comet* showed up on her sensors, the prize crew that's flying her turned the *Actaeon* around and tried to make it look like she was heading for Ceres. But they didn't quite have time to lock in the right course. Still, I had to be sure."

"And what convinced you?" Vass asked.

"The prize crew already knew Captain Wildasin's name and home port, so he had to correct me when I addressed him using the wrong ones. Still, he found another way to let me know what had happened."

"Which he clearly did. And what was that?"

"Fuel's expensive, Mr. Vass—a captain who doesn't set an exact course is burning up profits, and an engine restart is just as wasteful. So no captain heaves to without a direct order."

"Will the prize crew know that too?" Vass asked.

"They might. Captain Wildasin's risked his safety and that of his crew. So let's get on board before they pay the price."

"And might I—" Vass began.

"Not until the *Actaeon*'s secure."

Diocletia adjusted her headset.

"Mr. Grigsby, I want starboard gun crews on full alert. Assemble the boarding party at the port airlock. Yana, eyes on your long-range scans—let's not step in the same trap twice. Mavry, you'll lead the boarding. Take Tycho with you. Are you willing to go, Dad?"

"When's the last time I passed up a boardin' action?" Huff growled.

"Very well. Mr. Grigsby will be expecting you, then."

Grigsby had handed the chrome musketoons to Mavry when Tycho and Huff made their way belowdecks to join the throng of crewers. Huff had three carbines tucked into a cracked leather harness across his chest and a wicked-looking sword at his hip, while Tycho carried a pistol of his own.

Mavry nodded at Tycho and Huff, then turned to the tattooed Comets. Several of them had been part of Richards' unlucky prize crew. Their knuckles were white around their carbines and knives. Richards himself was peering into the airlock, his shoulders rigid.

Tycho raised an eyebrow at his father, and Mavry responded with a slight nod.

"Go easy, Comets," he said. "Keep your eyes and ears open and follow me to the bridge. And then . . . and then we'll see."

"Three cheers for First Mate Mavry!"

"Quarterdeck, we're ready to open her up," Mavry said.

"Acknowledged," Diocletia replied. She sounded tense and unhappy, and Tycho wondered how many times she had sent loved ones through the airlock of a seized ship without knowing what awaited them.

"Tycho? You in there, kid?" Mavry asked, waving his

hand in front of Tycho's face.

Tycho shook his head. "Sorry, Dad."

"Want me to take point, Master Mavry?" asked Richards.

"I do. But no shooting anybody—not even if the emperor of Earth himself is on the other side of that door."

The *Comet*'s airlock door hissed open. The *Actaeon*'s airlock was open too, and the Comets' shirts rippled as the atmospheres mixed. Three burly men in royal-blue uniforms were standing just outside the freighter's airlock, hands held carefully away from the pistols at their belts. Huff's forearm cannon whined eagerly.

Richards and Laney strode forward, carbines raised, but the two Actaeons offered no resistance.

"Good morning, gentlemen," Mavry said mildly, chrome musketoons still holstered in their bandolier. "I'm First Mate Malone, of the Jovian privateer *Shadow Comet*. Will you please lead the way to the bridge?"

The Actaeons exchanged a glance.

"Follow me," said one. "Just don't expect a warm welcome. If we're late making port at Ceres, it comes out of our pay."

"We won't keep you a minute more than is necessary," Mavry said as they headed deeper into the ship. "Heard anything about Earth privateers in the area?"

"Hear a lot everywhere," the Actaeon said with a shrug. "Whatever trade route you're on is about to be overrun with Earth privateers. Or Jovian privateers. Or Ice Wolves, Martian separatists, and little green men from the Oort cloud. Hearing it ain't the same as it meaning anything."

"You're a wise man," Mavry said as they reached the *Actaeon*'s main ladderwell. He followed the two Actaeons up to the bridge, out of Tycho's sight. The rest of the Comets followed, with Huff's metal footsteps echoing throughout the passageway.

The *Actaeon*'s bridge was lit softly by work lights. Through her wide viewports Tycho could see the immense glowing river of the Milky Way. A middle-aged man sat in the captain's chair. Tycho supposed he must be Captain Wildasin. One finger yanked irritably at the collar of his green uniform, which was dark with sweat.

Tycho looked around the bridge. The four men and two women at the consoles were wearing green. But there were five other Actaeons on the bridge—the two who'd met the Comets at the airlocks and three others. And all of them wore royal blue.

"It sure is crowded on this bridge, Captain," Mavry said.

Wildasin wiped his brow and nodded at one of the blue-clad Actaeons.

"Mr. Haines is our engineer," he muttered. "These are his people."

"Now that much I believe," Mavry said.

He drew his musketoon and aimed at the spot between Haines's eyes. His hand was perfectly still. A moment later the Actaeons wearing royal blue found themselves with carbines in their ears, under their chins, or between their shoulder blades, their weapons taken from them. Tycho noticed with annoyance that his own pistol was wavering in his hand.

"Oh thank goodness," Wildasin said when the last crewer in royal blue had been disarmed.

Haines's fingers twitched. He was breathing hard.

"Gently, please, Mr. Haines," Mavry said. "Now then. You want to tell me who you really are?"

"Like the captain said—"

"They're a prize crew from His Majesty's privateer *Kerensky*," Wildasin said. "She jumped us two days ago, pretending to be a patrol out of 617 Patroclus. They were taking us to Hygiea when you spotted us."

Huff stomped across the bridge and stepped so close to Haines that Tycho could see the distorted reflection of the man's face in his grandfather's chrome skull.

"So this stuffed-shirt Earthman wants to play pirate," he growled.

"I am a member of His Majesty's naval forces!" Haines bleated. "Taking part in a lawful action against enemy commerce according to the terms of our letter of marque!"

Huff's metal fingers closed around the front of Haines's uniform.

"Yer an Earthman what talks like a lawyer," he roared, hurling Haines across the bridge to land in a heap on the deck. "Dunno which part I like least."

"No need for that, Huff," Mavry said, hastily interposing himself between his father-in-law and the fallen Haines. He holstered his musketoon and adjusted his headset.

"Dio? Did you hear all that? Then come meet our new friends."

"The man refuses to be reasonable," Vass said in disgust, turning away from where Haines sat sullenly in the chair that had belonged to the *Actaeon*'s actual engineer, recently released from captivity in the freighter's hold.

Diocletia was leaning against Captain Wildasin's station.

"Must you be difficult, Mr. Haines?" she asked, then looked over to where a glowering Huff was pacing back and forth by the *Actaeon*'s ladderwell, his metal feet striking sparks from the decking. "It's a dreadful cliché, but we have ways of making you talk."

"My prize crew and I are lawful combatants, Captain Hashoone," Haines replied. "Neither you nor this . . . *bureaucrat* has the right to interrogate us outside of a military tribunal. And it is your obligation to guarantee us good treatment and swift repatriation."

Haines glared at Huff. "Seeing how you have already failed in that obligation, I can assure you the proper authorities will be told that I was assaulted in clear violation of—"

"Things can go wrong while securing a prize, Mr. Haines," Diocletia said, studying her fingers. "Terrible things, sometimes."

Six bells rang out. The *Actaeon*'s recording had a bad case of static, Tycho noted.

Diocletia looked up at Haines. "But I'm familiar with the laws of war. And I have every intention of taking you to a neutral port—in this case, Cybele. There, I'm sure His Majesty's representatives will secure your release."

"You're finally acting civilized," Haines said. "Therefore, as an officer in His Majesty's service, I give you my parole. My men can bunk in the common area of your ship, but I will of course expect to be housed in proper quarters. And to have my sidearm returned at once."

"Mmm," Diocletia said. "Mr. Richards? Take these men and put them in the *Comet*'s brig. And fetch Mr. Haines a crate to sit on. A fancy one befitting his status as an officer in His Majesty's armed forces."

Haines stared at Diocletia, his face mottled with rage.

"Into the brig or out the airlock, Mr. Haines," she said. "Let Mr. Richards know what you decide."

"This is outrageous!"

"Or you can answer Mr. Vass's questions, in which case we *might* find room for you to bunk belowdecks with one of the loblolly boys. Let's get moving, Comets.

Captain Wildasin has a journey to resume, and so do we."

"You just wait, Captain Hashoone!" Haines roared. "You Jovians will learn some manners when you meet Jean-Christophe Allamand!"

Diocletia shrugged. "I'm always looking for ways to improve."

9

A VETERAN OF 624 HEKTOR

Tycho wasn't on watch for a while yet, so he retreated to the *Comet*'s top deck as the *Actaeon* resumed her interrupted course for Jupiter.

He paused at the door to his own cabin and then headed aft, passing the galley and the cuddy, the enclosed ladderwell that led from belowdecks to the *Comet*'s top gun turret, and the head. Huff's cabin was the last one on the starboard side. Tycho knocked, then thumbed the door control open when he heard his grandfather's grunt.

Huff's cabin was cramped; next to his rarely used bunk was a humming power unit, connected by multi-colored cables to a long, low metal tank. The lid of the tank was closed, with Huff's head and shoulders emerging from a hatch at one end. His metal legs were lying on the floor of the cabin, next to his artificial hand, forearm blaster cannon, and a scattering of clothing.

"Yer mother send yeh up here, boy?" Huff asked, turning to peer at his grandson.

"No, Grandfather," Tycho said, sitting on the chair bolted to the deck near Huff's worktable. "I just wanted to see how you were doing."

"Been better. That Earthman still squawkin' 'bout the laws of war?"

"Mom's letting him think things over in the brig. But she allowed the other members of the prize crew to give their parole and sling hammocks belowdecks. She thinks a few hours of reflection might make Mr. Haines cooperate with Mr. Vass a little better."

"Arrr. Don't like that Vass, but 'ave to admit he don't scare easy."

"Mr. Vass wasn't doing anything bad earlier, Grandfather. We were talking about the Securitat, and the JDF, and what's happening in the solar system. It was interesting."

Huff turned and Tycho could hear the contents of the tank sloshing as he moved—it was filled with salt water that kept Huff's flesh from developing sores at the attachment points for his mechanical limbs.

"Listen, Tycho," Huff said. "I've seen yeh learn so much these last few years, an' it's made me proud. But there's things yeh still don't know, lad. Like how to deal with these intelligence types. They start by flatterin' yeh, actin' like what yeh know will help the Jovian Union, an' all they want is to listen. But then . . ."

Huff's voice trailed off and he leaned back against the padded rim of the tank, closing his living eye as something beeped irritably inside the tank.

"I'm sorry, Grandfather," Tycho said. "I should let you recharge."

Huff opened his eye again.

"No, boy, I'll be fine. Listen to me. What spies like this Vass want ain't information—it's *people*. People they can use for their own purposes."

The old pirate leaned forward, both his living and artificial eyes ablaze.

"Don't let them do favors for yeh, Tycho. Because them favors ain't free. Sooner or later they'll ask yeh for somethin' back. Won't be nothin' important, not at first. But eventually it'll be something yeh don't feel quite right doin'. An' if yeh agree, they've got yeh. Yeh understand me, Tycho?"

Tycho nodded, his heart thudding in his chest.

Seven bells rang out—it was 1530.

"I know yeh think it can't happen to yeh," Huff rasped, sinking lower into the tank. "But it can. Seen it happen to boys as honest as yeh, with futures as bright as yers."

Huff's eye closed, and Tycho watched him for a moment. His grandfather's beard was more gray than black where it covered the living half of his face, and the flesh was sagging and deeply lined. The tattoos on his flesh-and-blood shoulder had faded, the mermaids and old sailing ships dull and blurred.

He's an old man, Tycho thought, and even as he rebelled at the thought, it was replaced by a worse one: his grandfather wasn't even that. Less than half of him was living flesh—the rest was metal and machinery, circuits and ceramics, grafted to cauterized tissue and sheared-away bone.

Did he ever wish he'd died at 624 Hektor, when an Earth destroyer's missile had ripped through the *Comet*'s quarterdeck? Would he have preferred to be sewn into a shroud and set adrift in eternity, rather than forced to spend several hours a day trapped in this tank? Did he wish he'd never seen the once-mighty Jupiter pirates reduced to privateers and outlaws and hermits?

The scarred, gray-haired old head shifted slightly, living eye still closed.

"Look like yeh seen a ghost, boy," Huff grunted.

Tycho started in surprise, then realized Huff's artificial eye never shut, not even while the living remnant of him slept.

"Sorry, Grandfather. I was just thinking."

"That's a sure road to trouble," Huff muttered, but

a smile creased the living half of his face, and Tycho smiled back.

Tycho opened his mouth to excuse himself, to leave the old man in peace. But then he hesitated. What had happened at 624 Hektor had been a forbidden topic throughout his childhood—a tale pieced together from furtive searches through information databases and overheard snatches of conversation, whispered about when grown-ups weren't listening. But all at once, there in the dim room that smelled faintly of salt water, he discovered he was tired of wondering.

"I know the Securitat gave you the software programs that were supposed to protect against the jamming, Grandfather," he said, relieved to hear his voice was strong and clear. "Did they lie to you about what they were for?"

Huff's eye opened. He turned his head slowly to stare at Tycho, who forced himself to look right back at him. A muscle in the old pirate's cheek spasmed.

"I know you don't want to talk about it, Grandfather. But it *matters*. And I need to know. Did the Securitat have something to do with it?"

Huff said nothing for a long moment. But then he raised his chin until he was staring at the hull above their heads.

"I forget yeh ain't a child no more," he muttered. "Seems like just a couple of weeks back yeh an' yer siblings were mere babes, but then I realize it's been years. Yer practically a man now, Tyke. An' I'm proud of the man yer becomin'. Proud of all of yeh."

Huff sighed. "Hard to think of anythin' in this coffin. But yeh deserve to know. So ask me yer question agin."

Tycho swallowed.

"Did the Securitat have something to do with 624 Hektor?" he asked, forcing himself to say the forbidden name.

"Arrr, of course they did."

Tycho drew back, surprised. But he said nothing, fearful of breaking whatever spell had unbound his grandfather's tongue.

"The freighters in the Martian convoy we ambushed was carryin' United Collective hardware to the warehouses of Ganymede Quint-X. Never found out exactly what, but it was sophisticated stuff, worth a fortune. Part of some sweetheart corporate deal. Our commerce ministry didn't like an Earth corporation gettin' that much control over one of our own, but a Jovian court had said the deal could go ahead. So the Union leadership decided 'twas best for the shipment to go missin', on account of pirates. It had to be a secret, of course. That's where the Securitat came in. We didn't know that Earth was behind it all—that they were pullin' strings, plannin' to destroy us an' embarrass the Securitat by trickin' 'em into helpin'."

"I understand the Securitat was involved," Tycho said. "But who sabotaged the program? Was it Earth? Or was it the Securitat, and they just blamed it on Earth?"

"Arrrr, that's just a grog-shop yarn, boy," Huff

muttered. "An' 'fore yeh say it, I heard what that old witch Oshima tole yeh, back on Io. It ain't true, Tyke. It was Earth, an' it was Oshima."

"But she said you and Mox were the ones who distributed the program. She said she wasn't involved."

"She didn't distribute it. But that ain't the same as not bein' involved."

"What do you mean?"

"Oshima didn't like to get her hands dirty—she'd rather work in the shadows, pulling strings. Most impossible person in the solar system, even 'fore she turned traitor. If she got a hint of a better deal she'd sell yeh out in a second. Her daddy, Blink, was a decent sort, but he never taught Oshima that we don't swindle our own. The way I peg it, she used Mox for her plan 'cause she knew no other Jupiter pirate would listen to her."

Huff laughed, then grimaced as the laugh turned into a coughing fit that sent water sloshing in the tank. Tycho extended his hand, concerned, but Huff shook his head.

"We all did a lively business poachin' crewers from Oshima, y'know. Good captain, but a right hard horse to her own people. She drove all the Yakata family retainers away within a few years, so after that she had to use hired hands. The time to get one of Oshima's crewers was after his second cruise with her—if he didn't have any brains she'd sack him after the first, an' if he had any sense he'd be ready to sack himself after the second."

"Why? What would she do?"

"Arr, what wouldn't she do? Articles for each cruise

longer than a flight manual, an' she'd use the fine print to chisel her crewers out of prizes. Even traveled with a pet lawyer to draw up the articles an' settle disputes with other pirates—fella by the name of Satterwhite, what couldn't practice no more cause he'd shot someone for bein' slow to pay him."

"But if Oshima was so bad, then why did Mox trust her?"

"He didn't. But Thoadbone thought everybody was out to swindle him, so he didn't take it personal when Oshima tried to do it. An' he'd listen to any fool plan from somebody what had two livres to rub together."

"And . . . where did you come in, Grandfather?"

Huff leaned forward, his living eye shut. The lines around his mouth deepened into furrows.

"Mox came to me," he said quietly. "At the Hygiea roadstead. I figgered he was cross 'bout somethin' an' fixin' to kill me for it—that was usually the case—so I drew my persuader and stuck it 'tween his eyes 'fore his brain got around to sayin' how-do. But he jes put up his hands an' smiled, real reasonable-like. That weren't like Thoadbone, an' truth be told it kinda stumped me."

Huff let his head settle with a bump against the top of the tank.

"What a fool I was," he said. "'Bout that an' so much else. If only I'd settled his hash right then an' there, like I wanted to. It would 'ave saved so many good people so much grief."

Then why did you let him go after we captured the Hydra?

Tycho wondered. But he knew that asking would end the conversation immediately—and perhaps forever.

"So Mox told you he was working with Oshima?" he asked.

"No. Connected them dots later. Thoadbone told me 'bout the convoy, an' what it was carryin', an' how the Securitat planned to make it disappear. Sounded like an easy prize, Tyke—solid intelligence, a big reward, an' no questions asked."

The tank began beeping insistently again.

"Give me a minute, lad," Huff muttered.

He closed his living eye, his breath low and labored. For a moment Tycho thought he'd fallen asleep. But then, with his eye still closed, he began to speak again.

"It was a big score when we needed one. I let that blind me, when I should 'ave been askin' questions. An' . . . let's say there were family reasons, too."

"What do you mean, Grandfather?"

For a long moment Huff said nothing, the only sign of life a lone muscle leaping in his cheek. Then he opened his eye and began to speak, his eyes fixed straight ahead, avoiding Tycho's gaze.

"Yeh know yer aunt was engaged to Sims. She'd run off with him—said she didn't care 'bout the captaincy no more. Said yer mother could have it, because she was goin' to serve aboard Cassius Gibraltar's ship instead."

Tycho had never heard that. Huff's face twisted at the recollection.

"My own daughter, willin' to give up the captaincy of

the *Comet*—everything she'd worked for—to take orders on a Gibraltar quarterdeck. Left me in a right clove hitch, lad. I couldn't let that happen—would 'ave been the ruin of the family, one of ours signin' on with our archrivals. Yeh see that, don't yeh?"

Tycho nodded, but Huff had continued talking, not even looking at his grandson.

"Centuries of history an' honor, all reduced to bilge. So I did what I had to do."

He paused, then bit his lip. The expression made for a strange contrast—the anxious, flesh-and-blood side of his face next to the grinning half of a chrome skull.

"I said I'd make Carina my successor, an' let Sims serve on our quarterdeck. But then yer mother . . . yer mother an' Mavry . . ."

"They made a deal with Cassius instead. To join his bridge crew."

"Aye."

Huff shook his head, staring into the recesses of his gloomy cabin.

"It's hard on the ones what ain't named captain—I know that," he said. "But the ship is the family, an' that's more important. Every Hashoone has accepted that rule, for centuries. But yer mother . . . yer mother decided it didn't apply to her and Mavry. Everythin' I'd done, they was determined to undo. I thought a big score like what Mox had brought us . . . well, I thought it would make 'em reconsider. I thought it would remind 'em what we could do together, as a family."

"But Mom still wouldn't have become captain."

"No. It's nothin' against yer mother, lad, but Carina had earned the chair. Yer mother an' Mavry would 'ave had a place on the quarterdeck till yer aunt's children came up the ladder. An' then we'd 'ave found somethin' for them, like we always have. Water Authority, Callisto Minerals, one of the guild halls—somethin' easy, with plenty of livres."

Tycho nodded, but he was thinking of the Hashoone cousins who worked at those places, and the resentment on their faces during privateering discussions at Darklands. Of his mother saying how she and his father had refused to accept spending the rest of their lives as dirtsiders. Of Yana insisting she'd rather die than live as a nobody.

And how would Tycho feel to know the captain's chair would never be his, and he would be replaced by one of his siblings' children?

"But I still don't understand why Oshima would agree to help Earth," he said.

"Neither did any of us, for a while. Oshima was on hard times herself, boy. She'd gone missin'—at first rumor had it she was dead, an' then that she'd caught a sentence. If so, it weren't no Jovian jailer what put her in irons—nobody who did time on 1172 Aeneas saw her there. Always figured Earth had her locked up on Vesta or even Mars. Yeh ask me, that's when she turned traitor—they broke her while she was in the brig."

"You told me Oshima sold her ship after the battle.

Sold her ship and retired to the outback on Io."

Huff nodded. "Nobody saw her for a few years after she hightailed it out of the asteroids—the survivors looked, believed me. By the time she turned up on Io, I figured 'twas better to let her rot, out there alone with what she'd done. She's still there, so I s'pose the others felt the same."

"But I've seen where she lives. It sure didn't look like she was rich."

"It wouldn't. Oshima could squeeze a coin till it bled. Kept her ship near cold as space, air scrubbers dialed to the minimum so everythin' stank, short commons throughout a cruise. Still, I don't think she did it for the money."

"Then why?" Tycho asked.

"Revenge. She was desperate. Just out of prison, no luck huntin' prizes, an' more an' more trouble findin' able spacers who'd sign her endless articles. She hated the rest of us for it. Hated us for stealin' her crews an' for swindlin' her, though that last was only in her mind. If she had to hang up her musketoons, this was a way to take us all down with her."

"She hated all of you enough to plot against the Jovian Union?"

"Oshima weren't no patriot," Huff growled. "She ain't never believed in any country or cause 'cept her own. An' neither has Mox."

His voice rose, the flesh of his cheek darkening.

"Answer me this, boy: If she was innocent, why didn't she install the program that was supposed to protect us?"

"Grandfather—"

"Why didn't she do that?" Huff demanded through clenched teeth, as a chorus of alarmed beeps rose from inside the tank. "How'd she know, if she didn't know it was booby-trapped? If she wasn't in on the plot?"

"Grandfather, please. I didn't believe her. Not then and not now."

"That's better."

Tycho waited until the beeping had subsided and the angry color had faded from his grandfather's cheek.

"Forget Oshima for a minute," he said tentatively, trying to keep straight in his head what he had learned and what he still had to ask. "So it was Mox who told you about the Securitat, and why they wanted to stop the convoy?"

Huff nodded, his living eye closed.

"Got the full story from them spooks meself, though. Fool though I was, no way I was signin' on to somethin' on just Thoadbone's say-so. The Securitat's dirty business weren't new to us, Tyke. A pirate could profit from it, provided he was careful. They tole me 'bout the convoy, an' the jammers, an' their plan to protect us against 'em. An' I agreed to recruit more pirates for the ambush— pirates what wouldn't listen to Oshima or Mox."

Tycho hesitated.

"Who did you meet with? From the Securitat?"

Huff grunted and looked away. "Don't remember his name. An' it don't matter. All them spies use fake names anyway."

Tycho nodded. DeWise had told Tycho that wasn't his real name, without the least bit of shame.

"And the Securitat gave you the software to give to the rest of the pirates?"

"No. Got it from Mox. Vesuvia looked it over six ways from Sunday an' concluded there weren't anythin' wrong with it. She's a paranoid ol' bag of circuits, yeh know that. So then Mox an' I passed the programs on to the rest of 'em. I didn't know we were flyin' into a trap. A trap what killed Thane D'Artagn an' Stearns Cody. Habadon Alkasis. Helga von Stegl. An' . . . an' . . ."

Huff's eye shut and he swallowed convulsively. Beads of sweat had appeared on his brow.

"And the Gibraltars," Tycho said gently. "Cassius and Sims."

"An' them. Tyke, could yeh . . . would yeh fetch me that cloth?"

Tycho picked a rag off the desk. It was damp and cool. Huff lifted his head and water sloshed inside the tank.

"Let me do it, Grandfather," Tycho said, wiping the sweat from Huff's forehead. The old pirate's eye closed and he exhaled gratefully.

"Thankee, lad. That's better. Yeh met Simsie once, when yeh were naught but a babe. Did yeh know that?"

"No. I didn't."

"Had no use for his father, but Simsie was a good

lad," Huff said quietly. "Would 'ave made yer aunt a fine first mate. That was my hope, yeh know—Carrie in the captain's chair, Simsie as first mate, an' yer father flyin'."

"And what about Mom?"

"Sensors and navigation. Wish I could 'ave seen that crew come together—I might 'ave asked yer aunt to let me stay on an' run the commo board, just to be a part of it. An' it would 'ave worked, yeh know, if everythin' hadn't gone so wrong. If we'd had a little more time, it would 'ave worked. I know it would 'ave."

Eight bells rang out, signaling the end of the afternoon watch. Tycho tried to imagine his aunt in the captain's chair, turning to bark orders at the children she would have had with Sims, the ones who'd never had a chance to be born. What would he and Yana and Carlo be doing now, if that had happened? He might never have left Jupiter's moons. Perhaps he and his siblings would be working in one of the family businesses in Port Town, arguing about whose turn it was to drive the grav-sled back to Darklands and dreaming of the next time they might get to go somewhere as exotic as Ganymede.

"The thought of that spy in your aunt's cabin . . . ," Huff muttered.

"I meant to ask you," Tycho said hastily, hoping to steer his grandfather away from that unhappy topic. "What would have made Aunt Carina such a good captain?"

"Arrr. Brilliant strategist, cool under fire. But most of all, she was sure of herself. That's what yer mother's always struggled with—she's learned to keep it hidden, is all. Once Carrie made a decision, she never doubted it—an' she made everyone around her believe in it too. That belief can make or break a starship crew, once things start to go wrong."

Tycho crossed his arms over his chest. Sometimes he felt like he'd doubted every decision he'd ever made on the quarterdeck.

Huff saw his reaction and smiled.

"Go easy on yerself, lad. Yer still young, still learnin'. Far as I know, yer mother ain't ready to pick a captain yet."

"What if it was your choice, Grandfather? Who would you pick?"

Huff's living eye widened. "Arrr. Yeh sure yeh want me to answer that, lad?"

Tycho nodded.

Huff looked away, his yellowed teeth working at his lip, and Tycho suddenly regretted his question. His grandfather wasn't the captain anymore, and it was wrong to ask him to play that role, even here in his cabin.

He opened his mouth to apologize, but before he could get the words out, Huff turned to look at him.

"I'd pick yer sister. Reminds me of yer aunt at that age, Yana does—always arguin', even when she knows it ain't no good idea. Looks like her, too—sometimes I get them mixed up in my mind, an' have to recall me heading agin. But yer mother will never do that. Dio would be too worried Yana's temper would get her killed. Her an' everyone else. An' she might be right about that."

"If Mom won't pick Yana, who then?"

"I'd bet on you," Huff said, and Tycho felt his heartbeat accelerate. "Yer brother's the easy choice, but Carlo ain't got no head for people. He can give orders, but he don't listen to the people he's givin' 'em to. A leader has to do both. Yeh can learn how to fly, Tyke, but Carlo ain't gonna learn how to lead—if he could, he'd 'ave done it already. An' yer mother knows it."

Tycho looked away, trying to calm himself.

"The chair could be yours, Tyke," Huff said. "Most important thing is yeh learn to trust yerself—which is the hardest thing for any captain. Yeh have to trust yerself that yeh know what's right, and that when it matters yeh'll do the right thing."

10

ASTEROID CONVOY

As the *Comet* followed the main spacelane that led to 65 Cybele, she passed pinwheeling lumps of beige, gray, and reddish rock, dodged slabs of tumbling black debris, and flew through loose clouds of stones and dust, the remnants of asteroids blasted to pieces in ancient collisions.

It was the third day of the voyage, and alertness had eroded into boredom, as it tended to do on an uneventful cruise. Tycho and his siblings sniped and snapped at each other on the quarterdeck, drawing Diocletia's ire, while everyone vented their frustration at Vesuvia, whose programming at least allowed her to remain unperturbed. Nor was the *Comet* a happy ship belowdecks—the morning watch began with Grigsby bellowing about scurvy malingerers and plenty of room in the brig.

Grigsby was midrant when Vass ascended the ladderwell to the quarterdeck at impressive speed, looking pale and shocked.

"The language belowdecks . . . it's like being inside a cell on 1172 Aeneas," he muttered.

"In my day, Minister, there weren't no difference 'tween the two," Huff said with a grin. He had finally returned to his regular routine on the quarterdeck the night before, though he and Diocletia were limiting themselves to the absolute minimum of conversation.

Vass gave the old pirate a wary nod and took his now-customary position on the other side of the ladderwell.

"Don't forget to strap in, Mr. Vass," Diocletia said.

"Oh, I thought I'd forgo that blasted contraption today, Captain. I'm quite proud of my space legs by now, if I do say so myself."

"As you like. And how is Mr. Haines this morning?"

"More talkative. I bribed him with some coffee and asked Mr. Speirdyke to season his crowdy with cinnamon sugar."

"Hmm—that might've worked on me too," Mavry said.

"No thanks," Carlo said. "Spooning sugar's about the extent of Speirdyke's skills, and his coffee's always burned. If we make a few livres on this cruise, how about we pick a cook for some reason besides he's missing a limb?"

"And what would Mr. Speirdyke do after that?" Diocletia asked. "His family's served ours since Anna Barbara Hashoone was captain, and he lost his leg manning a gun to protect this ship from harm. Should we abandon him—a one-legged spacer—to beg for alms in Port Town?"

Carlo raised his hands placatingly. "I just wanted better coffee!"

"Then why don't you learn to make it?" Yana asked.

"If you've touched the coffeepot five times in your whole life I'm the emperor of Earth," Tycho said.

"That's enough," Diocletia said. "Yana, step up your scans. Tycho, get up on the comm board. If everything's on schedule, we should run across our freighter convoy within a half hour or so. But there's a lot of ship traffic in these parts, not all of it friendly. So eyes peeled."

"Never thought I'd see the barky reduced to shepherdin' a flock of tea wagons," grumbled Huff, his forearm cannon whining in agitation.

"You've made your feelings on this subject clear, Dad," Diocletia said without turning. "But that's the mission, so let's see that it's done properly. Your starship, Carlo."

The convoy soon appeared on Yana's scopes: a trio

of bulk freighters and a massive dromond, with seven smaller hoys interspersed among the bigger ships.

"And I've got two frigates—one at point, the other trailing," she said.

"That would be the *Izabella* and the *Berserker*," Diocletia said.

"Min Theo's ship?" asked Huff, brightening.

"Morgan Theo's in the captain's chair now," Mavry said. "Min retired to Ganymede about six months ago."

"Arrr, I hadn't heard," Huff rumbled, then added mournfully: "Now why'd ol' Min go an' do a thing like that?"

"Vesuvia, display colors," Carlo said. "Tyke, get Captains Andrade and Theo on the comm."

Tycho entered the command to raise the *Comet*'s communications mast from its housing atop the ship and began transmitting her identity to the convoy ahead.

"Channel established," Tycho said. "The comm's yours, Carlo. Wait—incoming transmission."

"Nice to see you, *Comet*," said the smooth, cultured voice of Garibalda Marta Andrade, the veteran privateer commanding not only the *Izabella* but also the Jovian privateers assigned to the Cybeles. "Be advised this has been a hot zone. The *Berserker* will protect our port flank. Take the trailing position and mind the hoys and the dromond."

"It's Carlo Hashoone, Captain Andrade. The *Comet*'s faster than the *Berserker*. I'd suggest the reverse formation."

Tycho saw Diocletia and Mavry exchange a glance, but neither said anything.

"We've been running these lanes for three weeks and have a sensor profile of every rock and snowball along the route," Andrade said. "On this run we need you at trailing."

"Understood," Carlo said sullenly.

Tycho eyed the main screen and the line of crosses that marked the location of the Jovian convoy. After a few minutes the ships became visible through the viewports, a cluster of bright lights in motion against the seemingly fixed stars. Closer still, and those bright lights took on shape and definition, becoming the bulbs of long-range tanks, their starships tucked beneath them. Their ion engines were a blinding blue.

"That dromond's throwing ions halfway back to Jupiter—careful of her engine wash," Yana said, inclining her chin at the giant freighter in the center of the convoy. A quintet of massive fuel tanks cradled the ship's vast bulk.

"Don't tell me how to do my job, Yana," Carlo said.

He reduced speed and guided the *Comet* into position at the tail of the column, behind the last three hoys—needle-nosed freighters about twice the length of the privateer. The *Comet*'s bulky long-range tanks robbed her of her speed and grace, but Carlo still guided her with an expert hand, maneuvering the frigate with practiced ease that bordered on nonchalance. Tycho knew if he'd been flying the *Comet*, he'd have wound up goosing the engines repeatedly, wasting fuel while he struggled to properly align her with the rest of the convoy.

"We're in position, *Izabella*," Carlo said.

"Nicely flown, *Comet*," Andrade said. "We're just shy of the first buoys—and it's three hours to port after that. Don't let those hoys creep up on the dromond—their pilots have been flying with heavy feet."

Scanners identified the three hoys as the *Marcus*, the *Camden*, and the *Hambrook*. Tycho couldn't blame their pilots for riding the throttle too hard—the massive dromond maneuvered like an artificial asteroid, barreling ponderously through space in whatever direction she'd been pointed.

"Locking in course," Carlo said. "Keep your sensors on active scan, Yana. Particularly the port array."

"Don't tell me how to do my job, Carlo," Yana said, smiling innocently at Diocletia's warning look.

Curious, Tycho called up the dromond's sensor profile: She was the *Nestor Leviathan*, little more than a bridge and engines separated by half a kilometer of cargo holds. He wondered how much the cargo she was carrying was worth. Hundreds of millions of livres? Billions? Whatever the amount, it was enough money to throw legendary shindies for at least a decade.

"You ever capture a ship that big, Grandfather?" Tycho asked Huff.

"Arrr, yeh read my mind, lad. Tough prize to take— yeh'd need yer own fleet of tugs, an' in my day a ship that big carried gangs of roughnecks to repel boarders.

Answer's not to take her as a prize at all—with a beast that big, yer in it for the ransom, not the condemnation."

Tycho glanced at his screen.

"I'm picking up pings from the buoys. They're thirty thousand klicks ahead."

"Roger that," Carlo said, easing his control yoke slightly to the right. "Heading looks almost perfect . . . there. We're in the pipe. Next stop, Cybele."

"Wait, Huff," Mavry objected. "Didn't Ursula Hashoone take a dromond as a prize in the Themistians?"

Huff tapped at his chrome temple, frowning.

"A dromond? Don't believe so, no."

Diocletia turned in her chair.

"That's the way I heard it too. The ship Ursula took was called the *Capistrano*—she wasn't a dromond?"

"Arrr, lemme think. No, the *Capistrano* was a converted Lophelia-class bulk hauler. Dromond-*sized*, p'raps, but a different configuration—basically a cylinder covered with magnetic grapples for attachin' deep-space containers. She could carry sixty or seventy of 'em when fully loaded. Made loadin' an' offloadin' a snap, but meant she was a ridiculous-lookin' scow. Father always said a fully loaded Lophelia looked like a pine cone."

"What's a pine cone?" Yana asked.

Huff shrugged.

"Some kind of mountain, I s'pose. Like a volcano. They got cones, don't they?"

"A pine cone is a—" Vesuvia interjected.

"What kinda mountain it is ain't the point, yeh useless compendium of trivia," Huff growled. "See, takin' the *Capistrano* weren't Ursula's goal. She sent in two boardin' parties. First one headed for the bridge, but that was just a feint—second boardin' party were the important one. They stormed the supercargo's control room an' performed an emergency decouplin' of all the magnetic grapples."

"Oh my," Vass said.

Huff chuckled. "Would 'ave liked to see that one meself—sixty-odd containers firin' their release jets an' hurtlin' off into deep space in every direction. Ursula pulled the boardin' parties, an' they let the *Capistrano* go while they started huntin' down the containers. They say some of them are still out there—Father plotted their probable courses an' programmed Vesuvia to sing out whenever the *Comet* was within two million klicks or so of one. Ain't that right, Vesuvia?"

"Your account contains a number of inaccuracies," the *Comet*'s artificial intelligence said. "Fifty-six containers were deployed in all. Twenty-one were recovered by three generations of captains of the *Shadow Comet*, the last one hundred nineteen years ago. Sixteen containers were recovered by Earth merchant vessels or their agents. Pirates and other unaffiliated vessels are believed to have recovered twelve. Four were either destroyed during recovery operations, impacted celestial bodies, or incinerated on close approach to the sun. Three have yet to be recovered. The nearest one is currently an estimated twenty-four billion kilometers from our current position, bearing two hundred eleven degrees."

"Unless you want to extend this cruise by a year or so, I think we'll let that one go," Carlo said.

"Prolly best," Huff said. "The problem was that Ursula didn't get the *Capistrano*'s manifest. So nobody huntin' them containers knew what was in 'em. Father said on one cruise Ursula intercepted a container filled with high-density computer cores, an' made a fortune fencin' 'em on Ceres. Next cruise, she took the *Comet* out halfway to Uranus an' reeled in a container full of tubs of freezer-burned synthetic butter."

Tycho joined in the laughter on the quarterdeck. Even Vass grinned.

"An' that particular trick never worked agin. The shipwright what made Lophelias locked the supercargoes out of the emergency decoupling procedure, but insurers was so spooked, it became too expensive to fly 'em. They cut up the last Lophelia for scrap above Mars when I was a middie."

"Master Hashoone?" asked Vass, peering over Tycho's shoulder. "What's that red light?"

Tycho gaped at his console in horror.

"Priority signal from the *Izabella*," he told the quarterdeck. "Patching it through."

"Repeat, we have sensor contact at three hundred and ten degrees," Andrade said.

"That's outside our current scanning cone," Yana said. "Can't see a thing out here. Wait, I've got it now. Looks like three—no, make it four bogeys."

"Sensor profile?" Carlo asked.

"That's a negative," Yana said. "We're out of range and in the back of the line. *Izabella* will have them painted while I'm still collating position data."

"Understood. Pass on whatever you've got as soon as you get it."

"Aye-aye. They're coming hot, I can tell you that. Too hot to be attached to tanks."

"Vesuvia, stand by to detach on my order," said Carlo.

"Acknowledged."

Tycho listened to the chatter on the convoy's shared communication channel, trying to pick out anything useful to pass on to his brother. The freighter pilots were frantic, screeching about bandits and arguing about defensive formations.

Tea wagons, he thought with a sigh.

"*Marcus, Camden, Hambrook,* maintain your position and await orders," Tycho said sternly into his microphone. "This is the *Comet*—we've got your back."

Captain Andrade's voice filled the channel. "*Berserker, Comet,* we're transmitting sensor data to you. We have four frigates, flying black transponders. Easy on the triggers and stick with your freighters."

Tycho's eyes jumped to the main screen and the mysterious triangles off to port. Three were inbound, while the fourth was hanging back, screened by the tumbling asteroids of the Cybeles.

"Bogeys are activating transponders," Vesuvia said. "They are flying Earth colors."

11

EARTH'S PRIZE

Tycho could hear Huff's forearm cannon squealing.

"Verifying transponder codes," Vesuvia said. "Bogeys identify as the *Loire*, the *Resolution*, the *Kerensky*, and the *Gracieux*."

"Captain Allamand, I presume," Diocletia said.

Tycho glanced at his mother in the captain's chair and saw Carlo's eyes turn that way as well. Diocletia's gaze was fixed on the main screen, but she said nothing else, fingers steepled beneath her chin. The *Comet* was still Carlo's to command, and Tycho fought to keep a scowl off his face—his brother couldn't ask for a better opportunity to show off his piloting skills.

"Vesuvia, tag all four bogeys as hostile and beat to quarters," Carlo said. "Mr. Grigsby, get the crews to their guns, but no firing till I give the word—and then let's not damage the merchandise."

"Aye-aye, Master Carlo," Grigsby said as the bosun's pipes shrilled. "We break it, we buy it."

"Mr. Grigsby, one of the bandits is the *Kerensky*," Carlo said. "We have some of her crewers belowdecks. What's their status?"

"They've given parole, Master Carlo. I trust them to honor that and not interfere. They've been sent to the wardroom to assist Mr. Leffingwell if needed."

"Privateers, hold your positions and stay with your freighters," Andrade said. "Don't let them split us up."

"*Gracieux*'s hanging back," Yana said. "Other three are closing to combat range."

"Mr. Grigsby, no blaster cannons," Carlo said. "Missiles only."

Mavry turned to Carlo.

"If you fire missiles within the convoy and one of those Earth ships breaks the missile lock—" he began, but Diocletia held up her hand, silencing him.

"Carlo's starship," she said.

"Mr. Grigsby?" Carlo said into his headset. "Belay that last order and hold your fire."

"Here they come," Yana warned.

The three Earth frigates swooped out of the tumbling rock to port of the lumbering convoy, moving perpendicularly to the freighters. Tycho leaned forward in his seat as a bat-winged frigate—sensors painted it as the *Loire*—passed between the hoys and the dromond, waggling its wings but not firing.

"Arrogant Earth dogs!" roared Huff.

The middle hoy broke to starboard, forcing its neighbor to pull up.

"Back in formation!" Tycho yelled into the microphone.

"They're coming around for another pass," Morgan Theo warned over the shared channel.

"The *Gracieux*'s paralleling us, screened by the asteroids," Yana warned. "She's creeping toward the head of the column."

This time the *Loire* didn't pass through the convoy but turned her nose and joined it, flying just below the dromond's engine wash. The hoys' pilots screamed for the *Comet* to fire. Carlo's knuckles were white around the control yoke.

"Earth-flagged starships, this is a Jovian merchant convoy," Captain Andrade said. "Your current maneuvers violate sections sixty-four through sixty-six of the interplanetary commercial code. If you do not immediately move outside the legally mandated hundred-kilometer navigational buffer, your actions shall be treated as hostile."

"Garibalda's playing it by the book," Mavry said. "Let's see what they do."

"Arrr, what's on the starboard scopes?" Huff asked, peering at Yana's board.

"So far I have nothing—just the bandits that came in from portside."

"So far," Huff rumbled.

Ahead of them, the *Berserker* had dropped back to fly alongside the *Resolution*, keeping pace with the Earth warship. Tycho knew the two ships' gun crews were at their stations, waiting for the order to fire.

"Are they going to try to take the convoy?" Vass asked.

"They don't have enough ships," Tycho said. "It's probably just harassment—they're hoping to provoke us. Don't you think so, Grandfather?"

"Arrr, depends if there are more of 'em to starboard. If I was Allamand, I'd look to cause chaos, then cut out a hoy or two to steal."

Ahead of the *Comet*, the *Loire* cut her speed, dropping back behind the dromond and forcing the trio of hoys to break formation.

"And how would you do that?" Vass asked Huff warily. "Cut out a hoy, I mean?"

Huff inclined his chin toward the main screen. "By doin' what they're doin'."

"Carlo—" Mavry began.

"I see it!"

The *Marcus* and the *Camden* nearly collided, while the

Hambrook broke to starboard, her nose veering from side to side in the dromond's engine wash. The pilots were all hollering at the same time, their voices drowning each other out.

"Tycho, tell them to hold their positions!" Carlo said.

"They can't! Not with that bandit running them off course!"

The *Loire* raised her nose and accelerated through the dromond's wash, with the *Kerensky* flying alongside her. The two Earth frigates shot past the *Resolution* and Morgan Theo's *Berserker*, heading for the *Izabella*'s position at the front of the convoy.

"Captain Andrade, you have bandits inbound," Yana said.

"I see them, *Comet*," Andrade said. "Maintain your position."

"The *Gracieux*'s on the move off to port, behind the asteroids," Yana warned. "She's accelerating toward the front of the convoy."

"It'll be three against one," Carlo said. "We have to help the *Izabella*."

All eyes turned to Diocletia—but she kept staring straight ahead, out at the blue blazes of the convoy's engines. Carlo was on his own.

The *Loire* and the *Kerensky* took up positions on either side of the *Izabella* as the three ships raced through the asteroid corridor at the front of the freighter convoy.

"Range between the *Gracieux* and the *Izabella*?" Carlo asked.

"Estimate eight hundred klicks and closing," Yana said. "Sensor contact is unreliable with all this junk floating around out here."

"Earth warships, disengage immediately or you will be treated as hostiles," Captain Andrade said. *"Berserker, Comet,* prepare to detach tanks on my order."

The bells *clang-clang*ed—it was 1700.

"All Jovian craft detach tanks," Andrade said, her words going out not just to her fellow privateers but to the freighters and the Earth craft menacing them. "Respond to hostile actions accordingly."

"You heard her, Vesuvia," Carlo said. "Detach."

"Acknowledged."

A clank sounded above their heads and the *Comet* shook slightly as Vesuvia decoupled and retracted the fuel lines connecting the frigate to her long-range fuel tanks, then demagnetized the grapples.

Carlo rolled the *Comet* to port and then back to starboard, checking that she was maneuvering properly.

Tycho stared at the symbols on the main screen. If the Earth ships were going to break off, they'd most likely do so now—freed of their tanks, the Jovian privateers could match their maneuverability.

But the intruders maintained their positions.

"We're all burning fuel fast now," Mavry said. "Whatever their play is, they'll have to make it soon."

"Yana, what's the *Gracieux* doing?" Carlo asked.

"Still closing on the *Izabella.* Two hundred klicks."

"And what else do you see on the scopes?"

"Only thing to port is the *Gracieux*. I have no readings to starboard."

Carlo stared at the main screen for a long moment. Tycho understood his brother's dilemma. The convoy was undefended to starboard—yet the *Izabella* was badly outgunned ahead of them.

"I'm going after the *Gracieux*," Carlo declared, swinging the *Comet* up and out of her place behind the convoy. "Tyke, tell the hoys to tuck in between the two bulk freighters and sit tight. Yana, eyes peeled."

"Acknowledged," Tycho said.

Carlo banked the *Comet* between a pair of tumbling rocks, then cut hard to the right to avoid a scree of ice, accelerating hard enough to press them back into their seats. Behind him, Tycho heard a yelp and a series of thuds.

"What was that?" Diocletia demanded.

"Yer pet spy fell down the ladderwell," Huff rumbled.

"Oh, for God's sake."

Wherever Vass had ended up, things weren't getting any easier for him—Tycho's stomach lurched as the *Comet* dipped below a slab of ancient black rock, then rolled over onto her port wing.

"*Comet*, return to your position," Captain Andrade said. "We've got all we can handle over here."

"It's time Captain Allamand learned that we won't be pushed around," Carlo replied. "And I'll be nearby if you need me."

"Seven hundred klicks and closing between us and

the *Gracieux*," Yana said. "She's still paralleling the *Izabella* and the other two Earth ships."

"Let me know when she sees us coming," Carlo said, slapping at his comm controls. "Mr. Grigsby, we are closing on a bandit. Hold your fire, though—for now we're just trying to run her off."

"Got it, Master Hashoone."

"Five hundred klicks," Yana said. "The *Gracieux*'s breaking to port. Heading deeper into the asteroid field."

"Pursuing," Carlo said.

"The hoys' captains are demanding that we return," Tycho said.

"They'll be fine—all the action's up at the front of the convoy," Carlo said. "Vesuvia, give me more power. Don't sweat the fuel efficiency—I need to catch that bandit."

"Acknowledged."

"*Gracieux*'s still running," Yana said. "But we're faster than she is—distance four hundred klicks."

"And we've got a better pilot," Carlo said, sending the *Comet* into a barrel roll to duck a scattering of rock.

"Three hundred klicks," Yana said. "*Gracieux* is turning to heading two-seven-niner."

Carlo banked to port, altering the *Comet*'s course with a casual grace that Tycho envied.

"Two hundred klicks," Yana said. "We should have a visual soon."

As the distance between the two ships shrank, Tycho alternated glances between the sensor scope and the chunks of rock and ice filling the main screen.

"*Comet*!" yelled Captain Andrade. "We are under attack!"

Carlo looked up in shock. "What?"

"The *Loire* and the *Kerensky* have opened fire on the *Izabella*," Yana said, fingers drumming on her keyboard. "The *Resolution* and the *Berserker* are exchanging fire as well."

"Range to the *Gracieux*?" Carlo demanded.

"One hundred fifty klicks," Yana said. "She's maintaining the same heading."

"Which is takin' us away from the fight," Huff muttered.

Carlo turned to look at his mother. Suddenly all the hoy pilots were yelling at once over Tycho's channels.

"*Marcus*, say again," Tycho said, trying to make sense of the cacophony. "Convoy is reporting multiple sensor contacts," he told the rest of his family.

"Contacts from where?" Carlo asked, diving under a trio of boulders.

"I have no reading," Yana said. "We're too far away."

"Pilots say they came from starboard," Tycho said. "Multiple small attack craft."

Carlo brought one fist down on his console.

"Do you need me to take back command?" Diocletia asked him.

Carlo looked at his mother, his face gone pale, and Tycho felt sorry for his brother—even though the mistakes he'd made would benefit Tycho in the Log. Could he really say he wouldn't have tried to hunt down the *Gracieux*, as Carlo had done?

"I'm fine, Captain," Carlo said, yanking back on the control yoke and cutting hard to starboard. "We're on our way, *Izabella*."

"Look out!" Mavry yelled.

A pillar of rock loomed ahead of the frigate, a dark shape against the stars. Carlo tried to dodge beneath it, but the Hashoones bounced in their harnesses and a sound like the blow from a giant hammer left the hull ringing. The *Comet* shuddered with a low groan of distressed metal, followed by the hooting of alarms.

"Impact," Vesuvia said. "Dorsal hull, port side."

"Damage report?" Mavry asked.

"Initiating assessment," Vesuvia said.

"We're fine, we're fine," Carlo said, racing through the rocky field as the *Comet* continued to vibrate alarmingly around them.

"Damage to dorsal armor plating," Vesuvia said. "Hull integrity reduced to sixty-four percent over a three-meter area. Partial damage to sensor suite."

"Rerouting sensor feeds," Yana said.

Tycho contacted the convoy. "Jovian craft, we're on our way. Report your status. If you have been boarded by hostiles and are unable to communicate, signal that by double-clicking your microphones."

The frantic pilots began talking all at once in his headset. As Tycho checked each ship off in turn, steps sounded on the ladderwell. Vass ascended carefully, looking sheepish. Someone belowdecks had found a harness for him.

"I'm securing myself," he said hastily.

He was just in time—a moment later Carlo turned the *Comet* on its starboard wing, pushing the engines as hard as they could go. The vibration above their heads made Tycho's teeth clack together.

"We are inbound and hot, *Izabella*," Carlo said. "Send us targeting data."

"Too busy," Captain Andrade said brusquely, and they could hear her bridge crew barking out orders.

"Do you need assistance?" Carlo asked uncertainly. Yana smirked at Tycho, who knew what she was thinking. Of course the Jovian privateers needed assistance—they'd needed it most while the *Comet* was engaged in her fruitless pursuit of the *Gracieux*.

"They're not shooting to kill—just keeping us pinned down here," Andrade said angrily. "Protect the convoy, *Comet*."

"Will do, *Izabella*," Carlo said, angling farther to starboard. "Yana, what do you have on sensors?"

"Collating partial data. That scrape severed the portside data leads."

"We'll have to eyeball it, then."

"*Comet*, this is Captain Cromer of the *Nestor Leviathan*," a calm voice said in Tycho's ear. "We have multiple boarding parties entering our vessel."

"Acknowledged," Tycho said "How many craft are boarding, Captain?"

Carlo heard his brother's question and turned as the bells clanged three times.

"What ship are they attacking, Tyke? One of the bulk freighters? Or the hoys?"

"None of them. They're boarding the dromond."

Yana's eyes went wide.

"O-ho," said Mavry.

"Arrr," Huff said. "He's a bold one, this Captain Allamand."

They could see the battle ahead of them now, amid the whirling asteroids of the Cybeles. At the front of the column of freighters, bright flashes of light surrounded the *Izabella*, the *Berserker*, and the Earth ships tormenting them.

"At least the *Leviathan* will have onboard security to repel boarders," Carlo said.

"Not enough of it," Vass said. "Most freight lines have reduced shipboard security to a minimum—there's too much worry about accidentally hiring Ice Wolves. That's why we instituted the convoy system."

"Terrific," Carlo said. "Yana, get me a scan of the *Leviathan*—and look for any other Jovian craft with hostiles attached. Tycho, give me updates from any of the captains. Mr. Grigsby, prepare boarding parties—the *Leviathan* is under attack by Earth boarders."

"Aye, Master Hashoone," Grigsby said, and a moment later the bosun's whistle shrilled below.

"Captain Cromer, we are inbound with boarding parties ready," Tycho said.

"You're a little late, *Comet*. They're all over the ship—we're trying to hold the bridge."

"Then we'll catch them in a crossfire," Tycho said with forced bravado.

They could see the huge shape of the *Nestor Leviathan* now—and tiny bright lights surrounding it. Several of those bright lights streaked toward the *Comet*.

"Attack craft inbound—they profile as pinnaces," Yana said.

"Mr. Grigsby, fire at will," Carlo said.

All heard the sharp report of the *Comet*'s bow chasers as Grigsby's crews began firing at the Earth pinnaces. One vanished in a ball of flame, and cheers rang out belowdecks.

"That's one who wishes he'd stayed home," Yana growled.

"And an Earth ship destroyed by Jovian fire," Vass said quietly. "We may all wish we'd stayed home, before this is over."

The pinnaces zipped past the *Comet* on either side. Her port and starboard guns roared out, shaking the frigate. Other pinnaces lay between the *Comet* and the bulk of the *Leviathan*, which still barreled along beneath her long-range tanks.

"Yana, let me know where we can dock," Carlo said, studying the huge ship.

"Nowhere," Yana said.

"What do you mean, nowhere?"

"The *Leviathan* has four freight docking rings and four airlocks. Scan shows enemy craft attached to all of them."

"We'll have to burn our way in, then," Carlo said grimly. "Mr. Grigsby—"

"Wait," Yana said. "There's something else. Those aren't standard pinnaces. Their engines and onboard tanks are oversized."

"What does that mean?" Carlo asked.

As if in response, the *Leviathan* began to turn to starboard, and all on the *Comet*'s quarterdeck saw bright flares emerge from the pinnaces attached to her port side.

Mavry glanced back at Huff. "What was that you said about a fleet of tugs?"

"Arrr, never thought I'd see it," Huff said, grudging admiration in his voice.

"Captain Cromer," Tycho said. "What is your situation? Captain Cromer?"

The two hoys that had been flying to starboard of the *Leviathan* dodged below the massive dromond as she continued to angle away from the convoy.

Diocletia activated her headset.

"My starship," she said, and Carlo sagged in his seat. "Captain Andrade—"

"We see it, Diocletia," said the captain of the *Izabella*. "The other Earth privateers are disengaging and following the *Leviathan*."

"What are your orders?"

There was no reply for a moment, and Tycho could picture Captain Andrade studying her scopes, trying to choose among several unhappy options.

"Protect the rest of the convoy and bring it in to Cybele," Andrade said.

"Mr. Grigsby, defensive fire only," Diocletia said. "Tycho, tell the remaining ships to close up the line. We'll guard the rear."

When the *Comet*'s guns ceased firing, the Earth pinnaces streaked back the way they'd come, following the dromond.

"Mom, we can still catch the *Leviathan*," Carlo pleaded. "Those tugs can't have enough fuel for long-term operations. If we catch her, and the other privateers form a perimeter . . ."

"No, Carlo. They'll have other tugs out there—and other privateers, for all we know. Flying blind got us into this mess—let's not compound the error. Captain Allamand's won this round."

12

CYBELE

The rest of the journey to Cybele passed in near silence, with Carlo hunched miserably behind the *Comet*'s control yoke.

The asteroid called 65 Cybele was a lumpy sphere nearly three hundred kilometers in diameter, its dark surface given definition by a spiderweb of lighted lines and dots. Attis, a smaller but still massive chunk of brownish-gray rock, orbited above the surface of the asteroid, crowned with sensor masts and towers. Between Attis and Cybele, a sprawling station hung in space, ringed by docking cradles and spindly umbilicals for servicing larger craft. And everywhere there were starships—angular warships bristling with guns, massive spherical tankers, boxy freighters, and tiny scout ships, gigs, and ferries.

The three Jovian privateers waited above the station while the bulk freighters and hoys docked, then headed for their own cradles. Tycho couldn't help feeling a bit nervous as they passed into the shadow of Attis above them—he knew gravity had kept the satellite safely in orbit above Cybele for eons, but it still felt like the massive rock was about to smash down upon them.

"Those corvettes are military models or I'm a middie," Huff said with a growl, peering out the viewports at a trio of dart-shaped starships hanging in space below Attis. "But they ain't a model I'm familiar with."

"Right you are, Captain Hashoone," Vass said. "That, officially speaking, is the Cybelean navy."

"Arrr, three corvettes ain't no navy."

"Agreed. The Cybeles' importance is best measured economically, not militarily."

"Tycho and Yana, muster out the crew belowdecks," Diocletia said. "They're to report to the Jovian fondaco, where they'll get passes. There will be Jovian officials awaiting them to arrange everything, but warn them to watch out for crimps—Cybele is plagued with them, and they don't always respect a pass. All hands are at liberty tonight, but as of 0800 tomorrow they should be ready to respond to a recall order with thirty minutes' notice."

"Thirty minutes?" Yana asked. "They won't like that."

"And yet those are my orders," Diocletia replied. "We'll be using Cybele as a base of operations, which means we have to be ready to fly on short notice. The rest of us will head dirtside as soon as the crew departs. Minister Vass, you can ride down with us in the gig, or we can have Vesuvia summon a ferry for you."

"I'll go with you, if that's all right," Vass said.

"What's a fondaco?" Tycho asked the minister.

"A compound reserved for Jovian citizens. While we're on Cybele we're required to sleep there, though we can get passes to go most anywhere else on Cybele. Until curfew, that is."

"A nicer kind of prison, in other words," growled Huff. "Ain't seen a place with fondachi since Mars."

"Cybele has one reserved for citizens of Earth as well," Vass said.

"Bet it's nicer than ours," Huff said as Tycho followed Yana down the ladderwell.

"Yes, I'm afraid it is," Vass said.

The Comets knew what the loss of the dromond meant for the Hashoones and the Jovian Union, and took their leave with little of the normal boisterousness of crewers headed for shore leave. Tycho eyed his sister when Immanuel Sier came through the line, but the young Saturnian crewer put his knuckles to his forehead and nodded respectfully to Yana, who nodded back and even offered him a small smile. The last crewer to depart was

Grigsby, accompanying Haines and the paroled Earth crewers. The Jovian consulate would decide whether to detain them further or exchange them for captive Jovians.

"So I guess you've forgiven Mr. Sier," Tycho said as they shut down their mediapads and walked back through the now-empty lower deck.

"Immanuel? Oh, he's not so bad. I saw him every day on the journey here—Mr. Dobbs is teaching us both unarmed combat."

"Unarmed combat?"

"Sure—I'll show you," Yana said, putting her media-pad down on the deck. "But you'll want to back up first."

Tycho retreated until Yana told him to stop. His sister exhaled, then sprang forward onto her hands. Then she exploded forward onto her feet, cartwheeling across the deck in a blur of arms and legs that ended with her fist a centimeter from Tycho's face.

"Okay, that was impressive," Tycho said. "But I'd just shoot you."

"Try it. Pretend you're drawing on me."

Tycho shrugged, then stepped back. His hand shot to his hip, but next thing he knew he was on his back, with one of Yana's knees pinning his wrist and one of her hands under his chin, fingers around his neck. Her other hand was up, fingers spread and aimed at his eyes.

"Point taken," Tycho said. "Let me up already."

Yana disengaged, grinning, as Tycho rubbed the back of his head.

"When everything went bad on the *Lampos* I felt helpless," his sister said, suddenly serious. "That's never happening again."

"Welcome to Cybele," Mavry said after a port official verified the Hashoones' identities and recorded their arrival. "Now, I understand we're to report to the fondaco, Minister?"

"Yes," said Vass, staggering along with his valise. "While I am bound for the consulate. I believe transport has been arranged for us."

"Arrr, gimme that parcel or we'll never get there," Huff grunted, ignoring Vass's protests and snatching his bag away.

"Well, if you insist, Captain Hashoone," the minister said with what dignity he could muster.

They followed a long tunnel from the ship terminal. Its walls were of thick plastic, cloudy with dust and accumulated scratches. Beyond, Tycho could dimly see 65 Cybele's charcoal-colored plains. It was bitterly cold. He zipped up his jacket and huddled against the chill.

At the tunnel's end stood a dour-looking man bundled in synthetic fur and scowling beneath a matching hat, both dyed a brilliant orange. He held a sign that said "Vass." Behind him other men and women in furs were standing next to wheeled rickshaws, which were little more than benches on either side of platforms for baggage. The holographic banner of the Jovian Union rippled above one vehicle.

"I want that flag turned off," Diocletia said as the orange-clad pilot loaded the bags.

"Diplomatic requirement, I'm afraid," Vass said, nodding gratefully as Tycho helped him on board. "The driver will take you to the Jovian fondaco, but first I need to go to our consulate to be briefed on preparations for tonight's banquet."

"Did you say banquet?" Yana asked as the rickshaw started forward with a whine of motors.

"I did. The Cybeleans have invited the Jovian delegation to a gala tonight. All of Cybele's power brokers will be there, from financiers and officials to shipbuilders, merchants, and mining executives."

"Sounds awful," Yana said. "Why all this fuss over us?"

"Oh, it's not just for us. Earth's delegation is invited as well."

"After what happened today?" Carlo asked, his question accompanied by a puff of breath.

"Yes," Vass said. "Which makes it even more important for us to be good guests. But I agree with your sister that it sounds awful. The Cybeleans have made a great deal of livres in the last few years, and they love showing that off."

"We're privateers, Minister, not diplomats," Mavry said. "Sparkling conversation isn't our specialty."

"That's why we're meeting with the assistant secretary for protocol before the banquet. All the privateers currently based here in the Cybeles have been requested to attend tonight's affair."

"Includin' yer new pirates?" Huff asked with a grin. "That'll be a fine shindy."

"It's not a shindy, Grandfather—it's a banquet," Carlo said.

"If there's pirates attendin', it may start as a banquet, but 'twill end as a shindy."

Carlo shook his head and turned his attention back to Vass. "Does that include the privateers from Earth, Minister? Such as Captain Allamand?"

"I have no doubt he will be in attendance."

Carlo's face reddened, turning his scar white.

"That's intolerable," he sputtered. "It's a provocation."

"No, my boy—just politics," Vass said with a small smile. "But for now, a bit about security on Cybele. The Well is safe enough, and if you get an invitation to the Northwell you have nothing to worry about. But watch your step elsewhere—particularly beyond the Westwell."

"What's the Well?" Tycho asked as the rickshaw bumped through an open airlock.

"You're looking at it," Mavry replied with a smile.

Tycho whistled in surprise as the rickshaw exited the lock. He'd expected to find himself in a pressure dome set on the asteroid's surface, but instead a bridge crossed a gigantic cavern hewn from the rock of Cybele itself. A maze of walkways filled the space above their heads, supported by a web of guy wires that had been attached seemingly at random to pillars, other bridges, and the distant rock. High above were enormous mirrors that directed light down into the depths below. The walkway shivered beneath the rickshaw's wheels, and the guy wires around them whined and sang as they flexed.

"Impressive, isn't it?" Mavry asked. "This area was so heavily mined that the second generation of settlers just cored it out to make room for all this. Things don't fall down as often as you might think, but make sure you get a map. I've been here a dozen times and I still get lost."

"So do I," Vass said, pointing up the shaft to where a collection of what looked like glass bubbles clung to the rock wall. "Those are the Cybelean government offices—with the Jovian and Earth consulates on either side. Keep going that way and you'll find yourself in the Northwell, which includes Earth's fondaco. But they won't admit you unless you have business there. Behind us is the Southwell—you'll find our fondaco there, as well as depots, mercantile offices, and the like. Same in the Westwell, but all manner of shady business takes place there."

"Is there an Eastwell?" Yana asked.

"It was filled in to create the spaceport," Vass said. "Like I said, don't go beyond the Westwell unless you have a very good reason—your pass will offer theoretical protection, but the Honorable Constabulary of the Cybeles doesn't patrol that far. The Securitat operates beyond the Westwell, but even they watch their step."

"Why, Mr. Vass?" Tycho asked. "What's out there?"

"Dozens and dozens of pressure domes—some

abandoned, others not. You'll find ice mines, factories, and fab units—but also crimps, smugglers, crime rings, Ice Wolves, and who knows what else."

"We can handle ourselves, Minister," Yana objected. "We aren't children."

"Then you understand I wouldn't tell you this without a good reason. Cybele is a port of call for the Jovian Union, for Earth, and for the Ice Wolves—with the Cybeleans playing all of us against each other. There are wheels within wheels here, some set spinning by us, others by our enemies, and a few by those whose loyalties aren't clear. Open hostilities are rare in the main Wells—no one wants to offend the Cybeleans. But elsewhere? Anything goes."

They were crossing the center of the Well now, where a number of bridges met. A market had sprung up at the nexus, with hawkers calling out from tents and stalls. The rickshaw's driver honked irritably as the crowd forced their vehicle to slow to a crawl. Tycho spotted sign walkers carrying holographic imagers that displayed starships with flags that morphed continuously, circulating among the colors of Earth, the Jovian Union, and a black circle surrounded by stars.

Vass noticed Tycho's curious look.

"Registration transfers. With all the privateering going on, insurance rates are soaring for ships moving through this area of space. Cybele is reregistering ships under its own flag—and Cybelean companies are buying up starships on the cheap from both Jovian and Earth shipping firms that are tired of losing cargoes to priva-teering. Ah, but here's our first stop."

The rickshaw pulled up to an elevator bank guarded by soldiers in Jovian uniforms. They wore mirrored eyepieces and had forearms sheathed in metal. Tycho nudged Yana.

"Those are Gibraltar Artisans cyborgs," he said. "Like Lord Sicyon's bodyguard on Ganymede. Remember?"

Yana shrugged. "At least they're on our side."

"I wish they weren't. Those guys give me the creeps."

Vass hopped off the little vehicle and reclaimed his valise, nodding to the impassive soldiers.

"I'll see you an hour before the banquet," he called as the rickshaw puttered off in the direction of the Southwell.

"Arrr, thought we'd never be rid of that cursed spy," Huff growled.

"The spy whose luggage you were kind enough to carry, Grandfather?" Yana asked with a smile.

"He has pluck, I'll give him that. I ain't above the occasional good deed, y'know."

"Yeah, you ought to be careful about that, Grandpa," Tycho said. "Someone might get the impression that you were fond of Minister Vass."

"Quiet, you two," Carlo said.

Yana stuck her tongue out at Carlo. Tycho rubbed his arms, his head wreathed by his own breath.

"If the Cybeleans are making all these livres, why don't they spend a few on some heat?" he demanded.

* * *

The Southwell was a smaller version of the Well, dotted with merchants' stalls, hostels, grog shops, and kips. A pair of liveried Cybelean constables guarded the Jovian fondaco's gates, armed with pistols and staffs whose tips crackled with electricity. To Tycho's relief, he saw no sign of any Gibraltar cyborgs.

"Are they to keep others out or us in?" Yana asked as the constables checked the driver's credentials.

"Bit o' both, I suspect," Huff said.

Beyond the gates was a spacious compound with a mess hall, offices, warehouses, and three-story dormitories hugging the rock wall. A uniformed Jovian official led the Hashoones to the third floor and gave them their passes, complete with shimmering holo-seals. Their rooms consisted of a sparse living room and kitchen, with a bedroom for Diocletia and Mavry on one side and four smaller, identical bedrooms down a short hall past the bathroom.

"Clean enough," Diocletia said after a cursory inspection. "With any luck we'll spend most of our time in space. Your father needs to work with Vesuvia on the hull repairs, and I have business at the consulate. So I need you three to get the *Comet* restocked—assuming you can find a chandler who isn't completely crooked. Dad, will you go with them?"

Huff nodded and grunted, but Carlo looked up in dismay.

"I was going to get the flight simulator set up," he

said, belatedly adding: "It's for all of us to use, of course."

"We can handle the restocking on our own," Tycho said, before Diocletia could tell his brother no.

"As long as Carlo also figures out how to get the heat on," Yana said with a shiver.

Diocletia shrugged. Carlo gave his brother a small smile of gratitude, then turned away, escaping to the room he'd chosen.

But the restocking wasn't as simple as Tycho had expected—prices at the first three chandlers ranged from outrageous to rapacious. Huff clanked out of the third one roaring about greedy dogs what needed to be keelhauled.

"Come on, you lot—there's better prices in the West-well," he growled.

"Isn't it dangerous there?" Tycho asked, cinching up the fur-lined cloak he'd thrown over his jacket before leaving their rooms.

"So's blowin' the whole budget for the cruise and leavin' the *Comet* half restocked. Jus' watch yer back is all."

"Oh, come on, Tyke," Yana said. "We'll be fine."

Tycho followed his sister and grandfather through the maze of tunnels that led to the Westwell. The passages were thronged by a mix of Cybeleans wearing synthetic furs in a rainbow of colors and burly, bearded spacers in merchant-association uniforms. Many wore carbines on their hips.

"Ice Wolves, do you think?" Yana asked.

Huff shrugged. "If yer mother's spy was right, they won't try no foolishness. An' if they do, well, that's what me persuader's for."

He tapped his built-in forearm cannon against his gleaming chrome skull, grinning at his grandchildren.

Tycho was so busy gawking at the spacers that he turned too late and walked right through a sign walker's holographic image of a starship under construction, cycling from skeletal struts around engines to a completed gleaming hull and back again.

"Come build starships, son," the sign walker urged, clamping a hand on Tycho's shoulder. "Safe work and good livres! Sign up today and I'll give you a pass—keep the crimps from snapping you up."

"Building starships where?" Tycho asked.

"Don't worry about that, young man—all of our facilities offer safe, profitable working conditions. There's entry-level work here on Cybele and big jobs out there, provided you're rated for zero-G work. Now, if you'll just sign here—"

Up ahead, Yana turned around and beckoned irritably at Tycho.

"Let go—I was just asking," Tycho said, shaking the man off and hurrying to catch up with his grandfather and sister.

The passage exited at the bottom of the Westwell, which was much shallower than the Southwell, with only a few levels of walkways above their heads. Power conduits spilled out of a central shaft, leading to a jumble of stalls and open-air cafés surrounded by rickety tables.

"Arrr, I wonder," Huff muttered, craning his neck to peer into the upper levels. "Well, ain't that a sight for sore eyes. It's still there."

"What's still there, Grandfather?" Yana asked.

"One-Legged Pete's," Huff said, gesturing with his forearm cannon to a collection of metal rooftops above their heads. "That there's the finest grog shop in the outer solar system. Raised many a mug there over the years."

Laughter and music spilled from the bar above them.

"Good place to hear what ships might be ripe for the takin', too. Y'know, kids . . ."

"We can get the ship restocked, Grandfather," Yana said, elbowing Tycho in the ribs.

"Arr, I don't know. Yer mother wouldn't like it."

"Yana's right—we can handle it," Tycho said. "Besides, you might find some valuable intelligence for us to use aboard the *Comet*."

"Good thinkin'," Huff said with a grin. "But yeh two watch yer step in these parts. Don't go beyond the Westwell—it ain't safe. An' here—yeh best take these."

The old pirate opened his ancient leather jacket and extracted a pair of wicked-looking musketoons from his bandolier, handing one to each of his grandchildren—a gesture that instantly cleared a meter of space between the three of them and the rest of the crowd.

"Don't draw on nobody 'less they need shootin'," Huff rumbled, already clomping toward the ramp that led to the grog shop. "An' if they do need shootin', don't miss."

"This blaster's heavy," Tycho complained, tucking it into the pocket of his jacket.

"Glad to have it, though," Yana said, putting hers in her parka. "I don't like the look of folks around here."

"Neither do I."

The two of them poked through the marketplace, keeping a wary eye on the spacers around them.

"What do you think Mom will put in the Log about today?" Yana asked as they extricated themselves from an old woman who swore she'd give them a great price on leather boots from Earth—guaranteed as natural and not vat-grown.

"Nothing good," Tycho said. "I bet Carlo wishes he'd come with us. Mom's probably giving it to him with both barrels now—and in person, not just in the Log."

"All of which is good for you, you know."

Tycho shook his head.

"Who cares? We *lost a dromond*, Yana. It's a disaster for the Jovian Union—and don't think those Earth captains won't be crowing about it tonight."

"That's right—I forgot about that stupid banquet," Yana said, wrinkling her nose. "But what happened wasn't our fault. It was Carlo's. He just had to show off, trying to chase down Allamand."

"So you knew he was doing the wrong thing? Because I didn't."

Yana shrugged. "I was just worried Mom would take

command back before he made things worse for himself."

Tycho stared at his sister in amazement.

"If she had, we might not have lost the *Leviathan*. Don't you feel even a little sorry for Carlo?"

Yana snorted. "Would he feel sorry for us?"

Tycho knew she was right—Carlo would have found ways to bring up such a failure for months. And perhaps Yana was correct that Tycho's recent run of luck had given him a new opportunity to win the captain's chair—which was only what he'd wanted his entire life.

But Earth had seized an unfathomable amount of livres' worth of Jovian cargo and a Jovian crew—one the *Comet* had been protecting. And he took no pleasure in remembering his brother's misery. Carlo's smug self-assurance had annoyed Tycho many times—but the sight of his older brother stunned and despondent had left Tycho feeling hollow and somehow ashamed.

Prices at the two depots in the Westwell proved no better than in the Southwell. As Tycho and Yana huddled to consider their options, a grizzled tout leaned into their conversation.

"Restockin' a ship? You need to go to the Last Chance—all services and fair prices. All I ask is you tell the boss lady that Merle sent you."

"And where's the Last Chance?" Tycho asked.

Merle pointed a grimy finger at the rock wall leading deeper into Cybele's maze of passages.

"In Bazaar—it's the next dome over, just a few hundred meters that way."

"Beyond the Westwell?" Tycho asked.

"Only a few hundred meters. Safe enough for two strapping young spacers such as yourselves."

"I don't know," Tycho said when they'd freed themselves from Merle.

"Tyke, honestly—we're carrying enough firepower to outfit a strike fighter," Yana said, patting the blaster beneath her parka.

Tycho surrendered, and they passed through an open airlock that connected the Westwell with a dim, dank tunnel hacked out of the rock. The passageway reminded Tycho of the lower levels of Port Town on Callisto—a frigid dumping ground for the luckless and those who preyed on them.

But the tunnel was as short as Merle had promised. Tycho saw a bright square of light ahead, and then he and Yana emerged into a pressure dome that had been erected on the surface of Cybele and inflated over curved struts adorned with clusters of brilliant white lights. Multicolored flags and wind chimes made of scrap metal hung from the girders above, giving the dome an oddly festive atmosphere.

Bazaar was filled with shacks and stalls made out of metal and plastic, where fur-clad shoppers bickered and bargained. Tycho and Yana stepped over forlorn men, women, and children who sat cross-legged behind blankets covered with a miscellany of repaired machinery, or who mutely held up bowls in hopes that some passer-by would drop in a livre or two. In the center of the dome was a larger structure, a multilevel assemblage of old shipping containers and scrap metal that had been fused into a sprawling depot topped with a holographic sign that read "The Last Chance," in neon colors bright enough to leave afterimages on Tycho's vision.

Tycho looked around the riot of stalls, trying to get his bearings amid the astonishing profusion of goods for sale. Bazaar offered everything from common spacer gear scuffed and yellowed by solar radiation to diaphanous silks that would have passed muster at a Ganymedan fete. Yana stopped at one stall to examine a cowl that switched from yellow to deep green as it moved in the dealer's hands.

A tout buttonholed Tycho to extol the virtues of an apprenticeship with a freight tender, then stopped in midsentence, looking anxiously over Tycho's shoulder. He blanched, then hurried away from the twins. The silk merchant snatched the cowl out of Yana's hands, causing the fabric to erupt in bursts of purple and rose, and reached for the metal shutter above his head.

Clangs and rumbles sounded all around them as the owners of stall after stall brought down their gates. The peddlers bundled up their merchandise and scampered away. A hard-eyed man slammed the last shutter at the Last Chance, transforming the depot into a blank fortress. Only the seekers of alms remained, faces grave yet expectant, their children peeking out from behind their shoulders.

A half dozen men swaggered into the deserted marketplace. The leader had a cybernetic eye and animated tattoos chasing themselves up and down his arms. A blaster pistol rode low on his hip, and he carried a constable's staff over one shoulder, its tip flaring with white light. The others were armed as well—Tycho spotted guns, knives, and clubs in holsters, waistbands, and hands.

"Crimps," Yana said. "I hate crimps."

The leader saw the Hashoone twins and grinned.

"Hello, what have we here?" he asked. "Ever consider a career in space, kids?"

"Already got one," Tycho said, willing his voice to be firm and deep. "We're midshipmen on the privateer *Shadow Comet*, operating under a letter of marque from the Jovian Union."

The man with the cybernetic eye grinned.

"Fancy that. And I suppose you have passes that testify to your gainful employment and prestigious occupation?"

"We do."

"I'll see them, then," the leader said, as the gang moved forward.

"That's close enough," Yana said, reaching her hand into her parka and emerging with Huff's pistol.

The crimps stopped. Their leader grinned, tapping

his staff absentmindedly on the ground. Curlicues of energy chased each other around his feet before dissipating.

"Mighty big gun for a little girl," the leader said. "Careful it doesn't go off."

"You take one more step and it will," Yana said. "My brother will show you his pass. But just you—and you can look at it without that stick."

The crimps laughed, but the merriment had an uncertain edge now. Their leader grinned again, but he also gave the energy prod to the man next to him before striding over to stand in front of Tycho.

Tycho handed over the pass, which the crimp eyed suspiciously.

"Looks legit. Or perhaps Mommy and Daddy have enough livres to pay for a good fake."

"It is legit and you know it," Tycho said, reaching to reclaim his pass. The crimp held it away from him, baring a mouthful of yellowed teeth.

"Relax, kid," he said, turning to regard Yana. "And where's yours, missy?"

"Right here," Yana said, inclining her head minutely toward the barrel of Huff's pistol.

"She's my sister," Tycho said. "And a midshipman on our quarterdeck. Her pass is the same as mine."

"Passes can get lost. And if two kids wake up belowdecks on a construction barge, it can take a while to sort things out."

"That's not going to happen," Yana said. "Give my

brother back his pass and go bother someone else."

"Six against two ain't great odds, girlie. What if we'd rather bother you?"

"Then this gun turns your head into steam. What happens after that won't be your problem."

"I hear there's easy pickings in the next dome, boss," one of the crimps said after a moment.

The leader narrowed his eyes, then nodded. He let go of Tycho's pass, which fluttered to the ground. "Looks like it's your lucky day, kids."

"Uh-uh," Yana said. "Pick up the pass and hand it to my brother. Right now."

The crimps' leader was no longer smiling.

"You that tough, kid?"

Yana said nothing. The lead crimp eyed her for a moment, then snatched the pass off the ground and thrust it against Tycho's chest.

"You two caught me in a good mood—but if I see either of you here again, I won't be so merciful," he warned, then shot a last look at Yana. "Your sister's a piece of work, kid," he told Tycho.

Tycho tucked the pass back under his cloak and managed a small smile. "You should meet our mother."

When the last of the crimps had departed, Yana exhaled and lowered Huff's blaster.

"First thing I do when we get back is ask Mom for a gun that weighs less," she said.

Shutters rattled upward around them, and within a minute Bazaar was nearly as crowded as it had been before the crimps' interruption. The vendor held out the cowl Yana had been looking at.

"Synthetic chromatophores, miss," he said. "The color changes in response to sound and movement. Just look at this workmanship—"

"I was looking before you left us to the crimps," Yana said. "You're giving me a discount for that."

The merchant shrugged as Yana stretched out the silk and watched ripples of red and blue chase themselves across its length.

"Wouldn't this be great for the banquet?" she asked Tycho, their encounter with the crimps apparently already forgotten.

"It's coming out of your allowance, not the restocking fund. I'm going to check out the Last Chance."

He left his sister to her haggling and entered the sprawling depot, which was piled high with everything one might need to outfit a starship: cargo containers were stacked next to pyramids of batteries and bins of high-intensity lamps, while signs promised the best rates on Cybele for water, air, and foodstuffs. A short flight of steps led to a small café where spacers were comparing notes on their mediapads, and a brightly lit video board was crammed with blinking and flashing starship logos, the calling cards of captains seeking to fill out their crew rosters. Clerks scurried about, and big, hard-eyed men with iron bars in their hands stood around the depot's perimeter, ready to roll down the shutters or attend to other trouble.

Tycho's mediapad beeped. He looked at the device and scowled—it was his mother.

"Where are you?" Diocletia asked when he answered.

Tycho hesitated.

"The chandler's depot in a dome called Bazaar."

Diocletia said nothing for a moment, and Tycho knew she was looking at a map of Cybele. He braced for impact.

"That's beyond the Westwell."

"Just a few hundred meters. We'd need a year's worth of condemnations to meet any other depot's prices."

"I see. Stay there. I'm on my way."

Tycho put the mediapad away, wondering what his mother wanted. He supposed they'd find out soon enough.

"Like I told you the last two times, Jenks, no goods on credit," a woman said in an angry voice. "I can't pay the rent with rumors about mineral deposits, you know. Which is all you ever have for payment."

The woman stood behind a triangle of counters in the center of the Last Chance. She was tall and broad shouldered, with sharp features and black hair gone gray. She waited with her hands on her hips while the unfortunate Jenks's pleas turned to imprecations. One of the men with bars took a step forward, prompting Jenks to scuttle out of the Last Chance with a final offended glance.

The woman turned and gave Tycho an appraising look. "If you're cabin boy on some broken-down ore boat, I'll save us both some time and trouble—the answer is no."

Tycho shook his head as Yana joined him at the counter, a parcel of opaque plastic tucked under one arm.

"Merle sent us," he said. "We're restocking a frigate. Um, assuming you can service a ship that big . . ."

"I've outfitted prospector convoys trying their luck in the Kuiper Belt, kid—I can handle a frigate."

Her eyes narrowed, then lingered on Yana.

"You and that girl are the ones who just faced down Jasper One Eye. Free advice—be careful of him. Whoever he's working for, they've got plenty of livres—and they're snatching up anyone who looks like they can figure out the right end of a power wrench. And Good Samaritans are in short supply around here."

"I noticed that," Tycho said.

"Well, don't forget it. Now show me your shopping list and I'll get you a price."

Tycho specified the *Comet*'s needs and studied his surroundings while the woman entered numbers into her mediapad. A knot of bearded spacers were arguing over the merits of different models of air scrubbers while a young clerk hovered nearby, looking for a break in the dispute.

"Those spacers look Saturnian," Tycho said, keeping his voice carefully neutral.

"Are you asking me if they're Ice Wolves?" the woman asked with a raised eyebrow.

Tycho shrugged.

"Don't know and don't care," she said. "Saturnians, Jovians, asteroid dwellers, Martians, Earthfolk—we get them all in here. Their livres are legal tender, which is good enough for me. Anything beyond that is information, kid. And information isn't free."

"Hey, jump-pop," Yana said, peeking at a cooler behind the counter. "I'll take an orange—as long as it's cold."

The depot owner eyed Yana, then placed a jump-pop in front of her. The bottle was covered with frost.

"Could I get a lime one, please?" Tycho asked.

"That's ten livres," the woman said.

"*Ten?*" Yana asked in shock. "They're two for seven in the Southwell."

"They're also warm and left over from last year's imports. Up to you."

"Fine," Yana grumbled, passing over a coin and downing a long swallow of jump-pop.

"All right," the woman said, turning her mediapad around so they could see it. "Water, air, consumables as specified."

"I think you put a decimal point in the wrong place," Yana said.

"This does seems awfully high," Tycho said.

"It's correct. And what I sell will weigh the same on the landing-field scale as it's listed on the manifest. Which won't be true if you buy in the Southwell."

"It's still outrageous," Yana said.

The depot owner sighed.

"Did you see all the ships in orbit when you made port, kid? This little rock is booming right now. That's the price. If you don't want to pay it, within an hour I'll have two captains who will."

Tycho and Yana looked at each other uncertainly.

"Does that include delivery to the landing pad, at least?" Tycho asked.

"It does not. We'll prepare a shipment for transport by your own people, but delivery is extra."

"Last time we restocked on Ceres, it was half this price," Yana said.

"So restock on Ceres," the woman said, pointing. "It's one hundred million kilometers that way."

Tycho started to argue, but the woman was looking past him, a curious expression on her face.

"So it's you," she said. "It's been a long time."

Tycho turned and saw Diocletia standing behind Yana, arms folded across her chest.

"It has, hasn't it?" Diocletia said. "Hello, Mother."

13

TABLE MANNERS

Yana was the first to recover, peering curiously at the depot owner.

"You're our grandmother? That means your name is . . . Elfrieda?"

The woman nodded. "Elfrieda Stehley. You must be Yana. I should have guessed—you're the spitting image of Carina when she was your age. And this would be Tycho, then."

Tycho started to say something, but Elfrieda's

attention had returned to Diocletia. The two women eyed each other in silence.

"Last I heard, you were running a hostel at the Hygiea roadstead," Diocletia said at last.

"Gave that up years ago. So where's Carlo?"

"Back in our quarters. Dad's here too." Diocletia's eyes jumped to Tycho and Yana. "In fact, he was supposed to be with the two of you."

"He's at One-Legged Pete's," Tycho said. "Uh, gathering intelligence on shipping."

"That's one way of putting it."

Elfrieda brightened for the first time. "Glad to hear the old pirate is still kicking. Send him by for a nip, will you?"

"I'll tell him you've fetched up here," Diocletia said, glancing down at the mediapad. "So is our business concluded?"

"We were discussing that when you arrived," Elfrieda said, passing the mediapad over. "That price doesn't include delivery."

"I figured it wouldn't," Diocletia said, studying the numbers on the mediapad. "And is there a family discount? Considering we're the only people you have left in the solar system?"

"Never mix business with personal. Didn't I teach you that, at least?"

"You did. Along with not to count on you for anything."

Elfrieda took her mediapad back and shut it off with

a snap. "Since we have nothing further to discuss, I have other customers to attend to."

"Oh, I'll take the deal," Diocletia said. "I'll expect these goods to be ready for my crewers by 0600 tomorrow—a minute after that and I'll leave everything here and sue you for each and every livre you don't refund. Is that understood, Mother?"

"Perfectly. My people are never late, Diocletia. Have your crewers here ready to load up at 0600—a minute after that and you'll pay a restocking fee. And I know every lawyer in the asteroid belt, so don't think you'll get out of it."

Diocletia nodded and the two completed their transaction in silence. Then Diocletia was striding out of the depot with Yana in her wake.

"It was nice to see you, Grandmother," Tycho said, turning and hurrying after his mother and sister.

"Call me Elfrieda," his grandmother replied.

It was clear from Diocletia's determined stride and baleful gaze that she wasn't interested in discussing Elfrieda, but Tycho and Yana could barely keep their curiosity in check, and each began a silent campaign of stares and hand gestures meant to goad the other into breaching their mother's wall of silence.

As they returned to the Westwell, Diocletia grew weary of her children's scowling and rolling eyes at each other on the periphery of her vision.

"Whatever you want to ask, ask it now. I'll give you

until we reach the fondaco. After that, no more questions."

Tycho and Yana looked at each other, unsure of how to proceed. Then Tycho rushed ahead.

"Why didn't you tell us our grandmother was on Cybele?"

"Because I didn't know. Mother's set up shop everywhere from Mars to Titan. She's not one to leave a forwarding address."

"Did you ever try to find her?" Tycho asked.

"It was fairly obvious she didn't want to be found."

"We had no idea that was her, you know," Yana said. "It's not like we were trying to find her."

"Well, now you have—you'll find it's no great privilege. I'm not angry that you ran into Mother. Finding you beyond the Westwell, on the other hand . . ."

"We stayed together," Yana said. "When did Elfrieda leave again? I don't remember her."

"When you were three or four. It was a long time ago, Yana."

"*Why* did she leave?" Tycho asked.

"You'd have to ask her that. Now listen—we have more important matters to discuss."

That was breaking the deal she'd just struck with them, but neither twin dared argue the point.

"We're exchanging Haines and the Earth privateers we captured for the crew of the *Nestor Leviathan*," Diocletia said. "Allamand brought them in an hour ago."

"And what about the *Leviathan* herself?" Tycho asked.

"No sign of her. Perhaps the consulate will address that before the banquet. If there's enough time after we talk table manners."

Tycho and Yana exchanged a baffled look.

"Did you say table manners, Mom?" Tycho asked.

"I'm afraid I did."

Tycho glowered at the formal suit waiting for him on a hanger in the bathroom, but he'd already showered, shaved, and made a vague effort to subdue his hair, so he couldn't put it off any longer. Carlo was staring into the mirror, unhappily activating and deactivating various color schemes for his tie.

"Go with the alternating yellow and red," Tycho suggested. "Colors of the Jovian flag, right?"

"And what a fine son of Jupiter I've shown myself to be today," Carlo muttered.

"I heard Dad say the hull damage is minor and we'll be able to fly in the morning," Tycho said, hoping to offer his brother some small comfort.

Carlo shrugged. "The damage in the Log's a little tougher to repair."

"Did Yana tell you about our grandmother? About Elfrieda?"

That made Carlo look up, puzzled, and Tycho told him the story.

"I thought she was dead," Carlo said.

"I did too. Mom said she left when we were three or four. Do you remember her?"

Carlo stared into the mirror.

"I remember her," he said quietly. "She left a week before I started my apprenticeship. The *Comet* was coming back from a cruise to Vesta. I was eight."

"Oh. And do you know why she left? Mom didn't want to say."

Carlo sighed. "For once in your life, Tyke, leave it alone."

"But she's our family."

"She *was* our family. She hasn't acted like it in more than a decade."

Tycho started to argue, but there was a knock at the door.

"Ready to learn about forks?" Mavry asked with a grin.

"This whole thing is insulting," Carlo muttered. "I already know about forks."

"Well, that's a relief," their father said with the same grin. "Ready to teach the rest of us about forks?"

The Hashoones knew better than to wait for Huff, and left his gaudiest yellow tie for him to find in the living room before setting off for the Well. When they arrived at the Jovian consulate, Vass was waiting for them in a black velvet suit that Tycho suspected had been made for a child. The minister complimented Yana on her cowl, which responded with a flurry of brilliant green, then bowed low over Diocletia's hand. The *Comet*'s captain was wearing a plain black dress with a red and yellow shawl—about as fancy an outfit as she ever wore.

Inside the consulate, a dozen privateers had gathered in a conference room with a vertiginous view of the Well. Tycho recognized Morgan Theo and Garibalda Marta Andrade, standing with their crews. He saw Carlo go rigid when he spotted Andrade—and he also saw the hard look in the veteran privateer's eyes when she saw him.

A gray-haired woman with a pinched expression entered the room and stood next to Vass, towering over the diminutive minister. Behind her, two of Gibraltar Artisans' cybernetic soldiers took up positions on either side of the door.

"Unfortunately some members of our party seem to have been delayed, but let's begin," she said. "Ladies and gentlemen, I'm Elspeth Hastings, Madam President's assistant secretary for protocol. We know that your . . . *unconventional* job descriptions have kept some of you from attending a formal banquet in the recent past. So we thought we would provide a refresher in the more complicated aspects of etiquette."

"That was delicately said," Mavry observed, one eyebrow raised.

Diocletia shushed him.

"Before you you'll see a typical table setting for a formal dinner," Hastings said.

Tycho studied the broad plate sitting in front of him. A smaller plate rested on top of it, crowned by an elaborately folded napkin. A bewildering number of forks, knives, and spoons flanked the two plates—there was even a fork and spoon above them, between yet another small plate (with a knife) and a diagonal line of ever-smaller glasses.

"Looks busier than a docking queue above Ganymede," grumbled one of Andrade's officers.

"It does seem like a lot, but you'll see it's not so hard to get straight," Hastings said. "Let's start with the basics. . . ."

Some kind of commotion was happening outside the door. It opened to admit Huff Hashoone, bellowing laughter. Behind him came a squat, slab-faced woman with dark skin and spiky white hair, blinking tattoos, and a big grin.

"Dmitra Barnacus, as I live and breathe," Mavry said, smiling and shaking his head.

Huff was wearing his yellow tie, though it had wound up thrown over one shoulder. A line of spacers entered the conference room behind him and Dmitra, all of them sporting scars and missing body parts and in the middle of a raucous conversation.

"Why do I get the feeling there was a lot of intelligence gathering at One-Legged Pete's?" Mavry asked Tycho.

Tycho grinned, then peered at the new arrivals.

"Wasn't Dmitra at 624 Hektor?" he asked Yana.

His sister nodded. "But she never got a letter of marque. Last I heard, she was running cargo out around Neptune. And, they say, hunting Earth haulers and prospectors as a pirate."

Huff nearly smacked into Assistant Secretary Hastings, pulling up with perhaps a millimeter to spare, then eyed the impassive soldiers.

"Beggin' yer pardon, madam," he said. "Had pirate business what needed attendin' to."

"Privateer," Tycho said automatically. A couple of the grizzled new arrivals looked at him curiously.

The assistant secretary tried to restore order, then gave up and waited for the spacers to finish laughing and yelling and locate seats.

"Canaan Bickerstaff, the Widderich brothers, and I do believe that's Zhi Ning," Mavry said in wonder. "It's like old home week."

"On 1172 Aeneas, maybe," Carlo grumbled.

Huff swaggered over and executed a landing of sorts in the seat next to Diocletia, while the other newcomers navigated their way toward what empty seats remained. Introductions were made, which took a while, given the privateers' need to roar out hellos and exchange cheerfully obscene insults with old compatriots.

"My goodness, no, don't say that at the banquet table," Hastings gasped. "Please be seated. Now, let's discuss the setting before you. The napkin goes in your lap, not around your neck. Then, to the left of the plates, you'll see a salad fork, a fish fork, and a dinner fork."

"Y'know, you could melt these down and have a serviceable cutlass," mused Canaan Bickerstaff.

Assistant Secretary Hastings chose not to hear that.

"That large plate on the bottom is the service

plate—you won't actually eat off it," she said. "When the first course arrives, it'll be on a salad plate, placed atop it as shown. Now, to the right of the plate you'll see a dinner knife, fish knife, teaspoon, soup spoon, and shellfish fork."

Tycho stared at the seemingly infinite utensils in dismay.

"If one of those utensils is missing, it means you won't be enjoying that course tonight. We included them all because the Cybeleans haven't shared tonight's menu with us—they want it to be a surprise."

From the assistant secretary's expression, Tycho could guess what she thought of surprises.

Huff raised his blaster cannon in the air, drawing the baleful gaze of the cyborg soldiers. Hastings looked at the twitching weapon nervously.

"Do you have a question, Captain Hashoone?"

"Arrr, I'm allergic to shellfish. Had 'em once on Ganymede an' blew up like a hatch seal."

"I shall inform our hosts. But just in case, your waiter should know if any dish contains shellfish."

"But what if one of these thrice-cursed rock burrowers is fixin' to poison us?" demanded one of Barnacus's crew.

"That would be a serious diplomatic incident. I'm quite sure no one at tonight's event will be trying to poison anyone."

Other privateers had their hands in the air now too. Captain Andrade's navigator was gluten-free, two members of Morgan Theo's bridge crew didn't eat dairy, Kanoji Ali kept halal while two other members of his crew kept kosher, and several privateers ate only synthetic meat and were suspicious about the sourcing of the night's menu. Hastings fielded their complaints, looking increasingly flustered, while Vass stood next to her with a dazed smile.

"If your waiter can't tell you what's in a dish, you can of course politely decline it," Hastings said. "Now, why don't we move on? Above and to the left of your service plate—"

"What's this blasted extra fork and spoon up here for?" Huff asked Diocletia in a whisper that could be heard halfway down the table.

"I have no idea, Dad," Diocletia said.

"Yeh don't know?" Huff asked, looking surprised. "After all them governesses I got for yeh an' yer sister?"

"They ran off with pirates."

Hastings had stopped her lesson and was waiting for the discussion to cease.

"*All* of 'em ran off with pirates?" Huff asked in shock.

"Or Mother got rid of them."

"Huh. Deuced waste of livres, that."

"The spoon and fork above your plate are for dessert, Grandfather," interjected Carlo.

"That's correct," Hastings said gratefully. "And the small plate to the left of them is for bread—you'll find your bread knife atop it."

"If yeh need to stab someone, don't use that one—it

won't do nothin' unless yeh get 'em right between the ribs," Huff said. "Picked up the wrong knife once in a dustup at Hygiea. Embarrassin', that."

"Don't stab anyone with any utensil!" gasped a suddenly pale Hastings.

"Well, of course not," grunted Sanco Paz, Canaan Bickerstaff's grizzled first mate. "Stabbin' people ain't proper company manners."

Several privateers grunted their assent to this.

"Well said, sir," Hastings said. "Now then, let's consider glassware. Who knows what this largest glass is for?"

"Grog!" declared a member of Dmitra's crew. "With any luck, they're all for grog!"

Several privateers cheered, and a couple raised their empty glasses and clinked them in mock toasts. Tycho heard glass break somewhere at the far end of the table. Hastings winced.

"Ladies and gentlemen, please! The largest glass is not for alcohol, but for water."

The privateers began to boo.

"This next glass is for red wine, and this one is for white wine," Hastings said, raising her voice. "And then this flute is for champagne, and this smallest glass is for sherry."

"What's sherry?" Tycho asked his father, as the privateers debated how many of those beverages counted as grog.

"It's for cooking," Yana said. "Mr. Speirdyke always

has a bottle of it open in the galley."

"Oh dear," Mavry said.

Karst Widderich raised a hand—or rather, the stump of one.

"Begging pardon, ma'am, but where do you extinguish a cheroot?"

"That one's easy—in the water glass," said his brother, Baltazar. "Ain't you got no manners, you bilge-born cur?"

"Duty compels me to correct you—" began Hastings.

"I didn't know, Balty, which is why I was asking," Karst told his brother in a wounded voice. "So can the water glass be used as a spittoon too? Or is that another glass?"

Dmitra brayed laughter. "You nitwit. You really would spit in your own water glass, wouldn't you?"

"SHUT UP!" Hastings bellowed. "ALL OF YOU! THIS INSTANT!"

The privateers looked at the assistant secretary in shock.

"*No* glass should be used as a spittoon! Or for extinguishing smoking materials! Neither activity is permitted at tonight's banquet!"

"All these glasses and not one of 'em's a spittoon?" muttered Karst Widderich. "That ain't proper planning."

Hastings breathed deeply and closed her eyes, then opened them and attempted a smile.

"You will all receive place cards when you enter the banquet hall," she said in a voice that now sounded only slightly strained. "You'll find your table assignments on them. Please do not rearrange the cards or engage in disputes over them."

"That means no stabbin' people, you lot," Huff said, gesturing emphatically with his forearm cannon.

"I believe we have covered the etiquette of stabbing. Now, with each course you should alternate whom you speak with at the table—the person on your left and then the person on your right."

"First port and then starboard," Dmitra growled as Karst Widderich regarded his hands.

The privateers looked left and then right, shrugging agreeably.

"As this is a diplomatic event, I have some subjects I suggest you avoid with your tablemates. Politics, for one. As well as piracy and privateering."

"These options do not leave much about which to converse," observed Zhi Ning.

"There's grog," Canaan Bickerstaff said.

"And weapons," said Kanoji Ali. "Can we talk about them things, ma'am?"

Hastings sighed. "I suppose so. Grog and weapons it is."

Vass whispered in her ear and Hastings nodded.

"I have an idea," she said, smiling brightly. "Perhaps we could speak to our hosts about an alternate seating arrangement. How many of you would prefer the company of your fellow privateers at this banquet?"

Most of the privateers put up their hands—or in

some cases, lifted forearm cannons and other artificial appendages. Mavry raised his hand, only to have Diocletia haul it back down and shake her head warningly at Tycho and Yana.

"Very well, I shall see about the arrangements," Hastings said. "I . . . look forward to seeing you all shortly for what I'm certain will be a memorable evening."

And with that the assistant secretary fled, leaving the privateers arguing about points of etiquette.

"I think that went well," Mavry said.

The banquet was held at the pinnacle of the pressure dome sheltering the Well, which meant the Jovian officials and privateers had to wait patiently for room in the lone elevator serving the consulate.

Tycho had noticed that Huff's indicators were flashing yellow and decided to make sure his grandfather was monitoring his power levels—he occasionally got too excited to pay attention. Tycho waved for the rest of the Hashoones to go ahead and pushed his way back to where the privateers were laughing about old times.

"Arrr, yer a good lad, Tyke," Huff said, ruffling Tycho's hair affectionately with his artificial hand. "Brought along a spare power pack, so don't yeh worry about me."

Tycho nodded and tried not to wince as his grandfather patted him on the head again—Huff's artificial hand didn't provide much in the way of feedback, so the pats were more like slaps. He squeezed into the elevator with Huff and several other privateers, winding up with his nose wedged in Canaan Bickerstaff's armpit.

"You ever see so many rich prizes around one rock?" Canaan asked Huff as the doors closed.

"Not since the old days. There's enough livres in orbit for the whole lot of us to spend the rest of our days sleepin' soft an' eatin' dainty. Blasted shame we can't scoop 'em up."

"And who says we cain't?" asked Baltazar Widderich from the back of the elevator.

"Yeah, who says we cain't?" his brother, Karst, echoed.

"You boys ain't too clear on what a letter of marque means, I'm guessin'," Bickerstaff said with a grin.

"It's clear enough," Baltazar replied, sounding offended. "Jes' ain't never cared much about papers and lawyers. The pirate trade was a fair sight better without them."

"Arrr, ain't that the truth," Huff said.

The doors opened and Tycho extracted himself, a bit woozily, from the sweaty privateer and then the elevator. They were above the rim of the Well, looking out at the starships surrounding Cybele, the bulk of Attis looming overhead, and the infinite stars.

"Now that's a view," Huff breathed appreciatively as they joined the end of a long line of privateers and officials. "But what's this holdup, then?"

"I heard no weapons," said Slack Robin, a cadaverous privateer who served with one of the Widderiches. "They'll stow them for us, but you can't take them into dinner."

"Arrr, that's why I don't like formal affairs—too stuffy," Huff said, tugging at his tie. "Yeh go ahead, lad—no sense waitin' for me."

"I'll stay, Grandfather," Tycho said, then hesitated. "Did you hear who we ran into beyond the Westwell?"

"No one tells me nothin' no more," Huff said, and then the living half of his face darkened. "Yeh better not mean crimps."

"No. Well, yes. But that wasn't what I meant. We ran the crimps off."

Huff peered at him, curious.

"Elfrieda's here on Cybele, Grandpa. Running a shop in a pressure dome called Bazaar."

"Is she now? Wondered where she'd taken herself off to."

Tycho tried to figure out what his grandfather was thinking. He couldn't tell, but Huff didn't seem upset.

"She said you should come by for a nip."

"Arrr, p'raps I will. Thankee, lad. Be good to see yer grandmother again. Though I'd keep her an' yer mother separated, for both their sakes."

Ahead, four Cybelean constables flanked the double doors to the banquet hall, eyeing the readout on a weapons detector, while a young man and woman in black uniforms waited behind a table, handing the privateers tickets for their carbines and sidearms.

"Anything to declare, sir?" the young woman asked Huff, retreating a step as his forearm cannon squealed.

"Oh my. We'll definitely need to ask you to check that."

"Yeh take good care of me persuader now," Huff said, unstrapping the cannon and setting it on the table. "That baby's let me end more'n a few unpleasant conversations."

"We'll keep it for you in a secure locker," the woman promised, handing Huff a ticket and delicately hefting the cannon.

"Jes' a minute, lassie," Huff said, noticing the weapons detector. "There's a couple more."

He opened his coat and extracted the carbines he'd lent to Tycho and Yana, thumping them down on the table. Then he bent to unbuckle the sword on his hip.

"Uh, I'll get some more claim checks," the woman said.

Huff held up a finger, fumbling in his jacket. He extracted a small but deadly-looking pistol, then frowned and reached behind his back, his artificial hand emerging with a punch dagger of black ceramic.

"All right, this will take me a couple of trips," the woman said.

"Hang fire a moment, girlie. Oh, that's right."

He touched the middle two fingers of his artificial hand to its thumb and twisted his wrist. A hidden hatch opened in his palm and a small baton slid out.

"What's that one do, Huff?" said a privateer whose name Tycho remembered as al-Adabi.

"Sonic emitter," Huff said with a grin. "Look here,

Hasan—I touch that button three times and there wouldn't be an intact eardrum within ten meters of here."

"Wouldn't that include you?"

"Arrr, ain't had natural eardrums for near on forty years. Delicate little blighters—the Almighty weren't thinkin' on space battles when he created 'em."

"Sure you ain't got a bow chaser tucked somewhere in that metal carcass of yours, Huff?" asked Dmitra Barnacus with a grin.

"Not yet. Arrr, if a body's still kickin' after that lot, I reckon I can chomp 'em."

He clacked his jaws together a couple of times and departed, a sheaf of tickets jammed in his metal fist.

They passed through the weapons detector without incident and into the banquet hall, where waiters were rushing about with trays of drinks and finger food.

"Arrr, first place I've been on this miserable rock what's warm," Huff muttered.

In the center of the room was a small stage where four musicians were playing—Tycho spotted what he thought were three violins and a larger instrument he'd never seen before. No one was seated yet; Tycho saw naval uniforms of both Earth and the Jovian Union next to the formal black suits of ministers and functionaries and the cheerful riot of clothes worn by privateers.

The Cybeleans were easy to spot. They wore luxuriant-looking furs or velvet in deep, rich colors.

Their fingers and ears glittered and sparkled with rings, and a number of them wore gravity-defying hats. And they were beaming and gesturing grandly.

It's their party and they want to impress all of us, Tycho thought.

"Now don't let the Earthfolk intimidate yeh, Tyke," Huff said in his ear as they scanned the front table for their place cards. "Ain't no shame growin' up under a dome instead of breathin' air. Can't nobody pick where they're born or who they're born to—it's what yeh do with the life yer given that counts."

"I know, Grandpa," Tycho said with a smile, reaching for what he thought was his place card. His name was written with so many flourishes and curlicues that he had to look twice to make sure it was his.

"Are you Huff Hashoone, from Callisto?" a gruff voice behind them asked as the musicians began to play.

The empty socket of Huff's forearm cannon squealed and twitched. Tycho and his grandfather turned and saw an older man standing behind them, wearing a dark-blue tunic, red vest, and a ruffled orange shirt.

"That's me, sure enough," Huff said. "An' whom am I addressin'?"

"Ripton Ferdinando Zombro, captain of the *Argent Raptor*," the man said stiffly. "Operating under letter of marque granted by His Majesty, the emperor of Earth."

"I've heard of 'im," Huff said, eyeing the Earthman. "This here is my grandson Tycho Hashoone, midshipman aboard the *Shadow Comet*."

Captain Zombro nodded at Tycho and offered him a small bow.

"Your grandfather doesn't remember my name, but he ought to remember my old command in His Majesty's navy. Back in the seventies I was captain of the HMS *Perseus*. We fought an engagement once, above—"

"—above 43 Ariadne, in the Floras," Huff said. "That was seventy-four—I remember it well. We'd boarded a bulk freighter through the starboard docking ring. An' yer crew—"

"—boarded through the port ring," Zombro said with a grin. "We met in the middle. I recall it was warm work, Captain Hashoone."

"Warm work indeed," Huff said, hitching up his right sleeve. "See this scar, the one starting below the elbow? One of yer marines gave me that, with a bayonet. Ruined a nice mermaid tattoo I'd had done on Ceres."

"I have my own souvenirs from the encounter," Zombro said, parting his hair above the ear. "See that scar? A centimeter to the left and I'd have been in a shroud. You did that, Captain Hashoone."

"I did? Thought I was a better shot back then. But wait, Captain Zombro—look here."

Huff opened his jacket and tugged at his shirt, sending buttons flying.

"See that burn mark? The one right above the heart? Breastplate kept the bolt from going through, but blistered me something fierce."

Zombro peered at the rippled scar.

"Lucky thing, that," he said, then turned partially around. "My right buttock? Entirely artificial. Blast damage as your crewers were retreating. Say, I hear they've imported genuine Earth brandy for tonight. How about a snifter before it's all gone to waste?"

"Capital idea," Huff said, clapping Zombro on the back with his artificial hand. "Yeh don't mind, do yeh, Tyke?"

Tycho shook his head, though he would have been happy to hear more of the old combatants' war stories. But Huff and Zombro had already set course for the bar.

He looked around the banquet, feeling ill at ease, then caught sight of the rest of his family and hurried to join them. Diocletia and Carlo looked miserable, but Mavry was studying a waiter's tray of snacks appreciatively, and Yana had talked someone into fetching an orange jump-pop.

"Some party, huh, kid?" Mavry asked, popping a piece of fish into his mouth and gawking at the musicians. "Never seen a real live fiddler before, let alone four. Gotta hand it to the Cybeleans—they spent plenty on this shindy."

"I'm surprised they don't just throw livres into the air," Carlo muttered. "What a vulgar display."

"Oh, it's definitely that," Mavry said, looking for another waiter to ambush. "But most vulgar displays don't fill your belly."

A burst of laughter came from the bar, lost to sight

behind a mob of privateers.

"At least Grandfather's having fun," Yana said.

"Well, of course he is," Mavry said, a bit wistfully. "This is like how it used to be—the pirate life, I mean."

"Oh, please," Diocletia said, eyes flashing. "I don't remember going to a lot of parties with the captains of the Earth warships that were trying to kill us. In fact, I don't remember a single one. Carlo's right—this a game played by the Cybeleans. To test us, and to amuse themselves. And I don't like it."

Mavry had learned when it was wise to let a subject drop.

"And what table are you at, Tycho?" he asked brightly.

Tycho peered at his place card. "Six."

"That's the kids' table," said Yana, looking disgusted. "I'm there too. Carlo, on the other hand, is considered a grown-up."

"Someone has to be," Carlo said.

"Which means he gets to listen to old people rattle on about the past," Mavry said. "Lucky Carlo."

Heads had turned to the banquet hall's entrance. Tycho looked over, curious, and saw a beefy, florid man with a bald head and a long red mustache, standing in the middle of a circle of people that included Garibalda Marta Andrade.

"Who's that?" Tycho asked.

Diocletia's eyes narrowed. "Unless I'm mistaken, that is Captain Cromer of the *Nestor Leviathan*. They must have already exchanged the *Actaeon*'s prize crew for the

Leviathans. We have to pay our respects."

"We do?" Carlo asked.

"We most certainly do," Diocletia said, walking that way. The rest of the Hashoones hurried after her, joining the circle around Cromer, who was standing next to a silver-haired man in a suit of navy-blue velvet and a crimson cloak.

"Your ordeal has been a source of dismay for us all, Captain Cromer," Diocletia said after the introductions, bowing slightly. "It's a relief to see you safely returned to your countrymen."

Cromer bowed his head in response.

"I beg you not to be too heavily burdened by today's misfortunes, Captain Hashoone," he said. "If it hadn't been for your family's heroic action, my crewers and I might still be prisoners. Fortunately Captain Allamand here is a man of honor—he even remembered the banquet and insisted I take my formal clothes from the *Leviathan* before our departure."

The Hashoones' eyes leaped to the man in the red cloak. He smiled.

"Any honorable captain would have done the same. Captain Jean-Christophe Allamand, of the *Gracieux*, at your service. I am humbled to meet such worthy adversaries."

"Captain Allamand," Diocletia said stiffly. "I'm—"

"Captain Hashoone, of the *Shadow Comet*, of course," Allamand said, taking her outstretched hand and bowing low over it. "And this would be your first mate, Mr.

Malone, and Masters Carlo, Tycho, and Yana. It is a distinct pleasure to meet you all, at long last."

Tycho murmured something he hoped was appropriate.

"I must thank you, Captain Hashoone, for your treatment of my prize crew. Mr. Haines kicked up quite a fuss, but he's always been a bit excitable. Still convinced he's in the navy, I'm afraid."

"And I must thank you for the treatment of our own prize crew," Diocletia said. "Mr. Richards told us of your kindness in offering parole."

Allamand smiled. "It's an unpleasant business, this conflict we find ourselves in. But let the politicians hurl barbs and vitriol—there's no reason we cannot conduct ourselves in a more agreeable fashion."

Tycho smiled back, but he was certain his expression looked fake. Just hours before, this regal-looking captain had stolen countless livres from the Jovian Union, an embarrassment that had been broadcast all over the solar system by now. Ships under his command had exchanged fire with ones commanded by the people he was now making small talk with, and crewers on both sides had died.

Now their conversation was polite and almost pleasant—and Tycho found he didn't like that any more than his mother and brother did.

"But where are my manners?" Allamand asked, turning and beckoning to someone behind him. "This is my daughter—Kate, as she insists on being called."

Allamand ushered forward a slim young woman about the same age as Tycho and Yana, wearing a dress of deep burgundy with a silver necklace that set off her long neck and pale skin. She had a mop of black hair and dark eyes.

Kate Allamand smiled and curtsied to the Hashoones. Yana elbowed Tycho in the ribs and he bowed hastily, feeling himself flush.

Captain Allamand's daughter was the most beautiful girl he'd ever seen.

14

THE CAPTAIN'S DAUGHTER

The next few minutes of small talk barely registered with Tycho, who alternated sneaking looks at Kate Allamand with telling himself not to look at her at all. He tried to imagine that a few hours earlier she'd been on a starship he'd been pursuing. It seemed impossible. What if Carlo had caught the *Gracieux* and they'd fired on each other?

Soft chimes pealed out five times, prompting a privateer to bark that "someone's gettin' keelhauled—it ain't 2230!" Then a waiter paused at the periphery of the Hashoones' group and asked everyone to take their seats.

Captain Allamand headed in one direction with Diocletia, Mavry, Carlo, and the other Jovian privateers, chatting amiably, while Tycho stumbled after Yana in search of table six, taking a last look over his shoulder at Allamand's daughter.

"What's wrong with you?" Yana hissed. "Have you been struck in the head? Or did you get into the grog?"

"What? Neither."

"Well, quit acting like a spacesick dirtsider," Yana said, eyes scanning the tables. "If we keep our ears open, maybe we can learn something we can use. Remember what Mom always says about cruises succeeding or failing because of what happens in port."

"I remember," Tycho said. "Do you remember any of that stuff they said about forks and soup?"

Yana scoffed as they reached table six. "I wasn't listening in the first place. Here's my place card."

Tycho walked around to the other side of the table, where a snow-white card bore his name, written in the same elaborate script he'd encountered earlier. Their table held eight, and the other chairs were filling up with young people in formal clothes. Yana was already chatting with a young woman in a navy-blue and red dress when Tycho found his hand vanishing into the paw of a massive youth with a patchy beard and a luxuriant silk doublet. He was sitting to Tycho's left, his rich furs flung over the back of his chair.

The young man introduced himself as Thaddeus Sewickley and immediately began explaining his work as an apprentice analyst in his father's investment house here on Cybele. Tycho nodded and tried to keep up with the bewildering stream of terminology coming out of Sewickley's mouth, glancing repeatedly at the empty seat next to him.

Kate Allamand was standing a few steps behind Yana, nodding politely at something said by an old man with a walrus mustache who was holding her hand and patting it. Tycho glanced once more to his right, but that place card was turned slightly away from him, and he couldn't see what it said.

He looked around the room, murmuring assent to something Sewickley said. A rotund young man and a sharp-faced woman, both teenagers, were finishing a conversation and starting to walk in Tycho's direction.

Go away, Tycho thought. *Go away go away go away.*

Kate finally extracted her hand from the grip of the man with the walrus mustache. She glanced at a place card in her other hand as the two teenagers passed behind Tycho's table.

"I mean, have you ever seen a more favorable interest-rate environment?" asked Thaddeus Sewickley.

"Huh? No, never. Amazing!"

"That's what I say!" Sewickley exclaimed, and began to talk again. Tycho peered past him and saw the sharp-faced teenaged girl walking by herself. Kate was across the table, peeking over Yana's shoulder with her brows knit. Waiters surrounded their table and began setting down salads festooned with nuts and fruits in unlikely colors.

"Excuse me," a voice said in clipped tones behind Tycho. He turned and saw the rotund boy looking at him in puzzlement.

"I say, is this table seven?"

"Six!" Tycho all but crowed.

The boy gave him a curious look and headed back the way he'd come. Tycho turned back to Sewickley and spotted Kate behind the young Cybelean, hitching her dress up slightly as she walked his way.

"Oh, don't get up," she said with a smile, and Tycho kicked himself mentally that getting up hadn't occurred to him.

And then she was in the empty seat right next to him. She smiled at him and started to say something, but Sewickley all but spun Tycho's shoulder around to tell him about debt ratios. When Tycho was able to turn back to Kate, she was deep in conversation with the young Cybelean woman next to her.

You're supposed to turn and talk to the other person after each course, he reminded himself, and turned back to Sewickley, who was sopping up salad dressing with an entire dinner roll.

"So as I was saying, our ROI—that's return on investment, you know—for shipbuilding has been off the charts," Sewickley said, accidentally spitting a chunk of half-chewed dinner roll onto his plate.

"Right, right," Tycho said around a mouthful of salad. "Wait. Did you say shipbuilding?"

"I did," Sewickley said, flinging the half-chewed piece of roll on the floor. "Cybele's been a center for shipbuilding for centuries, of course. But we can't keep up with the demand right now. Firms are doing work for local customers, for Earth, and for independents."

"Independents like who?"

"Oh, mostly shipping firms with operations on multiple worlds. From their perspective this dispute is an annoyance more than anything else. They can fly whatever flag is convenient on a given run—and perfectly legally, too. Lots of them are reregistering ships as Cybelean, though—takes the guesswork out of it. But registrations isn't our business—too many lawyers, not enough fun."

"How interesting. So building all these ships must take more facilities than are here on Cybele. Where else does this work happen?"

Sewickley eyed him. "I forgot your name. What is it you do again?"

"Tycho Hashoone. I'm a midshipman aboard the *Shadow Comet*, operating under a Jovian Union letter of marque."

He risked a quick glance at Kate as he said this, but she gave no sign that she'd heard him.

"You're a pirate, then?" Sewickley asked.

"Privateer," Tycho said icily.

"Right, of course. I forget there's a difference. Still,

given the situation, I'm not sure how much I should be telling you."

Sewickley followed this remark with a nervous bark of laughter, then blew his nose in his napkin.

"Oh, ships under construction are no use to us as prizes," said Tycho with a casual wave of his hand. "I'm curious because my family has shipbuilding interests of our own at Jupiter, and we've talked about expanding. If we can find the right partner, of course."

"Ah. What was your question again?"

"I'm interested in the shipbuilding facilities you've invested in. You must visit them, right? To see how your livres are being spent?"

Sewickley shook his head.

"I get spacesick something awful. We just put up the livres and make connections between interested parties. All of that happens down here. Most of our construction facilities are in orbit, but there are plenty of asteroids within a day or so of here where your family could establish an operation."

"I understand," Tycho said, trying not to sound disappointed.

He glanced in the other direction as Sewickley tore into his salad. Kate Allamand was still talking with the Cybelean woman. Tycho admired Kate's delicate ear, graceful neck, and black curls, then forced himself to turn back to Sewickley.

"But what about the people?" he asked. "You know, the labor. Where do you get them?"

"Oh, you know, local contractors."

"You mean crimps," Tycho said sharply.

Sewickley shrugged, his face a mask of bland indifference. "Like I said, we just move the livres—and try to make our stack grow, of course. That's how it's been done on Cybele forever, you know. We've got nothing to mine except water, so we've always been traders and connectors. Fortunately, there's never been a better time to be in that business than right now."

"That's apparent," Tycho said, looking out over the lavish banquet hall—and then up at the ceiling, and the graceful curve of the spacedocks above.

"Still, shipbuilding . . . that's a tough business for a newcomer right now," Sewickley said. "There are real shortages in both raw materials and labor, because of this one shipbuilding project we're not part of."

Tycho leaned toward Sewickley.

"What project is that?"

Someone was tapping on a glass—a barrel-chested Cybelean noble three tables over, standing next to a rail-thin, frail-looking man with white hair. The noble tapped more insistently until the conversation level finally dropped.

Tycho fidgeted through the white-haired man's speech, and the one given in response by Earth's envoy to Cybele, and the one following that from the Jovian Union's envoy. The waiters were clearing the salads by the time he was able to lean back over to Sewickley.

"Sorry, I asked what shipbuilding project you meant,"

Tycho said. "You mentioned a big one that's taking up all the raw materials and labor."

"I don't know what it is—wish I did. Then maybe Dad and I could get some of the action on it. Whoever the client is, though, they've got plenty of livres. And they don't want attention."

Waiters reached over their shoulders to put down covered plates, then lifted the lids to reveal some concoction that appeared to be made up of fish and flowers and sticks. When Tycho looked up from poking at it, Sewickley had turned to address the person on the other side of him.

Oh, now *he remembers his manners.*

The arrival of the new course meant it was time for Tycho to switch conversational partners as well. His heart fluttered in his chest and his mouth felt dry. He lunged for his water glass, almost knocking it over, and forced himself to turn to the right, where Kate was smiling at him. Her irises were deep brown, nearly black, and startling against the bright whites of her eyes.

"So I understand you're a privateer, Master Hashoone?" she asked.

"Yes—a midshipman aboard the *Shadow Comet*, operating under letter of marque for the Jovian Union," he said, wincing at how stilted and formal he sounded.

"And what do midshipmen do, exactly?"

"Whatever the captain tells us to, but I typically handle navigation and communications. But wait . . . aren't you part of your father's bridge crew?"

"Me?" Kate looked astonished, then faintly amused. "Oh no. I have a room aboard the *Gracieux*, but while my father's in space I stay here in our fondaco."

"Oh," Tycho said, trying to get his bearings. "So what do you do, then?"

"Homework, mostly," Kate said, then nodded at the musicians. "And I practice the viola—though I'll never be good enough to be part of a real string quartet. I want to be an ambassador. Or a minister—preferably in the commerce ministry."

She scowled, and Tycho thought to himself that somehow it made her look even more beautiful.

"Though I'll be lucky not to be married off as soon as I'm of age," she said. "And then I'll never be allowed to do anything ever again."

"Married off?"

Kate nodded, looking morose. "Girls like me don't have the same opportunities you do out in the colonies. My father brought me out here so I could see the solar system."

It had been centuries since anyone in the Jovian Union had referred to their home moons as colonies, but Tycho decided to ignore that.

"So you've never left Earth before?" he asked.

Kate shook her head and smiled. "I'm sure I must sound very sheltered to you."

"Of course not," Tycho said, though he'd been thinking exactly that. "So now that you're out here, what do you think?"

Kate wrinkled her nose. "It's very strange not to be able to go outside. Or for there not to *be* an outside. I feel cooped up all the time. And . . . well, everything smells bad. No, not *bad* exactly. More like *stale*. My father says it's because the air's been recycled so many times."

Tycho nodded, trying to wrap his head around the idea that air might smell different other places, that it wasn't simply air.

"It seems strange to me that you could open a door and just walk outside," he said. "Where I come from, if that happened you'd be dead in less than a minute."

"So you've never been to Earth? Or even Mars? Never stood under a sky?"

"No. I mean, in simulations, sure. But even with the best ones you know they're fake."

"Oh, I wish you could see Earth. It's so beautiful. Maybe after all this is over."

They smiled uncertainly at each other, then ate in silence. Tycho had to admit that the flowers and sticks were delicious.

"Do you do homework?" Kate asked. "I mean, you don't go to school. . . ."

"Oh, I do plenty of homework. Vesuvia's our instructor for most everything."

"Vesuvia? Is that your mother's name? It's very nice."

"No, Vesuvia is our starship's artificial intelligence. She's kind of a pain."

"Your teacher is a starship?" Kate asked, looking skeptical.

"Sure. She's programmed for instruction in most any-thing you'd need to learn. Like I have a paper due next week on how Shakespeare's works have been turned into motion pictures and interactive dramas."

"But when do you have time to study? Aren't you on duty aboard your ship?"

"We call it being on watch. But mostly that means looking out the viewports and waiting for something to happen. There's plenty of time for homework, unfortu-nately."

"But you must have been in battles."

Tycho nodded, resisting the urge to add that this morning's battle had involved her father.

"It sounds terrifying," Kate said. "I've been going crazy while my father's away. It's nerve-racking sitting around thinking something might have happened to him. Don't you get scared?"

Tycho smiled and raised his chin.

"Of course not—I've been a privateer all my life. I don't know what scared is."

Even before the first word was out, he knew his grand and heroic declaration sounded thin and uncertain.

Kate cocked her head at him.

"That didn't sound too convincing, did it?" Tycho asked.

Kate shook her head. But then she smiled at him, and he found himself smiling back.

"Can I try that one again?" he asked.

"Please do," Kate said, leaning forward expectantly, her eyes bright.

"I get scared," Tycho said.

"This version is more convincing already."

Tycho smiled but then found himself turning serious. "The thing is, I've trained for this since I was eight. You keep from getting scared by focusing on your responsibilities. And by having faith that the person next to you will do that too."

They resumed their silence. The string quartet sounded beautiful, Tycho thought—he'd heard classical music before, but never as it was actually being made by hands on instruments.

Kate looked over at him tentatively.

"Have you ever killed anybody?" she asked in a small voice.

Tycho's mind jumped back to four years ago, spinning in zero gravity aboard the *Hydra*. To screaming and firing his carbine over and over again, until old Croke took hold of his shoulder and assured him it was over.

"I don't know," he said. "I was part of a team that invaded an enemy ship during my first boarding action. I was twelve. My brother got hurt and I had to go in after him. I was firing my carbine at people, but I'm not sure if I hit anybody. Everything happened so fast—it was just a blur. I still dream about it, though."

"A boarding action? Who were they?"

"Pirates. They were seizing Jovian ships and kidnapping the crews."

"Oh," Kate said, and he could see she was relieved. "I was worried you'd say it was an Earth ship."

"It wasn't," Tycho said, thinking that it easily could have been. Kate's father was his enemy. What did that make her?

"But the pirates were working for Earth," he said reluctantly. "It was part of a scheme cooked up by an Earth bureaucrat on Ceres."

"I see."

They were silent for a moment. Tycho hesitated, then jumped. "That bureaucrat's now your father's boss, you know."

"What are you talking about?" Kate asked.

The warmth was gone from her dark eyes now. But Tycho felt she needed to understand who her father worked for.

"Your emperor's new war minister, Threece Suud. A couple of years back he was hiring every thug in the asteroid belt. He pretended they were diplomats and put them on merchant ships so privateers like us couldn't seize them. And he hired a bunch of other thugs to serve as crewers for pirates led by a man named Thoadbone Mox."

"I remember the incident you're talking about," Kate said stiffly. "The emperor was furious—he'd been lied to. And my father had nothing to do with it. He'd never associate himself with something like that."

"I'm sure that's true," Tycho said, trying to be gallant. "I didn't mean to suggest otherwise."

She smiled at him. "But . . . misguided though they were, the ministers behind what happened were responding to a real problem—piracy in the outer solar system."

Tycho shook his head. "If they were trying to do that, they would have been trying to capture Mox. Instead they were paying him. Their real goal was to stamp out privateering."

His voice was raised, he realized—Yana was looking his way, her expression quizzical.

"Which shouldn't exist," Kate said, raising her own voice. "How are corporations supposed to do business knowing their cargoes will be stolen, or their factories won't be supplied? They're caught in the middle of a political disagreement that isn't their fault. You're attacking people who have never attacked you."

"We're defending our interests the only way we can."

"By stealing from us?"

"By targeting your economic interests. We can't compete with your military power, and we have no voice in your parliaments or corporations."

"You have no representation because you declared independence! And you *do* have a voice in Earth corporations."

"You just called them Earth corporations," Tycho said smugly. "Which is correct, because they serve you, not us."

Kate dropped her fork, which clattered on her plate.

"You know what I meant," she said, snatching up the utensil. "Those companies have shareholders and operations all over the solar system, not just on Earth."

"Even if we do have a voice, it isn't heard," Tycho said. "There are, what, twenty-five billion of you and a couple of million of us? Anything decided is always going to be in Earth's favor."

Kate smiled, and Tycho wondered what trap he'd fallen into.

"Shouldn't what benefits twenty-five billion people outweigh what benefits two million?"

"Not if it means the two million people aren't treated fairly."

"And what would fair treatment mean?"

"That's easy—freedom. What happens to our homes should get decided on Ganymede, not Earth. We need to be able to develop our own industries, without having to compete with yours at the same time. And we should be able to figure out these things without worrying that your war fleets will show up to stop us."

"That seems fair to me—in a few hundred years," Kate said.

Tycho blinked at her.

"Why's that?"

"Because it cost Earth trillions and trillions of livres to establish colonies in the asteroids and outer solar system. And it wasn't just our government that did that—our corporations spent trillions of their own livres. That's why they got a charter for the asteroid belt."

"You're talking about something that happened six hundred years ago. They've made their money back by now."

"They haven't come close, because of the independence movements. We did the work and are now expected to give you the rewards."

"You didn't do the work," Tycho objected. "Settlers and miners and prospectors did—people like my ancestors."

"We put up the livres, didn't we?"

"That's not the same thing."

"Without the money, none of the work would have mattered."

They glared at each other for a moment.

"So you're saying we should all work for you," Tycho said. "That we should be slaves paying off a debt we inherited from our ancestors."

Kate shook her head. "I'm not saying that at all. I'm saying that there are obligations in both directions."

"What you're *saying* sounds reasonable," Tycho said, and Kate glanced at him suspiciously. "Except I've seen what Earth corporations do when no one's looking. It was my family that found the secret Earth factories where Mox's prisoners were taken, you know. They were slaves—and they'd still be there if we hadn't found them."

"We already discussed that. What happened was illegal, and a lot of people on Earth paid the price for it."

"Threece Suud didn't, apparently. I believe you that

your father's an honorable man. But he works for someone who's anything but."

Waiters were taking away the plates now. The string quartet took a break to scattered applause.

"My father can't control who's war minister," Kate said.

"Fair enough. Why did he become a privateer, anyway?"

Kate bit her lip.

"He gave up his commission in the navy when I was a baby. He tried to rejoin the service a few years ago, but they wouldn't take him—they said he was too old. So he responded to the call for privateers. He missed the adventure, I guess."

Tycho nodded.

"The adventure. For us, what's happening in the solar system isn't a game. My grandfather nearly died when an Earth destroyer fired on his ship. He lost his remaining hand fighting the pirates Threece Suud hired. And my brother will have a scar for the rest of his life."

"You can't blame my father for that!"

"No, but I can blame him for being part of it. And I do."

"And apparently you blame me as well," Kate said, color flaring in her cheeks.

When Tycho said nothing, she rose abruptly from her seat, nearly knocking over her chair, and stormed off before he could react. The other people at their table were staring at him.

"What was that about, Tyke?" Yana asked.

"Politics, I guess," Tycho said helplessly.

The waiters busied themselves picking up utensils and cleaning up crumbs.

"Better to avoid such a dreary subject at dinner," a young Earthman across the table said disapprovingly.

Tycho frowned, folding his arms over his chest and trying to figure out what he'd do when Kate returned.

"She's probably in the head trying to calm down," Yana said. "Maybe you should do the same."

He mumbled an excuse and got to his feet. He decided against the bathroom, fearing if he headed that way he'd run into a still-upset Kate. Instead, he'd get himself together outside the banquet hall.

One of the tables of privateers exploded into laughter, with Jovians and Earthmen banging glasses together and then guzzling wine amid cheers from the other tables. One bearded privateer crept over to the string quartet's stage, returning with a violin and bow and a huge grin.

Tycho felt ashamed. The occupants of those tables had fought each other, sometimes hand to hand aboard ships, and they were managing to get along well enough. So why couldn't he do the same thing with a girl making her first trip off Earth? He'd not only lost his cool but also fallen into the Cybeleans' trap by squabbling openly in front of their hosts.

He slipped out of the hall, thinking the dazzling view of the asteroids and stars might give him some perspective. He passed the Cybelean constables and the check-in desk, then followed a curving corridor past the elevators, his eyes on the jeweled expanse of the heavens above.

Which meant he almost plowed directly into Kate. Apparently she hadn't gone to the bathroom after all.

She dodged and stood staring at him, lips set and eyes flashing.

"It's you," she said.

"It's me. Um, I'm sorry. I was . . ."

"Wrong?" Kate asked, eyebrows raised.

"No, not wrong. Impolite."

"You certainly were that. Rude, intemperate, naïve . . . the very definition of a colonial."

Tycho found himself grinning.

"What can possibly be funny?" Kate demanded.

"You're right. I *am* a colonial. Never seen a sky or grass, never breathed fresh air, never been outside of a pressure dome or starship."

Kate looked away, flushing.

"Never read a book that wasn't a prospecting manual."

"You said it, not me."

"Never held a fork that wasn't made from a mining implement."

"All right, cut it out."

"In fact, before tonight I don't think I'd ever held a fork at all. On Callisto we prefer shovels."

"I said cut it out! You're absolutely infuriating!"

She stared at him, chest heaving, and then the distance between them had shrunk to nothing and they were in each other's arms, her lips against his and his hands in her hair. Their noses kept colliding and their teeth clacked together, but neither of them cared.

Tycho didn't know how long it was before they finally separated—it seemed like simultaneously forever and no time at all. His heart was pounding, and he felt dizzy. Kate reached up with one shaky hand in a doomed attempt to attend to her mussed hair, then mumbled something and hurried toward the banquet hall.

15

INTO THE LABYRINTH

Tycho lurched in his seat when the *Shadow Comet* accelerated away from Cybele, his headset falling forward over his eyes.

Yana snickered, and both of his parents turned around at their stations.

"Tycho? Are you with us this morning?" his mother asked.

"Sorry. I was thinking. Uh, about optimum search patterns."

"Really?" Diocletia asked, one eyebrow raised. "Then you won't mind calculating those patterns and feeding them to Vesuvia. It'll save your sister some work."

Tycho sighed but found himself smiling as he began the tedious task of mapping out search vectors. The Jovian privateers had each been given a different section of the Cybele asteroids to explore in hopes of finding the missing *Nestor Leviathan*.

"What's gotten into you?" Yana asked, perturbed that she'd lost out on a chance to gloat. "You've been acting strange all morning."

Tycho shrugged, looking away so his sister couldn't see his face. The night before, he'd waited a couple of minutes before returning to the banquet hall, to find an Earth privateer standing atop a table playing a ditty on the violin while the other privateers sang along at the top of their lungs and threw rolls at him. Tycho had settled back into his place next to Kate and spent the rest of the evening sneaking looks at her—and repeatedly found her sneaking looks back at him.

She'd slipped him her messaging recognition code as the party broke up, and then he'd spent much of the night tossing and turning, staring up at the unfamiliar ceiling of their new quarters.

The Hashoones had just started eating breakfast when Diocletia's mediapad began pinging. She'd excused herself, then returned and ordered all crewers to be aboard the *Comet* in half an hour. Amazingly, nearly every Comet had responded to the summons; the last to report had been Huff Hashoone, who shuffled up the gig's ramp looking ashen, then retired to his cabin on the top level without even pausing on the quarterdeck.

It had been that kind of night. By the end of it most of the privateers had been snoring at the table, and a good number of Cybelean grandees had misplaced their hats and furs. Tycho imagined a lot of the other Jovian privateers—and any Earth ships that had taken to space—were struggling with surly quarterdecks this morning. Fortunately, his parents had either moderated their own consumption or were doing a good job being brave.

"Captain Andrade, we're beginning our sweep," Diocletia said over her headset.

"Acknowledged, *Comet*. Good hunting."

The bells clanged eight times—it was 0800.

"All right then," Diocletia said. "We'll search outbound for the forenoon watch, then inbound for the afternoon. Tycho, when you've got the route calculations, give them to Vesuvia and let's fly."

"On the way," Tycho said, giving the numbers a final look and transmitting them.

"Course information received," Vesuvia said in her clipped voice.

"Locking it in," Carlo said. "Keep the sensors peeled, Yana."

"Dialing them up to max," Yana said. "But I don't know what we're expecting to find. Allamand stashed the *Leviathan* somewhere yesterday—he had enough time to bring her entire crew back to Cybele, and we know they didn't take a direct course. So there'll be no ion flux or anything we can trace."

"Not from the *Leviathan*, agreed," Diocletia said. "But we might find a trace left by an Earth ship taking goods off of her, or bringing supplies to her, or maintaining whatever installation Earth's stashed her in. And if nothing else, we're looking—that's important to keep the Union from blowing its collective stack."

Carlo glanced over at his mother, and Tycho knew he was wondering if he was being blamed. But Diocletia wasn't looking his way—she was staring straight ahead at the starfield and the course information Vesuvia had projected over it.

"Are we expecting Allamand to bring the *Leviathan* in for condemnation?" Tycho asked.

"No," Diocletia said. "Cybele doesn't have an admiralty court. If Captain Allamand wants to bring her in as a prize, he'll have to take her to Ceres or even Vesta."

"Which means he'll want to keep her hidden," Tycho said.

"It's what I'd do. Keep her under wraps until the politicians work out a deal that lets me bring her in."

"But why are we assigned to the search?" Yana asked.

Diocletia cocked an eyebrow at her daughter. "Any number of reasons. One, this is a fast ship."

"Which makes us ideal for raiding shipping. We could be taking prizes instead of turning over rocks."

"Two, Captain Andrade doesn't trust the newly

commissioned privateers to give the *Leviathan* back if they find her," Diocletia said as if she'd never been interrupted.

Yana considered that and nodded.

"And three, the *Leviathan* was taken on our watch. So it's only right and proper that we try to get her back."

Carlo winced at that.

Tycho, who'd been thinking about the way Kate twirled a curl of dark hair around one finger, jerked himself back into alertness. The route calculations were still on his screen, describing a meandering thread through the vast field of shattered asteroids orbiting in concert with Cybele.

"Wait a minute," he said. "What if Allamand doesn't intend to bring the *Leviathan* in at all?"

"What do you mean?" Diocletia asked.

"At dinner I was sitting next to this Cybelean kid whose father is some kind of big investor in shipbuilding. He said they can't keep up with the demand, and there's a big shipbuilding project that's taking up a lot of the available raw materials and labor. It's *got* to be Earth's."

"What makes you say that?" Mavry asked.

"And what does it have to do with the *Leviathan*?" Carlo asked.

"One at a time," Tycho said. "Whatever this big project is, we know it's not ours—and remember what Minister Vass told me about Earth wooing the Cybeleans by dangling shipbuilding contracts in front of them. So whose project could it be but Earth's?"

"How do we know it's not the Ice Wolves'?" Mavry asked.

"They don't have the livres for anything that big," Diocletia said.

"This mysterious project you were told about *can't* be Earth's," Carlo objected. "Because they don't have a shipbuilding contract like that yet. One of the reasons we're here is to make sure they don't get one."

"Maybe they do, but they're trying to keep it secret," Tycho said.

"And why would they do that?" Carlo asked.

"I can answer that one," Yana said. "Because the Cybeleans want both deals—the shipbuilding contract with Earth *and* the raw-materials agreement with us."

Mavry grinned at Diocletia. "Can you believe our innocent children have become this cynical?"

"It was bound to happen eventually."

"But the Cybeleans can't get both deals," Carlo said. "It's one or the other."

"That's what the politicians are saying, which means you shouldn't believe it," Mavry said. "Our industries want this raw-materials contract too."

"But how do you know it isn't our project, Tyke?" Yana asked. "Is it because you think the Securitat wouldn't lie to us?"

"I don't think that at all, believe me."

"Even if we could keep a project that big a secret, I doubt we could compete with what Earth can offer," Diocletia said. "Go on, Tycho."

"Whoever's project it is, they don't have the labor they need. Sewickley—that's the Cybelean kid—admitted workers are being supplied by crimps, which is why things are so dangerous on Cybele right now. He also said they're short on raw materials. What if they're trying to solve that problem by using seized ships for parts? Ships such as the *Leviathan*?"

"That would be an outrageous violation of interplanetary law," Carlo said.

"Like Earth cares," Yana interjected. "They strike a deal with Cybele, and a few months from now they admit wrongdoing and pay off the *Leviathan*'s owners."

"That does sound like a very Earth thing to do," Mavry said.

"So does building warships for its navy with seized Jovian craft and raw materials supplied by Jovian companies," Tycho said.

"Any Jovian companies that were part of such an arrangement would be guilty of treason," Carlo said.

"I'm sure they'd find a way to justify it," Mavry said.

"One thing, though: Allamand would never collect the prize money for the *Leviathan* if they did that," Diocletia said.

"He wouldn't mind," Tycho said. "This is just an adventure for him."

"From the way he and his daughter dress, they have plenty of livres," Yana said.

Diocletia nodded. "It's an interesting idea, Tycho.

When we get back to Cybele, I'll run it by Mr. Vass and his ministers and see what they think. But for now, we search."

Tycho knew he should have been pleased by his mother's praise. But Yana's mention of Kate had frightened him into silence. The last thing he needed was his sister recounting his argument with Kate, which might start their mother asking questions, which might in turn cause him to slip up and reveal something. And that would lead to Diocletia learning everything.

He winced at the thought of his mother lecturing him about enemies and being irresponsible, then leaving a blistering report about whom he'd kissed in the Log. But was he sure that's what she'd say? As a veteran privateer, his mother knew perfectly well that any scrap of intelligence gathered in port could be valuable, and she wasn't squeamish about how such information was obtained. What if she saw his connection with their enemy's daughter not as a danger to be avoided, but as an advantage to be exploited?

Tycho couldn't decide which was worse. But he knew he didn't want either to happen.

The airlock had barely closed on the last of the *Comet*'s departing crewers when Tycho messaged Kate asking when and where they could meet.

He sent the message, then checked that it had sent properly. It had. He looked at his message queue for a moment, then checked to see if any new messages had come in. Then he checked again. And then one more time.

He looked up from his mediapad, worried that Yana would notice him obsessively resending the same command. But his sister was engrossed with her own device.

A clank and a slight rattle under their feet indicated the ferry containing the crewers had detached itself from the privateer and was on its way to Cybele below. Tycho activated his headset.

"Last crew ferry is away," he said.

His message indicator pinged. Stabbing at his mediapad's screen, he navigated hurriedly over to his message queue, reminding himself that it was probably a junk message or a cranky homework reminder from Vesuvia.

But the message was from Kate.

"Tycho, did you hear what I said?" Diocletia asked in his ear.

"Um—"

"I'll take that as a no. I told you to get any gear you need for the trip down. We'll be dirtside for a day or two, unless something happens. Gig's leaving in ten minutes."

"Right," Tycho said distractedly, vaguely registering his mother's annoyed huff of breath before she broke the connection.

CAN YOU COME TO NORTHWELL AFTER LUNCH? I PROMISE WE WON'T TALK POLITICS. KA

Tycho reread the message four times while packing his duffel bag, his smile getting bigger each time. But as the gig detached from the *Comet*, his smile faded away. Should he get Kate a gift? He decided that wasn't necessary, then that it was, and by the time they cleared customs and entered the passage that led to the Well, he had no idea what to do.

He glanced at the rest of his family. The idea of asking Yana was obviously insane, as was broaching the subject with his mother.

His father? Mavry would be able to help, and probably wouldn't immediately interrogate him. But despite his easygoing nature, Tycho's father was all business when it came to privateering. He'd figure out that Tycho had met someone at the banquet and need to know who it was, and when it turned out that someone was Captain Allamand's daughter . . .

No, his father was out.

Tycho's eyes lingered on Carlo. His older brother had been on dates—he even remembered a couple of girlfriends from the Helmsmen's Guild and another who'd been the daughter of someone important in Port Town. And Carlo could be helpful if it meant an opportunity to demonstrate that he knew something his younger siblings didn't.

But his brother was self-absorbed on his best days, and racked by misery at the moment over his decision to abandon the *Leviathan*. And he never missed a chance to gain even the smallest advantage in the Log.

No, it was too dangerous to ask Carlo.

Then there was Huff. Tycho looked appraisingly at his grandfather. He'd been married long enough to have two daughters, hadn't he?

"Arrr, they oughta space the dimwit what decided this tunnel should go halfway to Vesta," Huff growled, then began to cough raggedly.

"Are you all right, Grandfather?" Tycho asked.

Huff pounded on his chest with his forearm cannon, then spat out something vile that hit the wall of the passageway with a glutinous splat and stuck there.

Tycho decided not to ask him either.

But then he thought of someone who might be able to help.

Tycho's shoulder holster didn't fit quite right and kept riding up into his armpit, forcing him to reach under his heavy cloak and paw at his jacket to push the carbine back into place. But the weapon's weight was still a comfort as he left the Westwell for the dim, frigid tunnel that led to Bazaar.

He wasn't used to carrying a weapon and kept thinking the carbine was horribly conspicuous, even under a thick, fur-lined jacket. Tycho and Yana had told their parents about the crimps that morning. Diocletia had listened with a grave expression, then summoned Mavry to their bedroom for a brief consultation. She'd reluctantly agreed that they could carry carbines, then given them a stern lecture on the importance of not using them unless there was no other alternative.

Tycho had worried that Yana would want to go with him, but she'd said vaguely that she had things to do. Tycho had wondered idly if that meant she wanted nothing to do with their grandmother, or if she just meant to spend more of her free hours practicing unarmed combat. Whatever the case, he'd been glad not to have to ditch her.

He pushed through a crowd of spacers, worried about another encounter with Jasper One Eye or one of his crimps, but arrived at Bazaar without incident. The dome was less crowded than on his first visit, with several stalls shuttered.

One of Elfrieda's toughs stood aside as Tycho approached the Last Chance, though the man's eyes stayed fixed on him. The little café was more crowded than the rest of the depot, with a handful of grim-looking spacers glumly examining pallets of freeze-dried noodles and krill.

Prospectors, Tycho guessed, lowering the hood of his cloak. And not particularly lucky ones, judging by their threadbare jackets and worn boots.

Elfrieda was behind the counter, crabbily explaining something to a young, baffled-looking clerk. She looked up to survey the customers in the depot, her eyes flicking over Tycho and then returning.

"Hello, Grandmother," Tycho said.

"Call me Elfrieda. Don't you know it's dangerous to come here alone?"

"I'm being careful," Tycho said, pushing the holster back down again.

"That's good. So what can I do for you?"

"I need . . . a present."

Elfrieda looked baffled. "A present? What kind of present?"

"I don't know exactly. It's . . . for a girl."

"Does this girl like the kind of things a chandler's depot would sell?" Elfrieda asked. "Like replacement air scrubbers or lavatory disinfectant?"

"I don't think so. It's . . . it's more that I don't know what to buy. And, well, I don't have anybody I can ask."

Elfrieda leaned her elbows on the counter and sighed, and Tycho was certain that in another moment she'd tell him to go away. But then she shook her head and smiled ruefully.

"Burke, try not to mess anything up for the next ten minutes," she said to the flustered clerk next to her. "I'm going to get a cup of tea. Would you like one, Tycho?"

Tycho nodded gratefully and followed Elfrieda up a low flight of stairs to the collection of battered couches and salvaged flight chairs that passed for the Last Chance's café. She pulled aside a clerk, who hastily started preparing tea.

"Tea's three livres," Elfrieda told Tycho.

He smiled, then realized Elfrieda wasn't kidding. Flushing, he dug in his cloak for coins.

"So who's this girl you can't tell your family about?" Elfrieda asked once the tea was served. "Not that your mother's the person to ask about gifts anyway. Diocletia actually would want a new air scrubber."

"This girl . . . she's the daughter of the captain in charge of Earth's privateers."

Above the rim of her teacup, Elfrieda's eyebrows shot up. "Well, that's complicated."

"I know. That's why I haven't told anybody. It would cause . . . trouble."

Elfrieda waved a hand dismissively. "At your age, all love is trouble."

"Was that true of you and Grandfather?"

Elfrieda looked amused. "Oh, definitely. Did he tell you I agreed to have a nip with him? He's coming by later tonight, after we close up."

"Really? That's great!"

"Now don't go and get everybody all riled up. We both moved on a long time ago. Getting along for a few hours was never the problem for me and Huff. It was after that when things would get messy."

"Oh."

"So, your captain's daughter . . . I'm guessing she isn't a spacer or anything like that."

"No. This is her first time off Earth."

Several bearded spacers had entered the Last Chance and were examining cutting torches. Tycho eyed their jackets. He saw no sign of the white wolf on a black background that the Ice Wolves had adopted as their symbol, but that meant nothing—the Saturnian revolutionaries were keeping a lower profile these days.

"This girl's first trip off Earth is to Cybele?" Elfrieda asked. "Isn't she lucky? This rock's half a meter too low to be the armpit of the solar system. And while it galls me to talk myself out of a sale, I don't think you'll find a good present in the Last Chance."

Tycho glanced from the Ice Wolves—he was certain that was what they were—to the Last Chance's counter and out into the common area under the dome. The man who'd sold Yana her scarf was showing a similar one to a spacer.

"What about a scarf like my sister was wearing last night?" Tycho asked eagerly.

"The 'like my sister was wearing last night' part should tell you no."

"Oh," Tycho said, crestfallen. "Maybe a ring then?"

"*A ring*? Slow down before you make a mess, Tycho. Besides, I have an idea."

Elfrieda reached into her jacket and extracted a marking stylus and a piece of scrap paper that was coffee-colored from repeated recycling.

"Here's the name of a stall in the Well where you'll find something. The owner's name is Hugo—tell him I sent you and that I said not to rip you off too badly. And tell Hugo it's a gift for a well-bred Earth girl. He'll know what that means."

"Thank you, Grandmother," Tycho said, trying to see what the Ice Wolves were doing.

"You're welcome. Now please stop staring at my customers."

"They're Ice Wolves. Aren't you worried about your safety?"

"Not in the least. A millimeter outside the Last Chance and whatever they do isn't my problem. A millimeter inside and my hired slabs of beef swing into action."

"I wonder what they're up to," Tycho said, furrowing his brow. It seemed unlikely that the Saturnians would know anything about the *Leviathan*, but they were in the depot for a reason.

"I don't know why they're here and it's not my business to care."

"Well, you'll have to forgive me, Grandmother, but it's mine. They're enemies of my country, and they've spent more than a year trying to kill members of my family."

He looked up to find Elfrieda calmly finishing her tea.

"You're a good kid, Tycho. But take an old woman's advice. Find a cause and pretty soon you'll find politicians. And politicians will get you killed without a second thought. Fools dig for treasure, Tycho—the wise sell shovels."

The Ice Wolves had finished their inspection of the Last Chance's wares and headed back out into Bazaar. Tycho wrapped his cloak around himself.

"I hunted for buried treasure once, Grandmother," he said. "Found it, too. Now, if you'll excuse me, I'm going to do my duty as a Jovian."

* * *

Tycho walked about ten meters behind the bearded spacers as they headed west from Bazaar, trying to keep several other people between himself and them. As he walked, he passed miners caked in gray dust, spacers carrying duffel bags, and people muffled in furs against the cold.

His pursuit took him through several domes, through chilly passages dug into the rock and ice of Cybele and ones laid down across the surface, their thick plastic walls covered with a hodgepodge of old patches and seals. He eyed the patches suspiciously, ears straining for the faintest hiss of escaping air. Sudden decompressions weren't unknown, particularly on the outskirts of asteroid settlements. In the event of a blowout or some other disaster, airlocks at the ends of corridors and around the perimeters of pressure domes would automatically slam shut. But that wouldn't help those caught inside the passageway or dome that ruptured.

Tycho shoved his shoulder holster down for at least the twentieth time, annoyed. Then he stopped. The spacers were no longer in sight ahead of him—while he'd been daydreaming, they'd picked up their pace and left the tunnel. And the traffic in the corridor had dwindled to three people, all in a hurry to be elsewhere.

A leathery-faced miner passed Tycho going the other way, leaving him alone in the corridor. Tycho came to a halt, hand creeping toward his carbine. Ahead of him, the passage climbed slightly to end at the open door of an airlock. Through the walls of the tube Tycho could see the outline of a dimly lit pressure dome ahead. There was no sound except the hum of air circulators.

Tycho wondered if he should draw his weapon. He decided against it. But should he go back?

Suddenly he wished Yana were here—normally his sister's brash confidence annoyed him, but a little of it would be welcome now.

Relax—they just got a little ahead of you is all.

He exhaled and forced himself to go forward, cinching his cloak more tightly around him. If his sister were here, he thought, by now she'd have snorted dismissively and stomped off after the Ice Wolves, forcing him to hurry after her.

The pressure dome was small, dim, and chilly. A bank of freight elevators sat in the center of the space, signs indicating they were out of service. A handful of stalls stood nearby, shuttered and locked, and two brightly lit tunnels led deeper into the labyrinth of Cybele. Tycho paused in the center of the dome, peering down each tunnel in turn. He didn't see anybody in either tube.

The click of a carbine's safety being released was his only warning, and it wasn't enough.

16

THE ICE WOLVES

They came out of the shadows, carbines raised. Before Tycho could reach for his own weapon, two of them grabbed him, holding him tightly by the arms. He found himself staring down the seemingly gigantic barrel of a blaster.

If I'd gone for my gun I'd be dead now.

"Tole ya someone was followin' us," growled one of the spacers.

"Who are you, boy?" demanded the man with the gun.

"Another one of them sneaking Cybelean rats," grumbled another.

"An *armed* Cybelean rat," said a fourth, yanking open Tycho's jacket.

The leader looked appraisingly at Tycho's carbine where it sat useless in his shoulder holster.

"And what were you going to do with that, boy?" the leader asked.

"Protect myself," Tycho muttered, trying not to shiver in the cold air.

"And how's that working out for you?" the leader asked with a nasty grin as a rat-faced Ice Wolf with a ginger beard stepped forward to search Tycho, extracting his pass from his pocket.

"This one ain't Cybelean—he's *Jovian*," the red-haired Ice Wolf said, handing the pass to the leader. "Probably spying for their blasted Securitat."

"Thought we had a deal that they'd leave us alone," growled the Ice Wolf who'd found Tycho's gun.

"I'm not a spy," Tycho managed. "I want to join up."

"Oh? And just who do you think you're joining, boy?" the leader asked.

Tycho swallowed. "You're Ice Wolves."

The leader nodded, his eyes cool and calculating. He looked over Tycho's pass.

"This ain't no ordinary boy," he said. "This here's a Hashoone."

"What's a Hashoone?" the red-haired man asked.

"Family what owns one of them Jovian privateer

ships," the leader said.

Muttering greeted this news, and the hands on Tycho's upper arms tightened.

"Then he's definitely a Securitat spy," the red-haired man said.

"Maybe," the leader said. "Now why would you want to join us, Master Hashoone?"

"Because I believe in the same thing you do. Freedom for the outer planets!"

"Hear that, boys? Master Hashoone's gone and become an idealist. Must have been reading fancy books."

As the Ice Wolves laughed, Tycho heard footsteps. A slim man in tattered furs entered the dome and stared at the Ice Wolves in horror. Tycho locked eyes with him hopefully, but the man turned his face away and hurried deeper into the labyrinth of tunnels.

The Ice Wolf leader waited until the man had gone, then smirked at Tycho. "Membership's closed, kid."

"You don't understand," Tycho said, thinking desperately. "The boss told me to come by!"

"Really? Come by where?"

"He wouldn't tell me—said if I wanted to join that badly I'd figure it out. Which is why I was following you."

The Ice Wolves laughed.

"Boss told you to come by, eh?" asked the red-haired Ice Wolf. "What's he look like, then?"

"Big man," Tycho stammered. "Um, with a beard . . ."

Laughter surrounded him.

"You've never seen the boss, Master Hashoone," the

leader growled. "But he's seen you."

"We got things to do, Jake," muttered the rat-faced Ice Wolf. "Let's shove the kid out an airlock."

Tycho's knees were shaking. He tried to will them to stop. He wouldn't give them the satisfaction of hearing him beg.

"Alarm'll go off," said another. "Shoot him and we'll drop him down the elevator shaft. By the time someone finds him, won't be nothing but bones."

Tycho struggled futilely in the Ice Wolves' grip. But Jake was shaking his head.

"Keeping a low profile was part of the deal, remember?" he said, lowering his weapon. "Which means it's your lucky day, Master Hashoone. But if I find you sticking your nose in our business again, I'll cook it off your face. Now get lost before I change my mind."

The two Ice Wolves let go of Tycho. He hurried back the way he'd come, careful to keep his hands away from his jacket. He half expected the Ice Wolves to reconsider. The energy of a carbine beam traveled far faster than sound, so at this range his ears would give him no warning of what was coming—he'd hear the shot only after it tore through him.

If he heard it at all.

He hurried through the dome's empty airlock and found himself alone in the tube on the other side. He wanted to look back but forced himself not to. He was still jittery—it felt like there wasn't enough air to fill his lungs.

Something about the face of a man coming toward him struck him as familiar. He slowed to a walk, trying to think where he'd seen him before.

Then he realized it was DeWise—and the Securitat agent looked furious.

"Keep going, you fool," DeWise said, pivoting smoothly to walk alongside Tycho. "What in God's name did you think you were doing?"

"You were following me!" Tycho said.

"I was following *them*. But a lot more carefully than you were. You're lucky to be alive."

"You struck a deal with them! They said so!"

"Not a deal—a truce of sorts. We don't try to disrupt their operations here, and in return they leave our citizens alone and stay out of this competition with Earth that the Defense Force thinks is so important."

"And you trust them to keep their end of the bargain?"

"Fortunately for you, they just did."

That shocked Tycho into silence.

"Now, what happened?" DeWise asked.

When Tycho looked reluctant, DeWise's expression turned hard.

"It's important, Tycho."

"All right. They searched me and looked at my pass. They acted like they knew who I was, and claimed their boss knew me too. Oh, and the leader was called Jake."

"We know him—one of the Shupe brothers. So they said Jake was the boss?"

"No, just the leader of the group I followed. I said I

knew the boss and they asked me to describe him."

They had returned to a more populated part of Cybele, with the passageways getting crowded again.

"Go on," DeWise said.

"I said he was big, with a beard," Tycho said, looking away from DeWise's scornful expression. "They started laughing. Said I'd never seen him."

"The irony is that you have. We know who their boss is—it's Thoadbone Mox."

"What?" Tycho said, staring at DeWise in shock. "That's impossible—the Ice Wolves kicked Mox out at Saturn. I was there, remember? When your big plan turned into bilge."

"Hodge Lazander relieved Mox of command, yes," DeWise said, refusing to be baited. "But Lazander is the Ice Wolves' political leader, not their military commander."

"What does that matter?"

"The political leaders want more power for the outer solar system, but a lot of the captains are just pirates looking for a license to steal. It's a split in their ranks that we've worked in secret to make as big as possible."

"I bet you have," Tycho said. "Manipulating others is your job, after all."

"My job is protecting the Jovian Union," DeWise said. "If you want to argue about how we do that, we'll go somewhere else."

"I'm not going anywhere with you."

"Fine. Then remember this: Mox is still seizing ships

for his fellow Ice Wolves—and he's based here on Cybele."

"Maybe, but if so he's not the boss," Tycho said. "You're wrong about that."

"And you know that how?"

"By the way they acted. It was like the boss was someone I didn't know—no, more like someone I *couldn't* know. Like it was a test I couldn't pass."

Tycho could almost see DeWise's brain sorting through this new information. The passageway was thick with people now. From the looks of the fur-clad men and women around them, some mining operation had just changed shifts.

"Whatever Mox's rank is in their operation, the point is that he's here on Cybele," DeWise said. "And he's got a score to settle with your family. Stay away from the Ice Wolves, Tycho—I doubt you'll be as lucky next time."

A broad-shouldered miner passed between them. Tycho turned to say something to DeWise, but the Securitat agent had vanished in the crowd.

17

AMONG THE EARTHFOLK

At least two differences between the Northwell and the rest of the pressure domes on Cybele were immediately apparent to Tycho—it was warm inside the Northwell, and Cybelean constables were everywhere. He was stopped twice on his way to Earth's fondaco, and the guards at the gates refused to let him proceed unless he unloaded his carbine and handed over its power pack.

Earth's fondaco was a massive building in its own

right, constructed around an atrium filled with trees and plants and extending to the curve of the pressure dome overhead. The air felt wet and smelled strange, and Tycho blinked against the bright light. He shielded his eyes and peered up to find a brilliant spotlight trained down on the atrium. The pressure dome, he saw, was hidden by a hologram of a blue sky dotted with clouds.

Strolling in the atrium with his furred cloak over one arm, Tycho couldn't resist poking a finger in the dirt of a planter. His finger came out wet and black with loam, and he brushed at it, sniffing the dirt, then wiped it on the seat of his pants. He heard birdsong above and looked up to see a blur of wings among the trees. He had not the slightest doubt that the birds were real.

"You there, boy, what are you doing?" someone barked at him.

Tycho looked down to see a gendarme striding his way.

"You're no Earthman," the gendarme said, staring at Tycho. "What are you—"

"He is a guest and is to be treated accordingly," said a steely voice.

Captain Allamand, wearing a dark-blue uniform, was walking up behind the gendarme, with Kate trailing behind.

"Begging your pardon, Captain Allamand," the gendarme said. "This one didn't identify himself. I was only doing my duty—"

"Understood, and you are to be commended for it.

But I assure you all is well."

The gendarme made his getaway, and Allamand offered his hand to Tycho, who took it, reminding himself to make eye contact and shake hands firmly.

"So how do you find Cybele, Master Hashoone?" Allamand asked, turning to stroll with him through the garden, Kate following a pace behind.

"It's interesting," Tycho managed. "Wish they'd turn the heat up, though. Your fondaco and the banquet hall are the only places on this rock that aren't freezing."

Allamand smiled. "Apparently the Cybeleans prefer to spend their livres on furs in supernatural colors."

Tycho laughed politely, risking a glance behind him at Kate. She was dressed simply: a white blouse above dark-green trousers and black boots.

"My daughter tells me you've never been to Earth. I hope one day you'll do us the honor of being our guest at our estate outside Avignon."

"Um, you're very kind."

"I've had the good fortune to visit Jupiter on a couple of occasions. One gains valuable perspective from an hour spent at a window in Ganymede High Port, staring at Jupiter and watching the Great Red Spot continue its eternal journey across the surface. I hope one day my daughter will be able to see that as well."

"As do I, Captain."

Allamand smiled.

"The gallantry of our way of life can be intoxicating, Master Hashoone. But peace between our countries would be better. Ah well. In time, I hope. Perhaps one day we can recall this conversation in Avignon. Or above Ganymede."

Tycho fumbled for a reply, but Allamand had halted.

"And now duty calls," he said. "Until we meet again, Master Hashoone."

The Earth captain strode away down the path. Kate smiled at Tycho, cocking her elbow in his direction. After a moment of free fall Tycho realized what was expected of him and took her arm.

"I hope that wasn't too painful," she said.

"No, not at all. Where is your father going?"

Kate sighed. "Into space. On some dreadful new mission."

Tycho went cold. "Into space?"

"Yes. But please let's not talk about it."

Tycho frowned. He ought to at least send his mother a quick message. But he looked at Kate, admiring her dark eyes and the tiny silver studs that glinted in her ears, and couldn't bring himself to step away from her for even a moment.

"Uh, I brought you something," Tycho said, disengaging and fumbling in the innards of his jacket.

"Is it that pistol?" Kate asked with a smile. "Honestly, Tycho. What kind of reception did you expect from us?"

"Oh, that was for . . . well, somewhere else."

"I'm teasing you. Though I'm sure I could learn to be a wicked pirate."

244

"Privateer. Here. I hope you'll like it better than a carbine."

They sat down on a bench tucked into a nook along the garden path. Kate opened the little box he'd bought at Hugo's stall and smiled at the gleaming black stones inside.

"They're lovely. What are they made of?"

"Carborundum. From Jupiter's Trojan asteroids. It's extremely rare as a natural substance on Earth, but you can scoop it up from asteroids and moons out here. A little souvenir from the rest of the solar system."

"I think they're beautiful," Kate said.

Thank you, Hugo, Tycho thought.

"So are you," he said, and leaned forward. But Kate pulled back, blushing.

"I'm sorry, Tycho. The other night—that was crazy. Nice, but crazy. Can we . . . can we go a little slower?"

Tycho nodded, embarrassed, and Kate leaned forward to let her lips brush his cheek.

"Thank you," she said, then looked down at the earrings. "They really are beautiful."

She handed him the box and her hand went to her ears. She placed her silver earrings in the box and replaced them with the teardrops of black carborundum. "How do they look?" she asked.

"Perfect," Tycho said, and she smiled and reached over to lace her fingers through his.

The artificial sun was lower now—it moved on some

mechanism he hadn't seen before—and the holographic sky was edging from blue into purple.

"Is that what Earth is like?" he asked.

Kate looked up at the sky appraisingly.

"More like a cheap holo-drama of it than the real thing. But the trees and the birds are real. That's nice."

"It is," Tycho said, squeezing her hand. She smiled, but her fingers slipped out of his and she colored faintly.

"Tycho," she said. "It's a funny name. Where's it come from?"

"He was an astronomer from Earth. Actually, Tycho's my middle name."

"It is? What's your first name, then?"

"You'll laugh."

"I will not."

"It's Herschel."

Kate put a hand over her mouth.

"See?"

She reached over to squeeze his hand by way of apology.

"I'm sorry, Tycho. I have to ask, though: Why Herschel?"

"Another astronomer from Earth."

"I see. I think you made a good choice there."

"So do I," Tycho said. "The dread pirate Herschel Hashoone doesn't quite work, somehow."

"Oh, I think it sounds *terrifying*. Herschel Hashoone, scourge of the spaceways."

"Stop it. What's your middle name?"

"It's long. And a bit ridiculous."

"Try me."

"It's le Bondavais."

"Kate le Bondavais Allamand? No, wait. It would be Katherine, wouldn't it?"

"Katarina, actually."

"Katarina le Bondavais Allamand. Too complicated and fancy for a colonial like me to pronounce. I'd better stick with Kate."

"I like that more anyway."

"And where did le Bondavais come from?" he asked, eager for an opportunity to tease her back.

"It was my mother's name. She died giving birth to me. My father gave up his commission in the navy to raise me."

Tycho lowered his head.

"I'm sorry, Kate."

"It's all right," she said, and smiled when he took her hand again. They sat there, hand in hand, as the birds fell silent and the holographic sky dimmed and disappeared, revealing the real stars overhead.

The chiming of Tycho's mediapad marked the end of his time with Kate—Diocletia was summoning her children to dinner.

Besotted by thoughts of Kate, Tycho managed to walk nearly to the other side of the Westwell, completely missing the bridge that led to the Jovian Union's fondaco. He was about to turn around when he spotted

Carlo emerging from the passageway that led to Bazaar and the unpatrolled domes and tunnels of Cybele.

Their eyes met, and Carlo looked surprised.

"Mom wants us back for dinner," he said.

"I know—I missed where you turn right. Where were you? Visiting Grandmother?"

"No," Carlo said with a scowl.

"Are you ever going to? I think she'd like to see you."

Once again Tycho wondered how three siblings could regard the same thing so differently. He was still worrying over the question of Elfrieda and why she'd left. Yana had pumped their mother for information, then moved on once her curiosity was satisfied. And Carlo had been instantly dismissive.

"Quit trying to fix everything, Tycho. I don't want to see her—not now and not ever."

"Why not?"

"You wouldn't understand. You were just a little kid."

"So explain it to me."

They were near the center of the Westwell now, surrounded by girders and guy wires.

"There's no point," Carlo said, but then he leaned on the railing of the walkway and looked up at the pressure dome high above them. "You and Yana don't even remember her."

Tycho shook his head. "I've tried, but you're right—I don't."

"Well, I do."

Tycho peered at his brother, puzzled. "Was she bad to you, growing up?"

"No. She was kind. She meant a lot to me, in fact."

Tycho just looked at him, hoping he would explain. For a moment he thought Carlo wouldn't—his fingers opened and closed on the railing. But then he looked at Tycho and began to talk again.

"When she left, I thought I'd done something wrong," Carlo said. "I spent months belowdecks on the *Comet* in my hammock wondering what it was, trying to figure out what I'd done."

"You were eight—you couldn't have done anything."

"Of course I didn't do anything! She couldn't have waited just a little longer? She was just selfish and not thinking of anyone but herself. It took me a long time to figure that out, while she was missing. But I did. And so she can stay missing."

Carlo stared up at the struts of the pressure dome above them, his face pale. "Now do you understand?"

"Yes. And I'm sorry."

Carlo waved dismissively. "It's fine. Forget it."

"But if you weren't in Bazaar, then where were you?" Tycho asked, remembering the Ice Wolves and the deserted dome. "It's dangerous out that way, you know."

"I can take care of myself. I had something to do. Where were *you*?"

"I had something to do too."

Carlo nodded, and Tycho realized they'd somehow

reached an unspoken agreement: they didn't believe each other, but they also weren't going to pry into each other's business. But he couldn't keep from peering curiously at his brother. Did Carlo have a girlfriend too?

"Aren't you tired of this awful place?" Carlo asked suddenly. "Being cold all the time, and not knowing what Earth is up to, and trying to figure out the Cybeleans and their double-dealing games?"

"Keep your voice down. We're guests here, remember?"

"I don't care. They're toying with us—with all of us. It's dirty and dishonorable. And now we've stooped to their level. Paying pirates to fly the Jovian flag. Remember when only Earth did that?"

Tycho nodded.

"It's terrible for us as a family," Carlo said. "It makes the JDF see us as all the same—like there's no difference between Mom and Dmitra Barnacus, or between Captain Andrade and the Widderiches."

"But they've always seen us that way," Tycho said. "That's what Yana and I were trying to tell you. We're irregulars—expendable. Remember?"

"That's where you're wrong. This is making things worse for us. Making it harder for us to do what we need to do."

"And what's that?"

"What I told you before—win a place in the JDF. A way to continue the family business after they outlaw privateering and leave us with nothing. Which is going to happen sooner rather than later, if we keep letting unreformed pirates bring shame to our flag."

Carlo turned to Tycho. His jaw was set, his fists clenched.

"I'm not going to let that happen to us, Tyke. I'll do anything to stop it. You understand that, don't you?"

"I don't think Mr. Vass sees us as pirates," Tycho said, taken aback by his brother's fervor. "He flew here with us and saw how we worked. He knows we're not like the Widderiches."

"He's just one man. And what did he see, anyway? He saw us lose a dromond."

"Which we're trying to get back. Besides, the Union wants us here. We're a part of its plan."

"But what *is* that plan? It feels like we're all in over our heads—caught between Earth and the Ice Wolves, and trying to figure out what the Cybeleans are up to."

"We're trying to take Earth prizes and protect our own merchant ships to show the Cybeleans that Earth isn't all-powerful. And stop them from making a ship-building deal with Earth. And recover the *Leviathan* if we can. I agree, I don't like the Cybeleans or their games either. But sometimes not playing isn't an option. And if that's the case, you may as well win."

Carlo turned to Tycho, studying him. After a moment he nodded.

"What is it?"

"Nothing. I was thinking that's good advice. About a lot of things."

Carlo looked like he was going to say something else

but then ducked his head, staring down into the lower levels of the Westwell. He swallowed, and Tycho could almost see whatever had possessed him drain away, leaving him looking tired and unsure of himself.

"I'm a great pilot," he said hesitantly. "And you're . . . well, you're not so hot."

"I really hope there's a 'but' coming," Tycho said.

"There is, if you'll be quiet and let me get to it."

Tycho studied the contours of the pressure dome high above them—the thin membrane that kept the life-giving air around them from vanishing into the black void beyond.

"I'm a great pilot, but it's taken me a long time to understand there's more to being captain than piloting," Carlo said. "In that respect, Tyke, I could learn a lot from you."

"Thanks," Tycho said, then laughed nervously. "I don't suppose you'll ask Mom to put that in the Log?"

Carlo's eyes came up and met Tycho's for a moment. Then he looked away, grimacing. "Come on. Before we're late for dinner."

When Tycho and Carlo entered their temporary quarters, Yana was standing at the dinner table, breathing hard, her face red and her hair dark with sweat.

"Unarmed-combat sims," she said in response to her brothers' questioning glance.

"They're a lot noisier than pilot simulations," Mavry said, wrapping an arm around Carlo's shoulder.

"And smellier," Tycho said.

"Mr. Speirdyke needed hot water to cook," Yana said with a shrug. "Would you rather eat next to a dirty sister or starve next to a clean one?"

Somehow Tycho doubted that Earth's fondaco was ever short on hot water.

"And where have you two been, anyway?" Diocletia asked as Carlo and Tycho settled themselves at the table. "I was about to comm Mr. Grigsby and have him lead a search party."

Carlo and Tycho muttered excuses without looking at each other, prompting an amused look to pass between Yana and Mavry.

"Never mind us—where's Grandfather?" Tycho asked.

"Visiting my mother," Diocletia said in a tone that indicated the subject was not to be pursued further. "I'm afraid salad dressing is beyond Mr. Speirdyke's skills, but this burgoo isn't bad. And there's duff for later."

Tycho gave the stew a sniff, then scooped it into his bowl. He wondered what Kate was eating, and if she had company. He imagined a table surrounded by handsome young Earth nobles, each with a liveried servant behind him, eating some delicacy he'd never imagined existed.

"Tyke, quit glaring at the burgoo and pass it already," Yana said.

"Huh? Oh. Right."

It was odd to eat as a family accompanied neither

by bells nor by the quiet, dignified presence of Parsons, waiting to bring things to the table or take them away as needed. The Hashoones ate in silence for a few minutes, each lost in his or her own thoughts.

"Are we heading back into space tomorrow?" asked Yana.

"Most likely," Diocletia said. "There's a meeting at the consulate in the morning. It seems Captain Allamand has taken another prize."

Tycho looked up from his burgoo.

"When was this?" he asked.

"I just received word. The *Gracieux* and the *Argent Raptor* snatched a couple of ketches making the run from Ceres to Ganymede."

"Did any of our captains try to intercept?" Carlo asked.

"Dmitra was on station and made a run at Allamand, but he moved fast—put prize crews aboard the ketches and sent them back inbound before she could get there."

Tycho's appetite vanished. While he'd been sitting in the garden with Kate, the Jovian Union's enemies had been ambushing his countrymen in space. And he'd done nothing to warn them.

"They're not huge prizes, but the insurers are screaming," Diocletia said with a sigh. "So I suspect we'll be back looking for the *Leviathan* tomorrow. That or this shipyard of yours, Tycho. I shared your idea about the *Leviathan* being turned into parts, and Mr. Vass and his ministers got very interested."

Yana offered her brother a small smile, while Carlo stared into his burgoo. Tycho knew what both of them were thinking: he'd get credit for his theory in the Log.

"Whatever this big shipbuilding project is, our ministers suspect it's almost finished," Diocletia said. "They've been keeping an eye on the Cybelean shipbuilders for a while to get a better sense of what kind of deal Earth might offer them. In the last couple of days the sign walkers have basically stopped recruiting."

"Does that mean we're running out of time?" Yana asked.

"Well, Vass says there's no indication of any life-support systems being procured yet—intelligence can trace those more easily than orders of steel and ceramics," Mavry said. "But yes, it sounds like they're well along in the construction process."

"Or Tycho's right and Earth's just stealing components from one of the missing ships," Yana said.

"That's possible too," Diocletia said. "Anyway, be ready for a recall order."

"And in the meantime, eyes and ears open," Mavry said. "Our side could use a win pretty badly, if only to change the conversation."

"I heard something," Tycho said. "Mox is here on Cybele."

Mavry and Diocletia exchanged an alarmed glance.

"Where did you hear that?" Mavry asked.

Too late, Tycho realized he couldn't tell his father the truth.

"In Bazaar," he said vaguely.

"Overheard it from who?"

"Spacers were talking—Ice Wolves," Tycho said, then became aware of his mother's disapproving gaze. "Bazaar is a good place to find information, Mom. That's important, right?"

"And how do you know they were Ice Wolves?" Mavry asked.

Tycho shrugged. "Burly guys with beards talking about Thoadbone Mox?"

"I think that area's too dangerous to visit," Diocletia said. "This is just more proof of it."

"I had my carbine," Tycho said, thinking that it hadn't done him any good.

"They have carbines too," Diocletia said. "The shipbuilding work may be slowing down, but we had two crewers snatched by crimps beyond the Westwell yesterday—and three Comets needed medical attention after battling it out with someone or other. And those are veteran spacers, not teenaged members of a bridge crew."

"Is this about the Ice Wolves or about you not wanting us to talk to Grandmother?" Tycho asked.

It wasn't his siblings' faces that told him he'd gone too far but the way his father's expression went from surprised to disappointed to carefully blank.

"I'm sorry, Mom," he said in a small voice.

He risked a glance at his mother, expecting volcanic rage, but she just looked tired. No, he thought, more than tired—she looked exhausted.

"Forget it," Diocletia said, her voice uncharacteristically quiet. "The three of you are getting a little old to be told how to conduct yourselves in port. So I'm asking you to be careful. Remember, you only have to be unlucky once."

18

CARLO'S PRIZE

The next morning, Tycho was retyping a message to Kate when Carlo burst into the Hashoones' quarters at the Jovian fandaco.

"What's with you?" Tycho asked, hurriedly covering his mediapad.

"Sign walker," Carlo said, stripping off his hooded parka. "Tried to recruit me."

"And this is news why?"

Both brothers could hear Huff snoring in his quarters,

the sounds coming through the door echoed by the gurgling of his tank.

"See, I was in the passageway to Bazaar—" Carlo began.

"You heard what Mom said—that area's dangerous. You should at least carry a carbine out there."

"Would you forget about carbines and listen to me?" Carlo said in exasperation as Diocletia emerged from her bedroom, curious about the commotion. Mavry was aboard the *Comet*, attending to a faulty fuel-balancing sensor.

"The sign walker was hiring people to unload freight and said it was from an Earth ship, and he guaranteed no pirate trouble," Carlo explained. "That's what made me listen. I asked him how he could promise that and he said the ship wasn't coming all the way here. He told me its owners had made an arrangement to transfer its cargo to Cybelean coasters before reaching the area where there's been pirate activity."

"When was this, exactly?" Diocletia asked.

"Fifteen minutes ago, I guess. Mom, we were talking about needing to change the conversation, remember? This is the perfect opportunity to do it."

As Diocletia gnawed on her thumbnail, Yana emerged from the bathroom, hair wet from the shower.

"We're supposed to conduct more sweeps of the asteroids," Diocletia said. "I was just about to issue a recall order."

Yana stopped drying her hair and demanded to know

what they were talking about. Her eyes narrowed when Carlo got to the part about Cybelean coasters.

"Are the Cybeleans offering our freighters the same help in keeping their cargoes safe?"

"Not that I've heard," Diocletia said, poking at the coffeemaker's controls.

"Of course not," Tycho said, hand still over his media-pad. "This is just another one of their sleazy deals."

"We can make them regret this one," Carlo said pleadingly.

"That would be fun," Yana said with a predatory gleam in her eye.

"It would be," Diocletia said. "But it would be more fun to find the *Leviathan* and steal her back."

"We've got ships all over the asteroids and nobody's found so much as a stray ion from the *Leviathan*," Yana objected.

"That's true."

Diocletia drummed her fingers on the kitchen counter. Huff continued snoring in the next room. Tycho, Yana, and Carlo waited, knowing their mother's habits. The drumming fingers meant she was making up her mind, and further campaigning would only annoy her.

Her fingers stopped drumming. The coffeemaker pinged.

"Carlo, patch into Vesuvia remotely and see if you can get a fix on the likely point where they'd be transferring cargo on that route," Diocletia said. "Then cross-reference that with anything you can find in the freight database on expected deliveries, cargo vessels, and so forth. I want to make sure we're not chasing a ghost."

"On it," Carlo said with a grin, then turned to his brother and sister. "Will you two help?"

"For prize money?" Yana asked. "You have to ask?"

"Tycho?"

Tycho reluctantly erased his half-written message to Kate.

"Something about this doesn't feel right," he said. "What if it's a trap?"

"Then we start shooting," Yana said. "Is that what's bothering you, Tyke? Or is it that you can't stand the idea of someone else having a bit of luck?"

"Belay that," Diocletia snapped, but the rebuke sounded halfhearted. There was a difference to their mother's tone when she thought you were wrong, as opposed to when she thought you were right but being obnoxious about it. Tycho knew perfectly well that this was the latter—and judging from her smile, so did Yana.

"Carlo, my lad, yeh need to breathe," Huff growled from his perch near the *Comet*'s forward ladderwell. "Trust an ol' pirate—more worked up yeh get awaitin' a prize, the slower she is to appear."

Carlo nodded and exhaled, his shoulders rising and falling. But a moment later he was staring out through the *Comet*'s viewports again.

The frigate had detached from her long-range tanks and was sitting just off a secondary spacelane connecting

65 Cybele with the inner asteroids, running silent and dark. They'd been lurking there for half a watch, and everybody on the quarterdeck was getting antsy. Judging from the vile oaths and blood-curdling threats bouncing up the forward ladderwell, the same was true below-decks.

When the bells clanged out 1030, Diocletia sighed.

"The ship will be here, Captain," Carlo said. "I *know* it will be."

The certainty in Carlo's voice was strange—he was normally one to scoff at hunches and feelings. Tycho glanced at Yana to see if she'd noticed the same thing, but his sister was busy performing another scan of the area.

"Arrr, if believin' were the difference maker, lad, wouldn't be a poor pirate anywhere in the solar system," Huff said.

"We'll hold our position, but surely the rest of you have something better to do," Diocletia said. "You're excused, Carlo—you couldn't concentrate on anything else right now anyway."

"I'm caught up with my homework," Tycho said before his mother could suggest that as a way to fill the time.

Mavry raised an eyebrow. "Vesuvia? Is that true?"

"Tycho has two overdue homework assignments—a Shakespeare essay and a calculus exercise," Vesuvia replied. "And Yana is four exercises behind in her self-directed History of the Solar System studies."

"Hey!" Yana protested. "Leave me out of this."

"For shame," Mavry said.

"Oh, come on, Mom," protested Tycho. "During an intercept?"

Diocletia gestured to the scattering of rocks visible through the main screen. "When there's something to intercept, you can quit. Until then, hit the books."

"I'll do mine later—I'm too busy running scans," Yana said.

"Nice try," Diocletia said. "Vesuvia, switch scanners to my console. And Mavry will take communications."

Tycho and Yana sighed and called up their overdue assignments. But Tycho found it impossible to focus. Why was their brother so certain a prize was headed their way?

Because he's desperate, Tycho thought.

But was he desperate enough to risk wasting their time because he'd heard something from a sign walker beyond the Westwell? That didn't feel right—particularly not for Carlo, whose instinct was to doubt anything that didn't come from official sources or show up on a sensor reading.

"Do you require a review of your homework assignment, Tycho?" Vesuvia asked.

"I'm thinking," Tycho told the ship's AI.

"Careful you don't break anything," Yana said.

Carlo offered his sister a flicker of a smile. His eyes met Tycho's, then slid away, his expression turning grim as he returned to his vigil.

He knows *the ship is coming. This isn't a hunch or a feeling. He* knows.

Tycho stared at the back of his brother's head as the pieces of the puzzle he'd been working on rearranged themselves, rotated, and locked into place.

He knows the same way I knew about the Portia—*because someone told him. There was no sign walker. Just like I never found a mediapad on Ceres.*

The Securitat would have known about Carlo's mistakes during the raid on the convoy—every Jovian official had received an account of that. And they almost certainly would know that he feared losing out on the captain's chair—it was their job to know such things. They would have zeroed in on him as desperate, vulnerable, and ripe for recruitment.

Tycho had turned his back on DeWise and the Securitat, rejecting further help in winning the captain's chair. So they'd watched and waited for the chance to recruit his brother instead. Waited for the chance to propose a meeting and offer him a prize. There would have been no strings attached, or at least none that Carlo could see—just a little gift to help him even up the competition.

Them Securitat types spin their webs, an' little by little they wrap yeh up. Until yeh can't find yer way out, an' yeh realize they own yeh.

Tycho closed his eyes, furious at his brother but also at himself. He'd been such a fool—both for cheating and for failing to understand what turning his back on the

Securitat would lead to. Why had he thought the Securitat would just walk away from his family? Why had he never imagined that he could be replaced?

When something finally did appear on the *Comet*'s scanners, it was two somethings, not one. And the two somethings were coming from the wrong direction.

"Mr. Grigsby, we have bogeys inbound from Cybele," Diocletia said.

"Aye, Captain," said Grigsby, and a moment later the bosun's pipes shrilled belowdecks.

"I'll take back sensors," Yana said, even as Tycho was asking Vesuvia for control of communications.

"Hold on a moment, you two," Diocletia said. "There's time to figure out what we're looking at."

"The bogeys are coming from Cybele?" Yana asked with a smile. "Your sign walker seems to have been a bit confused, Carlo."

"Not if those are the coasters, coming to meet the freighter and unload her cargo," Carlo said.

Tycho frowned. Carlo was calm and confident now—and why shouldn't he be?

"They're too big to be coasters," Diocletia said. "They're frigates at least."

"That . . . doesn't make any sense," Carlo said, and Tycho couldn't resist a small, mean smile.

"Sensor contact," Vesuvia announced.

"No kiddin', yeh blind calculator," Huff growled. "Tell us summat we don't know."

"This sensor contact is a single ship heading for 65 Cybele from the inner solar system," Vesuvia said with a hint of smugness.

"*Now* you two can take over," Diocletia said. "Carlo, your starship."

"Thank you, Captain," Carlo said, hauling the control yoke back and elevating the *Comet*'s nose. "Vesuvia, beat to quarters. Mr. Grigsby, we are intercepting a third bogey inbound from the inner solar system."

"The first two ships are hailing," Tycho said as the bosun's pipes squealed beneath their feet once more. "It's the Widderich brothers."

"What are they doing here?" Carlo demanded. "We don't need help, least of all from the likes of them."

"Tryin' to horn in on our prize," Huff rumbled. "Been a bad habit of theirs for years."

"Patch them through," Diocletia said, looking annoyed.

"Heard you might need some help, *Comet*," said Baltazar Widderich.

"Give me the comm, Tycho," Diocletia said, activating her headset. "You heard wrong, Baltazar. Right now we're a little busy."

"Where did the Widderiches come from?" Yana asked when Diocletia had fended off Baltazar's complaints.

"I had to tell Garibalda that we weren't taking part in today's search of the asteroids," Diocletia said. "Someone on her quarterdeck must have talked. Word gets around, someone in traffic control's getting slipped livres to share information, and pretty soon you've got company."

"I'm more worried about our other company," Carlo said as he swung the *Comet* into the spacelane. "What's on the scopes, Yana?"

"New arrival looks like a Minke-class, but confidence only fifty-eight percent. She's about to see us—her sensor cone will overlap our position within forty-five seconds."

"Baltazar an' Karst will be playin' by pirate rules," Huff warned.

"What does that mean, Grandfather?" Carlo asked.

"Means they'll expect a snack if they're within firin' range at the time of the capture," Huff said. "Least that's how we used to settle these things. Kept us from puttin' holes in each other. Well, at least sometimes."

"We better get there first, then," Carlo said, hitting the throttle hard enough to mash the Hashoones back in their chairs. "Tycho, plot us a course back to our tanks in case our bogey turns out to be a warship. Vesuvia, display colors."

Tycho began computing the requested course, trying to keep his anger in check: Carlo was not only flying with his usual precision but also smoothly issuing the orders expected of the ranking officer during an intercept. Tycho could guess what he'd done to put himself in that position, but there was nothing he could say about it—not now and not ever.

"Flying Jovian colors," Vesuvia said.

"Tyke, I'll hail the bogey," Carlo said. "Mr. Grigsby, we're going in hot."

"The comm is yours," Tycho said. "You've earned it, after all."

Carlo gave Tycho a puzzled glance, then activated his headset. "Unknown ship, this is the *Shadow Comet* operating under letter of marque of the Jovian Union. We are on an intercept course. Activate transponders and identify yourself immediately."

Seven bells rang out.

"Ninety percent confidence that she's a Minke," Yana said.

"Target craft has activated transponders," Vesuvia said. "Cybelean colors."

"Incoming transmission," Tycho said. "All channels."

"*Shadow Comet*, this is the *Blue Heron*, finishing our run from Ceres," a polite, cultured voice said over the bridge's speakers. "You've seen our colors. We're on a tight schedule for a rendezvous with our coasters to unload cargo, so I'll need to ask you to stand down. And the same goes for whoever that is coming up behind you."

"Negative, *Heron*," Carlo said. "Sorry to hold you up, but we're going to need an in-person inspection."

"If you disrupt our operations, my board of directors will take the additional cost out of your performance bond," the *Blue Heron*'s captain said. "I have to warn you that the cost will be considerable."

"We'll take that risk, *Heron*. We invoke our right to inspect your vessel under the articles of war governing interplanetary commerce. Heave to and prepare for boarding."

They could see the freighter now, a point of brilliant light moving against the backdrop of stars.

"Yana, how far away are the Widderiches?" Carlo asked.

"Eight thousand klicks."

"This interference is outrageous, *Comet*!" the *Blue Heron*'s captain said.

"I won't say it again, Captain—heave to immediately," Carlo said. "Mr. Grigsby, send a shot near their main mast."

"Be a pleasure, Master Carlo," Grigsby said with a purr of satisfaction.

The *Comet* shook and a line of brilliant green fire streaked between one of her bow chasers and the freighter.

"The next one won't miss, *Heron*," Carlo said. "Now heave to."

"Hold your fire, *Comet*," the *Blue Heron*'s captain said disgustedly.

"They're stopping—ion emissions dropping to zero," Yana said. "But the Widderiches are fifteen hundred klicks off and closing."

"We can dock before they get here," Carlo said, his head swiveling to his parents. "If we're docked, does that count as a capture under pirate rules?"

"No, lad—it's when they strike the colors," Huff said.

"Then perhaps Mr. Grigsby can encourage them to do

that," Carlo said, reaching for his headset.

"Carlo, give the Widderiches their snack," Diocletia said.

"No way!" Yana sputtered.

"Those two lowlifes didn't do anything for this prize," Carlo protested, and Tycho gritted his teeth.

Neither did you, he thought, but another thought came right on the heels of that one: *And neither did I, back when we captured the* Portia.

"Baltazar and Karst are dangerous men," Diocletia said. "They've never been too clear about the difference between friends and enemies. We're trying to change the conversation, remember? If the Cybeleans hear we wound up trading shots with our own countrymen during an intercept . . ."

"Are you giving me an order, Captain?" asked Carlo.

"No—your starship. But consider it highly expert advice."

Carlo said a bad word, then nodded. "Fine. They can have their snack. But it better be a small bite. Mr. Grigsby, prepare the boarding party—I'll meet you at the starboard lock."

Once his vessel was boarded, the *Blue Heron*'s captain admitted his true allegiance was to Earth and cooperated with Carlo and Huff—after all, he said with a shrug, it wasn't as if GlobalRex's insurance adjusters were willing to die for him. Mindful that Earth's ships might arrive and attempt a rescue, Mavry hastily recruited a prize crew from belowdecks, while Yana kept scanning the area and Tycho plotted a course that would take the *Blue Heron* back toward Ceres before turning and running to Ganymede for condemnation.

Throughout the capture, the Widderiches' frigates, the *Romulus* and *Remus*, hung in space a few hundred meters away from the *Comet* and her prey, with Diocletia assuring each brother in turn that he would get a share of the prize money and sternly insisting that he keep his distance.

"It's Baltazar again," Tycho said wearily, hands on his headset.

"Why is it always Baltazar?" Yana asked.

"Oh, Karst probably forgot how to work his comm board," Diocletia said. "There's a few genius pirates, and then most of us, and then a bunch of idiots, and *then* there's Karst. Put it through, Tycho."

"Ach, Captain Hashoone, been reviewing your boy's course," Baltazar grumbled. "Some rescue ship will scoop up our prize before she makes the Kirkwood Gap. Smarter by far to divide the cargo now."

Diocletia said nothing for a moment, and Tycho knew she was trying to calm herself. A Hashoone who could see the way her shoulders were set would have stopped arguing immediately—but then Baltazar was neither present nor a Hashoone.

"Give him both barrels, Mom," Yana muttered.

"Silence on the bridge. Captain Widderich, the boy you're referring to is a veteran midshipman. And if you're worried about an Earth ship making a rescue, the best thing for all of us to do is get out of here as soon as possible."

"But Captain Hashoone—" Baltazar said, then stopped. They could hear the low buzz of conversation on the *Romulus*'s quarterdeck.

"Two new sensor contacts," Vesuvia said. "Inbound from Cybele."

"Get me a scan," Diocletia said. "Tycho, inform our boarding party. Baltazar, do you see them?"

"Hailing 'em now," Baltazar said, his voice turning gleeful. "Since you'll be too busy to assist with this next capture, Diocletia, my brother and I will intercept."

"The incoming craft are flying Cybelean colors," Vesuvia said. "Transponders identify them as the *Townsend* and the *Northwind*."

"Must be the coasters they hired to unload the freighter," Diocletia said. "Captain Widderich, those are the Cybelean merchant craft that the *Heron* was due to meet."

"So?" growled Baltazar.

"So our letters of marque allow us to intercept only Earth craft and Saturnian vessels."

"Lawyer talk," Baltazar growled as the *Romulus* activated her trio of engines and began to turn in the direction of the coasters. "They's prey, and we's predators. Karst, get that wreck of yours in gear! Don't just sit there like a grog-addled sloth in a gravity well!"

"Captain Widderich, listen to me," Diocletia said. "An

inspection will find those coasters' papers in orders. That means any damage you do to cargo or craft will come out of your performance bond, and could result in revocation of your letter of marque. And any harm to the crew will be treated as an act of piracy."

"And who's gonna know? Lot of room for ships to get lost out here."

"The court of inquest will know. Based on my testimony and that of my crew."

Tycho risked a glance at Yana, who was watching their mother intently.

"You'd turn on yer own like that?" Baltazar asked. "You ain't no Jupiter pirate."

"No, I'm not. None of us are anymore. And that includes you, Captain."

19

DOWN THE WELL

B y the time the *Comet* returned to Cybele, Tycho
was in a foul mood—one made worse by Kate's
message that she was stuck at some official Earth
function and didn't know when she'd be able to
get away.

Tycho stewed as the ferries collected the boisterous
Comets, and sulked on the short ride down to the landing field in the gig. Carlo piloted the little craft like the

sixty-second jaunt was a journey through Saturn's rings, and Diocletia never said a word. Tycho fell behind the others in the endless tunnel on the far side of customs, and barely looked up when his sister dropped back to walk alongside him.

"What's eating you this time?" Yana asked.

"Nothing."

"Come on—you've barely said a word since the intercept."

Tycho shrugged, but his sister was peering at him in a way that reminded him of their mother.

"This wouldn't be about Carlo getting credit for taking a prize, would it?" she asked.

Tycho kicked at the grimy decking. That wasn't it *exactly*, but it was close enough—particularly since he couldn't tell Yana the real reason.

"It all goes in the Log, doesn't it?" he grumbled.

"I don't think taking a freighter quite makes up for losing a dromond."

Yana's mediapad beeped and she glanced at it, which reminded him once again that he wouldn't even get to see Kate.

"Well, at least it's good for the Jovian Union," he said, trying to sound dutiful.

Yana smiled at something on her mediapad, then shut the device's cover with a snap.

"I'm glad none of this bothers you," Tycho said peevishly.

"Why should it bother me? I'm not going to be captain of the *Comet*. I figured that out a while ago."

Tycho looked at her inquiringly. There had been no bitterness in Yana's voice, no hint that she wanted him to disagree with her. She'd simply said what she meant.

"I mean, I'm going to be captain," Yana said. "Just not of the *Comet*."

"We've talked about this. It's against every rule—"

"Oh, there you go again," Yana said, smiling sweetly at him. "You know what's funny, Tyke? I'm your twin sister, and yet it's like you don't know me at all."

Tycho knew it was a bad idea, but he couldn't help himself. After checking his mediapad yet again for a message from Kate, he typed in the password that unlocked the secret folder inside the device's memory. There were DeWise's messages—the ones that, if ever discovered, would reveal his involvement with the Securitat.

He glanced at the doorway to his room. He could hear Mr. Speirdyke clattering pans as he prepared dinner, and the thuds and gasps of Yana pushing herself through another unarmed-combat sim.

He entered DeWise's recognition code, then began to type.

SO I GUESS YOU HAVE A NEW RECRUIT. YOU NEED TO TEACH HIM TO LIE MORE CONVINCINGLY. BUT WHO BETTER TO LEARN FROM THAN YOU?

He sent the message, making sure to hide it in the folder. He checked to see if Kate had made contact, saw she hadn't, checked again, and tossed his mediapad onto his bunk with a sigh.

Mr. Speirdyke finished the cooking, said his farewells, and hobbled off to his own quarters with the other Comets. Tycho maintained a cautious silence during dinner, worried that any conversation would cause him to lose his temper. That could only make things worse—criticizing his brother would either come off as sour grapes or lead to disaster for both of them.

But there wasn't much conversation to be had. Carlo seemed oddly subdued, eating mechanically and staring off into space. Yana was silent too, probably tired after her unarmed-combat session, and Huff had gone off to carouse with the Jovian privateers.

It made for a quiet table—until Mavry looked quizzically around at the rest of his family.

"Does anyone remember that we took a prize today?" he asked. "It feels like we're gathered for a funeral."

"I seem to recall taking a prize today, now that you mention it," Diocletia said.

Carlo smiled quickly and nodded, but barely looked up from his food.

"She's not a prize until she's safe and sound at Ganymede," Tycho said. "And with all the Earth ships prowling out here, that's no guarantee."

"True," Diocletia said. "But remember, our mission here is to complicate Earth's plans—to make the Cybeleans think twice about an alliance. Even if the *Heron*'s retaken, we've shown the Cybeleans that Earth isn't untouchable. Which is exactly what your father meant when he talked about changing the conversation."

Carlo looked off across the room. Tycho picked morosely at his stew.

A mediapad chimed somewhere in their suite of rooms. Tycho turned his head hopefully, but Yana was already out of her seat, recognizing her personalized tone pattern. A minute later she reappeared wearing a fur-lined coat, with her color-changing scarf around her neck.

"And just where are you going?" Diocletia said.

"The combat-sim rig I ordered from Ceres just came in."

Diocletia and Mavry looked at each other.

"The shop's in the Well," Yana said, then patted her coat below the armpit. "And I'm armed."

"All right," Diocletia said. "Be careful."

"Worry about whoever gets in my way," Yana said as she departed.

Carlo stopped staring off into space and shook his head.

"I'm just glad what I overheard turned out to be true," he said quietly. "I was afraid it wouldn't be."

Unable to help himself, Tycho darted a poisonous look his brother's way. Carlo saw it and drew back slightly, looking surprised. And guilty, Tycho thought.

"It was a good tip," Diocletia said. "All three of you performed admirably out there today. Even with the Widderiches doing their best to interfere."

"I gather they almost turned pirate on us," Mavry said.

Diocletia nodded. "I don't think Baltazar and I will be celebrating this capture together."

"The Widderiches *are* pirates, plain and simple," Carlo said. "The Jovian Union never should have issued them letters of marque."

"I know," Diocletia said. "It's a sign of how desperate the Union is. They didn't let the Widderiches become privateers fifteen years ago, and no one's wanted to inquire too carefully about how they've made a living since then."

"You could say the same about Dmitra," Mavry pointed out. "And a few others besides."

"Too many others," Carlo said.

Tycho heard his mediapad chiming in the other room and pushed back his chair.

"Really?" Diocletia asked.

"Sorry!"

He hurried into his room and picked up the device, hoping it was Kate. But there was no message showing in the queue. It took him a moment to remember his earlier message and open the hidden folder where his exchanges with DeWise were kept.

I'M SURE I DON'T KNOW WHAT YOU'RE TALKING ABOUT, TYCHO. YOU HAVE FRIENDS HERE, DESPITE YOUR BEST EFFORTS. IF WE HAVE SOMETHING TO DISCUSS, THAT CAN BE ARRANGED.

Tycho snorted—DeWise had immediately contradicted his own halfhearted denial—and flipped back to his mediapad's main screen, hoping a message from Kate might have arrived in the last couple of seconds.

Which actually had happened.

FREE—COME TO OUR FONDACO AS SOON AS YOU GET THIS! KA

All at once the disturbing day seemed full of promise. He grabbed his jacket, put an arm into the wrong sleeve, tried again, and made a doomed attempt to slick down his hair. Should he shave? He decided he should, thought about how long that would take, changed his mind, and rushed out of the room.

"Not you too," Mavry said.

"Sorry Dad, I've got—"

"Go ahead, Tycho," Diocletia said. "But tomorrow night, all mediapads are getting shut off before dinner."

To Tycho's surprise, Kate was waiting just inside the gates of Earth's fondaco, peering out of an oversized coat of synthetic fur and looking furious. When she saw him, she turned her head to speak sharply to someone, then marched out into the Northwell past the pair of Cybelean constables.

"What is it?" Tycho asked. "And why did you bring a coat?"

"They won't let you in. I'm sorry, Tycho."

"Who won't let me in?" he asked, and peered suspiciously at the Cybelean constables. They stood stock-still, pretending to be unaware of the conversation happening in front of them.

"No, not them—our people," Kate said. "No Jovians are to be given access to the compound. Not even for diplomatic meetings. Something about a captured freighter."

"Ah. Well, never mind then. Let's take a walk around the Well."

He reached for her hand and she entangled her fingers with his. She was wearing the earrings he'd given her, he saw with a smile. But a moment later she glanced over at him and frowned.

"Wait a minute. You know something about this. I can tell."

Tycho sighed. "Yeah, I do. Um, it was my ship that captured the freighter."

Kate pulled her hand away and looked at him, disbelief and anger and embarrassment chasing each other across her face.

"It's what my family *does*—we're privateers," Tycho said, embarrassed at how defensive he sounded. "It's what we *all* do. The first time I ever heard of your father, it was because he'd stolen a prize back from *us*."

Kate lowered her eyes.

"You're right. I guess I didn't want to think about it. It's just . . . it's so *complicated*."

"I know," Tycho said, then reached for her hand again. "But *this* doesn't have to be."

She offered him a small smile and made no objection when he put his arm around her shoulders. The smell of her made him slightly dizzy. He tried to identify the components of that intoxicating scent—soap, definitely, and perhaps a hint of perfume.

"The garden would have been nice," he said. "But there are other places to go on Cybele."

"I know," she said. "But . . . well, my father's away. And I was so excited to see you."

Tycho must have looked surprised, because Kate blushed.

"I just meant that we could have a little privacy. Away from all these eyes."

"So let's go find some," Tycho said. "I think we've created scandal enough here."

She smiled and nodded, and they walked away from the gate, into the hubbub of the Well.

"What about that top level?" Kate asked. "Where we met? It's beautiful up there. I felt like I was surrounded by stars."

Tycho shook his head sadly. "The Cybeleans'll never let us in. That was one night only, for their entertainment."

"What about the Jovian fondaco, then?"

Tycho raised his jacket's fur-lined collar against the cold. "It's . . . not as nice as Earth's. You'd be disappointed."

"You don't really think I care about that, do you?"

"No. Of course not. But . . . look, our people are even more paranoid than yours are. If your side didn't let me in—"

"Oh, let's not talk about sides. It's awful. All right then, the Well it is."

She extended one hand into the air, letting it hang there like she was a queen. "Lead on, good sir."

"I've never been so honored," Tycho said, bowing over her hand and kissing it, and then lingering to do so repeatedly. She pulled her arm away and swatted at him, but she was smiling.

The Well was quieter now, with most of its offices and banks dark and silent behind blank shutters. Tycho and Kate took an elevator to the lower levels, which were filled with a mix of cafés, restaurants, and high-end shops and stalls. Tycho saw few spacers—this level was the domain of wealthy Cybeleans, with a sprinkling of foreigners in formal clothes and not a privateer or crimp to be seen. The café tables were softly lit and heated, surrounded by a buzz of low conversation, with Cybelean constables keeping a discreet but watchful eye on things.

A dim passageway sloped down into a tunnel beneath a sign that read "Guild Offices." Planters filled with dark-green vegetation lined the corridor. Kate's fingers trailed over the plants and she shook her head.

"Plastic," she said.

Tycho smiled, trying to imagine living in a place where you assumed plants were real.

He raised his eyebrows and inclined his head down the corridor.

"Are you sure it's safe?" Kate asked.

"It's the Well," Tycho said, then patted his side beneath his armpit. "And I've got a carbine. It'll be fine."

They were halfway down the corridor when Tycho heard a small sound and saw a flash of blue and green. Two figures were ahead of them in the gloom, separating hastily. He slowed his pace, stepping forward to block Kate's body with his own, and the fingers of his free hand crept toward his shoulder holster.

"Tyke?"

Yana emerged from the gloom, followed closely by Immanuel Sier. Her eyes widened when she saw Kate.

"You're with her?" Yana asked.

"You're with him?" Tycho said at the same moment.

They started to talk over each other again, then stopped, staring at each other in disbelief. With a sigh of annoyance, Kate shook her head and stepped forward.

"We met at the banquet," she said to Yana, then extended her hand to Immanuel. "But I fear you and I haven't been introduced. I'm Katarina Allamand."

Immanuel muttered his name as he nodded over Kate's hand.

"Are you insane?" Yana asked, red dots chasing each other around her scarf. "She's from Earth."

"So?" Tycho replied. "He's Saturnian *and* from belowdecks."

Immanuel stepped forward, eyes cold.

"And what do you mean by that, then? If'n I didn't know better, *Master* Hashoone, I'd think I was bein' insulted."

"I didn't mean it that way," Tycho muttered.

"Yes you did. So which is worse: Saturnian, or belowdecks?"

Tycho blinked at Immanuel for a moment, conscious of Kate's eyes on him. Anger flared in him but almost immediately withered away into embarrassment.

"I'm not sure what I meant, Mr. Sier," he said. "But I owe you an apology either way."

Immanuel's eyes narrowed, but then he nodded.

"All right then," he said. "No harm done."

"Come on," Yana said to Immanuel, taking his hand and leading him back up the ramp. A last flurry of colors marked her departure.

Tycho exhaled, looking at his boots, then reluctantly raised his eyes to meet Kate's.

"Well," she said. "That was certainly exciting."

"I shouldn't have said that."

"Which part?" Kate asked, taking his hand again.

"Any of it," he said disgustedly.

"The first part wasn't your best moment," she said, drawing him toward her. "But the apology was gracious. There are plenty of important men and women on Earth who can't own up to a mistake. It's part of the reason the solar system's in the mess it is."

"That's true where I come from as well," Tycho said.

"So that's settled," Kate said. "Now here we are surrounded by fake plants in a deserted corridor on a freezing asteroid—what could be more romantic? Come here, Master Hashoone."

20

ELFRIEDA'S STORY

Tycho stared at the ceiling of his room, wishing sleep would come while knowing it wouldn't. Finally he gave up, activating his mediapad and blinking unhappily at the sudden glare, then glowering at the numbers displayed there: 0549.

He padded into the kitchen and found his sister already there, face illuminated by her own mediapad. She glanced at him and grunted—Tycho wasn't sure whether that was because of the early hour or their unexpected encounter the night before.

"I was thinking about bells," Tycho said quietly, taking the seat next to her.

"That's way too random a statement for me to deal with right now, Tyke."

"I was thinking it's hard to sleep without them."

His sister sighed. "I thought I was the only one."

They exchanged quick smiles. Then Yana looked back down at her mediapad.

"But that's crazy," Tycho said after a moment. "If you want people to sleep, the last thing you should do is ring a bell every half hour. Yet apparently that's what I need."

"Right."

"How did I learn to sleep with them in the first place? It must have driven me crazy, when we started bunking belowdecks. But I don't remember."

Yana looked skeptical. "You don't? Really?"

Tycho shook his head.

"It *never* bothered you," Yana said. "I was so jealous. It took me most of our first cruise to get used to those stupid bells."

Tycho tried to remember discussing that with his sister, back when they were apprentices, but if they'd spoken about it, he'd forgotten. He found that faintly disturbing—it hadn't been *that* long ago.

"The bells aboard the *Gracieux* drive Kate crazy," he said.

"That's because she's a civilian—they drive all civilians crazy. On the way here I'd find Mr. Vass in the cuddy at all hours, working because he couldn't sleep."

Tycho frowned, wondering if his sister had had her own conversations with the intelligence minister.

"So I guess you and Kate made up after your argument at the banquet," Yana said.

"You could say that. How did you and . . . Immanuel get together?"

"Unarmed-combat drills. Dobbs made us partners."

"That must have been awkward at first," Tycho said, getting up.

"At first," Yana replied, eyes back on her mediapad. "Then . . . well, not so much."

Tycho paused, then looked at his sister. "What do you think Mom would say?"

"I'd rather not find out. What do you think she would she say about you and Captain Allamand's daughter?"

"I feel the same way you do."

"So that's settled then."

Tycho opened the wall cooler. "Do you want a jump-pop?"

"We're out. Mr. Speirdyke should be here before long to start making breakfast. I'm hoping he bought some."

"Not likely," Tycho said, sitting back down. "But hey, there'll be burned coffee."

Yana made a face.

"What are you reading so avidly over there, anyway? Love notes from Mr. Sier?"

"Belay that, Tyke. There's a big scandal on Titan. Jovian Union investigators discovered someone's been diverting funds from refining operations to secret accounts for the last two or three years."

"Diverting funds? Like for a concubine or something?"

"Not with this many livres. Unless whoever did it was supporting a whole moon full of concubines."

"Right," Tycho said. He was too tired to worry about some scandal on distant Titan, yet he knew he wouldn't be able to get to sleep—and he hated the idea of sitting around waiting for the rest of their family to get up.

"You know, Grandmother has jump-pop," he said.

Yana looked up, considering the thought. "Is her place even open now?"

"If Grandmother can earn a livre, she's open. Our recall order isn't till 1000, right?"

"That's right," Yana said. "Fine, I'll go—someone has to keep the crimps off your back. Another day of searching for ships that don't exist. I can't wait."

Tycho couldn't see what had alarmed Bazaar's merchants and early-morning shoppers, but he heard the familiar rattle and bang of shutters coming down and saw anyone young and fit enough to catch a crimp's eye hurrying to make themselves scarce.

He and Yana turned toward the brilliant sign adorning the Last Chance, where clerks had brought half the shutters down while Elfrieda's goons stepped forward, ready to swing their heavy iron bars like clubs.

"Come on," Tycho said, hurrying toward the depot.

One of the guards stepped into their path.

"Get lost," he growled.

"But we know Elfrieda," Tycho protested, catching sight of her at the center of the depot. "Grandmother!"

She turned at the sound of his voice, frowning. "Let those two in, Bix."

The goon stepped aside, and a minute later Tycho and Yana were inside the shuttered depot with the rest of Elfrieda's customers. The spacers and shoppers trapped inside peered wearily at monitors hanging from the ceiling that showed the nearly deserted dome outside. They sighed and muttered about lawlessness and what they were going to say if they were late.

Tycho craned his head to see past the shoulder of one of the guards. A woman in threadbare robes was alone in the dome, possessions bundled in a blanket, looking frantically from shuttered stall to shuttered stall.

"Hey!" Tycho said, shaking the guard's shoulder. "We need to let her in!"

"No we don't. Shove off, kid."

"Elfrieda!" Tycho said, getting his grandmother's attention.

Elfrieda shook her head. "Don't know her."

"Forget it," Yana said when Tycho started to object. "She doesn't care."

Tycho stared anxiously at the feed from the security camera until the woman moved out of range.

"Whoever she was, she's fine," Yana said. "Probably scooted into the next tunnel."

Yana elbowed her way to the counter. After a moment, Tycho followed her.

"Two jump-pops, please," she said. "An orange and a lime."

Yana handed over a few coins and Elfrieda counted them, then placed the bottles on the counter. Tycho stood beside his sister, peering up at the monitors.

"So how's the buried-treasure business, Tycho?" Elfrieda asked.

"What? Oh. So far it's not working out. Um, how was your nip with Grandfather?"

"Oh, we had a good time," she said, her eyes turning to Yana. "I do adore that old pirate. He's always been trouble. But then trouble's part of the fun, isn't it?"

Yana smiled thinly and extracted her mediapad from her jacket. Elfrieda's gaze lingered on her granddaughter for a moment, then returned to the monitors overhead, where a group of men in jumpsuits was looking around Bazaar with puzzled faces.

"Those are mine inspectors, not crimps," she scoffed. "Everybody around here's acting like a bunch of old biddies recently. Bix! Open up!"

As the shutters rose, Yana nudged Tycho. "I'm going back to the fondaco. Are you coming?"

She saw he was about to protest and rolled her eyes. "If you must know, Immanuel messaged me."

Tycho glanced at his grandmother, then back at his sister. "I'll see you at the ship, okay?"

"Gotcha. Watch out for mine inspectors." And with a smirk, Yana was off.

Elfrieda watched her go, then turned and found Tycho looking at her. "I suppose that's another member of the family who doesn't much like me," she said.

"I think she thinks you want to be left alone."

"That hasn't run *you* off," Elfrieda muttered, and anger swelled in Tycho. But then he saw that his grandmother's eyes were sad and felt his anger drain away, replaced by pity.

"Word of advice, kid—don't listen to grouchy old battle-axes," she grumbled. "Especially first thing in the morning."

He supposed that was an apology, or the closest thing to one that he would get. Elfrieda was watching his sister stride off toward the Westwell.

"It's amazing how much she looks Carina. Or like Carina did, before it happened."

Some mean little part of Tycho wanted to ask Elfrieda how she remembered what Carina looked like, considering she hadn't seen her in years. But he held his tongue.

"And your brother?" Elfrieda asked.

"He's fine. Got a tip yesterday that led to us capturing a prize, in fact."

"You make that sound like bad news."

When Tycho just shrugged, his grandmother nodded.

"Oh, of course—the battle for the captain's chair. The

competition that's been tearing Hashoone families apart for centuries."

"It's—it's not like that."

"It isn't? Then why are you unhappy about a prize?"

"I'm not unhappy about the prize . . . ," Tycho said, groping for words and finding them all inadequate.

For a moment he was tempted to tell her everything. Perhaps if his grandmother knew what he had done, how he had conspired with the Securitat, she'd be able to advise him how to react to Carlo having made the same mistake.

But that was crazy. Elfrieda was his grandmother, but he barely knew her.

"I'm . . . it's complicated," he said.

"It always has been. And now it's come between you and your brother."

Tycho shook his head emphatically. "No. That isn't true. I . . . I love my brother, of course. But we've never been close."

"And why do you think that is?"

"I don't know. We're just different, I guess. And maybe because I barely knew him, before the *Comet*. He left Darklands when Yana and I were little kids."

Elfrieda nodded. "I remember. As long as you've known your brother, you've been competitors. What if he becomes captain and you don't? I've seen what that leads to, you know. I saw it rip apart Huff and my daughters. By now you know your grandfather was going to name your aunt as the next captain, right?"

"Yes. And I know my mom and dad weren't going to accept that. I know they planned to join Cassius Gibraltar's crew."

"That's right. Which made Huff angrier than I'd ever seen him. He ranted that he'd been betrayed, that Carina had dishonored the family and now Dio would destroy it. And that was on his good days. On his bad ones he told me it was all a plot of Cass Gibraltar's, a plan to eliminate the family starship and then the family name. Carina marrying Sims, Dio and Mavry joining the *Ghostlight*— he saw Cass as behind all of it and swore he'd stop it somehow."

"By doing what?" Tycho asked.

"Oh, it wound up not mattering. Sims and Cass died. Huff nearly did too. Carina . . . well, you've seen what happened to her. And so Dio became captain while knowing she wasn't his choice. Just like your grandfather always knew she'd planned to defy him and walk away from it all. They've spent every day since then living in the shadow of that."

"I know what Mom and Dad's plan was," Tycho said. "But since she became captain, Mom's followed the old tradition. She's done everything she can to teach that tradition to us and to make it work."

"I know she has. And of all the bad decisions your mother has made in her life, that's the one I find hardest to forgive."

"But it *wasn't* the wrong decision!" Tycho said. "Yana and Carlo and I have talked about this. We have our differences, but we know the stakes—and we've never let the competition get in the way of our shared goals as a family."

"That's because you haven't lost yet. You all still think you're going to win. But two of you will be wrong."

"I know. We *all* know. But . . . the tradition is bigger than any of us. We have an expression, 'The family is the captain—'"

"Don't you dare say that horrible old proverb in here!" Elfrieda said, loud enough to make heads to turn in her direction. "Huff was whispering that bilge to my children before they could even sit up. It's cherished by the winners and despised by everyone else. You think Ulric Hashoone still recites it at his home? Or Josiah? Or Philemon? Do you?"

Tycho remembered the resentment on the faces of his great-uncle and his cousins—the ones who'd been passed over for the captain's chair and consigned to a life spent dirtside.

"Probably not," he admitted.

"Believe me, they don't," Elfrieda said. "I know because I was rotting away at Darklands when Ulric and Josiah were left dirtside—and I was still rotting there when Philemon quit. They felt abandoned. They *were* abandoned. Just like I was."

Elfrieda picked up a box of carbine batteries and began to sort through them, separating the different models and slapping them down on the counter one by one. Tycho stood silently as his grandmother's voice rose.

"Oh, it was all such fun at first," she said, shoving a mislaid battery into the proper pile. "Huff would sweep in with silks and jewels, flinging livres around and regaling everyone with his latest adventures. When Johannes gave the crew leave, we'd be off to Ganymede—or Huff would send tickets for a liner and tell me to meet him on Vesta, or even Mars. But the waiting? That wasn't so much fun. Saying something and waiting for your husband to hear the words and react? Or sending a message into the void and fearing there would never be a reply? No, that wasn't fun at all."

Slap slap slap went Elfrieda's hands on the counter. She flung the empty box aside, heaved another one onto the counter, and smacked its magnetic release.

"Huff wasn't there when your aunt was born, did you know that?" she asked. "Or your mother. It was me and a pack of flea-brained nurses and governesses—all of whom thought I was the luckiest woman in the solar system to be wed to a dashing pirate. The luckiest woman in the solar system, sitting in a hole on Callisto."

She stopped and looked down at the batteries scattered across the counter, her anger momentarily spent.

"Is that why you left?" Tycho asked hesitantly.

Elfrieda looked up and Tycho wondered if she'd forgotten he was there. Then she laughed, a curt bark without a trace of humor.

"Oh, I left a few times. But yes, you could say that was why. Do you know the worst part? In a terrible way, I was glad when your grandfather came home after 624 Hektor."

She stopped for a moment, drumming her fingers on the counter, then shook her head and continued.

"He was so badly injured that the doctors on Ganymede said he might not live unless they turned him into a brain in a tank—some experimental procedure the scientists had in mind. I told them no. I knew he'd rather die than become like that. I prayed for him to live, and he did. And I thought at least I had half a husband back, after all these years of not having one at all."

Elfrieda looked down at her hands, the box of carbine batteries forgotten.

"He lived—and then he went back into space," she said. "Not to be captain, not to be anything. Just to be on that ship of his."

Her eyes scanned the little kingdom of her depot.

"Your brother packed his gear a month before his birthday, do you remember that?" she asked, smiling faintly. "He was that excited—told everybody he was sure he'd get to fly the ship on his first day. And I saw what the rest of my life would be like. I'd sit in that hole with a shattered daughter and two more grandchildren who'd grow up counting the days until they could go into space themselves. And then I'd wait for two of them to come home bitter and broken, if they came home at all."

Tycho just stood there, stomach churning and cheeks hot. He'd been too young to remember Elfrieda at Darklands, but he did remember many childhood afternoons he'd spent asking adults about the day he'd get to leave, or telling them the amazing adventures he'd have once he did. Then he *had* left, and his family's ancient homestead had become a place to endure, an interruption of life aboard the *Comet*. And he'd rarely if ever thought of those for whom the fractured plains of Callisto represented normal life.

Elfrieda shook her head. "I couldn't do it, Tycho. Not even for another day."

"I understand," he said, while knowing that wasn't really true and never could be.

21

THE *GRACIEUX*

Tycho had just reentered the Southwell when his mediapad began to trill. He looked down and saw it was his father. He thought about not answering—he'd be back in the Jovian fondaco in a couple of minutes, after all—but then reconsidered.

"I'm almost there, Dad."

"Almost where? I hope you don't mean here, because you're wanted elsewhere."

Tycho came to a stop, forcing a burly man in a freight

hauler's uniform to perform an awkward pirouette to avoid crashing into him.

"I can't figure out what that means," Tycho said as the freight hauler departed with a shaken fist.

Mavry chuckled. "It means you're wanted at the consulate."

"Ugh. All right. I'll be there in a minute and we can all walk over."

"Oh, we weren't invited. Just you. Mr. Vass requested you specifically."

"For what?"

"Seems like a logical first question for the minister, kid. Anyway, the rest of us are going to relax over bowls of hominy and gossip about the Titan scandal."

"Terrific," Tycho said with a sigh.

"We'll see you at the *Comet*. Oh, and Tycho? Give the minister our fondest regards."

Vass's office was near the apex of the Well, guarded by a Gibraltar Artisans cyborg who turned his mirrored eyepiece in Tycho's direction.

Tycho stopped when the soldier's weapons system powered up. Sparks shot from the electro-prod clenched in his left fist, and lights blinked on the console in his chest armor.

"I have an appointment with the minister," Tycho said, annoyed and a little frightened.

"You are armed," the soldier replied. His voice sounded gravelly, as if from disuse.

"I'm a Jovian privateer. I'm not going to shoot one of our own ministers."

"You are armed," the man repeated, taking one step to the side so that he blocked Vass's door.

"And you're repeating yourself. I had business beyond the Westwell—I needed to be armed."

The soldier just stared at him, and Tycho wondered what Gibraltar Artisans' technologists had done to his brain in augmenting him for bodyguard duty. Did the man think, feel, and dream like he always had, with an additional layer of threat awareness through which he could view his surroundings? Or had the human part of him been removed? The thought made Tycho suppress a shudder.

The door to Vass's office opened, and the minister tried to peek around the cyborg's bulk.

"What's this, then? Ah, Tycho. Come in, come in."

The soldier blocked Vass's way, his eyepiece fixed on Tycho.

"He is armed."

"That's perfectly all right," Vass said. "Tycho isn't a security threat. You may stand down."

The soldier's expression didn't change, but after a moment he stood aside, the sparks from the electro-prod vanishing.

Inside his office, Vass was standing behind his desk, looking up at the black bulk of Attis suspended overhead.

"Interesting thing, working beneath one's own sword of Damocles," he muttered. "Sit down, Tycho.

Thank you for coming. It's already a busy morning—we're trying to figure out where those livres missing from Titan wound up."

"Yeah, I heard about that," Tycho said as he perched on one of the plastic chairs in front of Vass's desk. "I apologize, Minister, but I need to be at our ship by 1000."

"Ah yes. The hunt for the shipyard. Good work there, Tycho. We hadn't considered the idea that Earth was seizing ships to use in construction."

Tycho nodded. "Thank you, Minister. But we're looking for the shipyard *and* the *Nestor Leviathan*."

Vass waved that away. "All things considered, the loss of the ship is merely an embarrassment. The shipyard is far more of a concern."

"You'll forgive my family if we see it a little differently."

"Of course," Vass said, then hesitated.

"What is it, Minister? Do you have new information that might help us?"

"Not exactly. We have some promising leads—the Securitat has identified and interviewed a number of workers who returned from the shipyard, and is collating information in hopes of pinpointing its location. But that method brings no guarantee of success. Which is why I asked you to come in today. I wonder, Tycho, if you've made use of all the sources that might be available to you."

"I don't know what you mean, Minister."

Was it his imagination, or did Vass look embarrassed?

"I believe you have a . . . friend who is highly placed in Earth's community here."

Tycho stared at Vass.

"The two of you haven't exactly been discreet, Tycho."

"Kate doesn't know anything. Her father brought her out here to see the solar system. She's not part of any of this. She's innocent."

"I'm sure that's true." Vass got to his feet and stood by the curved window of his office, staring down into the Well's web of girders and wires. "But through her you might discover information about Earth's operations that we desperately need."

Tycho folded his arms. "You're asking me to use my relationship with Kate to spy for you," he said, his voice turning hard.

Vass turned from the window and locked eyes with Tycho. "Yes, that's what I'm asking you to do."

"I won't," Tycho said, staring back at him. "And you should be ashamed for asking me, sir."

"Tycho, the only scenario that fits the facts we have is that the craft nearing completion in that shipyard is an Earth warship. And you know as well as I do where this leads—to an Earth shipyard and possibly a military base. Both on our side of the Kirkwood Gap."

Vass's gaze crept upward again, to the enormous rock above them.

"Distance, Tycho, is the only real defense we have against the economic and military might of Earth. If that's taken away from us, our very survival is at stake. So no, I am not ashamed about what I'm asking you to do. I would ask you to do far more."

"And you'd get the same answer. I said no and I meant no. Good day, Minister."

Vass watched silently as Tycho rose from his chair and thumbed the control to retract the office door. As Tycho passed the cyborg soldier, he caught sight of his distorted face in the man's mirrored eyepiece and turned away in disgust.

When Tycho climbed the ladderwell to the quarterdeck, his mother was waiting for him. She inclined her head for him to follow and led the way aft, not turning until they'd passed the equipment bays that opened on either side of the passageway.

"Go back belowdecks," she said. "You and Carlo are on duty reading the hands in for this trip."

"It's Carlo's and Yana's turn, not mine."

"You're going to take your sister's turn anyway. I don't know what your problem is with your brother, but I'm tired of seeing you staring laser beams at him, so the two of you are going to work it out in the fifteen minutes or so before the crew ferries start arriving. Is that clear?"

Tycho hung his head.

"Use the aft ladderwell," Diocletia said, already striding back toward the quarterdeck.

Tycho passed the larder, auxiliary magazine, and head, following the passageway where it curved around the closed ladderwell that led from belowdecks to the *Comet*'s dorsal gun turret. He reached the aft ladderwell and climbed down, emerging in the narrow passageway between the port and starboard holds.

Carlo was waiting at the port airlock with his mediapad. From his unhappy expression, Tycho could guess that their mother had taken him aside too.

"Guess it isn't Yana's turn after all," Carlo said.

"Guess not," Tycho grumbled, taking out his own mediapad and getting ready to record which crewers were present and fit for duty. He knew he couldn't blame their mother. He and his siblings had arguments and resentments like in any other family, and there was no way Diocletia could know that this was something far larger—something that couldn't be fixed by a captain's order to get an uncomfortable conversation over with.

It was Carlo who broke the silence first.

"So are you going to tell me what I did?"

Tycho stopped tapping on his mediapad. The smart thing—the *sane* thing, really—was to say nothing, to stand in uncomfortable silence next to his brother until it was time for the *Comet* to fly.

But he was tired of saying nothing.

"You already know what you've done," Tycho said. "Your problem is that I know it too."

"I have no idea what you're talking about," Carlo said, but his face had gone pale.

"There was no sign walker," Tycho said, surprised at how calm he sounded.

"Are you calling me a liar?"

Tycho jabbed his finger at his brother's face.

"It's not just that you're a liar—it's that you're a *bad* one. The solar system's chattiest sign walker, standing in a tunnel telling everybody where Earth freighters are going to offload cargo? In an area of space prowled by privateers? You couldn't do better than that?"

"Back off or Mom will have a bigger problem to handle. Since you know everything, Tyke, tell me what it is you think I've done."

Tycho hesitated, kicking angrily at the deck beneath their feet. Then he leaped. He knew it was a terrible idea, but he had to see his brother's face when he was confronted with what he'd done.

"The Securitat *gave* you that ship," he said. "Told you where it would be and when. They gave it to you as a gift, and you took it to help your chances of being captain. I just hope you asked them what they'll want in return. Did you ask them that, Carlo?"

Carlo stared at Tycho, his mouth hanging open.

"The Securitat?" he stammered. "What would they know about Earth freighters?"

"Don't play dumb. It's their job to find out stuff like that—and to use it."

"You're crazy," Carlo managed. "Crazy and paranoid. That thing Yana said about you catching up with me has got in your head, and now you're imagining things."

"Maybe I should try imagining a sign walker," Tycho said, trying to ignore the little voice in his head reminding him that he'd imagined a lost mediapad well enough when he was the one who'd talked to the Securitat.

Carlo swallowed, and his hands balled into fists. Then Tycho saw him forcing himself to relax.

"Listen to me," Carlo said, his voice low and harsh. "I know what we need to do to survive as a family. I see how to get there, and I'm the only person to lead us. I'd rather do that with your help than without it, Tycho—but I'll do it either way. I'm not going to let anything stop me—particularly not some crazy fantasy you've concocted."

They stood in silence for a few moments. The bells clanged five times. It was 1030, just about time for the ferries full of Comets to start arriving.

"You know what, Carlo?" Tycho asked. "I believe you when you say you know what we need to do, and that you think you're the right person to get us there. I just can't believe that you, of all people, would sacrifice your honor to make that happen."

Carlo said nothing for a moment, his face expressionless. It frustrated Tycho that he couldn't figure out what Carlo was thinking—but then, he'd rarely been able to do more than guess at how his brother's brain worked.

Then Carlo simply turned his back on him, his shoulders sagging.

"Obviously you'll believe whatever you want to believe."

* * *

When Tycho and Carlo returned to the quarterdeck, neither bothered pretending that they'd patched up their differences—their mother was harder to fool than that.

As Grigsby bellowed out orders belowdecks, Carlo flopped into his chair and strapped himself in, then immediately started testing the piloting linkages. Behind him, Tycho reviewed their course and marked communications channels for the other Jovian privateers taking part in the day's sweep. Diocletia studied her sons, face impassive, then turned to look out through the viewports at the arc of docking ports and ships.

"Piloting systems check out," Carlo said.

"Course to our long-range tanks is locked in," Tycho said, wincing as Huff leaned forward from beside the ladderwell to tousle his hair too roughly.

"Got it," Carlo said. "We're ready to roll, Captain."

"Tycho, raise traffic control and get us a departure slot," Diocletia said.

"Aye-aye," Tycho said. "Cybelean Traffic Control, this is the *Shadow Comet* in Berth 33A, operating under Jovian flag. Requesting immediate clearance for departure on vector twenty-six-niner."

"Stand by, *Comet*," a controller replied, her voice tinny and modulated.

A tense silence hung over the quarterdeck, and Tycho found himself mourning that the family ship had become an unhappy one. Was that his brother's fault, or his? Or was it bigger than either of them—a consequence of everything at stake here at Cybele?

"Come on, let's get out of here already," Yana grumbled from her seat.

"Hold for departure, *Comet*—we're prioritizing a launch from the surface."

An annoyed Tycho could only sigh. "Acknowledged."

"What the heck?" Yana asked. "Who's cutting the line?"

"Someone willing to pay a premium for a dirtside berth," Mavry said. "Unless we're planning to shoot up the tower, we just have to wait."

"Arrr, is there anything I hate more'n console jockeys an' their shenanigans?" Huff growled.

"Since being named to the bridge crew of this starship on September 17, 2838, you have identified seventy-four individuals, collective entities, situations, or abstract concepts you purport to hate more than any other items that could be assigned to those categories," Vesuvia announced.

"An' how many times have I asked for yer opinion, yeh presumptuous blabbermouth stenographer?"

"All right, that's enough," Diocletia said. "It's another minute or two in a docking cradle—I don't think it will kill us."

"Whoever's cutting the line, they're taking off," Yana said. "And it looks like their vector will take them right past us."

A moment later, a sleek winged craft about the same length as the *Comet* rose smoothly into space in front of them, the light of the distant sun flashing off her chrome engine baffles.

"Ain't that an elegant little firecracker," Huff muttered. "Catamount-class, wouldn't yeh say, Mavry?"

"Looks like it. I believe that's the *Gracieux*."

"It is the *Gracieux*," Tycho said. "And she's hailing us."

"Patch it through," Diocletia said.

"Good morning, Captain Hashoone," Captain Allamand said. "Apologies for burdening you—we had to extend our launch window to receive new orders. Good hunting, my friends."

Diocletia maintained a stony silence as the *Gracieux*'s maneuvering engines ignited. She waggled her graceful wings as she accelerated away from them.

"Arrr, that ship would look a lot better with a few holes in her," Huff said.

The search was fruitless, leaving the Hashoones silent during the trip back down to Cybele in the gig and during the long walk back from the landing field. At the center of the Well, a glum Diocletia headed right, due for a briefing at the consulate, while the rest of her family turned left toward the Jovian fondaco.

When Mavry summoned them for dinner, Tycho emerged from his room and nearly bumped into his sister, who was sweaty from another unarmed-combat sim. Yana was breathing hard, but she was smiling too.

"Hot date tonight?" Tycho asked quietly.

Yana aimed a sidelong glance at their family assembling in the kitchen, but Huff was loudly explaining some strategy for boarding actions. A cruiser could have plowed into the fondaco without attracting attention.

"Just got the message," Yana said. "We're meeting right after dinner. And you? You look a lot happier than you did on the *Comet*."

"Same plan," Tycho said. Kate had messaged him to say that the formal dinner she'd feared would never end was, in fact, breaking up.

"Good for you," Yana said. "Now all you have to do is get through half an hour without killing Carlo."

Tycho glared at his sister, but she just fluttered her eyelashes.

As they were passing the trays of vat-grown meat, Diocletia returned and sank heavily into her chair.

"So what news from the powers that be?" Mavry asked with a brave attempt at cheer.

"It's pretty much all bad," Diocletia said, picking at her food.

"Out with it, Dio," Huff said. "Bad news don't improve with age."

"Let's see. Wages for shipbuilding workers have dropped by two-thirds since yesterday. How's that for starters?"

"Meaning that Earth ship's finished and ready to fly?" Carlo asked.

"Sounds like it. Except there's still no indication that

the life-support systems have been installed. Presumably you'd need workers for that. So go figure."

"That's another sign Tyke was right and they stripped those systems from a seized ship," Yana said.

"Which implies the *Leviathan*'s at the shipyard," Tycho said. "Find one and you'll find the other."

"Or, as has been the case so far, you'll find neither," Diocletia said. "Point is, we're out of time, or very close to it."

"I hate to bring this up, but did you say 'for starters'?" Mavry asked.

"I did," Diocletia said. "The Widderiches and Dmitra chased down what they thought was a convoy of Earth ore boats."

"Uh-oh," Tycho said.

"Uh-oh is right. It was a Cybelean convoy. They seized two of them and demanded ransoms for crew and cargo."

"It's not like the Union couldn't have seen that coming," Carlo said. "Sleep with snakes and eventually you get bit."

"We should all remember that," Tycho said, glaring at his brother.

"Arrr, serves them Cybelean swine right," Huff growled. "How much ransom did our guys get?"

"That's not the important part, Dad," Diocletia said.

Huff shrugged, his forearm cannon whining. "I'm interested is all."

"What interests me is who compensated the ore boats' owner. It was Captain Allamand—as a gesture of friendship and solidarity from the people of Earth."

Leaving the Southwell, a troubled Tycho turned up the furred collar of his jacket against the inescapable chill of Cybele. He pushed his way through the Well's usual evening crowds, then waited irritably as the constables at the entrance to the Northwell verified that he had a legitimate reason for being there.

His footsteps slowed as he caught sight of the gilded gates of Earth's fondaco and the holographic blue and red flag of Imperial Earth flying above them.

"Tycho!" Kate called, and he smiled when he saw her waiting just inside the gates, face framed by a halo of synthetic fur.

The gates opened and she hurried past the Cybelean guards, turning her face up to kiss him.

"Oh, your hands are freezing," she complained.

"Where do you want to go tonight?" he asked. "What deserted corner of this frozen rock shall we investigate?"

"I've got a better idea," Kate said, taking his hand and tugging him along. "Come on!"

She led him back to the center of the Well but then turned left, toward the long corridor that led to the landing field.

"Where are we going?" he asked, puzzled.

"You'll see," she said as they passed sign walkers pacing back and forth beneath their holographic ads and a morose gaggle of rickshaw drivers waiting for fares.

A gang of freight haulers walking down the seemingly endless tunnel looked at them curiously, surprised to see a beautiful girl in luxurious furs coming toward them with a young spacer in tow. Kate didn't break stride, and the freight haulers stepped to either side of the corridor, peering after her and Tycho before re-forming their ranks.

"Kate, wait—there's nothing down here. Just berths and customs offices and waiting areas for ferries."

"Would you please trust me, Herschel Tycho Hashoone?" she asked, eyes merry.

They reached the customs station, and Kate showed the two Cybelean officials her mediapad. They scanned it, then looked questioningly at Tycho.

"My guest," she said.

The officials looked at each other. Then one of them shrugged.

"Berth 12, ma'am."

"Come on," Kate said.

"Your father's ship? Really?"

"Really." She stuck out her lower lip theatrically. "Unless you don't want to come."

"I'm just worried you'll get in trouble."

"I can take care of myself, Tycho. I'm tired of ministers' lectures. Like I told them, I'll spend time with who I want and I'll go where I want. Which right now means spending time with you, in my room aboard the *Gracieux*. Don't get any crazy ideas, but this way we get to be alone—and without risking hypothermia."

Through the curved glass wall of the docking terminal Tycho could see starships sitting on the landing field, connected to the terminal by umbilicals. The *Comet*'s gig was just a few hundred yards past Berth 12, blocked from his sight by a bulky galleon.

Tycho found himself holding his breath as they reached the end of the umbilical, and he followed Kate up the gangplank. Belowdecks, the *Gracieux* was spotless dark steel and carbon fiber, silent except for the faint throb of air circulators. The *Comet*'s corridors were stained and pocked by centuries' worth of abuse, and smelled of sweat, oil, and cheroot smoke. The air in the *Gracieux* held only the faintest whiff of cleanser. Captain Allamand's frigate was far less claustrophobic than the *Shadow Comet*, and she looked like she'd just emerged from the docking cradle where she'd been built.

"Come upstairs," Kate said, then paused. "Oh. I should have known. You'll want to look around, of course."

"Maybe just for a moment," Tycho said. He headed toward the bow, his heels ringing on the decking. Above, hammocks were stowed in perfect lines. Eight bells rang out, the tone bright and clear. The gunports were pristine, down to the neatly coiled cables and gleaming pistons of the cannon housings.

He eyed the cannons unhappily. Those weapons had been aimed at Jovian starships, and the projectiles they'd hurled had killed Jovian crewers. And it seemed likely they would do so again.

He imagined looking up from Port Town and seeing the sleek shape of the *Gracieux* overhead, part of an occupation force. Not so long ago, he would have dismissed the idea as a paranoid fantasy. But now it seemed horribly possible. Earth could turn out dozens of frigates like this each month, if it had to—not to mention warships that would dwarf the *Gracieux* in both size and destructive capabilities.

"Are you all right?" Kate asked when he returned from his quick inspection.

"She's very . . . impressive," Tycho said, trying to keep his voice light and unconcerned. "A beautiful ship."

"She should be—the crew does enough work on her. I just wish it wasn't so cramped in here. Come on."

He climbed up the ladderwell after her and emerged on the spacious quarterdeck, gaping at the bridge crew's wide, comfortable chairs. He ran his hand over the tawny tops of the consoles. They were wood, set in gleaming black metal.

"It can't be that different from your family's ship," Kate said, noticing his dumbfounded look.

"Well, the layout of the quarterdeck is more or less the same."

"And my room is down here, toward whatever it is you call the back of the ship."

Tycho grinned. "Your cabin, Miss Allamand, is located aft, near the stern."

He followed her down the passageway, passing a compact, spotless galley and the door to the head. Kate's cabin was small, but as comfortable and well constructed as the rest of the *Gracieux*, with a desk running from bulkhead to bulkhead, opposite a berth. Between the two, cabinets were built into the starboard beam.

Tycho took off his jacket and sat in the chair, while Kate tossed her furs onto the berth. He peered at the ceiling, then smiled.

"What is it?" she asked, trying to see what he was looking at.

"It's silly. The ceiling of my cabin is covered with people's initials."

"It is? Why?"

"Family tradition. Everyone who occupies a berth leaves his or her initials on the ceiling. They go back centuries—there are dozens of them."

Kate considered that. "On my father's ship, I think someone would show up with a can of paint before you finished writing."

"I'm sure you're right."

"Anyway, this is where I spent most of the journey here from Earth, doing homework or practicing. It was crazy—our warrant officer had to disable the security on my console so I could play the viola. Something about the music simulator not working properly with the security settings."

Kate settled herself on Tycho's lap, then reached past him to the computer console set into her desk. Tycho jumped a little as a hologram shimmered to life around them. A man and a woman in formal clothes sat to their right, holding violins and bows. Tycho turned and saw a man with a larger stringed instrument sitting to his left. He heard the sound of tapping, and the three players around them nodded to each other. The violinists tucked their instruments under their chins, and all three musicians brought their bows up. They drew the bows across their instruments' strings, then immediately stopped, faces turning to Kate and Tycho.

"When I was little I wouldn't play because I thought it was more fun to make them stop and wait for me," Kate said with a smile.

As he moved to kiss her, the first violinist looked at him disapprovingly over Kate's shoulder.

"Um, could we turn them off?" he asked.

Kate cocked her head at him, puzzled, then laughed.

"You know they're not real, right? Just checking."

"I know it's crazy, but they're making me self-conscious."

Kate laughed again, delighted, then gave him an apologetic kiss and got to her feet.

"I need a few minutes to freshen up," she said. "And I was thinking of making some tea. Do you want some?"

"That would be great," he said, eager to chase some of the Cybelean cold out of his bones.

"I'll be back. You and my musicians can make friends while I'm gone."

And with a parting smile she was gone, the door shutting behind her. The musicians had lowered their hands and were waiting. Whenever Tycho shifted in the chair, they turned to see if he was ready to play yet. He knew the responses were programmed, a simulation of life, but the illusion was eerily convincing.

He swiveled idly in Kate's chair, the sumptuous leather beneath him creaking faintly as he turned his back on the musicians. The computer console was a state-of-the-art model. Tycho's knee bumped the desk and the touch screen lit up, open to a data stack labeled "Homework." Behind it, other stacks were grayed out.

Tycho looked from the screen to the door, then back. Thoughts chased themselves in his head. The *Comet* pursuing the *Gracieux*, bearing away from the Jovian convoy and into disaster. The blazing engines of the *Nestor Leviathan* shrinking as her captors bore her off. Vass staring up at the bulk of Attis, warning about an Earth shipyard and military base on Jupiter's doorstep.

He got up from the chair, walked through a perturbed-looking violinist, and opened the door, leaning out into the passageway.

"Kate?"

There was no answer. He shut the door, politely stepping around the holographic musicians, and sat down again.

He imagined the *Leviathan* being reduced to a metal skeleton by a swarm of spacesuited workers. In his vision another ship sat nearby—a military vessel, with workers shuttling parts from one to the other. He thought about the dry docks of Earth, suspended in space above an impossibly blue world, their questing metal arms cradling warship after warship, all nearing completion.

Tycho extended a finger toward the monitor. He closed the data stack holding Kate's homework. The stack on the top left of the screen said Flight Operations.

He hesitated, then reached for it.

It'll be locked. Please please please let it be locked.

It opened.

The screen now displayed rows of substacks within Flight Operations. He found Flight Logs in the third row.

Tycho tapped Flight Logs, and there were Captain Allamand's files, organized by month. He opened this month's file and saw a long list of navigational entries—an exact record of everywhere the *Gracieux* had traveled, when, and for how long.

"Tycho?" Kate called, making him jump. "Do you want milk?"

"Yes please," he said, reaching forward to close the flight log, to navigate back to her homework stack.

"It's coming up. I'll need a minute—I can never find where our cook keeps things."

Tycho reached into his jacket pocket and pulled out his mediapad. He tapped the connect icon, telling it to look for nearby computers it could exchange information with. He hoped it wouldn't find any, while knowing that it would.

His mediapad beeped, confirming it was connected. Tycho leaned forward and tapped the last two months' flight logs, selected the Copy command, set his mediapad as the destination, then confirmed the command.

Copying records: two minutes remaining, the screen read.

Tycho closed the flight logs, then backed out of Flight Logs and then Flight Operations. He tapped on Homework, shut off the touch screen, and slipped his mediapad back in his pocket.

The cellist seemed to stare reproachfully at him.

The door opened. Kate handed him a cup of tea. It was hot and he drew his hand hastily away, sloshing tea onto his pants and the leather cushion on the seat.

"Oh!" Tycho said. "Sorry!"

"Did you burn yourself?"

"No, I'm fine. But the chair . . . I'm really sorry."

"Tycho, it's a *chair*—don't worry about it," Kate said with a smile. "I'll just get a towel."

She returned and sipped her tea while he dabbed grimly at the spilled tea, unable to meet her eyes.

His mediapad beeped and he almost spilled the tea again. The file transfer was complete.

"What was that?" Kate asked.

"Incoming message or something. Probably just junk."

"Good," Kate said, settling back on his lap and leaning forward. Her lips tasted sweet from the sugar in the tea.

His mediapad beeped again—and kept beeping, filling the cabin with long trills of sound. The holographic musicians looked over questioningly.

"Oh, why don't you smash that stupid machine?"

"I can't—that's an immediate recall order," Tycho said dismally. "From my captain. I have to go."

"No," Kate said, burying her head in his shoulder. "Oh, Tycho. Please no."

"I'm really sorry," he said, gently moving her off his lap and getting to his feet, reaching for his jacket. "It's . . . it's my duty."

22

THE BLACK SHIP

Tycho was the first member of his family to arrive at the gate reserved for the *Comet*'s gig. Through the thick glass he could see the gig sitting on the landing field, and workers in spacesuits dragging a flexible umbilical corridor over to its stern.

He pulled out his mediapad and called up the files he'd copied aboard the *Gracieux*. Part of him hoped they'd been secured by some code that hadn't been apparent back in Kate's cabin—perhaps they could only be read within a few meters of a specific location, for instance.

But the flight logs opened immediately. Tycho scanned the list of coordinates the *Gracieux* had visited in the last month, looking for an entry that showed up multiple times. But there wasn't one. He frowned, then realized he'd neglected to account for orbital mechanics— like every other celestial body, 65 Cybele was in constant motion, slingshotted around the distant sun by gravity.

He scrolled to the bottom of the list and saw that the last entry had been time-stamped just a few hours ago. Those coordinates had to be 65 Cybele. But he couldn't make sense of the rest—there were too many numbers and he was too agitated to detect any patterns. He'd have to wait until he could take advantage of Vesuvia's computing power.

"Hey, look who's the first one here," his father called out as he arrived with Diocletia and Carlo. "Guess Tycho gets to ride up front."

Mavry was grinning, but Diocletia and Carlo looked anxious. Tycho wondered where his sister and grandfather were.

He nodded hello, then looked back down at his mediapad and the list of coordinates, trying to will some insight into being. Would the *Gracieux* have made multiple visits to wherever the *Leviathan* was stashed? Just one? Or none at all?

"So what's the mission?" he asked his father.

Mavry shook his head, looking around the terminal suspiciously. "Not here. Let's get into space."

He glanced at Tycho's mediapad. "Crunching numbers, kid?"

Now it was Tycho's turn to shake his head—and look sidelong at Carlo.

"More intel from our friendly neighborhood sign walkers?" Tycho asked his brother.

Diocletia raised a finger in warning. "Belay that. Like your father said, let's get into space."

Carlo gave Tycho a murderous glance and headed down the now-inflated umbilical to warm up the gig's engines.

By the time Yana and Huff appeared at the end of the corridor, Tycho was grimly certain that Carlo had been given another gift by the Securitat. What else could have inspired his mother to order a return to space just hours after they'd landed? He scanned the list of coordinates again, hoping something would match the various courses he'd set for the *Comet* recently and only half remembered.

"We're coming, we're coming," Yana said, seeing that her mother had her hands on her hips.

"Arrr, these legs are built for endurance, not speed," Huff complained, wiping sweat from the living half of his face.

The Hashoones strode down the umbilical to the gig, then up the gangplank. Carlo was already buckled into the pilot's seat, prepping for takeoff. The interior of the little ship seemed nearly as cold as space; breath wreathed the Hashoones' faces, and Yana's teeth chattered.

"Why do you always forget to turn on the heat?" she demanded as the whine of the gig's engines rose in pitch.

"You'll live," Carlo said. "We'll be on the quarterdeck in three minutes."

"Unless Captain Allamand has an errand he wants to run," Mavry said.

The gig's gangway clanked shut behind them.

"I want the *Comet* flying as soon as we're crewed," Diocletia said. "No grace period for stragglers. Tycho, are you planning to strap yourself in?"

"Right. Sorry."

He tucked his mediapad under his leg and buckled his harness, then looked around at his family. In a couple of minutes the *Comet* would be preparing for flight, with everyone's attention focused on whatever Carlo had discovered. The time to speak up was now.

He took a deep breath.

"I have the *Gracieux*'s flight logs."

Everyone—even Carlo—turned to look at him.

"*What* did you say?" Diocletia asked.

"I said I have Captain Allamand's flight logs. I copied them to my mediapad. There's a record of everywhere he's been in the last two months. That should show us where the shipyard is. Probably the *Leviathan* too."

Nobody said anything. Then Huff began to laugh.

"Arrrr, the biggest scoundrels are always the ones yeh had pegged as honest," he purred, reaching back to give Tycho a bone-jarring clap on the shoulder.

"And how exactly did you come by this information?" Diocletia asked.

"Well," Tycho said, then paused. His vocal cords seemed to have stopped working.

"I can't wait to hear this," Mavry said.

"Um, so . . . I've been, well, I guess the word would be *dating* Captain Allamand's daughter. Only we had nowhere to go after they said I wasn't allowed in Earth's fondaco anymore, and everywhere else on Cybele was freezing, so Kate invited me aboard the *Gracieux*—we just wanted a little privacy—and there was no security on the console in her cabin. So while she was making tea, I looked through the files and there were the flight logs."

Everybody just kept looking at him for a moment.

"We're talking about Captain *Allamand*'s daughter," Diocletia said. "The commander of Earth's privateers."

Tycho just nodded.

"And you got the logs from the computer aboard his ship."

Another nod.

"Oh boy," Yana said, as Huff began to laugh again.

"Well, you've certainly been busy," Mavry said, shaking his head. "I hate to tell you this, Tycho, but we already know the location of the shipyard—the Defense Force found it. That's where we're headed, along with four other privateers. I just hope we're in time."

His father said something meant to console him,

about how he was certain the information would still be valuable. But Tycho barely heard him. He had betrayed Kate's trust for nothing.

While Carlo and Yana read in the crewers belowdecks, Tycho plotted a course to the coordinates the Defense Force had given them. He nodded when his father reminded him to prioritize speed over fuel efficiency. Vesuvia double-checked his calculations. And then he had nothing to do but stare at his computer screen.

He wondered what Kate was doing. Was she still in her cabin—maybe doing homework? Had she returned to Earth's fondaco? And was there any way she'd discover what he'd done?

"Tycho?" Diocletia asked. "Is our course locked in?"

Tycho looked up guiltily. "Plotted and verified."

"And have you set up communications links with the list of Jovian ships I gave you?"

He nodded. "I was going to go through the *Gracieux*'s logs and see if anything stands out."

"You'll have to make it quick. This is a dangerous mission, Tycho—we all need to be focused."

She turned back to her own console, and Tycho activated his headset and selected the channel reserved for one-on-one communications with Vesuvia.

"Vesuvia, I'm uploading two files to you. I need you to plot the coordinates in them against the orbits of charted celestial bodies. Ninety-five percent confidence interval."

"Acknowledged. Beginning calculations. Shall I plot the positions on the main screen?"

"My console will be fine."

His monitor filled with a spaghetti of lines plotted against a map of the solar system. A sequence of straight lines led into the tangle from the inner solar system, while a loop headed out toward Jupiter. Tycho saw immediately that the initial sequence of lines represented the *Gracieux*'s trip from Earth to Cybele, with a refueling stop at Vesta, while the loop marked the trip on which Captain Allamand had rescued the cargo hauler taken by the Hashoones as a prize.

He zoomed in on the tangle of smaller lines and found a flurry of trips that began and ended at 65 Cybele, each position slightly different as the asteroid followed its clockwork path around the sun. He knew that a graph of the *Comet*'s recent journeys would look much the same.

"Vesuvia, exclude everything more than a week before the intercept of the *Nestor Leviathan*. Then zoom in on what's left."

"Do you want me to delete those coordinates from memory?" Vesuvia asked as the bells clang-clanged—it was 2100.

"No, don't do that," Tycho said, rolling his eyes. "Just take them off the screen."

"Greater specificity in formulating requests would make this process more efficient," the AI replied.

Tycho ignored that, peering at the screen. His eyes jumped to 65 Cybele, surrounded by loops of various lengths. The results looked vaguely like a child's drawing of a flower.

"Now, highlight the coordinates where the *Leviathan* was intercepted."

"Acknowledged."

Boots rang out on the ladderwell, and Carlo climbed up to the quarterdeck.

"Eight stragglers, Captain," he said. "Do you want to give them more time?"

Tycho stared at the blinking cross on his screen where the Jovian convoy had been disrupted.

"No," Diocletia said. "It's time to fly. My starship."

"Aye-aye," Carlo said, heading for his own chair. Yana's head appeared in the ladderwell.

"Show me any coordinates from the twenty-four hours after the intercept," Tycho told Vesuvia, then glanced at Yana. "What's wrong?"

Yana aimed a furtive glance at Diocletia.

"It's Immanuel," she said in a low voice. "He didn't report."

"Him and seven others," Tycho said, glancing from his sister back to the screen. "Crewers are late sometimes."

"We were together when the recall order came," Yana said. "He said he had to run back to his quarters to get his gear. He should have only been a couple of minutes behind me. What if the crimps got him?"

"Worry about the crimps, then. Mr. Sier can take care of himself."

He wanted to say something more to reassure his sister, but there simply wasn't time.

"Yana, I need you up on sensors," Diocletia said, and Yana spun away from Tycho in agitation, flinging herself into her own seat.

Tycho looked at his monitor. Two hours after the intercept of the *Nestor Leviathan*, the *Gracieux* had intersected the orbit of an asteroid whose sole designation was 124996.

"Vesuvia, show me every time the *Gracieux* intersected the orbit of 124996," Tycho said.

The Earth frigate had been there three times—its most recent visit coming four days ago.

"Highlight 124996's current position, and also plot our course to the shipyard," Tycho said. He leaned forward, eyes fixed on the mysterious asteroid's location, expecting to see their current course end at the same point.

"Vesuvia?" he asked after a moment. "I asked you to plot our course—"

"The requested course has been plotted," Vesuvia said.

Diocletia turned in the captain's chair. "Tycho, contact traffic control—we need clearance for departure."

"Will do, Captain," Tycho said automatically, turning back to his console. "Vesuvia, zoom out on that view."

"Do you think I mean next Thursday, Tycho?" Diocletia snapped. "Do it *now*."

Now he could see their current course. And its end-point—the site identified as the shipyard by the Jovian Defense Force—was nowhere near 124996.

"But Mom—" Tycho began.

"But Mom what?" Diocletia demanded.

"I plotted the course data from the *Gracieux*. She's never been to the site the Defense Force thinks is the shipyard."

"We don't have time for this, Tycho. We'll assess the information you found later, but right now we have a mission. And that means I need you to follow orders."

"Aye-aye," Tycho said reluctantly. He erased the tangle of courses and orbits from his monitor and hailed traffic control. A few minutes later, the *Comet* accelerated away from 65 Cybele and Attis in a graceful arc, attached to her long-range tanks with a shiver, and raced toward her target.

Flight time was less than half an hour; given the tension on the quarterdeck, Tycho decided not to revisit the puzzle of the *Gracieux*'s course data. The *Comet* and four other privateers—Garibalda Marta Andrade's *Izabella*, Morgan Theo's *Berserker*, Dmitra Barnacus's *Banshee*, and Zhi Ning's *Jin Chan*—converged and hurtled toward an oblong asteroid named Zephaniah.

"Why'd Captain Andrade bring two pirates?" Carlo asked disgustedly.

"She needed crews that could fly immediately," Diocletia said. "This is who was available."

"The *Izabella*'s hailing all Jovian craft," Tycho said, his ears catching the familiar hammer blows of Huff descending from the top deck. He put Captain Andrade on the main screen. The veteran privateer looked weary and grave.

"Captains, form up your craft and display colors," she said. "Our orders are to reconnoiter the shipyard and keep whatever's inside bottled up until the JDF issues further instructions. We're here to buy time and hopefully get control of the situation—not start a war."

"Arr, that last one's easier said than done sometimes," Huff growled.

"Detach tanks and take us in, Carlo," Diocletia said. "Yana, eyes peeled for ion emissions. Tycho, ears open—the shipyard will undoubtedly call for help when they see us coming."

All three Hashoone siblings acknowledged their mother's order. Diocletia leaned forward, eyes fixed on the darkness of space ahead.

A clank sounded above them, followed by a bump and a shudder.

"And we're detached," Carlo said, his voice cool and even despite the sudden acceleration shoving all of them back in their chairs.

"Mr. Grigsby, we are inbound and hot," Diocletia said. "Stand by."

"The lads are ready, Captain."

Four bells rang out.

"Initial scans of Zephaniah show a typical rock," Yana said. "Iron-nickel, too low-grade to mine. Trace ion signatures, but at this level it could just indicate local ship traffic—there's a secondary spacelane a few hundred thousand klicks to starboard."

Tycho's palms were sweating. He wiped them on his pants, scanning communications frequencies for any hint of a distress call emanating from the asteroid ahead of them.

Huff saw his grandson's nervousness and chuckled.

"Arrr, yeh never feel more alive than during moments like this. Rest of life, lad, is waitin' for the next such moment to come around."

"Silence on deck," Diocletia barked. "Vesuvia, tactical readout on the main screen."

"Acknowledged."

The Jovian craft advanced in a wedge, with the *Izabella* in the lead, flanked by the *Comet* to port and the *Berserker* to starboard, with the *Banshee* and the *Jin Chan* completing the formation.

"I've got a transmission," Tycho said. "Origin point is Zephaniah. Looks like an encrypted tight-beam transmission back in the direction of Cybele."

"Our Earth friends are calling for help," Mavry said.

"And I'm reading an energy source on the asteroid," Yana said. "Make that multiple sources. Pretty high power levels."

"If there are defenders down there, this is when

they'll show themselves," Mavry warned.

"*Comet*, I need eyes down there," Captain Andrade said. "I want you and the *Jin Chan* to make a pass around the asteroid."

Diocletia acknowledged the order and nodded to Carlo. The *Comet* dipped her nose and passed beneath the *Izabella*'s belly, taking up a position perhaps a kilometer from the portside cannons on the boxy *Jin Chan*.

"You lead, *Comet*," said Zhi Ning over their shared channel. "I will cover you."

Carlo goosed the frigate's engines, taking the ship down to within a few hundred meters of Zephaniah's mottled gray surface.

"Sensor contacts!" Yana yelped. "Multiple ships, inbound from Cybele!"

Tycho's eyes shot to the main screen, where several arrowhead symbols had appeared on the edge of the readout.

"Morgan, Dmitra, on me—defensive formation," Captain Andrade said calmly. "Diocletia and Ning, continue your run."

"Anything on transponders?" Diocletia asked. "Whose ships are those?"

"They're flying black," Tycho said.

"Sensors paint five ships—they're a mix of frigates and corvettes," Yana said. "Querying registration database for matches with known craft."

"Sing out when you have something," Diocletia said. "And keep your heads, everybody. We don't know what we're dealing with here. Let's figure it out before we do something rash."

The *Comet* was approaching one knobby end of bulbous Zephaniah, the surface of the asteroid bright against the spangled stars.

"Energy spike!" Yana yelled. "From the asteroid! It's big!"

"Look at that," Mavry said wonderingly.

The end of the asteroid had split open along a hidden seam, tons of rock sliding away from each other along cleverly concealed tracks. Carlo cut the *Comet*'s speed and hit her retro rockets, slowing the frigate and retreating stern-first as the opening at the tip of Zephaniah widened.

A matte black shape like a giant hammer emerged from the confines of the asteroid. Tycho watched in disbelief as meters of metal were revealed, his eyes jumping from the spines of sensor masts to the bumps of gunnery stations set along the hull. The ship moved slowly and steadily out of the secret hangar that had concealed it. The rear segment of her hull finally emerged, a cluster of cylindrical engines crisscrossed with power conduits. Then finally she was free of the asteroid, hanging in space in front of the *Comet* and moving slowly away from her.

"That is one mean-lookin' ship," Huff said with grudging admiration.

"Captain Andrade?" Diocletia said. "I'd estimate that's a heavy cruiser at least, maybe a battleship. Massive armament. Yana, scan everything. Carlo, hold here."

The warship in front of them seemed to shiver, and then her quintet of massive engines ignited. Tycho could hear the Comets belowdecks exclaiming and shouting, followed by Grigsby's bellows for silence and accompanying threats of medieval punishments.

Carlo turned the Comet to port and accelerated to keep pace with the huge black ship. Yana was glowering at her instruments.

"This doesn't make any sense," she said. "The weapons systems and propulsion are powered, but I only get trace readings from the other systems."

"Life support?" Mavry asked.

"She's cold as space."

"Maybe construction isn't complete," Diocletia said. "The crew could be in spacesuits. Tycho, any communications from her?"

"None. And transponders are black."

"If that thing isn't finished, I don't want to see the final product," Mavry said.

"I'm going in for a closer look," Carlo said, angling the Comet toward the massive ship's stern.

"Missile lock," Vesuvia warned.

Carlo hastily cut to port. Tycho braced himself for the sight of missiles streaking in their direction, but the massive ship held her fire.

"She's hailing," Tycho said. "All channels."

An eerie whine filled the quarterdeck as he patched

the transmission through.

"Keep your distance or die," said a male voice that made the hairs stand up on Tycho's neck. It was electronically modulated, but beneath that it sounded low and ragged, like speaking hurt the speaker's throat. And Tycho could hear something else that he couldn't quite place—a faint rumble or gurgle.

"What was *that*?" Yana asked.

"Mr. Grigsby, hold your fire," Diocletia said. "Carlo, keep your distance."

"Transponders activating," Vesuvia said. "Saturnian colors."

The massive black ship continued to accelerate away from them. While they watched her shrink into the distance, a frigate and two corvettes shot past the *Comet*, the last one waggling its wings. All were flying Saturnian colors as well.

"It wasn't Earth's shipyard at all," Tycho said. "It was the Ice Wolves'."

"But where did they get the livres?" Carlo asked.

"Titan, I'll bet you," Mavry said. "All that missing money wound up here."

They stared at the warship's blazing engines for a moment.

"What are we doing?" Yana demanded. "We can still intercept her!"

"That monster would blast us to scrap 'fore we could so much as dent her hull," Huff said.

"Dad's right," Diocletia said. "Our duty is to get back to the JDF with whatever information we can give them."

The bells clanged out five times.

"She's reached her long-range tanks," Yana said. "Heading for the outer solar system."

"Something tells me we'll see her again," Carlo said.

Mavry nodded. "No doubt. Funny—we fought with Earth, and the Ice Wolves won."

"Which means we both lost," Carlo said.

"How did Earth lose?" Yana asked. "They still have the *Leviathan*."

"Perhaps we can change that," Mavry said. "I seem to recall that someone on this quarterdeck has the *Gracieux*'s logs."

Tycho hung his head. For a moment he'd imagined that with the hunt for the shipyard over, no one aboard the *Comet* would see the need to dig into Allamand's flight logs. And he'd been fine with letting Earth keep the *Leviathan* if that would prevent his snooping from being discovered.

But there was no point delaying the inevitable. He switched back to the map of the *Gracieux*'s comings and goings and tapped his finger on the asteroid designated 124996.

"Vesuvia, put this on the main screen," he said. "This has to be Captain Allamand's hiding place. The *Gracieux* went there right after the taking of the *Leviathan*, and she's been back twice since then."

Diocletia studied the loops and lines for a moment,

fingers drumming on her console.

"Plot a course, Tycho. And share it with Captain Andrade. We missed our chance to stop the Ice Wolves, but maybe it's not too late to retake the *Leviathan*."

23

ASTEROID RAID

With a new objective identified, Diocletia was quick to hand out duties. While Tycho plotted a course to 124996, Yana researched the *Leviathan*'s likely deck plan and Grigsby began assembling boarding parties belowdecks. Meanwhile, Captain Andrade sent out a call for any other available Jovian privateers to head for the asteroid.

"Every ship in port will know something's up," Mavry said.

"It can't be helped—we'll just have to hurry," Diocletia said, activating her headset. "Mr. Grigsby? Please
report to the quarterdeck. And bring Mr. Dobbs with
you."

Tycho needed the fingers of only one hand to count
the number of times someone from belowdecks had
walked the *Comet*'s quarterdeck, but Grigsby expressed
no surprise at the order. Moments later, he ascended
the ladderwell with Dobbs right behind him. Unlike the
tough old warrant officer, the pale master-at-arms was
visibly uncomfortable at finding himself in forbidden
territory.

"Good evening, gentlemen," Diocletia said. "We're
twenty minutes away from Tycho's asteroid, so let's go
over the plan. Vesuvia, put the schematic of the *Leviathan*
on the main screen."

"Acknowledged," Vesuvia said, and all on the quarterdeck peered at the deck plan.

"I want two boarding parties—one to take the bridge,
the other to secure the engine room. I'll lead the bridge
party—Carlo, Tycho, and Yana, you'll be with me. I'd
like you along as well, Mr. Dobbs, with five crewers of
your choosing."

Tycho and Yana glanced at each other in surprise—
during a boarding action their mother normally remained
on the quarterdeck, and often kept Yana back as well to
watch the sensors.

Diocletia saw the look and knew what it meant.

"The other privateers will be our eyes and ears,"

she explained. "The key is to get the *Leviathan* flying as quickly as we can, so Captain Allamand thinks twice about risking another fight over her. Dad and Mr. Grigsby will take the engine room with eight crewers as backup. We take control of the bridge, get the engines online, and fly her at maximum speed to Cybele. Earth won't fight to take her back so close to there, not with everyone watching."

"Will two teams of ten be enough, Captain?" Grigsby asked. "That's a big ship."

"I suspect Allamand will have only a skeleton crew aboard. Recall that he gave all the Leviathans parole, and he doesn't have enough crewers to have replaced them. And if we're wrong, we fall back to the *Comet*, disengage, and decide things in space."

"What about other Earth ships defending the site?" Yana asked.

"Doubt we'll find any. With all the sweeps we've done in that area, one of our privateers would have turned up ion trails."

"Tycho's asteroid is too small to hold both the *Leviathan* and her long-range tanks," Carlo said.

Diocletia nodded. "They probably ditched them for retrieval later. Still, the *Leviathan* should have enough fuel in her maneuvering tanks for a straight shot to Cybele. After that, refueling her will be her owners' problem. For now, Carlo, make sure you simulate piloting a dromond—the *Leviathan* won't maneuver like a frigate, to say the least."

Tycho looked around the quarterdeck. Mavry was smiling as if they were on a pleasure excursion, but Tycho knew he was examining various scenarios in his head, sorting through what was of concern and what wasn't. Carlo was already browsing through Vesuvia's library of flight sims, Yana was leaning forward in her harness, and Huff was grinning at some private thought, his forearm cannon jerking eagerly.

"I want all boarders in spacesuits in case Allamand's people have purged the dromond's atmosphere—or decide to do so as a defense," Diocletia said. "The key is to hit them hard and fast. Got it? Good. We've all got jobs to do, so let's get to them."

The asteroid designated 124996 looked like any other chunk of rock until the *Comet* closed to within two kilometers and Yana detected energy readings. Closer inspection revealed that the asteroid was little more than a shell—thin layers of rock separated by a grid of metal, with a large opening at one end.

"Definitely reading a second mass within the asteroid—and chemical signature indicates it's artificial," Yana said. Like Carlo, Tycho, and Diocletia, she was wearing a bulky spacesuit that her harness could barely contain, with her visor raised and gloves off. Huff was in the gig with Grigsby and the rest of the first boarding party, waiting for the order to detach.

"Garibalda, we're going in," Diocletia said over her headset.

"We'll let you know if anyone's coming," Andrade replied. "Good luck, *Comet*."

The *Comet* left the other privateers behind and swept down toward the asteroid. Carlo cut the frigate's forward momentum, tapped her retro rockets, and eased the *Comet* into the shadowy confines of the asteroid.

"Vesuvia, bring up the bow lights," he said.

Ahead, they could see a trio of engines in the gloom, looming like massive mouths.

Yana whistled. "Definitely the *Leviathan*. Nothing else out here would have that engine configuration."

"This rock has only one entrance, right?" Tycho asked.

"Afraid so," Carlo said, scowling. "We'll have to back her out."

"Can you do it?" Diocletia asked. The question wasn't a challenge or a taunt, but a captain's need to know.

"I'm not looking forward to it, but I think so. I don't suppose Captain Andrade could blast off the other end?"

"As long as you don't mind the roof falling on us," Mavry said. He was the only one on the quarterdeck still wearing his usual shipboard jumpsuit—he'd be responsible for flying the *Comet* out of the asteroid ahead of the *Leviathan*.

"I'm against that," Carlo said.

The massive dromond was shrouded in darkness—even her running lights had been extinguished. The *Comet* crept along her port beam, passing her aft airlock and the first freight docking ring.

"She looks intact," Yana said. "I can't see any damage from the intercept."

"That's good," Diocletia said. "Tycho, is anybody hailing us? Any transmissions from the asteroid?"

"Negative on both counts."

"Garibalda, anything on your scopes?"

"Negative—nobody out here for now except us."

Diocletia switched channels on her headset.

"Dad, cast off," she said. "We're heading for the forward airlock. Wait for my signal to board."

"Headin' out, Dio," Huff said, and a moment later the *Comet* shivered slightly as the clamps holding the gig against her belly released.

The bells signaled 2330 as the blank slab of the *Leviathan*'s hull slid by to starboard. To port, Tycho knew, the web of girders was no more than thirty meters away. He realized he'd been holding his breath and forced himself to exhale.

"This must have been a shipyard once," he said. "A big one, too. What are the odds that the Cybeleans didn't know it was being used?"

"Zero," Diocletia said. "Our hosts seem to have struck secret deals with everyone except the Jovian Union. Mr. Dobbs? Stand by."

Carlo's eyes jumped between the viewports and images from the *Comet*'s starboard cameras as he lined up the frigate's starboard airlock with the dromond's forward portside lock. Tycho could only shake his head in admiration as his brother cut right, tapped the retro rockets, and eased the ship up against the far larger vessel.

"Vesuvia, deploy magnetic grapples. Good. We're locked."

"Let's go," Diocletia said, unbuckling herself from her chair and cinching her gloves tight.

Mavry checked Diocletia's suit seals, then leaned his forehead against hers briefly.

"Shoot straight and keep our kids out of trouble," he said quietly.

"See you soon," Diocletia said with a smile, one glove lingering on his cheek.

Tycho followed his mother down the ladderwell, with Yana and Carlo behind him.

"Captain Hashoone on deck!" bellowed Dobbs.

The *Comet*'s master-at-arms was waiting at the starboard airlock with a knot of crewers behind him. The Comets came to attention with a clatter of bootheels, eyes wide at the rare sight of their captain geared up for war. Their spacesuits were a riot of paint, decals, drawings, and scrawled graffiti—predators of species real and imagined competed for space with dire threats in multiple languages and prayers for deliverance addressed to several higher powers. The Comets clutched carbines and daggers in their fists and adjusted bandoliers holding ammunition and flash grenades.

The *Comet*'s airlock was open, and two crewers, Celly and Porco, were wiring up the *Leviathan*'s hatch, seeking to override its controls. They got to their feet as the

Hashoones approached, but Diocletia immediately indicated they should continue with their work.

"Boarding party of ten," Dobbs said, handing two chrome musketoons to Diocletia. "Ranking officer's weapons."

"Thank you, Mr. Dobbs," Diocletia said, looking at each crewer in turn. "Fast and hard to the bridge, ladies and gentlemen. That starship was stolen from our countrymen, and we intend to restore it to them."

"Three cheers for Captain Hashoone!" the crewers yelled.

Diocletia nodded. "Mr. Dobbs, you'll take point."

Dobbs made a quick sign of the cross above his pockmarked chest armor.

"Mistress Yana, on my left," he said. "Higgs and Corso behind Captain Hashoone, Master Tycho, and Master Carlo. Rest of you at the rear. Use your flash grenades and don't cross each other's paths."

Yana edged past Tycho to stand next to Dobbs. Tycho flipped off the safety on his carbine and touched the flash grenades on his bandolier, memorizing where they were.

"Ready to open her up, Captain," Dobbs said.

"Dad, what's your status?" Diocletia asked. "Good— we're going in. Do it, Mr. Dobbs."

"You know the entry procedure," Dobbs said to Yana, then nodded at Celly and Porco. The *Leviathan*'s outer airlock door rose slowly, compelled by the privateers' electronic tools. Dobbs flung a flash grenade through the opening, and Tycho heard the explosive device bouncing across the deck.

Wind rippled the stickers on the Comets' space-suits as the two ships' atmospheres mixed. The Jovians ducked their heads as the grenade detonated inside the *Leviathan*, filling the captured ship with blinding light. Tycho's faceplate automatically darkened against the glare.

Yana and Dobbs stepped across the threshold into the airlock. It was two meters deep; two meters beyond it was a T intersection.

Yana and Dobbs rushed forward into the intersection, with Yana dropping to her knees as Dobbs stayed on his feet. They flung flash grenades to either side; a moment later Tycho's visor darkened and sharp concussions made static cough in his ears. Diocletia strode forward, with Carlo and Tycho flanking her.

Two men in Earth uniforms were lying on their faces on either side of the intersection, hands over their eyes, blood dribbling from their noses. Their carbines were lying useless on the deck. None of the four was wearing a breath mask or spacesuit.

"Secure these men," Dobbs barked to the Comets bringing up the rear, and two hurried up, binding the fallen Earth crewers' wrists with zip ties.

"If that's the best they could do, no one aboard has combat training," Yana said, looking down at the men on the deck.

"You don't know that," Diocletia said. "There could be Earth marines deeper in the ship, trying to draw us in. Stay sharp and don't assume."

"The captain's right," Dobbs said. "Come on—forward."

The Comets were in a long, dimly lit passageway running the length of the *Leviathan*'s port beam. Tycho tried to remember the dromond's layout. There should be a junction twenty meters ahead, with the ladderwell to the bridge perhaps the same distance beyond that.

Dobbs and Yana jogged down the passageway, their breathing labored in the heavy suits. Diocletia hurried after them, with Carlo and Tycho at her heels.

"We're outside the engine room," Huff growled over their shared channel.

"Resistance?" Diocletia asked.

"Arr, they're tryin'. But they ain't got the numbers to make it a fair fight."

Yana and Dobbs stopped short of the junction, flinging grenades left and right. They went through the intersection low and fast, chased by laser fire.

Diocletia rushed forward, dropping to one knee as two Earth crewers emerged from cover and fired their carbines at Yana and Dobbs. A burst from her carbine left one Earth crewer lying on the deck; the other scrambled across the passageway for cover.

"Keep going!" Diocletia ordered as Yana turned to see what had happened.

Tycho pulled a flash grenade from his belt and twisted its cap to arm it. He counted one, one thousand, two, one thousand, and then tossed it to bounce into the portside corridor, knowing Carlo was doing the same with the starboard corridor.

Diocletia skidded to a halt in the corridor, blasts from her carbine lighting up the passageway. Tycho was a step behind his brother. One Earth crewer was lying motionless on his back; two others were on their knees, arms raised in surrender.

"Zip ties," Tycho barked at the Comets, keeping his carbine on the crewers. Ahead, Yana and Dobbs were hurrying back the way they'd come.

"They've sealed the bridge," Dobbs said. "We'll need charges. Celly, get up here."

Celly bared her pointy, black ceramic teeth behind the visor of her helmet.

"Quarter of a kilo ought to do it—don't want to make too big a hole," she said, chuckling as she extracted a lump of gray explosive from a pouch on her belt.

"Porco, cover her," Dobbs said, standing aside as the two Comets hurried forward. "Won't take but a minute, Captain."

The lights dimmed and a moment later the Comets' feet rose from the deck as the artificial gravity cut out. Tycho activated the magnets in his boots and gloves and adhered himself to the wall. With their hands tied, the luckless Earth crewers had no such option—they floated up to the ceiling and were stuck there. Two of the Comets grabbed the captives' wrists, dragging them back down the passageway like big blue balloons.

"Cutting the gravity helps us more than them," Yana said with a wolfish grin.

She removed her helmet and sent it spinning down the passageway with a casual toss, then started to shed her spacesuit. Her hair floated around her head like a cloud.

"Is that a good idea?" Carlo asked.

"Can't move in that thing," Yana said, adjusting her headset. "Don't worry, I know what I'm doing."

Diocletia turned to Dobbs, only to see the master-at-arms also shedding his suit.

"Your daughter's the best student I've ever had, Captain," he said.

Diocletia frowned, then nodded. "All right then."

"Engine room's secured," Huff growled in their ears. "No damage. We're bringing the engines online now."

"We'll be on the bridge in another minute," Diocletia said.

"Another minute? We ain't gettin' paid by the hour, Dio."

Diocletia ignored that—Celly and Porco were retreating back down the passageway by hurling themselves from one wall to the next.

"Ten seconds," Celly said with a feral grin. "I'd take cover."

The Comets ducked to either side of the intersection, spreading their hands and feet to stick themselves to the wall. A thunderclap of sound filled their ears and a shock wave of air shoved at them before dissipating.

"Go!" Dobbs said.

Tycho clawed his way into the passageway in time to see Yana launch herself down the corridor with Dobbs behind her. She alighted for a split second on the wall, then sprang down the passageway, seeming to pick up speed as she went.

"Come on!" Diocletia yelled.

Yana reached the ladderwell feetfirst, hooking it with her boots. That left her floating on her back, firing her carbine straight up to clear the hatchway. As the blaster's recoil pushed her upper body toward the deck, she used the momentum to roll herself into a ball, touching down on the deck with her knees bent. She threw a flash grenade above her underhanded, then sprang after it, arms raised, as light filled the passageway. Dobbs rushed after her, hands and feet kicking at the rungs of the ladderwell.

Tycho reached the ladderwell a step ahead of his mother and scrambled upward, trying to keep his feet beneath him. He emerged on the *Leviathan*'s broad bridge to find his sister floating serenely in midair, a carbine aimed in either direction. One Earth crewer was dead, while three others had their hands up. Through the dromond's broad viewports Tycho saw a wall of rock crisscrossed by the lines of gantries and observation decks.

"Bridge secured," Yana said with a smile.

"I'll get the gravity restored," Diocletia said as Dobbs

and the other Comets fastened zip ties around the wrists of the bridge crew. "Carlo, get us flying. Yana, sensors up. Tycho, make contact with Captain Andrade and your father."

Carlo was already strapping himself into the pilot's chair. Tycho overshot the navigator's station and had to struggle back to it by hauling himself along the tops of the other consoles. Yana kicked neatly over to the bulkhead behind the sensor officer's station, executing a forward roll that ended with her behind planted in the chair.

She grinned at Tycho.

"Nobody likes a show-off, sis," he grumbled as he strapped himself in.

"Gravity's coming up in five," Diocletia warned, and the Comets tugged the captive Earth crewers down to the deck so they wouldn't plummet out of the air. Tycho sagged in his seat as gravity once more pushed him down.

"They've locked out the piloting station," Carlo said.

"Really?" Diocletia glared at the three captured crewers through the bowl of her helmet. "Which of you is ranking officer?"

A distinguished-looking man with gray hair stepped forward. "Tyrus Sanford, of the *Loire.*"

"Captain Diocletia Hashoone, of the *Shadow Comet.* I'd appreciate it if you'd help us get up and running, Mr. Sanford."

"I'm afraid I can't do that, Captain. I have my orders to secure this ship at all costs."

"I see," Diocletia said, drumming her fingers on her

console. "Mr. Dobbs, please get your spacesuit and my daughter's."

"Will do, Captain," Dobbs said, clanking off across the deck.

"Captain Andrade is reporting Earth ships are inbound," Tycho said. "Twenty-five thousand klicks and closing."

"Understood," Diocletia said, turning her attention back to Sanford. "I'd very much like to avoid any further loss of life, Mr. Sanford."

"As I said, Captain, I have my orders."

Dobbs reappeared on the ladderwell, two spacesuits slung over his shoulder and helmets dangling from a loop on his belt.

"Thank you, Mr. Dobbs," Diocletia said. "Dad? Make sure all your crewers are suited up. I'm going to open the *Leviathan* to space."

Sanford turned pale. "You wouldn't."

"Tycho, check your sister's seals. Carlo, do the same for Mr. Dobbs."

"Aye-aye," Tycho said, unstrapping himself and waiting next to Yana's station as she zipped up her suit.

"Captain, I must protest this barbarism!" Sanford stammered.

Diocletia ignored him.

Yana rotated her helmet in the groove of her suit's collar, locking the two together, then cinched her gloves closed.

"Your seals are green," Tycho said.

"Green over here," Carlo said.

"Stand by to evacuate the atmosphere," Diocletia said.

"Wait!" Sanford said. "I'll unlock the controls!"

Diocletia nodded to Dobbs, who cut the zip ties on Sanford's wrists and marched him over to Carlo's station. The Earth crewer began hurriedly typing out commands.

"I am called Pathfinder," said the deep, calm male voice of the *Leviathan*'s AI. "How may I assist?"

"By giving me the sticks," Carlo said.

"Acknowledged," Pathfinder said.

"Earth ships are closing," Tycho said. "Twenty thousand klicks."

"Take these men below, Mr. Dobbs," Diocletia said. "Mavry, cast off. We'll be right behind you."

Carlo yanked his helmet and gloves off as the *Leviathan*'s control yoke rose from beneath his station. He gripped it and exhaled, peering at the view from the rear cameras half a kilometer behind him.

"We're detached and heading out," Mavry said over the comm.

The *Leviathan*'s bells clanged out eight times—it was midnight.

"Here goes nothing," Carlo muttered.

The deck shuddered beneath their feet, but nothing else seemed to happen. Tycho looked questioningly at his brother. But then he realized the dromond was moving slowly but steadily backward.

"This is like pushing a boulder with your nose," Carlo

said through gritted teeth, sweat running down his fore-head, and Tycho thought with a scowl that he felt that way when he was flying the *Comet*—a nimble ship barely a tenth the length of the dromond.

"We're clear of the asteroid, *Leviathan*," Mavry said in their ears. "But company's coming."

Carlo's eyes jumped between the viewports and his monitors.

"Gotta cut to starboard," he said to himself, pushing at the control yoke. "Come on, baby, *move*."

The rock wall ahead of them was more distant now, with a lattice of struts and girders stretching from the end of the hollow asteroid past their vantage point.

"Little more to port, I think," Diocletia said.

"I know!"

"Proximity alert," Pathfinder said.

Carlo shoved at the control yoke and the *Leviathan* shivered, a vibration passing through the hull.

"Ugh, too far," Carlo muttered.

"Impact," Pathfinder said, sounding disappointed. "Assessing damage."

"You just scraped her fenders, kid—that's what they're for," Mavry said reassuringly. "Keep coming!"

Tycho and Yana looked at each other anxiously.

"I've got it now," Carlo said. "She takes a long time to respond is all—makes it hard not to overcompensate. Let me line her up. Almost, almost . . . *there*. Okay, hang on!"

The *Leviathan* gained speed, the rock wall retreating rapidly in front of them. Tycho imagined he could feel the enormous weight of the huge ship now—her mass and her growing momentum.

The lattice inside 124996 became a blur on either side of them. Then they saw the entrance to the hidden hangar and the black expanse of space—the *Leviathan* had emerged from the asteroid. Carlo gasped, his head dipping forward momentarily, and Yana gave a cheer.

"Silence on the bridge," Diocletia said.

Carlo flipped switches and shoved the *Leviathan*'s control yoke hard to the right, sending the massive dromond's bow swinging to starboard.

"I have three Earth ships and several pinnaces at five thousand klicks—and six Jovian craft between us and them, in defensive formation," Yana said.

"That will be our friend Captain Allamand, I expect," Diocletia said.

"Patching the Jovian ships through to a shared channel," Tycho said. "And plotting a course back to Cybele."

"Pathfinder, display colors," Diocletia said with a smile. "Jovian, if you please."

Cheers erupted over the shared channel as the *Nestor Leviathan* began broadcasting her reclaimed identity.

"Nice flying, son," Mavry said, and even Tycho had to smile at the relief on Carlo's face. Then an alert on his console chased his joy away.

"It's the *Gracieux*—she's hailing all craft," he said.

"Captain Hashoone, I presume?" said Allamand. "It seems I must congratulate you on an elegant rescue—as well as a remarkable display of piloting. Let me assure you that the prize is yours, with no need for further hostilities. Your crewers will find the cargo untouched—our intention was to restore the *Leviathan* to her proper owners once the current regrettable situation was behind us. Which it soon will be, I'm pleased to report."

"What do you mean?" Captain Andrade demanded. "I don't know of any parley."

"Things are happening back on Cybele," Allamand said. "I'm informed that our envoys are negotiating steps to defuse this current confrontation. Captain Hashoone, may I ask after my prize crew?"

"We have five fatalities," Diocletia said. "I'm sorry for it. The remaining crewers will be freed at Cybele, of course."

"Thank you. One more bit of business, if you'll allow me. Might I address Master Tycho Hashoone?"

Tycho looked up in mingled surprise and dread, conscious of his siblings' eyes on him. Diocletia frowned, but nodded at Tycho, who hurriedly searched for the setting that would broadcast his voice across the open channels.

"I'm here, Captain," he said, trying to keep the quaver out of his voice.

"My AI informs me you've been a guest aboard my ship, Master Hashoone—along with your mediapad. Which explains why we are meeting at this particular location."

Tycho tried to force his vocal cords to work. "That's correct."

It was very hard not to call the man on the other side of the transmission "sir."

"My daughter . . . ," Allamand began, then paused. "My daughter is innocent in ways you and I can no longer claim to be. You have conducted yourself rather badly, Master Hashoone. All victories have a cost, but I suspect you will come to regret the price you've paid for this one."

I already do, Tycho thought, staring at his hands in his lap.

"That will do, Captain Allamand," Diocletia said.

"All in all, captains, it's been an honor to match wits with you," Allamand said. "I believe we've put on a splendid show—one I hope has satisfied our leaders back home, so that cooler heads may now prevail."

"They're moving off," Yana said. "Heading back toward Cybele."

"Time for us to do the same, then," Diocletia said. She freed her black hair from its ponytail, shaking it out, and closed her eyes for a moment.

The bridge was silent as the *Leviathan* churned steadily toward distant Cybele. Then Diocletia spoke again.

"Tycho, duty compels us to take actions we'd rather avoid. Things done for family, for country, or for both. And often that duty comes with regret."

She offered him a small smile, but he shook his head, determined to deflect the praise he'd so often sought.

"I didn't do the right thing," he said. "If I could do

it over again, I'd make a different choice. An *honorable* choice."

Diocletia's smile vanished. "Then the Jovian Union would be worse off. And so would your family."

Tycho nodded numbly, pierced by the realization that he'd never again see Kate smile at him, never see warmth in her dark eyes. He'd never get to lose his fingers in the tangles of her black curls, or watch her hurry to cross the distance between them more quickly. He had thrown all that away—not by accident or through inaction, but deliberately.

"Would you really have done it, Mom?" Yana asked. "Opened the ship to vacuum?"

Diocletia's eyes searched the stars spilled across the void beyond the viewports. "We had a mission. I would have completed it."

24

BROTHERS

t was an hour into the middle watch when the Jovian and Earth craft returned to 65 Cybele, holding their positions as various captains insisted—with the exaggerated politeness of recent enemies—that the other be first to dock or land.

The arrival of the *Leviathan* sent Cybelean traffic control into a frenzy, with a harried administrator first claiming that the dromond would have to wait until morning to dock. Diocletia's suggestion that she could park the *Leviathan* in the middle of the traffic-control tower probably didn't help, but it did frighten the Jovian consulate into waking up higher-ranking Cybelean officials, and they were able to coax the bureaucratic wheels into creaky motion.

Since docking was clearly going to take a while, Tycho got permission from Diocletia to leave the bridge, descending the ladderwell and wandering for a while until he found the officers' cuddy. He found Yana huddled in the corner with a jump-pop and her mediapad. Her eyes were red and watering.

"What's wrong?" Tycho asked.

Yana swiped irritably at her cheeks with the back of her hand, looking away.

"It's nothing."

"Come on. You don't need to act tough with me."

"I guess you already know anyway," she said, shoving her mediapad over to Tycho. "This message arrived as soon as we reached Cybelean local space."

YANA,
BY THE TIME YOU READ THIS I WILL BE GONE. I AM NOT
TAKEN BY CRIMPS OR STRAGGLING THO THAT WUD BE
EASY TO LET EVERY ONE BELEVE. YANA I AM A SON OF
SATURN AND I CAN NO LONGER DENY THAT. THE JOVIAN
UNION HAS NOT GIVEN US OUR RITES AND THEY WILL NOT
GIVE US OUR RITES THAT IS CLEAR TO ME NOW COS THEY
CAN NOT EVEN TREAT YOU AND YOUR FAMILY RITE AND
YOU ARE THER CONTRYMAN YANA. SO HOW CAN I EXPECT

RITE TREATMENT FOR ME A SATURNEAN. I MUST DO WAT
I BELEVE YANA AND THAT IS TO FITE FOR MY PEPLE
SO THEY HAVE THE SAME RITES YOU ENJOY AND THAT
PEPLE ENJOY ON EARTH. I AM SORRY TO HURT YOU YOU
HAVE BEEN GOOD TO ME. YOU WILL BE A GRATE CAPTAIN
ONE DAY YANA AND I MISS YOU ALREDY. REMEMBER ME.
IMMANUEL

"I'm sorry, sis," Tycho said.

"Your girlfriend's an Earth noble and my boyfriend's an Ice Wolf," Yana said with a small smile. "What's next, Carlo taking up with a Martian separatist?"

"What's that?" Carlo asked from the doorway. Tycho and Yana looked up, startled.

"Nothing," Yana said, her face turning hard. Stone-faced, she scooped up her mediapad and pushed past Carlo.

"Wait, I didn't mean . . . ," Carlo said to his sister's departing back. He turned back to Tycho, looking crestfallen.

"Just forget it," Tycho said. "It has nothing to do with you."

"Okay," Carlo said, perching uncertainly on the cuddy's padded bench, as far as he could get from his brother.

"I'm sorry about your girlfriend," Carlo said after a moment.

"I think it's safe to say she isn't my girlfriend now."

Carlo nodded. "I heard what you said about doing the honorable thing. Mom didn't seem to agree."

"I don't care what Mom thinks about it. Or anybody else, for that matter."

Carlo retreated into silence. Tycho glanced up and found him studying his hands on the tabletop, his teeth working at his lower lip.

"What would you have done?" Tycho asked. He wasn't sure if he was trying to bait his brother or if he was genuinely curious.

Carlo opened his mouth, closed it, and then shook his head. "I don't know. I don't know anything anymore."

They sat there for a while, listening to the thrum of the *Leviathan*'s air scrubbers.

"Do you think Mom really would have opened the *Leviathan* to space?" Carlo asked.

"Yeah."

"Would *you* have done it?"

"No," Tycho said. "I couldn't have. Would you?"

"No. I couldn't have either."

Morning came all too quickly, and along with it orders for the Hashoones to return to the Jovian consulate. They found themselves in the familiar conference room overlooking the Well, with the other privateer crews filing in slowly. By the fragile, haunted expressions on their faces, Tycho guessed there'd been a fairly legendary shindy to mark the end of active hostilities with Earth.

"Why are we here again?" Yana leaned over to ask Mavry.

Mavry yawned. "Maybe it's important to the future of the Jovian Union that we learn to fold napkins properly."

Huff was snoring contentedly in the chair next to Tycho when Vass and an aide entered the conference room and took seats by the door. Two Gibraltar Artisans cyborgs followed them in and stood at attention, studying the privateers.

"By now you've heard the rumors about negotiations between our envoy and Earth's," Vass told the bleary-eyed spacers. "I'm pleased to announce that the rumors are true. We've reached an agreement to cease hostilities here at Cybele."

Tycho elbowed Huff, who woke up with a snort, his living eye roving around the room.

"His Majesty has withdrawn the letters of marque issued to all Earth privateers," Vass said. "And talks about a closer relationship between Earth and Cybele have adjourned and are not expected to resume."

"So it's a draw, then?" demanded Canaan Bickerstaff. "What good is that?"

"Against the power of Earth, a draw is a great victory," Vass said with a smile. "His Majesty was embarrassed to see the return of the *Nestor Leviathan* hailed as a Jovian triumph, and furious to learn the Cybeleans used their neutrality to build a battleship for the Ice Wolves. His conclusion is that Earth has overextended its forces, and a pullback from the Cybeles would be a gesture of good faith in seeking a more lasting peace."

"Arrrr, I'll believe that one when I see it," Huff muttered.

"I share your skepticism, Captain Hashoone," Vass said. "But by stopping the rise of Earth in this region of the solar system, we have eliminated a considerable threat to the security of the Jovian Union. Ladies and gentlemen, your country owes all of you a debt."

"How big a debt?" asked Dmitra Barnacus, to laughter from the privateers.

"That will be established by the Defense Force upon review of your contributions here at Cybele. But all of you will be compensated. And those ships that responded to Captain Andrade's call for assistance will share in the reward for the rescue of the *Leviathan*. A rescue for which we have Captain Hashoone and her crew to thank—particularly Master Tycho Hashoone."

Tycho managed a pallid smile. He'd had only a couple of hours of sleep at their temporary quarters, during which he'd woken up repeatedly after dreaming Kate had sent a furious message to his mediapad. Each time he checked, he found his message queue empty, and by dawn he'd realized that no message would be coming—not today, not tomorrow, and not ever.

And that was so much worse.

"And what about the Ice Wolves?" asked Garibalda Marta Andrade. "There's a pretty big battleship out there somewhere, Minister."

"We are analyzing instrument readings and

communications logs from the encounter. We will find the ship, and eliminate it as a threat. And we are actively investigating the Titan affair that apparently funded its construction."

"In other words, we ain't tellin' you lot nothin'," Huff growled to Tycho.

"Now then," Vass said over the hubbub. "With His Majesty canceling privateering operations, President Goddard has decided on peace overtures of her own. Therefore, the letters of marque issued for this campaign are being withdrawn effective immediately."

"What?" demanded Baltazar Widderich.

"I assure you that all condemnations taken to date shall be honored if approved by an admiralty court," Vass said, pitching his voice to be heard above the privateers' angry voices. "Expenses incurred as you return to your home ports shall be paid, of course. And previous letters of marque remain valid. President Goddard thanks you for your service, captains—as do I. And now, if you'll excuse me, I'm afraid I have more meetings today than you can imagine."

The diminutive minister levered himself out of his seat and strode from the room, his aide hurrying along in his wake. The cyborg soldiers pivoted on their heels and exited as well, leaving the privateers all talking at once, fists and stumps pounding on the table.

"What was it they called us at Saturn?" Tycho asked Yana. "Irregulars?"

"I ain't standin' for this," Baltazar Widderich said,

his yellow teeth bared. "They can't give me a commission and then yank it away again without so much as a by-your-leave."

"It ain't right," Karst Widderich snarled.

"You heard the minister—you will be compensated for prizes and expenses," Andrade said, fixing the Widderiches with a steady gaze.

"Easy for you to say, Garibalda," Canaan Bickerstaff growled. "You three captains still have your fancy letters of marque. The rest of us have nothin'—if we do the same thing today we did yesterday, we won't be cheered as patriots but hanged as pirates."

"Ain't nothin' wrong with bein' a pirate," Dmitra Barnacus said. "'Cept maybe our saintly president not approvin' of it no more now that it ain't useful to her."

"There is also the prospect of being hanged," Zhi Ning said. "I dislike the idea."

"Eh, they can only hang you once," Dmitra said, looking around the table with a wolfish gleam in her eye. "Listen, you lot. When the excitement started, some of us set up camp at 588 Achilles—we've dry docks and lodgings and even a depot. And a grog shop or two, naturally. You're all invited to make it a new port of operations— unless you'd rather get back to haulin' freight and payin' taxes."

Huff leaned forward, his living eye bright and his forearm cannon quivering madly.

"Shouldn't discuss that around these respectable types," Baltazar said warningly.

"That's right," Karst said. "They ain't like us real pirates."

"Say that agin an' I'll settle yer hash," Huff warned Karst.

"I've served with all three of these captains," Dmitra said. "They won't betray us. And they're welcome to count themselves among us if they like."

The former privateers' eyes slid to the Hashoones and the crews of the *Izabella* and the *Berserker*.

"I serve the Jovian Union," Andrade said, getting to her feet. "And I will continue to do so."

"And does it serve you, Gari?" Dmitra asked.

Andrade said nothing, but led her bridge crew out of the room. Dmitra watched her go, then turned her eyes to Morgan Theo.

"This is a family decision," he said. "I'll have to consult with my father."

"You do that," Dmitra said. "And give old Min my love."

As Morgan and his crewers stood, Dmitra leaned back in her chair and eyed Diocletia.

"And you, Dio? What do you say?"

"Arr, Dio—" Huff began, but his daughter put up her hand, eyes flashing.

"When Carina and I were middies, many of you helped teach us the pirate trade," she said. "Some of you were at 624 Hektor when everything changed. And all of us knew Jupiter pirates who never came back from that place."

Some of the privateers scowled at the rarely uttered name of the battle, while others nodded.

"What's the use, she ain't gonna join—" began Baltazar Widderich, but Yana leaped to her feet.

"You shut your mouth when my captain's talking. And that goes for your parrot brother too."

"That will do, Yana," Diocletia said. "I've raised my children as privateers—not because it's what I wanted for them, but because it's what was possible. I've tried to teach them to abide by the laws of space, and to pursue our trade with whatever honor is possible—honor for our fellow privateers and our enemies alike. The heading you're on won't lead to glory, but to the gibbet. I won't risk that for my family."

Baltazar muttered something all of them chose not to hear. Diocletia got to her feet, and one by one the rest of the Hashoones did the same. Huff was the last to stand, grimacing as he braced himself on his forearm cannon.

"So be it, Diocletia," Dmitra said, her eyes jumping to Huff and then sliding to Tycho and Yana. "If any of you change your mind, you'll know where to find us."

Several Comets were coming at 1200 to collect the Hashoones' gear and bring it to the landing field. Tycho packed his duffel bag hastily, eager to leave Cybele—the Well, the Jovian fondaco, and even the persistent chill reminded him of Kate, of what he'd done and what he'd lost.

He'd finished zipping up his bag and was wondering how to fill the next hour when someone knocked. Carlo was standing in the doorway, wearing his parka.

"Uh, can I talk to you, Tyke?"

"About what?"

"I need to get something off my chest, I guess."

Tycho wanted to say no, but that would just delay the inevitable—there was no avoiding someone for three days on two decks of a sixty-meter frigate.

"Not here, though," Carlo said.

Tycho shrugged and grabbed his jacket. He thought of stopping to put on his shoulder holster but decided against it—his shoulder and side were still chafed from wearing it earlier. Zipping his jacket, he followed his brother out of their quarters and through the corridors of the fondaco, passing other spacers and Jovian bureaucrats with their own bags.

He wondered idly what was bothering Carlo. Probably something to do with the rebellious privateers angry about their lost letters of marque. Or perhaps he was still struggling with the ruthlessness their mother had shown in reclaiming the *Leviathan*.

He wasn't particularly surprised when Carlo led the way to the center of the Southwell and its web of wires. But he was taken aback by the look on his brother's face. Carlo looked ashen, and he was trembling.

"What's wrong?" Tycho asked, forgetting his anger for a moment.

"You were right," Carlo said, then stopped, his chin

falling to his chest. One hand came up and wiped at his eyes.

"Right about what?"

Carlo struggled to master his emotions, staring down into the levels below them. "There was no sign walker," he said, stumbling over the words in his haste to get them out. "It was the Securitat, just like you said. I *cheated*. I cheated and I don't deserve to be captain."

Tycho took a step backward, shocked—not that Carlo had done what Tycho had already suspected, but that he'd admitted it. His brother's eyes were red, his face twisted by misery.

"Just tell me what happened," Tycho said quietly.

"It started with a message. Right after I screwed up and let the Earth ships steal the *Leviathan*."

Tycho nodded, remembering DeWise's first message to him, the one he'd read on the quarterdeck above Ceres.

"Whoever sent it knew things about our operations that most people wouldn't know. About what had happened on cruises, about prizes taken and lost. And then they asked how I felt about my chances for the captain's chair. So I agreed to a meeting."

"A meeting where?"

"Out beyond Bazaar, in some dodgy miners' grog shop. They had all the information about that Earth freighter, the *Blue Heron*—where it would be and when. I asked what they wanted in return and they said nothing—just that they thought highly of me and wanted to help me. When I hesitated, they said they'd give the prize to some other privateer if I didn't want it. They said things had worked like this for years and there was no shame in it."

"And have they asked you for anything since then?"

"No. But what does that matter?"

Tycho leaned on his elbows. His anger had curdled into a nauseated regret. His brother wasn't confessing to anything Tycho hadn't done himself—except Carlo was admitting it and Tycho never had. Tycho had benefited from the Securitat's help, then turned his back on them. And he'd kept it a secret.

"Why are you telling me this?" he asked Carlo.

"Because it's the honorable thing to do. I've been thinking a lot about it. I wish I'd told the Securitat I'd take their tip, but only on behalf of my family. I wish I'd told them that's the rule for us—that the family is the captain, and the captain is the ship, and the ship is the family. Then things might have been different."

No, they wouldn't have, Tycho thought. *The Securitat doesn't work that way.*

"But it's too late," Carlo said. "I can't take back what I've done. All I can do is try to make it right."

"And you realize what that will cost you?"

Carlo smiled shakily at Tycho.

"It means you're going to be captain," he said, his voice breaking on that final word, the one that had meant so much to them over the years. "And I'm happy for you, Tyke. Maybe you don't believe me, but it's true. I really am."

Tycho felt his breath catch in his throat and tears start in his eyes. He turned away, unable to look at his brother.

"I mean it, Tyke," Carlo said, his hand on his shoulder. "You're going to be a *great* captain. I was even thinking I could help you with your piloting—show you a couple of things that will make a big difference."

"Stop it," Tycho said, shrugging off his brother's hand. "Don't touch me."

Carlo pulled his hand back. "I'm sorry, Tyke. I'm really sorry. And now I'm supposed to see my . . . my handler, or whatever you'd call him. I'm going to tell him that we're done. And then . . . and then I'll tell Mom, when we're back aboard the *Comet*."

"And then what?"

"And then it will be up to her." Carlo made a faltering attempt at a smile, then a better one, blowing out his breath. "I feel better having told you," he said. "That's crazy, isn't it? I just made sure I'll never be captain, and I feel relieved about it."

"Carlo, don't do this," Tycho said. "You don't have to do this."

His brother looked baffled.

"You don't have to tell Mom," Tycho said. "I understand. I really do. I . . . it can be our secret, okay?"

"I have to tell her. I don't think I could live with myself if I didn't."

"Then I have to tell Mom too," Tycho said almost before thinking about it. He stared at his feet, feeling his face flush.

"Tell her what? What are you talking about?"

Tycho forced himself to look his brother in the eye. "You're not the only one with a Securitat handler. Ceres, two years ago. A message, a man in a café, asking if I wanted to be captain. They gave me a freighter too, in fact."

Carlo's eyes widened in shock. "The *Portia*?"

"The *Portia*."

"You didn't find a mediapad?"

"No. Just like you didn't talk with a sign walker."

Carlo looked stunned, and Tycho found that he too felt a strange relief at having parted with the secret that had haunted him.

"I don't believe it," Carlo said.

"The Securitat was after the *Iris* cache, just like we were. I think they saw me as insurance in case they didn't find it. So I made a trade with them. There was a data disk in the boxes below Darklands. I swiped it when no one was looking and gave it to them—in exchange for giving us a clear title to the *Hydra*."

"But we never—"

"I know we didn't. They lied to me about the *Hydra*. Just like they would have lied to you sooner or later. Who was I going to complain to? Anyway, I haven't done anything for them since then. And I wish I never had."

Carlo nodded. "So what do we do now?"

Tycho took a deep breath. "Either both of us tell Mom or neither of us does."

"I have to. These last few days— I can't do this."

Tycho felt sick to his stomach. He'd not only done worse but also managed to live with himself a lot longer than his brother had.

"Then we both tell Mom," he said.

They stared at each other, letting that sink in.

"All right," Carlo said.

He extended his hand. Tycho took it, then hugged his brother, trying to remember the last time they'd done that. They parted after a moment, smiling awkwardly.

"I'll see you at the ship, okay?" Carlo said.

"Carlo, don't go see them—just send them a message. It's dangerous out there."

Carlo shook his head. "It's something I need to do. I'd feel like I was running if I didn't. It'll be fine, Tyke. The crimps don't have any more customers and the Ice Wolves are gone, remember?"

"I guess. Look, I'll go with you as far as Bazaar—I need to say good-bye to Elfrieda. Maybe you could—"

"No," Carlo said, looking away. "Don't, Tyke. She won't care. She won't care and you'll just be hurt."

"Maybe. But I'm still going to go. I guess it's my own thing I need to do."

It was probably just Tycho's imagination, but he thought Elfrieda's goons looked bored standing in their usual ring around the Last Chance. Bazaar was quiet, with just a scattering of shoppers and weary-looking merchants. But his grandmother occupied her usual spot at the center of her depot, barking out orders that made clerks scurry.

"I thought you'd be gone by now," she said when she saw Tycho.

"We're leaving in a couple of hours. I wanted to say good-bye."

Elfrieda nodded, and Tycho waited for her to turn away. But then she called Burke over to watch the counter.

"Cup of tea?" she asked Tycho. "My treat."

"All right. Thanks."

A minute later they were sitting in the Last Chance's café, mugs warming their hands.

"So how's your girlfriend?" Elfrieda asked.

Tycho shook his head, eyes downcast.

"Ah," Elfrieda said. "That's a shame. "

She let her eyes rove over the depot, then sighed. "Can't say I'm sorry to see your Ice Wolf friends move along."

"They're not my friends," Tycho said, but Elfrieda barely noticed.

"They spent livres, but they were an odd bunch. Told me they took orders from a boss they never saw—some kind of machine, one of them claimed."

"A machine?"

"That's what they said, at least. I didn't think much of it until the last wave of shipyard workers returned.

They said the ship they'd been working on never had any cabins built or life-support equipment installed."

Tycho's mind flashed back to the Ice Wolves' black ship and Yana's strangely low energy readings—and that ragged voice telling them to keep their distance or die.

"The solar system is full of wonders, I suppose," Elfrieda said. "Anyway, most of the Saturnians are gone. I've seen just a few this morning, on their way to space. Same with the Earthfolks and you Jovians. Gonna be quiet again on this chilly little rock."

"I wish you'd told me about the Ice Wolves and their boss," Tycho said. "We could have used that information."

"Not my business."

"I wish you'd told somebody, then. The Securitat, maybe."

Elfrieda put down her mug hard enough that tea sloshed out of it. "I wouldn't help those jackals if the fate of the solar system depended on it."

Tycho looked at her in surprise.

"They're dealers in misery," Elfrieda said. "They spend their days seeking weaknesses to exploit and puppets they can make perform. That's how they drew your grandfather in. Stay away from them, Tycho—they'll be the ruin of you. You understand me?"

Tycho's mug was burning his hands. He set it down.

"I understand," he said, thinking what an enormous

understatement that was. The Securitat had manipulated his grandfather into taking part in a scheme that had backfired and led to the Jupiter pirates' ruin. And then, years later, they'd ensnared Tycho and his brother.

But they'd never fool another Hashoone again. In an hour or two he and Carlo would have confessed what they'd done and no longer be in the running to become the *Comet*'s next captain. But at least their stories would be object lessons to future generations of Hashoones about the dangers of the Securitat's lures.

But which future generations? Tycho supposed that Yana would become captain. Ironically, the Hashoone sibling who had given up on gaining the captain's chair would be the only one left in a position to claim it.

Elfrieda sipped her tea for a moment.

"Grandmother? Can I ask you something?"

"No harm in asking."

"Do you believe in second chances?"

As Elfrieda started to answer, Tycho's mediapad trilled.

"Go ahead," Elfrieda said in response to his apologetic look.

It was a voice transmission, from an unknown recognition code.

It's Kate, he thought, fumbling to answer, his heart thudding.

"Hello?"

"Tycho," a male voice said. "Where are you?"

It was DeWise, he realized, his eyes jumping to Elfrieda, as if their discussion had somehow summoned the Securitat agent.

"Leave me alone," Tycho told DeWise. "And my brother too."

And then he disconnected him.

"I'd like to believe in second chances," Elfrieda said. "It's a lovely idea, really. But mostly they never come."

Tycho got to his feet. "I'll have to hope for the best, I guess. Maybe we'll see each other again, Grandmother."

"I'll keep a lookout," Elfrieda said. "For you and your sister."

Tycho edged around one of his grandmother's goons and exited the Last Chance, Bazaar's multicolored flags fluttering above his head in the breeze from the air scrubbers. His mediapad beeped again, muffled by his jacket. He recognized the sound as a message alert and kept walking, passing through Bazaar's airlock and into the tunnel leading to the Westwell. There was nothing DeWise could say that he cared to hear.

He'd left the Westwell behind and was just entering the main Well when his mediapad trilled once more, this time with another voice transmission.

"Take a hint already," he grumbled, but stopped to unzip his jacket and extract his mediapad. The new transmission was from his sister's recognition code.

"Yana? What is it?"

"I just got a really strange voice message. I don't know who it was from, but he was asking where you and Carlo were, and warning me about the Ice Wolves."

Tycho stopped, his mouth suddenly dry.

"Tyke? Are you there?"

"Yeah. I heard you. I better go."

He disconnected Yana and called up his message queue, fingers stumbling through the familiar steps. He tapped the message he'd ignored earlier and it began to play.

"Tycho," DeWise said. "You have to listen to me. The Ice Wolves are hunting you and your siblings. I tried to warn your brother, but he's refusing to answer. He needs to know—"

Tycho shoved the mediapad back into his jacket, DeWise's words of warning still sounding faintly beneath the fur lining. His brother had continued past Bazaar, going deeper into the warren of tunnels snaking across Cybele's surface. He reached for his holster before remembering he didn't have a weapon. Then he turned back toward Bazaar and began to run.

25

CYBELE INCIDENT REPORT AE-5362-H

A crowd had formed at the center of Bazaar. Tycho pushed at the backs of the people standing in the outer ring, yelling for them to let him through and finally shoving past them.

Carlo was lying on his back in the center of the dome. A Cybelean constable with a staff intercepted Tycho as he tried to get to his brother's side.

"Get back, boy!" the constable said, grabbing the

front of Tycho's jacket and pushing him back. "This don't concern you!"

"That's my brother!" Tycho said, and the man let go of him in surprise. Tycho shoved past him and sprawled beside Carlo. He reached for the charred hole in the center of Carlo's jacket, then drew his hand back when he saw the terrible wound underneath.

Tycho buried his head in his hands, struggling to breathe, to think, to do anything. He could hear the constables issuing orders, the muttering and murmuring of the crowd, the rattle of shutters on the reopening shops, and the faint tinkle of the chimes high above.

"All right, you lot, it's done," a constable barked at the crowd, rapping his staff on the floor. "Get back and let us do our jobs."

Tycho lifted his head as the crowd began to break up. A constable leaned down to him.

"Sorry for your loss, lad," he said. "Jovian, are you? We'll have to look at the security feeds since—as usual—there were no witnesses. But we'll find out who did this."

Tycho looked through the thinning crowd and saw Elfrieda's guards standing impassively in front of the Last Chance. Two clerks were struggling with a jammed shutter, while Elfrieda herself was standing just within the depot, arms folded.

Her eyes met Tycho's and widened in surprise. She took a step forward, then stopped, looking down at Carlo's body. Her hand flew to her mouth.

"I didn't recognize . . . I had no idea that he was . . . I didn't think that . . ."

"You didn't think it was any of your business?" Tycho asked, his hands balling into fists, his voice rising to a scream. "You didn't think you might help someone who needed it?"

All at once he began to sob, an explosion of tears that left his cheeks wet and his chest heaving. He reached out for Carlo and pulled his brother's head and shoulders into his lap. He could feel the stubble on Carlo's jaw and the ridge of the scar on his cheek.

Elfrieda stood frozen. Her mouth moved, but no sound came out. Then she turned, her steps slow and uncertain, and shuffled back into the shadows of the Last Chance.

After the Cybelean authorities took Carlo's body away, a hulking constable accompanied Tycho back to the Southwell, walking in silence a step behind him. Vass was waiting outside the fondaco with a pair of Gibraltar cyborgs. He rushed forward when he saw Tycho.

"My boy," the minister said, reaching up to put his hands on Tycho's shoulders. "I heard what happened. I can't tell you how much this awful news grieves me and every member of the Jovian delegation."

"Is my sister safe?" Tycho asked.

"Yes. But I'm afraid your family doesn't know yet. I wanted to make sure you were safe first."

Tycho nodded numbly. He turned and thanked the

constable, then followed Vass through the fondaco's corridors until they reached the door to their quarters. He could hear the buzz of his family's voices inside.

"Do you want me to tell them?" Vass asked.

"No. It's my duty."

He opened the door. A trio of Comets had piled duffel bags and stacked boxes in the small living room, next to Huff's empty tank. Mavry was peering into the coffeemaker, while Diocletia and Huff were chatting at the kitchen table.

"Arrr, tole yeh the lad wouldn't be late," Huff said with a grin as Diocletia looked up.

"Did you get a strange message like the one Yana got?" Diocletia asked, then frowned at the sight of Vass standing behind Tycho.

This was the last moment before everything would change forever, Tycho thought. Before he would leave everything in ruins.

Yana came out of her room, her dark eyes wide.

"We weren't expecting you, Minister," Diocletia said, puzzled. And then Tycho heard her voice change. "What's happened? Where's your brother?"

"It happened in Bazaar," Tycho said, having to force each word out of his mouth. "I got there as fast as I could, but . . ."

He shook his head, unable to go on.

His mother stared at him, not blinking. Mavry fumbled for a chair and sank into it, his eyes glassy.

"Carlo?" Huff asked, his living eye wild, his voice

strangled. Yana's head went back and hit the wall with a dull thunk. The Comets looked up in shock and dawning horror.

"You all have my deepest sympathies," Vass began, but Diocletia waved her hand to silence him.

"Who was it?" she asked in a quiet but firm voice. "You know by now, Minister. Who was it?"

"Captain Hashoone, I know this is a terrible shock. Perhaps—"

Diocletia slapped her hand down on the kitchen table, silencing him. "Tell me who it was."

"We received the security feed from the Cybelean authorities a few minutes ago. I haven't seen it."

"But you have it."

Vass said nothing.

"You're going to show it to me. Right now."

Diocletia got to her feet and walked into her bedroom. Vass followed reluctantly and shut the door behind him.

"He was jes' a lad," Huff managed, his forearm cannon still and silent at the end of his arm. The coffeemaker had begun to beep insistently.

Mavry looked up from the table. His face was ashen. His eyes turned to Tycho, barely seeing him, then moved to the shocked Comets.

"Gentlemen, would you please bring our gear to the gig?" he asked quietly.

The Comets hoisted the bags and withdrew with knuckles to foreheads and mumbled expressions of sorrow. Huff was repeating "jes' a lad," three words thick with grief and barely intelligible. Tycho shut off the beeping coffeemaker and slumped against the counter.

The bedroom door opened. Diocletia took two steps away from it and then stopped, as if she didn't know where to go. Vass came to a halt behind her.

"It was Mox," she said, her voice flat. "Mox and his thugs. Nobody helped our son. A dome full of people, and not one of them helped him."

She regarded Vass. "Please leave us, Minister."

"Your family's sacrifices will never be forgotten," Vass said. "Not by our president, or by the Jovian Defense Force. And certainly not by me."

He bowed to each of them, eyes lingering on Tycho for a moment, and then he was gone.

"Mr. Grigsby will retrieve the body and bring it to the gig," Diocletia said when the door had shut. "And that's where we need to be too."

"Mom?" Yana asked tentatively. "Are you okay?"

"No," Diocletia said, still motionless in the middle of the room. "No, I'm not. But this is a bridge crew. And I just gave that bridge crew an order."

Mavry got to his feet, moving like he was sleep-walking or couldn't see where he was going. One arm fumbled for Tycho, found him, and pulled him into his chest, clutching him there. Yana came to stand by her mother, her fingers clenching and unclenching.

"He was jes' a lad," Huff said again, his voice cracking.

Diocletia slowly turned her head to look at her

father where he was sprawled in misery at one end of the kitchen table. She reached up for her hair, her hands trembling slightly, and bound it into a ponytail.

"Not you," she told Huff. "You're not going."

"What did yeh say?" Huff asked, the flesh-and-blood side of his face going pale.

When she spoke again, Diocletia's voice was low and deadly.

"You let Mox go. You helped him escape the gibbet. Which led to Comets dying at Saturn, and now to this."

"Dio, yeh don't understand—"

"Don't you tell me what I don't understand," Diocletia said. "Because I understand this: your grandson is dead and you're to blame. So ask one of your pirate friends for a hole to hide in. Because you're never seeing the inside of Darklands or my ship again."

26

FLIGHT OF THE *COMET*

D iocletia said nothing as the rickshaw took them
through the Southwell and then the Well. She
seemed to have shut down, her eyes fixed straight
ahead, the holographic Jovian flag casting a flicker-
ing red and yellow light on her black hair and pale neck.
Mavry sat beside her with his head bowed, holding one
of her hands in both of his.

They disembarked from the rickshaw and walked in
silence down the long tunnel to the ship terminal. The

Cybelean customs officials saw them coming, and one of them hurriedly said something to the spacers waiting in the short line at their booth. They stood aside and the Hashoones walked up to the station, where their departure documents were presented.

The lead official was looking down the tunnel past them. Tycho turned and saw a cart piled with gear, trundling toward them. Three Comets sat on its sides, with Grigsby at the controls. The warrant officer's face was gray and drawn, his riotous tattoos extinguished.

The cart drew alongside the Hashoones, and Tycho saw the long form covered with a blanket, the boxes and duffel bags set carefully around it. Diocletia said nothing, while Mavry's head came up briefly, registered the cart and what it carried, then went back down.

Grigsby stepped off the cart and spoke quietly to the customs officials. Documents were stamped and the group walked forward again, the cart trailing them.

The docking terminal was filled with people. At the sight of the Hashoones the buzz of conversation stopped. Hands went to heads, and hats were removed. All of those waiting belonged to the bridge crews of the other Jovian privateers, Tycho realized. The captains stepped forward and stood in front of their crews, Garibalda Marta Andrade next to Dmitra Barnacus, who stood next to the Widderiches, and so on, until the slight figure of Zhi Ning at the end of the line.

The privateers stood at attention as the Hashoones passed. Then Diocletia held up her hand, stopping her family. She turned, her eyes taking in the line of captains and the crowd of privateers behind them.

"Thank you, captains," she said quietly, and then her eyes turned left and right. "Thank you, ladies and gentlemen."

The privateers remained still and silent until the cart had passed beyond their sight and vanished into the umbilical leading to the gig.

"Captain?" Grigsby asked over the *Shadow Comet*'s comm, his voice quiet and almost apologetic. "Full complement belowdecks."

"Thank you, Mr. Grigsby," Diocletia said into her headset from where she sat in the captain's chair. "Vesuvia, status for departure?"

"All systems are operational," Vesuvia said.

"Vesuvia, verify headings," Tycho said, finding himself grateful for the years of mind-numbing routine. Departure had long ago become a familiar, near-automatic checklist, one he could follow with minimal intervention by his brain.

"Course verified," Vesuvia said.

"Cybelean Traffic Control, this is the *Shadow Comet* requesting immediate clearance for departure," Tycho said.

"Granted," a voice said instantly. "And Godspeed."

"We're green for departure," Tycho said, and then slumped in his harness. With his checklist complete he had no idea what to do. His eyes crept to where Yana sat numbly beside him. It was strange not to hear the clatter of their grandfather shifting his metal limbs behind him on the quarterdeck, ready to quarrel with Vesuvia or share an old pirate yarn.

"Carlo, take us up—" Diocletia said, her head turning to the left, as it had so many times before. She stared at the empty chair for a moment, then turned her gaze back to the main screen.

"Mavry," she said. "Take us up to our tanks."

The *Comet* eased slowly away from her parking orbit, beginning her climb to the long-range tanks clustered above Cybele. Attis hung in space ahead of them. Mavry guided them smoothly beneath it. Diocletia sat silent and motionless in the captain's chair, staring straight ahead.

Mavry turned at his console, looking at his wife. Attis was below and behind them now, casting a shadow over the web of domes and corridors that marked the surface of its asteroid companion. Above them, Tycho could see pinpoints of brilliant light—long-range tanks waiting for their starships.

With a hum, the control yoke rose from beneath Diocletia's console.

"My starship," she said. "Vesuvia, beat to quarters."

"Acknowledged."

Belowdecks, the pipes shrilled and Grigsby began barking orders.

"Dio?" Mavry asked, but she had activated her headset.

"Yana, on sensors," Diocletia said. "Mr. Grigsby, gunnery crews to their stations."

"Captain?" Grigsby asked. "What's our target?"

"Bazaar."

Tycho looked at Yana in shock, but his sister didn't look back. She was activating her sensor boards, extending sensor masts and running hurried diagnostics.

"Dio, what are we doing?" Mavry asked.

"We're going to the place where our son died. Where nobody helped him."

The *Comet* banked to port and dipped her nose. Cybele grew from a spot of light into a shape once again, a gray lump made bright by the distant sun.

"Mom," Tycho said. "Elfrieda's there."

Diocletia said nothing.

"Mom?" Tycho tried again.

"I heard you."

Tycho looked helplessly at Yana. But it was Mavry who leaned over to Diocletia.

"Dio," he said quietly. "Don't carry that weight too."

"*Shadow Comet*, this is not an approved departure vector," a voice said over the comm. "Acknowledge."

Diocletia's hand went to her headset. "You have three minutes to evacuate Bazaar."

Below them, Cybele grew until its surface filled the viewports. Diocletia leveled off and the *Comet* cruised slowly over the barren plains.

"*Shadow Comet*, return to your departure vector immediately," the traffic-control official said, and Tycho could hear panic creeping into his voice.

"Three minutes," Diocletia replied.

"*Comet*, any hostile action against Cybelean citizens or property will be considered an act of war."

"If you think any of your toy ships can stop me, send them down here."

Tycho could see scattered domes, pits, and landing fields now—the outskirts of Cybele's settlements, farther from the Westwell than he'd ever dared to go. He wondered which of them had sheltered the Ice Wolves, and where the Securitat had made its headquarters. He could imagine the people below looking up, surprised by the unfamiliar shadow overhead.

And then he saw it—the pressure dome where his brother had died. He hoped Elfrieda had heard the warning and heeded it.

"Gun crews, prepare to fire on my mark," Diocletia said. "Counterclockwise rotation."

The *Comet* slowed, Bazaar dead center in her viewports.

"Mark," she told Grigsby.

The *Comet* shivered and bucked, and the first projectiles streaked toward Cybele's surface, delivered by the bow chasers. Two blossoms of flame sprang up below them, blindingly bright. Then Diocletia spun the *Comet* to bring her starboard cannons to bear, and Bazaar vanished behind a wall of fire and ejected dust and rock. The guns roared out from bow to stern, a continuous rolling thunder of sound, and the frigate rattled and shook. The

Comet continued to spin, and after a brief pause the port guns were firing, pouring destruction into the surface of the asteroid below.

Tycho's ears were ringing when the *Comet* completed her rotation and the firing stopped. The dust thinned, and Tycho saw there was no pressure dome below them anymore—only a low depression, its churned-up surface bubbling and glowing red.

"Target destroyed," Vesuvia intoned.

The bells clanged out three times.

"Cease firing," Diocletia said. She stared at the spot where Bazaar had been, the glow already fading as the rock cooled and began to solidify. Then she stood the *Comet* on her tail and accelerated toward the long-range tanks waiting above.

A crewer belowdecks began to chant Carlo's name. He was joined by another, and then by a third, and then by many more. After a few seconds of dissonance the chant found a common cadence, the syllables booming up the ladderwells accompanied by the stamp of boots.

The *Comet* reached her tanks. The stabilizers engaged and the fuel-line connectors mated, the familiar sounds faint amid the chanting below. The whine of the engines rose to a howl and the frigate shot into deep space, toward distant Jupiter.

Diocletia unbuckled her harness and got to her feet, one hand clutching the back of the captain's chair. Mavry hastily stood as well. He reached for Diocletia and she sagged against him. Then a sound emerged from her throat, a guttural moan that rose to a ragged scream, one that went on and on even as Mavry buried her in his arms, rocking her back and forth.

The chanting stopped belowdecks, leaving that dreadful keening wail to penetrate every compartment of the ship, from the lowermost hold to the top turret. It trailed away and then began again, inescapable and endless, and none of the Comets aboard that day would ever forget the sound of Diocletia Hashoone crying for her lost child.

27

CALLISTO

ycho and Yana sewed their brother's shroud in the cuddy that afternoon. In the evening they buried Carlo in space, with Grigsby reading the Spacer's Farewell while the Comets stood in solemn lines behind the Hashoones.

The voyage back to Jupiter passed in a crawl of miserable watches and near-silent meals. Yana spent every spare moment belowdecks, demanding that Dobbs push her through more-punishing unarmed-combat drills.

Mavry was a constant presence on the quarterdeck, his thoughts his own. And Diocletia vanished into the stateroom on the top deck, emerging only when one of them implored her to eat.

While on the quarterdeck, Tycho stood watches and did homework, offering the meekest of protests when Vesuvia insisted he redo assignments he'd barely paid attention to. When he wasn't on watch, he spent long hours in the cuddy, listening to the swish of the air scrubbers and feeling the hum of the *Comet*'s engines as she barreled through space.

It had been two days since Carlo's death, two days his brother would never experience. He and Yana had done nothing important—only their grief marked these days as different from others in the normal course of their lives, as they had pursued them for years and presumably would do for years to come. And Tycho thought about all the other lives around him, from those of the crewers belowdecks to ones he knew nothing about, lived by settlers on Vesta or Mars or Earth. Somewhere out there Huff was mourning and enduring hours in his relocated tank, and somewhere else Kate was practicing the viola and doing her own homework and thinking of the boy who had betrayed her. All these lives were going on, their stories continuing to be written in ways big and small. But not his brother's life. That had just ended, without warning. And that seemed impossible to Tycho somehow—that his life and all those others should simply go on while his brother's did not.

His thoughts kept creeping back to the pact he had struck with Carlo, in that last hour before his death. But he refused to interrupt his mother's grief to tell her what he had planned to confess—or to sully her memory of Carlo by revealing what his brother had done.

Grasping for something to do that had a purpose, he decided to find a holo of Carlo for the crypt at Darklands. He told Vesuvia to search her memory banks for possibilities, and was looking at candidates on his mediapad when Yana entered the cuddy, red-faced and sweaty from her latest combat session.

"Not that one," Yana said, peering at an image of Carlo smiling in a formal tunic, before he got his scar. "Something more serious. Maybe from a piloting sim."

"Vesuvia should have some of those. I'll show you what I find."

Yana hesitated.

"What happens now, Tyke? To any of us?"

"I have no idea. Mom's refused to even read the Defense Force's messages. But I assume our letter of marque is gone."

"We don't need one for what I have planned."

"And what's that?"

"Find Mox, of course. Find him and kill him."

"With what ship?"

"We'll go to 588 Achilles. We can get a ship and crew there."

"A pair of sixteen-year-old privateers? Who'd sign on with us?"

Yana shrugged. "We'll figure it out. This way we find Mox before he finds us. Or finds you, anyway."

"What are you talking about?"

"I've been thinking about how to tell you. I watched the security vid from Bazaar. There's audio. It's faint, but I've pulled up fainter signals while running sensors. It took some doing, but I was able to isolate it and enhance it."

She pulled out her mediapad, but Tycho shook his head.

"I don't want to see that. Not now and not ever."

"You think I wanted to? I made an audio file. It's just the parts you need to hear. Not the rest."

Tycho wanted to protest but found that he couldn't. His sister had found something—and if she said he needed to hear it, he believed her.

Tycho knew he'd hear the scraped-throat growl of Thoadbone Mox, but he still jumped at the sound of that voice, garbled and faint but recognizable.

". . . other two brats. Take the girl alive, but shoot the boy if you find him."

The reply was inaudible beneath the bang of a shutter.

"They won't interfere," Mox replied, and Tycho's hands balled into fists at the glee in his voice. "All but gave us an invitation."

"Wait," Tycho said, trying to keep his hands from shaking. "What did he say?"

Yana played it again, then let the transmission continue.

"We just have to be out of here before the constables arrive," Mox said. "And they never do nothing quickly."

The file ended. Yana looked questioningly at Tycho.

"What did that mean about someone not interfering?"

"I don't know," Tycho said, though that wasn't true. He tried to hide his fury, fearing Yana would see it. But his sister was staring down at the mediapad, brows furrowed.

"And why would Mox want to take me alive?" she asked. "Why am I different?"

"I don't know that either," Tycho said, telling the truth this time.

Yana pushed her mediapad aside, her thoughts her own.

"You're serious about going to 588 Achilles," Tycho said after a few moments, and Yana's eyes returned to his.

"I am. Like I said, I'm getting a crew and finding Mox."

"Grandfather will be there—it's the only place he could have gone."

His sister's expression turned hard. "Then he can help. It won't bring Carlo back, but he owes him that much. He owes *us* that much."

Tycho stared at the images of Carlo on his screen. "And Mom and Dad?"

"They're not going to let Mom fly for a long time, if ever. You know that. They may never let any of us fly again."

Tycho nodded.

"I'm sorry, Tyke. It's strange how it worked out. You were going to be captain, and now none of us will be."

Tycho turned away. His sister didn't know the secret he and Carlo had shared, and what they'd planned to do.

Tell her. If you can't tell Mom, at least tell her.

But to his shame, he found he couldn't do it.

He reached halfheartedly for the screen of his media-pad to look for more images of Carlo. But Yana leaned forward and grabbed his wrist, forcing him to look up.

"You're not going to be captain, and neither am I," she said. "But that doesn't mean we have to spend the rest of our lives as dirtsiders, Tyke. There's another way. Come with me to Achilles and we'll find it. Together."

His sister's grip was surprisingly strong.

"All right," Tycho said, putting his hand over hers. "Together."

Two days later the *Comet* eased into her docking cradle above Callisto. Tycho and Yana mustered out the crew, thanking them for their service and their kind words, and then returned to the quarterdeck, where Mavry was sitting in silence at his console. He raised his eyes and nodded at them, fetched Diocletia from the top deck, and then piloted the gig down in silence.

A grim-faced Defense Force officer was waiting at Port Town's transportation hub, flanked by two soldiers.

"Captain Diocletia Hashoone?" she asked.

"I knew you'd be here," Diocletia said.

"You are charged with piracy, illegal destruction of property, and unauthorized hostile action against a sovereign regime. Such charges are a violation of your family's letter of marque, which is hereby declared null and void, and your performance bond as a privateer is now forfeit."

Diocletia simply nodded and stepped forward, arms outstretched so they could handcuff her. But the official shook her head.

"That won't be necessary at the present time, Captain Hashoone. By order of Minister Vass, you are to consider yourself under house arrest pending resolution of this matter. You are forbidden to leave your homestead without specific permission from the Defense Force. Are these conditions clear, and do you agree to abide by them?"

Diocletia nodded. The official turned and signaled to the soldiers, who strode away.

Parsons, to his dismay, didn't know how to access the program that added holograms to the family crypt—he explained that Huff had always insisted on handling such things.

Tycho wasn't going to ask his parents or Carina, and Yana was in the simulation room fighting imaginary enemies. So he descended to the gloomy chamber alone, connected his mediapad with the hologram pedestal, and began struggling with the unfamiliar controls.

Machinery whined inside the pedestal, and the

image of Johannes Hashoone shimmered into existence. Tycho glared at his great-grandfather. He'd been a thief and a murderer, and it offended Tycho to think of him immortalized alongside Carlo.

But then, Carlo hadn't been perfect—he'd spent the last morning of his life tormented by that. Tycho had broken family covenants held sacred for generations. And Huff had made mistakes—terrible ones that had led to Tycho standing there in the darkness by himself.

Why did you do it, Grandfather? Why did you let Mox go?

On the third try he managed to get Carlo's hologram loaded, allowing himself a small smile as Johannes rippled and vanished, replaced by an image of Carlo at his console aboard the *Comet*, control yoke held loosely and confidently. His brother's expression was serene—he was exactly where he'd wanted to be, doing what he'd loved to do.

But then Tycho couldn't get the pedestal to *save* the hologram—it would only display it from the mediapad.

His frustration boiling over, Tycho brought his fist down on the control panel. It hurt badly, and he grimaced and rubbed the bruised heel of his hand. The panel was beeping now, and he could hear static.

Great, I broke the stupid thing.

"About time you checked in, Huff," a man's voice said from a speaker in the pedestal. "Our sympathies about your grandson. He was a fine pilot—and would have made a good captain one day. Now, what do you have to report?"

Tycho looked at the control panel in horrified realization. His grandfather had come here each time the *Comet* returned to Callisto, but it hadn't been to commune with the departed.

"Who are you?" Tycho demanded.

Silence, broken only by static.

"Never mind—you all use fake names anyway. I don't know who you are, but I know who you work for. You're my grandfather's handler for the Securitat."

After a moment the man on the other side of the comm found his voice.

"Tycho. Look, kid—"

"Shut up. Just shut up. You had my brother killed. He told you he'd made a mistake and wouldn't help you anymore, and you let him die for it."

"You saw the tape, kid. Mox killed your brother."

"I *heard* the tape. Mox killed my brother, but you let him do it."

Silence.

Tycho leaned closer to the pedestal, the image of his brother looming overhead. He wanted to be sure the Securitat agent on the other end of the transmission could hear him.

"I don't know how you ensnared my grandfather, or exactly what dirty deal you forced him into," he said. "But I'm going to find out. To honor what my grandfather was, before you ruined him, and to honor what my brother could have been."

The Securitat agent remained silent.

"I'm going to find out—that's a promise. And then I'm going to bring all of you down."

A SPACER'S LEXICON

A

abaft. To the rear of.

able spacer. The most experienced class of crewer aboard a starship. Able spacers are more experienced than ordinary spacers, while crewers with too little experience to be considered ordinary spacers are called dirtsiders.

admiralty court. A court concerned with the laws of space, including the taking of prizes. The Jovian Union maintains several admiralty courts in the Jupiter system and abides by the decisions of the admiralty court on the neutral minor planet Ceres, with privateers and warships expected to report to the admiralty court with jurisdiction over the area of space where a prize is taken.

aft. Toward the rear of a starship; the opposite of fore.

air scrubber. A collection of filters and pumps that remove carbon dioxide and impurities from the air aboard a starship, keeping it healthy and (relatively) clean.

amidships. In the middle of a starship.

armorer. A crewer in charge of a starship's hand weapons. Most crewers on privateers and pirate ships carry their own arms.

arrrr. Originally an acknowledgment of an order ("yar"), it has become a nonspecific pirate outburst, adaptable to any situation. The more Rs, the greater the intensity of feeling.

articles. A written agreement drawn up for each cruise, setting out rules and the division of any prize money and signed by all hands aboard a privateer or pirate ship.

articles of war. The body of space law governing hostilities between spacegoing nations and their starships.

avast. Stop!

aviso. A small, speedy starship used for carrying messages across space.

aye-aye. An acknowledgment of an order.

B

bandit. An enemy starship, typically a small, maneuverable one that's likely to attack you.

bandolier. A belt slung over an arm or across the chest that holds carbines, ammunition pouches, and other nasty things.

barky. An affectionate nickname for one's own starship.

beam. The side of a ship, always identified as port or starboard.

beat to quarters. A summons to battle stations, in ancient times accomplished by beating out a rhythm on a drum, in modern times achieved by playing a recording.

belay. A ranking officer's order countermanding a just-issued order.

belowdecks. The deck of a starship below the bridge or quarterdeck, generally reserved for spacers and officers who aren't members of the bridge crew. "Belowdecks" also refers collectively to these spacers.

berth. A sleeping place aboard a starship.

bilge. In ancient seagoing ships, the lowest part of a hull, which filled with foul water also called bilge. In modern parlance, anything foul or nonsensical.

blacklist. A list of spacers to be punished for failure to properly perform their duties or for other breaches of discipline.

blackstrap. Cheap, sweet wine bought in ports.

black transponder. A transponder that identifies a starship as belonging to a pirate captain or, more commonly, transmits a blank identification.

blaster. A pistol or other handheld cannon.

boarding action. The invasion of a starship with marines or crewers.

boarding party. A group of marines or crewers whose job it is to board and take control of a starship.

bogey. A starship that has been seen on scopes but not yet identified.

bosun. A crewer whose duties include daily ship inspections. The bosun reports to the chief warrant officer.

bow. The front of a starship.

bow chaser. A gun located at a starship's bow, designed for firing at ships being pursued.

bridge. A starship's command center, generally called the quarterdeck on warships, privateers, and pirate ships. On the *Shadow Comet*, the quarterdeck is the middle deck and is reserved for the bridge crew.

bridge crew. The officers who serve aboard the quarterdeck or bridge. On many privateers, the bridge crew is limited to the family that owns the ship or their close associates.

bridle port. A port in a ship's bow through which the bow chasers extend.

brig. A room used as a jail aboard a starship.

broadside. A volley of shots aimed at the side of an enemy ship and delivered at close range.

bulk freighter. A large merchant ship, typically corporate owned.

bulkhead. A vertical partition dividing parts of a starship. In the event of a breach, bulkheads seal to isolate damage and prevent the atmosphere from escaping.

buoy. A marker defining a spacelane. In the modern age, buoys send electronic signals to starships and maintain their positions through small, efficient engines.

burdened vessel. A starship that doesn't have the right-of-way; not the privileged vessel.

burgoo. A gruel made from shipboard rations, not particularly liked by crewers.

C

cabin. An enclosed room on a starship. Generally refers to an officer's personal quarters.

cannon. A general term for a starship's hull-mounted weapons. Cannons can fire laser beams or missiles and are designed for different intensities of fire and ranges.

captain. The commander of a starship. Traditionally, a former captain is still addressed as Captain.

carbine. A pistol.

cargo. Goods carried by a merchant starship.

cargo hauler. A no-frills class of freighter, typically corporate owned.

carronade. A powerful short-range projectile cannon used in combat.

cartel ship. A starship transporting prisoners to an agreed-upon port. Cartel ships are exempt from capture or recapture while on their voyages, provided they don't engage in commerce or warlike acts.

cashier. To discharge a crewer.

caulk. Thick rubber used to plug holes and seams in a starship's hull.

centaur. A celestial body with an unstable orbit and a lifetime of several million years, with characteristics of both asteroids and comets.

chaff. Scraps of metal released by a starship to confuse the sensors of an enemy ship or guided missile.

chamade. A signal requesting a cessation of hostilities and negotiations.

chandler. A merchant who sells goods to starships in port.

cheroot. A cheap, often smelly cigar.

chronometer. A timepiece.

clove hitch, in a. Dealing with a dilemma.

coaster. A starship that operates close to a planet or within a system of moons, as opposed to starships that make interplanetary voyages.

cold pack. Flexible packet kept cold and used to numb minor injuries.

condemn. To seize a ship for auction or sale under prize law.

container ship. A large merchant ship that typically carries cheap bulk goods.

convoy. A group of merchant ships traveling together for mutual protection, often with armed starships as escorts.

corvette. A small, fast, lightly armed warship.

crewer. A member of a starship's crew; the equivalent of a sailor on ancient ships. "Crewer" technically refers to all members of a starship's crew, but members of the bridge crew are rarely if ever called crewers.

crimp. A person who captures spacers in port and sells them to starships as crewers, usually by working with a press gang. Navy officers who lead authorized press gangs are never called crimps—at least, not to their faces.

crowdy. A thick porridge. More edible than burgoo, but not by much.

cruise. A starship's voyage.

cruiser. A fast, heavily armed warship.

cuddy. A cabin in which officers gather to eat their meals.

cutter. A scout ship.

D

dead lights. Eyes.

derelict. Cargo left behind after a shipwreck with no expectation of recovery. Any claimant may legally salvage derelict.

destroyer. A small warship with the speed to hunt down small, nimble attackers.

dirtside. A spacer's term for being off one's ship on a planet or moon. Said with faint derision and distress.

dirtsider. A spacer with minimal training and experience, limited to simple tasks aboard a starship. A hardworking dirtsider may eventually be rated as an ordinary spacer.

dog watch. Either of the two short watches between 1600 and 2000. At two hours, a dog watch is half the duration of a normal watch.

down the ladder. Tradition in which a midshipman spends a year or more belowdecks, learning the spacer's trade from an experienced crewer.

dreadnought. A large, well-armed, but slow warship.

dromond. A very large merchant ship, often one that carries expensive goods.

dry dock. A facility where starships are taken out of service for substantial repairs or refitting.

duff. A kind of pudding served as a treat aboard starships.

E

engineer. The crewer or officer responsible for keeping a starship operating properly.

engine room. The control room for a starship's engines. Sometimes the same as the fire room.

ensign. A flag indicating a starship's allegiance.

escort. A starship providing protection for another vessel, typically one that is unarmed.

F

fanlight. A portal over the door of an officer's cabin, providing light and air while maintaining privacy.

fenders. Bumpers on the sides of a starship, used to protect against damage in crowded shipyards, on landing fields, or in parking orbits.

fire room. The control room for a starship's reactor. Sometimes the same as the engine room.

fireship. A starship loaded with munitions and exploded among enemy ships to damage them.

first mate. A starship's second-in-command.

flagship. The starship commanded by the ranking officer in a task force or fleet.

flip. A strong beer favored by crewers.

flotsam. Debris and objects left floating in space after a starship is damaged or destroyed.

flummery. A shipboard dessert.

fondaco. An area of a planet, moon, asteroid, or artificial station reserved for citizens of a certain country, and within the bounds of which they are sometimes restricted. The plural is fondachi.

fore. Toward the front of a starship; the opposite of aft.

forefoot. The foremost part of a starship's lower hull.

freighter. A general term for a merchant vessel.

frigate. A fast warship used for scouting and intercepts, well armed but relying more on speed than weapons. The *Shadow Comet*, the *Ironhawk*, and the *Hydra* are heavily modified frigates.

G

galleon. A large merchant ship, particularly one that carries expensive cargoes.

galley. The kitchen on a starship.

gangway. The ramp leading into a ship, lowered when a ship is on a landing field.

gibbet. A post with a protruding arm from which criminals sentenced to death are hanged.

gig. A small, unarmed ship used for short trips between nearby moons or between ports and starships in orbit. An armed gig is generally called a launch.

grav-sled. A small wheeled vehicle used for trips on the surface of a minor planet, moon, or asteroid. Not a luxurious ride.

green. When referring to a system or process, an indication that all is ready or working normally.

gripe. A malfunction or problem with a system aboard a starship.

grog. A mix of alcohol and water, beloved by starship crewers. Also refers to alcoholic drinks imbibed in port, which shouldn't be mixed with water but often are.

gunboat. A small but heavily armed warship. Often found patrolling ports or spacelanes.

H

hail. An opening communication from one party to another.

hammock. A length of canvas or netting strung between beams belowdecks, in which crewers sleep.

hand. A crewer. Use generally limited to discussions of "all hands."

hang a leg. Do something too slowly.

hard horse. A stern, harsh, and/or stubborn captain.

hardtack. Bland starship rations that don't spoil over long cruises but aren't particularly tasty. Unlike in ancient times, hardtack is rarely actually hard.

hatchway. An opening in a ship's hull for transferring cargo to and from the hold.

head. A bathroom aboard a starship.

heading. A starship's current course.

head money. A reward for prisoners recovered.

heave to. A command for a starship to stop its motion.

heel. To lean to one side.

helm. Originally the controls for piloting a starship, but now generally a term indicating an officer is in command of a starship.

HMS. His (or Her, depending on who is the monarch) Majesty's Ship, a prefix for a warship from Earth.

hold. The area of a starship in which cargo is held. Hatchways or bay doors generally open to allow direct access to the hold.

hominy. Ground corn boiled with milk.

hoy. A small merchant coaster.

I

idler. A crewer who isn't required to keep night watches.

impression. Forced service aboard a starship during wartime.

in extremis. Unable to maneuver safely due to malfunction, damage, or some other condition. Privileged vessels must yield the right-of-way to starships in extremis.

in ordinary. Out of commission; said of a starship. Also applies to the crew of a starship while she is laid up in ordinary.

in soundings. Sufficiently close to a celestial body that its gravity must be taken into account during maneuvers.

intercept. The process of examining a starship for possible boarding, often followed by a boarding action.

interrogatories. Reports prepared about an intercept and boarding action, detailing events with evidence from the ships' records. Interrogatories are submitted as part of a claim in admiralty court.

invalid. A spacer on the sick list because of illness or injury.

irons, put in. To imprison.

J

jammer. A ship-mounted device intended to scramble the sensors and systems of nearby ships lacking software to counteract such effects.

jetsam. Objects jettisoned from a starship in distress.

job captain. A captain given temporary command of a starship while the regular captain is away or indisposed.

jolly boat. A small craft used for inspections or repairs of starships in orbit.

jump-pop. A sugary, caffeinated drink loved by children and crewers alike. Bad for you.

Jupiter Trojans. Two groups of asteroids that share an orbit with Jupiter, lying ahead of and behind the giant planet in its orbit. The group ahead of Jupiter is called the Greek node, while the trailing group is called the Trojan node. That naming convention developed after individual asteroids were named, resulting in an asteroid named after a

Greek hero (617 Patroclus) residing in the Trojan camp, and an asteroid named after a Trojan hero (624 Hektor) residing in the Greek camp.

K

keel. A long girder laid down between a starship's bow and stern, giving her structural integrity.

keelhaul. To abuse someone. Derived from the ancient practice of hauling a disobedient sailor under a ship's keel.

keep the matter dark. Keep something confidential.

ketch. A short-range merchant starship.

kip. A cheap lodging house in a port.

klick. A kilometer.

L

ladderwell. A ladder connecting decks on a starship.

lagan. Cargo left behind after a shipwreck and marked by a buoy for reclamation. Lagan can be legally salvaged under certain conditions.

LaGrange point. A stable point in space where the gravitational interaction of various large bodies allows a small body to remain at rest. Space stations, roadsteads, and clumps of asteroids are often built or found at planets' LaGrange points.

landing field. An area of a port where starships land. Typically, only small starships actually use landing fields, with larger vessels remaining in orbit.

larder. A room aboard a starship in which provisions are stored.

lash up and stow. A command, typically piped, for crewers to roll up their hammocks, clearing space for shipboard operations.

launch. A small, lightly armed craft kept aboard a starship, used for short outings and errands between ships. An unarmed launch is generally called a gig.

lee. An area where magnetism or some other measurable hazard drops to zero or close to it. A term borrowed from ancient ocean sailors.

letter of marque. A document giving a civilian starship the right to seize ships loyal to another nation, an action that otherwise would be considered piracy.

liberty. Permission to leave a ship for a time in port.

lighter. A starship used for ferrying cargo between ships and to and from ships in orbit above a port.

loblolly boy. A surgeon's assistant.

log. A record of a starship's operations.

longboat. A small starship primarily used for provisioning bigger starships.

long nine. A cannon designed to hit targets at very long range.

lumper. A laborer hired to load and unload a merchant ship in orbit or in port.

M

magazine. A section of a starship used for storing missiles and other ordnance.

marine. A soldier aboard a warship who splits his or her duties between gunnery and boarding actions. The term is typically reserved for formal military ships, though it is sometimes extended to soldiers serving for pay to defend merchant starships. Crewers who perform this role aboard civilian ships are never called marines.

mast. A pole attached to a starship's hull to maximize the capabilities of sensors and/or antennae.

master. A member of the bridge crew who is not the captain or first mate. A female crew member holding this rank is sometimes but not always called mistress.

master-at-arms. A crewer responsible for discipline belowdecks. On some ships the warrant officer or bosun serves as the master-at-arms, but wise captains avoid such an arrangement, as many crewers regard it as unfair.

matey. An affectionate word for a shipmate.

mess. Where meals are served belowdecks.

midshipman. A crewer training to be an officer. Midshipmen typically begin as children and spend years as apprentices belowdecks before being appointed to a starship's bridge crew. Low-ranking masters who are new to the bridge crew are often still called midshipmen. Middie, for short.

moor. To secure a starship during a period of inactivity, whether in orbit or on a landing field.

musketoon. A pistol with a broad, bell-like muzzle.

"my starship." A declaration of a captain or ranking officer indicating that he or she is assuming command. Command can be assigned through the order "your starship," etc.

O

off soundings. Sufficiently far from a celestial body that its gravity can be ignored during maneuvers.

ordinary spacer. A spacer capable of performing most activities aboard a starship, but not an expert. With work, an ordinary spacer may rate as an able spacer.

ordnance. A starship's offensive weapons and materials, from cannons to missiles.

ore boat. A starship hauling ore, typically owned by a prospector.

P

packet. A small passenger ship that carries mail and personal goods between ports.

parley. A negotiation, often informal, between enemies.

parole. A prisoner's pledge of good behavior while in captivity, or conditions agreed to if released.

pass. A document indicating a starship's allegiance, and good for safe-conduct from privateers aligned with a given nation. The validity of a pass is ensured by transmitting the proper recognition code. Also, a document attesting to a spacer's current service aboard a starship, offering theoretical protection from impression.

passageway. A corridor aboard a starship.

peg. To figure, as in "I didn't peg you for a lawyer/pirate/etc."

performance bond. A financial guarantee that a privateer will abide by the terms of its letter of marque. Fines can be levied against a performance bond by an admiralty court or by the government issuing the letter of marque.

persuader. Slang for a carbine, large knife, or other weapon that can sway the less well-armed participant in a dispute.

pinnace. A small, fast, highly maneuverable ship used for offensive and defensive operations by warships and other starships, and typically operated by either a single pilot or a pilot and a gunner.

pipe. A whistle used by the bosun to issue orders to a crew. Any spacer quickly learns to identify the unique tune for each order.

pirate. A civilian starship (or crewer aboard such a starship) that seizes or attacks other ships without authorization from a government. Piracy is punishable by death. A civilian ship with authorization for such seizures or attacks is a privateer.

pitch. A starship moving up or down through the horizontal axis. Sometimes an involuntary motion if a starship is damaged, malfunctioning, or being piloted poorly.

port. The left side of a ship, if a crewer is looking toward the bow from the stern. A starship's port hull is marked by red lights. Also, a planet, moon, or asteroid where a starship crew takes on supplies, offloads cargo, or has other business.

porthole. A small, generally round window in the hull of a starship.

press gang. A group of spacers that prowls ports, looking for men or women to impress into the navy, merchant marine, or crew of a starship. Press gangs are now rare in most ports.

privateer. A civilian starship authorized to take offensive action against another nation, typically by seizing merchant ships belonging to that nation. Unlike pirates, privateers possess a letter of marque, which requires them to abide by the laws of war and all other laws of space.

privileged vessel. A starship that has the right-of-way while navigating.

prize. An enemy vessel, crew, and cargo captured in space by a warship or privateer. The claiming of a prize is declared legal or illegal through a hearing in admiralty court. A legally taken prize is either condemned, and sold to a nation or on its behalf, or released for ransom and allowed to continue on its way. Either way, the proceeds (prize money) are divided among the ship's crew.

prize agent. An agent who sells prizes on behalf of a nation, pocketing a fee for his or her efforts.

prize court. A court that decides claims on captured starships.

prize law. The interplanetary laws governing the taking of prizes.

prize money. The proceeds from the sale of a prize and the ransom of its crew, shared out among the bridge crew and crewers at the end of a cruise.

purser. A crewer responsible for keeping a starship's financial records and distributing provisions to crewers. Typically a role assigned by the warrant officer to a trusted veteran spacer.

Q

quarterdeck. A starship's command center, often known as the bridge on civilian ships. Typically reserved for the officers of the bridge crew.

quittance. A release from a debt.

R

ransom. Money paid to pirates or privateers for the safe return of a ship and/or its crew. Also, money paid to privateers to allow a captured starship to proceed along its course without being taken to prize court for claiming and condemnation.

reactor. The power source of a starship, housed near the engines and heavily armored for protection and to prevent radiation from leaking and poisoning the crew.

read in. To make a spacer a member of a starship crew, typically by receiving an acknowledgment that the spacer has read the articles for a given cruise.

recall. An order to return to a starship and prepare for liftoff.

red. In reference to a system or situation, an indication that things are not ready or functioning normally.

rescue. The recapture of a prize by a friendly ship before it can be claimed in prize court and condemned. A rescue restores the starship to her prior owners.

retainer. A crewer whose family has served aboard a starship or for a specific family or shipping company for multiple generations. Many privateers and merchants are crewed in large part by retainers.

right-of-way. An indication that a starship has priority for navigating over other starships in the area. The starship with the right-of-way is the privileged vessel; other starships are burdened vessels.

roadstead. A safe anchorage outside a port or a port's orbit, often at a space station or isolated asteroid.

roll. A starship moving to port or starboard of the horizontal axis while changing its vertical orientation. Sometimes an involuntary motion if a starship is damaged, malfunctioning, or being piloted poorly.

rudder. The device used by the pilot to steer a starship. A physical object in ancient times, but now a series of software commands.

S

salvage. Abandoned or lost cargo (or a starship) that has been legally claimed or been claimed subject to a legal ruling.

scope. A screen showing the result of sensor scans or providing diagnostics about other starship functions.

scow. A dirty, poorly run starship.

scurvy. Originally a disease to which sailors were susceptible; now a term of contempt.

scuttle. To intentionally render a starship or an important system aboard a starship inoperable, so as to deny it to an enemy.

Securitat. The intelligence service of the Jovian Union.

settle one's hash. To subdue or silence someone, often violently.

shindy. A dance favored by boisterous crewers. Also: a good time had by same. A night of hijinks while at liberty in a port would be remembered as "a fine shindy."

ship of the line. A warship big and capable enough to take part in a major battle.

shoals. The area of space near a celestial body, within which particular care must be taken by a pilot. A term borrowed from ancient sailing.

shore leave. Free time in port granted to a starship's crew.

short commons. Thin rations.

sick list. The roster of crew members ill and unable to perform their duties aboard a starship.

silent running. Operating a starship with as few systems engaged as possible in an effort to avoid detection.

slew. A maneuver by which a starship turns around on her own axis.

sloop. A small, fast starship with weapons. Sloops are smaller than corvettes and typically used for interplanetary voyages.

slop book. A register of items given to crewers by the purser. The cost of these items is subtracted from their pay or share of prize money.

snack. A share of prize money given to a ship that was in firing range of a target vessel when it was captured. A tradition established to prevent violent clashes between pirates.

soft tack. Bread or cake, a treat during long cruises.

space. To expose someone deliberately to a vacuum, with fatal results.

spacelane. A corridor through space near a planet, a moon, or an asteroid, typically marked by buoys.

spike. To render a cannon inoperable.

squadron. A division of a fleet.

starship. Technically a starship is a spacegoing vessel capable of operating between planets or other distant points in space. In practice, any spacegoing vessel. Starships are called "she" and "her," with the exception of some commercial craft and small starships such as gigs, gunboats, and pinnaces. Military ships serving nations are usually called warships.

starshipwright. A designer or maker of starships.

stand. To hold a course for a destination.

starboard. The right side of a starship, as seen from a crewer at the stern looking toward the bow. The starboard side of a starship is marked by green lights on the hull.

stateroom. The cabin of a starship captain, another high-ranking officer, or an important person on board.

stern. The rear of a starship.

sternboard. A method of turning a starship when the pilot cannot maneuver forward. A real test of a pilot's ability.

stern chaser. A gun mounted at a starship's stern, used for firing at pursuing vessels.

sternpost. A thick beam rising from a starship's keel at the stern and helping to support her engines and reactor.

straggler. A crewer absent from his or her ship.

summat. Something.

supercargo. A crewer in charge of a merchant vessel's cargo. A supercargo is typically not a regular member of the crew but a representative of the shipping line or starship's owner. Not all merchant vessels have supercargoes aboard.

surgeon. A doctor aboard a starship, whose responsibilities include treating everything from common illnesses to wounds suffered in battle. Such medical care is often rudimentary.

T

tea wagon. A derisive term for a merchant vessel.

tender. A vessel that carries supplies, provisions, and personal deliveries to a warship in port.

ticket. A written document promising payment of wages or other compensation at a later date.

top deck. The uppermost deck of a starship. Often living quarters for the starship's officers and reserved for them.

transom. The aft wall of a ship at her stern. The transom is strong and heavily reinforced, helping to support the engines and often the reactor.

transponder. An electronic system that automatically broadcasts a starship's name, operating number, home port, and nationality. Many civilian ships travel with their transponders disabled, and some broadcast false identities to confuse pirates and privateers.

tub. A slow, ungainly starship.

V

victualing yard. A part of a port where the shops of many victuallers, chandlers, and other merchants are found. Typically, purchased items are delivered later.

victualler. A starship that sells provisions to other starships in orbit above a port. Also: the owner of such a starship or his or her shop in a port.

viewport. A large window in a starship, typically found on the bridge/quarterdeck.

W

wardroom. The cabin belowdecks reserved for the warrant officer and spacers assigned significant roles by him or her.

warrant officer. The ranking officer belowdecks, typically a spacer who has worked his or her way up through the ranks, but sometimes one drawn from the bridge crew.

wash. The ion exhaust of a starship's engines.

watch. A period of time during which an officer, a crewer, or a group of crewers is responsible for certain operations aboard a starship. The day is divided into seven watches: the first watch lasts from 2000 to midnight, the middle watch from midnight to 0400 hours, the morning watch from 0400 to 0800, the forenoon watch from 0800 to 1200, the afternoon watch from 1200 to 1600, the first dog watch from 1600 to 1800, and the second dog watch from 1800 to 2000.

watch officer. The ranking officer during a given watch. The watch officer retains command in the event of an emergency during his or her watch unless relieved by the captain or sometimes the first mate.

Y

yaw. A starship's motion to port or starboard of the vertical axis but maintaining the same horizontal bearing. Yaw refers only to an involuntary motion, as when a starship is damaged, malfunctioning, or being piloted poorly. A deliberate move to port or starboard of the vertical axis is simply a turn.

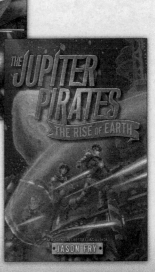